MUSIC
FOR
BOYS

MUSIC FOR BOYS

David Cavanagh

FOURTH ESTATE • *London* and *New York*

First published in Great Britain in 2003 by
Fourth Estate
A Division of HarperCollins*Publishers*
77–85 Fulham Palace Road
London W6 8JB
www.4thestate.com

10 9 8 7 6 5 4 3 2 1

A catalogue record for this book is available from the British Library.

ISBN 0-00-714872-0

Typeset by Rowland Phototypesetting Limited,
Bury St Edmunds, Suffolk
Printed in Great Britain by Clays Ltd, St Ives plc

MUSIC
FOR
BOYS

PART ONE

PART ONE

1
Going South

A snarl-up near Banbridge. Neither lane was moving and we saw the BMW in front of us bounce as its engine stalled. I had spotted horses half a mile back — now they too would be motionless, gazing down from the hillside on a country that had reached the end of the line. For a moment the world stood still. And that's when the first memory came.

We must have started moving again for the BMW was some distance ahead. In years gone by, the silent man to my right would have said 'Now that's a car I wouldn't mind driving' to the boy in the passenger seat. We might even have had a conversation about it. Hang on, though. No, I would have been in the back if we'd been going to Dublin. I would have been in the back seat on the right, waiting for the split-second *now* when you could see a hotel dramatically revealed through an archway as you drove into Castlebellingham. And before that I would have pleaded for a stop at the Roadhouse at Dundalk to inspect the wreckage of the crashed car, rusting and rotting in a ditch by the side of the road ... a car-wreck whenever we wanted to look. It had been there on a fine afternoon when David Hamilton played 'Midnight at the Oasis' on Radio One, and interrupted it to make a joke about camels being miserable because they always had the hump. 'Amused I wasn't,' we used to say in those days. 'A comedian you isn't.'

Shame on me — fancy reminiscing about babyish drivel at my age. That wasn't like me at all. I sucked at my gums and forced myself to think dull thoughts.

Thorburn, perched over the table, taking his time, no hurry whatsoever. They call him the Grinder, so patient and methodical is he when he's potting. He's deliberating about the red into the middle pocket . . . but I've a feeling he's going to leave it and play safe. Yes, it's safety-first at all times for Cliff. If he can just roll the cue ball on to the baulk cushion . . . He's having a good long think about this shot. He won't want to rush it.

The blushes abated, taking the memories with them, but it was hot in the car and I felt a dribble of dilemma. Grabbing a packet of tissues from the glove compartment, I wondered if any of them — or even all of them — would be able to deal with the fluid in my nose. I decided not. I did a bone-crunching sniff, snort and swallow that made Dad jerk his head with irritation. The soupy mucus tasted repulsive in my throat, but where else was I to put it?

'Interested in a trip down to Dublin with me?' Dad had asked an hour earlier as we met stiffly outside the bathroom. 'Just a routine visit to the usual suspects, but I'd appreciate your company. I know Hugh and Sylvia are looking forward to speaking some Spanish with you. Be nice to make an appearance.'

I could have weaselled out of it. But I'd been stuck in bed since Friday with only *Private Eye*, a flask of Lemsip and a supply of tissues, so I thought about the open road and said, 'All right if I bring some tapes?' I had the presence of mind to cough wretchedly as I hobbled to the car. I didn't want Dad making hints about me going back to school. 'Sounds bad,' he agreed, thumping my shoulder. 'Dirty old 'flu.' Then he added, 'I'll drive. You navigate.' He knew the route to Dublin inside-out.

We hadn't even got to the end of the Lisburn Road when an argument started.

'I wish you wouldn't go around telling everybody I'm fluent in Spanish,' I said. 'It's embarrassing. Knowing a few nouns and verbs is not the same as being fluent. By the time I've worked out what these people are saying, they're saying something else.'

'These people?' Dad said sharply. 'That how you talk about my brother?'

'Any people. People in general. It puts me in a difficult position.'

'Quite. Well, I'll have a word with old Hugh when we get there, and ask him if he wouldn't mind saying the odd phrase in English now and again for your benefit.' He paused. 'We wouldn't want you to be put in a difficult position.'

'If you're going to be sarcastic . . .'

'You'll find us quite flexible. We only try and embarrass you for the hell of it.'

'Here we go. Thank you and good night.'

'Unbelievable,' he said to his sun visor. After that, we travelled in silence. As usual I couldn't say a damn thing without upsetting somebody.

It was the early morning of May the fifth. Behind us in the city, the alarm clocks would soon be ringing — a pleasingly metaphorical thought until it was your turn to be confronted

with it. May was revision month for the Middle Sixth. In
the whine of the Fiat's engine I heard the Snoopy and
Kermit clocks striking up like an orchestra, and, seconds
later, the mothers of south Belfast knocking softly on bedroom doors. *I've made you a cup of tea, Stephen/Niall/Caroline/
Beverley. You'd better get out of your pit if you want those grades for
Sheffield/UMIST/Exeter/Trinity.* One of the Bigots needed
three As to get into Bristol. She only wanted to be a bloody
librarian.

There had already been reports of crack-ups and tears,
even a septic ulcer, as the Middle Sixth faced up to the
burden of building a life for themselves. 'I don't want a
fucking profession, I want a hug,' Joyce O'Connor had
sobbed to her friends in the sixth-form centre. Eight short
weeks, four to revise, four to do the exams. None of them
was ready. Most of them were addicted to vodka.

Andy, who was hoping to go to Queen's, would be
panicking now, no doubt about it. Those Rothmans he
smoked – the ashtray on his work-desk would be a tottering
pyramid of screwed-out butts. His mother would be back
and forth to the shop at the end of their road, filling the
boot of the car with boxes of Rothmans and adding them
to the pile outside Andy's door.

May the fifth. May the Lord bless us and preserve us.
May the sun shine out of our teenage arses today, tomorrow
and for ever and ever amen.

I'd been gripping the carrier bag of tapes between my
ankles since the fracas on the Lisburn Road. When I relaxed
and leaned back thirty minutes into the journey, some of
the tapes toppled over inside the bag. Not sure which ones
to bring, I'd packed sixteen: we'd have had to drive the
length of Ireland four times to play them all. But I would

wait until we were clear of the border before I suggested music. I knew Dad would want to hear the news at nine.

He turned on the radio at five-to, so we caught the end of *It's My Belief*. Maggie Kerr was interviewing a professor from Queen's. I flinched at the mention of the university, then remembered that the fear would be far worse for Andy. Then I imagined myself in a year's time opening my bedroom door and seeing a gigantic cigarette glaring down at me. The professor was saying something about econom-ists not getting a fair shout in the Bible, but it was hard to care about the conversation one way or the other, a problem I often found with local radio in the North. They seemed to insist on everybody having dreary discussions in monotonous voices, so as not to overexcite either side. Even when they played music, it was always something non-inflammatory like 'This Ole House'. Just the ticket for bitter-eyed pram-pushers married to men in balaclavas who went out at night with no explanation.

May the fifth . . .

In retrospect, it was fitting that we should drive into Newry as the news was about to begin. I didn't think anything of it at the time, though I remember feeling uneasy as we passed the barbed-wire fortress of a police station. Newry was not a town where you lingered to admire the panorama. It had a garrison dioxide of an atmosphere, and no particular inclination for traffic. But at nine o'clock precisely, several things happened that would etch the scene on my mind for a long time afterwards. First came the pips on the radio – then, as we pulled up at a red light, there was some chanting and I saw a group of people on the opposite kerb holding a large banner.

'This is the news at nine o'clock read by Eamonn Cook.'

7

A car behind us beeped its horn. Immediately, a cheer went up on the kerb and the banner gave a ripple. Dad grimaced into his mirror and beeped back. There was another cheer.

'Bobby Sands, the H-Block hunger-striker and MP for Fermanagh and South Tyrone, was pronounced dead shortly after one o'clock this morning.'

Suddenly there were three or four horns blaring simultaneously. The cheering from outside grew louder.

'Serves him right,' said Dad. 'What are those buggers beeping for? Can you see if the arrow's gone green?' He pressed the horn again. Another cheer. By now I could make out some of the words on the banner.

The newsreader continued: 'In protest at the Government's refusal to grant convicted IRA and INLA terrorists the rights of political prisoners, Sands had been on hunger-strike since the first of March.'

'That's his lookout,' Dad said, peering at the banner. 'Shouldn't have blown up innocent women and kids. *What* does that thing say?'

'I think they're CND,' I lied quickly.

'Those idiots? What the hell are they doing in Newry? Are they stupid or just thick?'

The lights turned amber ... green. We moved forward, waved on by the men with the banner. 'Beep for Bobby,' it read. 'Murdered by Thatcher 5/5/81. Political Status for IRA Freedom Fighters.'

Fuck. Now we were all for the high jump.

We could tell we'd crossed the border because the roads soon deteriorated to total shit. When I move to Prague to write my prize-winning novel, I thought, bobbing along, this is what driving will be like. So bumpy that you daren't put your tongue between your teeth.

Dad had switched off the radio. Every single frequency was Sands this and Sands that. The police were predicting riots across Ireland — what we'd seen in Newry was only the warm-up. And there would be more H-Block deaths in due course: the hunger-strikers had staggered their starting dates with a view to creating a new martyr every week.

The New Martyrs, I thought — not a bad name for a band. Not a bad name at all. In a flash, I pictured a leather-trousered five-piece with Ray-Bans walking on stage at the Pound. ('Evening, we're the New Martyrs and this one's off the album.') Or how about: 'John Peel here, thanks for tuning in. Sessions tonight from Josef K and the New Martyrs.' It was a lot better than all the useless Belfast band-names like Restricted Access and Diagnostic Limit.

I wondered what kind of music Bobby Sands had been into. Elvis? The Chieftains? Country and western? He wouldn't have been much of a Comsat Angels fan, that was for sure. The photograph of him in the papers showed a man with collar-length wavy hair who seemed to belong to a black-and-white time, a time long before punk rock, an ancient time of beards and moustaches on *University Challenge*. Ah, the challenge of university . . . I flinched again.

'Well, his mother must have loved him anyway,' said Dad ironically. 'You can play one of your cassettes if you like. Unless you prefer silence.'

I burrowed down into the Good Vibrations bag and came up with *Scary Monsters*. It was Bowie back to his best form. You had to marvel at the man's genius; the advert in *NME* said, 'Often copied, never equalled,' which was

absolutely spot-on. The only thing was, Andy had taped
the album for me on his Binatone stereo, which meant the
recording levels would be turned all the way up, the distor-
tion unbearable in places. Dad would probably sling it out
of the machine halfway through side one.

'Is she speaking Japanese?' he asked during the first song.

'Yep,' I replied.

'Interesting,' he said. 'Who's the group?' And so I made
a fatal mistake.

Because a minute or two later, without realizing what I
was doing, I was talking. Talking freely, talking rapidly,
talking *hungrily*, talking my imbecilic 'flu-ridden head off.
Nothing on earth could have stopped me. I talked about
Bowie ('Oh, if you like this you should hear *Station to Station*,
it's definitely his masterpiece. Starts with this big long track
that lasts for ten minutes . . .'). I talked about the record
shops in Belfast ('Good Vibrations is pretty good, the prices
are always reasonable. They have all the Beatles' albums for
three ninety-nine . . .'). I even talked about Andy ('No, no,
I didn't buy this in Good Vibes, a friend taped it for me.
You know the one that ate all the cornflakes that time he
came round? Yes, he *does* have an electric guitar . . .')

Stupid stupid cretinous moron. Months of careful work
undone in five minutes of pure thoughtlessness. It was a
serious lapse, my worst of 1981 so far. Didn't I know there
might be personal stuff in there that could be used against
me? Dublin was going to be a social catastrophe.

Thorburn at the table. Ice-cool, as always, under pressure. Not for
nothing is he known as the Grinder. Viewers at home may recall him
taking over an hour to compile a break of twenty-four against Dennis
Taylor in the Masters. Now, he just wants the brown to leave Reardon
needing snookers, so it's no surprise to see him having a good long look

at it. No, I think he's going to play safe. Quite right. He wants to make certain of this all-important first frame.

When I finally looked up again, side one of *Scary Monsters* was nearly finished and the black-green woods of County Louth were slanting upwards on my left. 'What say you?' Dad repeated. 'Yea or nay?'

'Nay,' I said emphatically.

I'd learned my lesson; no more slip-ups. The Rules of Conversation clearly stated that all questions of doubtful origin must be answered in the negative. Affirmative responses, however casual, opened up literally thousands of potential avenues of conversation. It was a pity I hadn't observed the Rules fifteen minutes earlier – it was a bit late to be complying with them now. But such was the insidious way in which conversation worked. Once you were in, it was impossible to get out. And once you started to talk, you subconsciously started to reveal. Was it the 'flu that had caused me to drop my guard? Was it Bobby Sands and all the carry-on in Newry? I made a mental note to tighten up the clause in the Rules about paramilitaries, and to add a sub-clause relating to drowsiness. I'd do it when we got home. I was too vulnerable at the moment.

'And what about on the way back?' Dad said. 'Yea or nay?'

'Nay.'

'You're the boss.'

We were snagged in a traffic jam in Balbriggan a little while later when it dawned on me what the question must have been. I must admit, in spite of myself, I smiled. Of *course*. He'd asked me if I wanted to stop at the Roadhouse to look for the remains of the car-wreck. Jesus aitch Christ, I thought – how bizarre. All those years ago and he remembered it too.

11

I reached once more for the tissues, this time to blow my nose properly. There'd been a treacherous forest of nettles in the clearing at the top of Foyle Crescent, I remembered, where no bungalows had been built. I'd fallen foul of them in my football shorts, crying and flailing at the ones that bit my thighs. And the nettles had been so prolific at the Roadhouse that Dad had had to lift me in the air so I could see the dead car.

Dublin was going to be a write-off at this rate. But then, Dublin was fifty miles away . . . Tearing the tissues steadily into quarters, I gave in to the memories and let them come. Maybe it was true what Joanne Adair said once in the clearing. About them only stinging you if you frighten them.

'Quick, he's in the nineties!'

Daddy and I walked back to the Vitesse where my mum was gesturing to the radio. Kanhai had just hit Geoff Arnold for four, she said, and two more of those would take him to his century.

'So what happened to the man who was in the car?' I asked Daddy. 'Would he have been killed?'

'Oh good God, no. Couple of days in hospital at the most.' He put on his driving gloves. 'Now if I know Geoff, he'll bowl a yorker at him. Take his middle stump out of the ground.'

I thought about the wreck in the ditch. It was dark red and brown, almost square in shape, and half-hidden by a bush. I wasn't sure if Daddy was telling the truth, or fibbing to spare my feelings. The man's body might be under the nettles for all he knew, buried too deep for the doctors to find him. He might be still alive!

I looked back in alarm, but the Roadhouse was out of sight now. My brother was asleep, worn out from eating his fish-finger. I'd had a bowl of lentil soup followed by plaice, but the woman had told me to *wait, please* until she served me the chips from her other dish, which had made me afraid, and Daddy said, 'Nice way to talk to your customers. Pathetic.'

We were going south to Wexford at the bottom of Ireland. I hoped our 1973 holiday would be better than Galway the summer before when it had rained all week. It wasn't raining today, but the rain in Ireland had a way of waiting until you were inside your chalet and unpacking the cricket stumps, and then it let you have it.

As soon as Kanhai made his hundred, I stopped paying attention to the radio and concentrated on *Pop Star*. Daddy had bought it for me at the Esso garage in Downburn when we filled up with petrol, because it was the best magazine for stories, pix and info. Unfortunately it wasn't an up-to-date *Pop Star*, it was an old one. It had info about Roxy Music, who weren't in the charts any more, and it had the song-words to 'Doctor My Eyes' when actually the Jackson Five's new song was 'Hallelujah Day'. The pic of the Jackson Five was weird. For some reason there were six of them.

I had never seen coloured men like the Jackson Five in Northern Ireland. We only saw them on *Top of the Pops* or on the cricket when the West Indies came over. There was Derek Griffiths on *Play School*, but I hadn't watched *Play School* for ages. Songs about elephants sounded silly once you'd heard Sweet and Geordie.

The magazine was so old that it had the song-words of 'Get Down' by Gilbert O'Sullivan, which had been at number one ... oh, heck ... when had 'Get Down' been at number one? February? I remembered it had been a duffel-coat time. If you wanted *Pop Star* to sell you a poster of Gilbert O'Sullivan, you could send away to England for it, except they would probably all be gone by now. I'd sent away to England in June to get 'Hell Raiser' by Sweet, because the record shop in Belfast had run out of it. I did an exchange with a girl in Worcestershire who put a pop-swop advert in *Pop Star* saying, 'I have Sweet, "Hell Raiser". I want Cliff Richard pix, info.' I couldn't believe my luck when I saw the advert – I had to look at it twice. We sent her a *Weekend* that had the song-words of 'Power to All Our Friends' and a pic of Cliff Richard in the Eurovision Song Contest. I was worried it wouldn't be enough, but 'Hell Raiser' came in a parcel three days later. My mum said I should write back and become pen-pals with the girl, but she was fourteen. 'Hell Raiser' must have been too loud for her. I wouldn't have pop-swopped a single for song-words and a pic.

'Don't do too much reading back there,' my mum was saying. 'You don't want to make yourself dizzy.'

It was a warm, summery day and the magazine had an important smell.

'I mean it now. No more stops until Dublin.'

'I won't.'

Hah! What she didn't know was that my eyes had become greedy for info, and they were going to guzzle *Pop Star* to find it. I'd already found some great stuff about the Jackson Five. Tito was older than Jermaine but not as old as Jackie. Tito, Jermaine and Jackie were all older than Marlon. Tito, Jermaine, Jackie and Marlon were all older than Michael. It was a bit like the puzzles they asked Raymond Adair in his eleven-plus. You know: Jermaine has five apples. If he gives one apple each to Marlon, Michael and Tito, how many more apples does Jermaine have than Jackie? That sort of thing. When I was in Mr MacLelland's class, I was going to pass my eleven-plus and go to Belfast Grammar like Raymond and Joanne. Raymond said it was enormous, the size of a palace. He said they gave you a bicycle to get to all the classrooms because they were so far away.

My favourite thing about *Pop Star* was the dates of birth. If you knew a pop group's dates of birth, you knew something interesting about them that not everyone knew. I could remember a date of birth for ever by looking at it twice. Jermaine Jackson was born on December the eleventh 1954. Brian Peter George St Baptiste De La Salle Eno in Roxy Music was born on May the fifteenth 1948. Blimey, look at all the posh middle names he had. His parents must have been viscounts.

The pic of Roxy Music was incredible. Bryan Ferry was hunkered down on his haunches and holding out his hands the way the Black and White Minstrels did, and Eno and the others were stood around him with who-goes-there? looks on their faces, pointing in different directions like hunters in a jungle.

I felt a bit dizzy. My chin was wobbly and I didn't want to read for a while. I put my forehead against the car window to cool down, but it only made me hotter. So I gulped in a breath and held it for twenty-five seconds, closing my eyes to watch Borzov run the 100 metres, turn on his heel and run back waggling the gold medal at the crowd. When I was sure I wasn't going to be sick, I started reading again.

I was disappointed that *Pop Star* didn't have any stories about Suzi Quatro – but then it wouldn't, I remembered,

because 'Can the Can' had come out after *Pop Star* was
written. 'Can the Can' had been out when the FA Cup was
on, so it would have been April or May. May had been
such a brilliant month. Sunderland had thrashed Leeds and
'Hell Raiser' had been on the radio every day. Mind you,
so had Perry Como, so May had been pretty terrible really.
You had to make snoring noises every time Perry Como
was on.

June was when we had the sunny days. We all ran out
into Foyle Crescent and played the Olympics. I usually
ended up near the back in all the races, so Raymond Adair
called me Slowpokovich the Slav. 'Come on, Slowpokovich,
everyone else has finished and gone home,' he'd shout as I
came puffing round the corner in the 800 metres. Raymond
was Pushova, from Siberia, the one who mostly won gold.
'And here comes Pushova,' Raymond would say, pretending
to speak into a microphone as he ran. 'Methinks ze invin-
cible Russki has defeated you another time, my friends.'
We decided that Pushova had walked to Munich from
Siberia for the Olympics because the airline wouldn't let
him take his bear on the plane.

The song I liked best in June was 'Rubber Bullets' by
10cc. It went to number one about a week before the
holidays, and Clare Beattie, who took a radio to school on
Tuesdays, gave us the news as soon as Johnnie Walker read
out the Top 30. Clare's favourite bit in 'Rubber Bullets'
was Deep Man saying how he loved to hear those convicts
squeal, which was my favourite bit too, but I changed my
mind because I didn't want to be a copycat, especially not
a copycat of Clare. I told her my favourite bit was when
High Man sang about the sergeant-major and the padre,
even though I didn't like it as much.

Clare said that 'Rubber Bullets' was about a jail in America, but I thought it was about the Troubles. The men on *Scene Around Six* said 'rubber bullets' some nights when there'd been a shooting, so there was obviously a connection. 10cc were singing about shooting bad people who were in the IRA. But I didn't understand why the men on *Scene Around Six* talked about rubber bullets in a serious way, whereas High Man, Deep Man and Smiley Man in 10cc made them sound fun — like springy bullets that bounced off your head and made you go, 'Ow, gerroff!' Shouldn't the soldiers have more dangerous guns to shoot bad people who were in the IRA? I needed more info about that. All I knew about soldiers was that they came on a ferry from Liverpool and they didn't have a sense of humour. You had to keep quiet in the back if a soldier ever stopped your car.

Boyce and Julien were batting on the radio when we arrived at Uncle Hugh and Aunt Sylvia's. I rolled up *Pop Star* into a tube and looked through it at the moss growing on the house. Daddy parked the Vitesse next to Grandad's Austin Healey in the yard, and we said, 'Form an orderly queue, please' to each other and laughed as we rang the bell.

The little shop selling pipes and tobacco had gone, I noticed, as we drove through the streets of north Dublin. It was now a Chinese takeaway called the Jade Garden. Well, it was no skin off my nose. I hadn't smoked a pipe as a kid, and I wasn't much in the mood for sweet and sour pork today.

I had been a *Pop Star* reader for a year, I seemed to

remember, but all of the issues now blurred into one. In 1974 I'd discovered *Record Mirror*, a weekly paper for the nine-year-old pop junkie, and had come to the conclusion that *Pop Star* was for toddlers. I hadn't played 'Hell Raiser' for the longest time ... I wasn't even convinced I still owned it. How did it start again? With the guitar riff? They hadn't gone straight to the chorus, or had they?

'I suppose you'll be looking forward to getting back to school,' said Dad, keeping an eye out for the turning. 'Let's aim for Thursday. Or shall we make it Friday?'

Back to the College. A double History period on Friday morning with a classroom full of Bigots telling hunger-striker jokes. Form an orderly queue, please. *What's Bobby Sands's phone number? Eight-nothing-eight-nothing-eight-nothing.*

'Monday,' I said wearily.

'It's a date,' Dad concurred, 'as long as your mother has no objections. You can use the weekend to brush up on the old Spanish.'

No, it didn't start with the chorus. I remembered now. It started with an explosion.

2
The Manuscript

Standing on a gradient that curved up and away from a busy main road, Belfast Grammar School was a sprawling estate of uneven buildings that had been founded during the reign of Queen Victoria and completed in the era of Ted Heath. The original 1880s mansion – where boarders were housed today – glowered down on the parked cars at the top of the winding drive like a grim asylum or haunted castle, putting the fear of God into any *Scooby Doo*-loving ten-year-old. Yikes, I'd thought in 1975 as I took my maiden steps up the drive. Six years later I still half-expected a flock of bats to fly out of the bloody thing at any minute.

In theory, the further west you walked through the school, the more modish and appealing it was supposed to be. But it didn't work like that in practice. The westernmost end was where the grey sanatorium backed on to the all-weather pitch, wafting a chickeny smell of illness to hockey players running up and down the touchline. Some of the most modern annexes of the school, meanwhile, had been built in the architectural golden age of 1968–69, when men with deep-rooted grudges against the young had been allowed to erect drab structures of mustard-coloured brick and ugly blue exterior panelling. Throw in a few hundred children and adults, and the visual effect of Belfast Grammar as a whole was that of a bustling urban hospital bolted on to a Transylvanian remand centre.

At some stage in the past, doubtless with a yearning to be perceived as an even more sombre institution than it already was, Belfast Grammar had acquired its enduring nickname, the College. Occupying a space in the College's main quad between the Modern Languages block and Assembly Hall was the sixth-form centre. Commissioned in 1972 by a previous headmaster, working in close alliance with an architect who had a dislike of windows, the sixth-form centre was a place where the Lower Sixth and Middle Sixth could go if they didn't have a lesson or if it was raining too heavily to smoke fags in the park. The centre had three storeys: lockers and pigeon-holes on the ground floor; then up a flight of stairs to a spacious, smartly furnished leisure area with a coffee bar, stereo and tennis table; and finally up more stairs to a long room partitioned into booths for studying in silence. The leisure area was traditionally more populated than the study floor by a ratio of twenty sixth-formers to one.

But it was to the study floor that I went now, on a lethargic Thursday in the middle of May, taking my choice of sixty-two empty booths and spreading my pieces of paper on the table. It was lunchtime and I could hear faint music from the stereo below. There were no other sounds to distract me.

I arranged the papers in chronological order around me, took out my fountain pen and wrote THE MANUSCRIPT on a fresh sheet of foolscap. Then I added the word REACTIVATED in brackets.

Owing to considerable ongoing changes in the outlook of the author of the document in question, I wrote, *it has not been possible in recent months to make headway with the diverse collection of writings known informally as the Manuscript.*

I read that back and went on:

However, in the light of certain new developments of a serious psychological nature, I now feel compelled to reactivate the Manuscript, and to broaden its scope to include matters confessional, environmental and documentary. Like a small shop that has undergone a change of management, the Manuscript is poised to enter a new phase.

Many of these developments of a serious psychological nature can be traced to intolerable strain resulting from educational pressures, traumas of adolescence, deliberate self-alienation from peers, existentialist dread, sleep deprivation, dieting, unrequited love, overwork, etc. Not the least dismaying consequence of these pressures has been an unwelcome tendency to remember scenes of childhood at inopportune moments, notably on a stressful visit to the Republic of Ireland whilst stricken by influenza. The occasion to which I refer was aborted at parental level, following a vehement altercation between family members in which my own involvement, while caused in great part by influenza-related symptoms, was not fully commendable.

The aforementioned unwelcome recollections of childhood have consistently failed to desist, and are now materializing with increasing frequency. By way of illustration, a state of inexplicable absent-mindedness led me to proceed on the afternoon of Monday, May 11 from the College to a bus-stop on the Ormeau Road — whence to catch an omnibus home to my erstwhile address in Downburn, County Down — rather than walk the short distance to the house in south Belfast where I have resided since 1978.

A repeat of this incident took place on Wednesday, May 13 (yesterday), when I belatedly became alerted to my error after voyaging on the omnibus as far as Belvoir shopping arcade, situated four and a quarter miles south of my official domicile. A sizeable hiatus then ensued, amidst light rainfall, before a northbound carriage became available.

These and other lamentable occurrences collectively provide the impetus for reactivating the Manuscript.

I paused as two Lower Sixth girls came upstairs with coffee mugs, walked slowly along the fawn-carpeted aisle and disappeared into the toilets at the far end.

Moreover, using details from within some of the recollections themselves, the Manuscript will now embrace more music, and less poetry, than at any time since the summer term of 1980, thereby bringing the Manuscript back into line with its initial objective to be first and foremost an entertaining dissertation on musical topics.

Now for the awkward bit, I thought, glancing at a sheet of narrow feint A4 on which PINK FLOYD had been written in biro.

Perhaps mercifully, I went on, few fragments of the prototypical The Manuscript: An A–Z of Rock (winter 1978/spring 1979) have survived. However, an entry for Pink Floyd, written in February 1979, has been found and reveals some naïve opinions and overall judgement of the group's work. Hereby recorded for reference purposes only, the entry reads, in part:

'*At the time of writing, nothing they've done will ever beat* Wish You Were Here *either for music or artwork. Every Pink Floyd fan should have this one in his collection. While exceptional in concept it may be,* Dark Side of the Moon *has grown tedious and besides it lacks the inspiration of "Shine on You Crazy Diamond". Their last album,* Animals, *which most people miss the point of, is recommended owing to its angry feeling about the society we live in, but it donates too much time to only three tracks whereas more numerous ones of shorter length would have been preferred. In conclusion, the group's next move is awaited with interest.'*

Nearly there, I said to myself. Just keep going.

In addition, an entry for the Who, written in April 1979, has been discovered and reads, in part, as follows: 'The tragic death of Keith Moon (RIP) shows no sign of stopping these rock veterans in their tracks. The news that he has been replaced by Kenny Jones (formerly of the Faces, and prior to that formerly of the Small Faces) will surely fill the hearts of all Who fans wherever they are. So come on, Roger, Pete and John, here's to another fifteen years. In conclusion, the group's next move is awaited with interest.'

A mere three lines exist of the next entry, for Wishbone Ash (also April 1979). 'If it's classic rock that you want, you can't go wrong with these boys from Devon. They make it sound effortless. With their duelling guitars and superb craftsmanship, they can always be relied —'

I drew a line under the last paragraph and wrote the words

DISCLAIMER & GUARANTEE.

Needless to say, the deficiencies all too apparent in my musical taste and phraseology as a fourteen-year-old will not, repeat not, be a feature of the reactivated Manuscript. The blame for those aberrations must lie with my then-friend Tinmeer, by whom, in my inexperience, I regrettably let myself be directed. The story of Tinmeer will be told in the Manuscript if and when it is deemed appropriate.

This brings me on to a crucial Tinmeer failing, which has become relevant in view of the recollections that have prompted the Manuscript's reactivation: namely, Tinmeer's unwillingness to take seriously any of

*the music that I had listened to in the years before we met. 'Derivative
garbage,' he would say if I were to raise the subject of the glam rock
acts Sweet, Suzi Quatro, the Glitter Band, Hello and Chicory Tip.
'Juvenile tripe,' he would declare of my one-time fondness for Status
Quo and Queen. 'Meretricious bluster' would be his appraisal of
Argent, Focus and Jethro Tull.*

*Among the objectives of the new, reactivated Manuscript must be
to acknowledge the role played in my formative life by glam rock, heavy
rock, progressive rock and other such 'music for boys', as Tinmeer
cynically called it, and to trace my journey, however painful or uncomfortable, from the days of Downburn Primary School to the threshold
of insufferable melancholia and confusion at which I now stand.*

When the bell rang at 2.20 p.m., I put the papers in my
carrier bag and headed downstairs to the coffee bar. I heard
raised voices as I passed the girls' toilets, but the coast was
otherwise clear.

Letter to Andy, May 27

Dear Lou,

Peel session arrived this morning – thanks. 'Hip Priest'
definitely a classic. See what you mean about 'Do the
Hucklebuck'(!)

How goes life in exile? Or should that be death row?
Eating a hearty breakfast and so on? Reassure me you're not
one of the crack-up cases we hear about. (Latest rumour: an
unidentified female has cut all her hair off and gone on
the run. Do you know who?)

I'm writing this in the sixth-form centre and believe
me, you're better off where you are. Toyah is everywhere,

but everywhere. You can't walk in here without hearing her or getting into a debate about her with our crimped-haired friends. Christ *alors*. Can you believe that 'I Want to be Free' has been acclaimed the most profound youth anthem ever to be played on the coffee bar stereo? *Sheep Farming in Barnet* and *The Blue Meaning* are now regarded as compulsory purchases by the Lorraine Dawsons of this world, who like to stare into their Slim-a-Soup and be mistaken for deep. Polemics have been raging about what Toyah's lyrics are going on about, only to end in Lorraine saying that we must delight in their ambiguity as they are unques- tionably the most intelligent lyrics of all time. I don't know what's got into everybody. Well, I do. Post-Sands trepidation and chaos. That's four of them dead now, as you'll have heard.

Meanwhile in the world of student fascism, I must tell you that our friendly neighbourhood Bigots seem to have invested their extortion monies in the year-old Rainbow LP *Down to Earth*, which as any Bigot will tell you has the same singer as that pitiful old rock cliché 'Night Games' that's just been in the charts. You might say the success of Graham Bonnet has led to full-scale Bigot mania for records that have Ritchie Blackmore guitar solos, and these are played relentlessly any time Doofus is on bar duty. Yes, our only respite from Toyah is being blasted with 'Child in Time' and 'Highway Star', which unlike Doofus you and I realized were bollocks as soon as we got into J. Rotten. Fatboy Wilkinson and that mob now opt to eat their Pot Noodles over the road. Sensible fellows.

Oh well. The Virgins, as per, are listening to their usual mix of Kim Wilde, Blondie and people that Bramerton's read about in *NME*. His current favourite is *Kilimanjaro*, which is not as bad as you said it was. Isobel accuses you of condemning it too rashly, and a few other accusations soon followed, but I'm sure you want the five-minute argument and not the full half-hour. (That was never five minutes.) Personally, as much as I like *Kilimanjaro*, I'm a little concerned that Teardrop Explodes may not be depressing enough for my requirements, but Isobel just sniggered when I told her that and said, 'Oh, I'm sure you're capable of finding misery in anything if you put your mind to it.' Mmmm. Touché Turtle. (She's now reading Muriel Spark with a wry look. Wait – she says hello.)

Enough about us. *Bonne chance* in the exams. Think they'll let you smoke? If you get a minute, write. Talking of which, got any new songs to play me? I wish you'd do me a tape.

Yours in gloom,

Doug

P.S. Were you ever a fan of early glam stuff – Sweet, Glitter, Hello, Quatro and co.?

Letter received from Andy, May 30

Hello Doug,

Everything fine. Looking forward to drinking again, playing etc. Decadents gig/party for my sister's 16th (July 9) if you're around. Venue not confirmed, probably here if we're quiet.

1. No, can't help on mystery girl.

2. Toyah is Lena Zavaroni with hair dye. She is a symbol of unity in our troubled times.

3. Ritchie Blackmore/Rainbow. Can't imagine anything worse.

4. *Kilimanjaro is* disappointing. 'Sleeping Gas' good, but the rest washes in and out. Too much of a happy-happy let-down. Tell Isobel I never rush to condemn an album till I've heard what the title is. Send her my love.

5. I will smoke wherever I please.

6. No songs written since the one you heard. No you can't have a tape.

7. I did like the Sweet, even bought 'Ballroom Blitz'. Glitter and Quatro were a bit too hairy and squeaky respectively. Who were/are Hello? Must have been into my (short-lived) Steve Harley phase then. Tell absolutely no one I said that.

Thanks for not phoning, sorry to be so anti-social. Hoping to sail into Queen's and buy lots of lovely records and vodka with my first cheque. I'll see you in the coffee bar next Friday lunch after the Lit paper.

Linger on,

L.

Monday, June the first was the day the A-levels began. It was expected that some of the Middle Sixth would congregate in the coffee bar at one o'clock to compare horror stories of the German Language and Biology papers. I wanted to be there when they did. I needed to see what the fear looked like up close.

Lest we forgot in all the excitement, though, the Lower Sixth had June exams too. The teachers' advice to us was to approach them as ersatz A-levels (as opposed to mock A-levels, which were not quite so ersatz and which we would take in December). But since the June exams held no great significance in career or university terms, it was difficult to feel any enthusiasm for them, or any energy, or anything at all save for a kind of philosophical listlessness.

Waking early on the Monday, I drifted back into a semi-doze until everyone else had left the house, only then poking one leg out of bed and yielding reluctantly to the morning. Malone Avenue was hushed and calm. It would remain so until the nurses next door returned in the evening, or until a helicopter flap-flapped on a security prowl above the rooftops.

I had a free morning ahead of me to revise for my 3 p.m. History paper, but to hell with that – I'd been trying to put the exams to the back of my mind. I poked out the other leg, lying prostrate and at an angle to the surfboard of my bed. The clock ticked later and later in my ear. I could score zero in every one of my exams and it would still be too late to back out of the contract. The only way out now was to be expelled for murder. Murder of a Bigot, murder of a canteen assistant ... murder of the self. But I'd resolved to put those thoughts to the back of my mind.

The last exam on my schedule was to be English–Latin translation (June 19). I had a perverse longing for it to be as tough as possible. The notion of translating a page of laborious prose into an extinct language in an immaterial examination in a politically tense Belfast in 1981 seemed to sum up the futility of all our lives just about perfectly. With a humourless smile to the mattress, I remembered the Seven Uses of Latin, much talked about by mad old Mr Menzicus when I was in the first form. 'Now some people will say to you that learning Latin is a waste of time. That nobody speaks it.' *Pacing the floor.* 'That it has no uses.' *Aghast look.* 'These people are liars. Latin has seven uses. Next week we will be looking at the Seven Uses of Latin.' But we hadn't. Nor the week after that. Nor ever.

As a thirteen-year-old I'd come up with the Seven Uses of Latin myself, jotting them down in pencil on a blank page at the rear of the *Aeneid*. One of the Uses was fabricating bogus Roman emperors and centurions, a pastime that my pal Eric Callaghan and I shared for several months before I found out that Eric was lifting names from *Monty Python's Life of Brian*. Another of the Seven Uses was conjuring up titles for prog rock album tracks, a hobby I did strictly in private. You could make them sound terribly authentic. 'Fuga Aquilae'. 'Vigilans Vulpis'. 'Semper ad Interim – Opus IV'. Sometimes I would note down the composers' credits and the time I thought the song should last. 'Mors Equitis Velocis' (Emerson–Lake, 22:45). Consisting of five sections: 'Cockcrow', 'Elevenses', 'Off to Blenheim', 'There Comes a Horseman' and 'Finale – in Valour Now Death I Meet for Thee'.

I smiled humourlessly again. Yea verily, that was how one had idled away one's third-form year at one's venerable academy whilst one had prayed for September to tick into June. Self-gratification by means of prog rock and Latin. I'd known better forms of masturbation in my time, to be honest. But I had been a peculiar sort of wanker at thirteen, more fascinated by non-existent Emerson, Lake & Palmer records than by any of their real ones. Small wonder, looking back, that even stoical Tinmeer had despaired of me. 'And this is how you spend your life?' he'd protested in that censorious Germanic tone that brooked no contradiction. 'Trapping yourself in a musical cul-de-sac like that cosy little what-you-call-it crescent in County Down that was only having one way in and out? Man . . . You're almost not worth it, you know that?'

Yeah, well, fuck you Fritz, I thought spitefully, rolling over in bed. *You never did understand me.* I squinted at the ceiling as prog rock memories flooded back to me from abandoned classrooms and textbooks. Names of prog supergroups – both factual and fictitious – tumbled out of forgotten hiding places or stirred from slumber. Renaissance, Tempus, Triptych, King Crimson, Royal Swan Motif, Green Regent. Frozen tableaux of prog life flickered, with a blink, into movement: handsome Yes bassist Chris Squire on the telephone to Roger Dean discussing the sleeve art for *Close to the Edge*; willowy Jon Anderson on a white stool, trilling a madrigal to the porcupine needle accompaniment of Rick Wakeman's harpsichord. Robert Fripp, frowning with a finger to his chin, pondering which one of his arsenal of electric guitars to use on 'Larks' Tongues in Aspic, Part Two', and not being able to choose between Black Evil and Angel of Armageddon. And now a spectacle that I had witnessed many times as a third-former: Jimmy Page standing regally with his double-necked guitar and fidgeting with his hair as Zeppelin prepared to record 'Achilles' Last Stand', but happy to wait while Robert Plant finished leafing through mythologies and chronicles that he'd procured on his travels in the East to enhance his colossal knowledge of history.

The vision of Zeppelin proved a flashback too far, for it reminded me of a letter I'd once written. I shifted distastefully in bed. Something was not right. (*Greetings* . . .) I tried to think of snooker, but no pictures came to me. Something was really not right. Reddening and squirming, cowering from the memory of the letter, I covered my face with the eiderdown and groaned. (*Greetings, mighty . . .*) Something was really and truly not right. Back in January or February, I wouldn't have remembered even liking Led Zep. Now I could recall my letter to them in hideous detail. (*Greetings, mighty James and fair Robert . . .*) I hoped to God they'd never read it. And if they had read it, I hoped they hadn't shown it to Genesis, Pink Floyd and Be-Bop Deluxe.

But then, with a louder groan, I resigned myself to the fact that the Zeppelin Letter would have to go in the Manuscript, every nauseating sentence of it. And all the prog inventions pre-Tinmeer. The rise of Johnny Hempridge. The fall of Green Regent. It would all have to be told. It would all have to be confessed.

What would I write? How should I handle it? *I confess to having bought the following albums and written letters to some of, if not all of, the musicians who made them. I also confess to inventing a parallel universe in which prog rock saw off the threat of punk with ease. I further admit that I listened to Genesis instead of the Clash in 1978. I don't mind if Phil Collins or Roger Waters get to read this, but for the love of God don't anyone tell Andy.*

I flopped out of bed with a sigh and trudged downstairs to get washed. Assembly would be starting in ten minutes, but the College was such a short walk that it was almost impossible to be late. How I wished we could move out of the city, out of the vortex, to a cul-de-sac somewhere with a clearing at the top and no nurses next door.

Extract from the Manuscript, written June 2

Let us say, for argument's sake, that I was a healthy, talkative, outgoing seven-year-old without a care in the world. Exuberant might even be the word I'm looking for. *Obedient* would be another good one. I did my best to oblige, whatever the circumstances. If I was asked to recite the Jabberwocky poem in a funny voice, I would recite the Jabberwocky poem in a funny voice. If I was told to have faith in God, I would have faith in God.

Whatever the circumstances, I did my best to oblige. When we came up from Dublin and the children of Foyle Crescent made fun of my ludicrous accent, I agreed with them that it was a ludicrous accent and helped them think of other ways to make fun of it. A summer boy with a winter birthday, I sprang towards autumn believing that the leaves were not dying but leaping to a better life on the ground. I had no phobias, no aggression, no enemies, no preference who won.

In my mind, now, or in my memory, there seems to be a difference — that is, a different feeling — between being seven and being eight, which I've always put down to becoming aware of pop music in Class 5 of primary school. Becoming aware and knowing that it was a change of circumstances. Becoming aware and remembering feeling alive and conscious at seven, but feeling more so now at eight, and remembering being patted on the arm and my mother saying, 'He likes all those groups with guitars,' so some of it must have happened in a dream before I woke up.

I've seen photographs of me at seven. I look as if I'm concentrating, but I wasn't. From eight, I see a different person in the photos. I can tell there's been a change. I'm surprised nobody else can see it.

I don't remember in what order these things happened. I became interested in the names Lieutenant Pigeon, Slade and Sweet, and began writing them on pieces of paper, in school books, in atlases, in my Dick & Dora stories — I did that more than once, I'm positive. This doesn't necessarily mean I'd heard any songs by those groups. I liked to deface literature at every opportunity. I would colour in the white parts of the French and Italian flags.

I saw a girl called Clare Beattie standing by the blackboard in the

Class 5 room at Downburn Primary that overlooked the cow field. We weren't allowed to play football in the field, because the Huddleston boys had guns and would kill us for trespassing. Clare, who I remember being rather round and having a straw-yellow bowlcut with a fringe like a lampshade, was holding a magazine — its colours attracted me. Though timid of Clare, I joined a group of taller children reading the pop gossip over her shoulder. 'My spies tell me that's Dave Bowie himself playing the mouth organ on "Jean Genie". Our Starman's not just a pretty face, ya know.' Clare didn't look amazed or shocked. She'd evidently read the magazine before.

On another day, before or after, in the same classroom, I asked somebody a question about Alice Cooper, but I don't recall the question or the reply. Weeks later, or maybe months previously, I ached with jealousy when Mary O'Keefe told me her parents let her watch Top of the Pops — but I can't remember why I knew that watching Top of the Pops was a desirable thing to do. Perhaps because by then I'd heard the pop songs.

The pop songs had numbers. Big fat yellow numbers on the charts on Top of the Pops when I had my tea at the O'Keefes' house with Conor, Fiona and Mary. The numbers didn't say 9, 8, 7 like numbers on a door. They said 09, 08, 07, and Conor, Fiona and Mary counted them out loud as the photographs flashed from 10 down to 02. 'They're your favourite group,' one of the girls said to me, and I shyly agreed. The name on the photograph was Sweet. I don't know if they became my favourite group in that instant, or if I'd already heard 'Blockbuster' and fallen under their spell. But that instant, for me, is when the clouds part and I can see a way through.

Friday the fifth of June had a petrified feel and I wasn't the only one who thought so. It was Day Five of the A-levels. The sixth-form centre at lunchtime was a hive of

Middle Sixth agitation, post-mortems, madding crowds and faster-than-usual games of table tennis, while we juniors stayed in the background and gave them space.

Days One to Four had been unnerving to put it mildly. There'd been a brutally high standard in the Sciences, together with a multitude of nasty surprises in the Languages. The tear-stained face of deputy head girl Norma Geary, ordinarily so icy, told its own tale. She had blundered in through the side door, slumped into a chair and just started weeping. A circle of sympathetic onlookers fussed over her with coffee mugs and hip-flasks, but she seemed oblivious to her surroundings. Norma had a Greek exam at 3 p.m. – nerves had obviously got the better of her.

I was one of half a dozen Lower Sixth taking up two rows of facing seats by the wall. We were drinking cups of soup, observing. The baffling caprice of our own exams, of which I had so far taken and in all probability narrowly passed three, was nothing compared to the outrage and disbelief which we could see and hear all around us.

'I'm getting my dad to ring the education and library board.' 'Chaucer! In an A-level!' 'Seriously, we should get a petition going. Make them mark us all up by thirty per cent. It's a travesty.' 'Is that their idea of proper English?' 'We were told to revise Jane Austen . . .' 'I know, and then it's George Eliot . . . I thought there was a page left out.' 'That's me on the dole. Monday morning, I'm signing on. I'm not even coming in for the results.'

The five people sitting with me were Piers Mawhinney, Isobel Clarke, Caroline Howard, Mark Coates and Owen Bramerton. They were a Lower Sixth splinter group, an outcast sect, who owed their solidarity to a cluster of coincidences. All born within days of each other in April 1964, all possessing an Uncle William and an elder brother whose Christian name began with a J, all hay fever sufferers and identity bracelet wearers, they also had in common a superior air, a mistrust of strangers and a penchant for innuendo. Not widely liked as individuals, they were shunned and derided as a clan. They called themselves the Virgins, because they were always talking or thinking about sex. Isobel Clarke, the friendliest of them, was in my Latin class and we sometimes met at Undertones or Stiff Little Fingers concerts in the Ulster Hall. Isobel was petite and doll-like, with hennaed auburn hair which she wore brushed back behind her tiny ears. She and Owen Bramerton accepted me as a satellite, a comrade. But Mawhinney, Coates and Howard were the Virgins' Politburo, and none of them so much as gave me the time of day. The chubby, blond-haired Coates, son of a wealthy Harland & Wolff executive, was said to have the biggest record collection in Belfast. Yet he and Mawhinney would roll their eyes whenever I attempted to chat to them about music. They only ever wanted to talk about sex.

Which was why, having positioned myself at the end of a row with my back to the wall, I had gradually moved leftwards so that I was detached slightly from the other five. It was a useful defence mechanism, I found. Should the Virgins get up and leave, I could pretend that I'd been sitting on my own all along. But they seemed content to stay. Isobel grinned at me occasionally.

In rare moments when they weren't talking about sex, the Virgins talked about the Bigots – their rival faction in the sixth form. Just as you didn't have to be a virgin to be a Virgin, you didn't have to be bigoted to be a Bigot. You just had to give a fuck about being a Protestant. Any viewpoint or stance on why the Church mattered or why religion had a bearing on a person's character, qualified a sixth-former to be a Bigot. And although they detested the name that Piers Mawhinney had conferred on them, the Bigots had no escape from Virginal damnation. They stood out a mile at the College and always gave themselves away – by moving their lips to hymns in assembly, by taking A-level Theology (the Superbigots), and in the cases of male Bigots who were both Bigoted and bigoted, by scrawling 'Motorhead', 'Rush' and 'AC/DC' in thick black ink on their denim rucksacks.

The most you could say for the Bigots was that at least they worshipped Jesus Christ and not Toyah. The ultimate compliment you could pay the Virgins was to describe them as an aloof clique of sex bores. There were more Bigots than Virgins in the sixth form. But I estimated there to be more virgins than either.

Andy was late. From my vantage point by the wall I could see both entrances, but I was pretty sure that the French A-level students would be arriving through the side door near the Modern Languages block, where they would have made a beeline to complain en masse to Miss Vincent about the arduousness of their Literature paper. I guessed they must be doing a question-by-question autopsy. If not, then something. Something that would explain why Andy hadn't appeared in the coffee bar for our lunchtime rendez-vous despite his exam finishing fifteen minutes ago.

Doofus had put Deep Purple's *Machine Head* on the stereo, but I knew he'd keep the volume low as long as there were Middle Sixth on the premises. I passed the time by eavesdropping on the Virgins. A wager was being made between Mark Coates and Owen Bramerton that Coates could get Norma Geary to go to the Botanic that evening for a consolation drink. I didn't fancy his chances. I'd been with Coates, Owen and Isobel after a U2 concert in February, and the Botanic had turned all the boys away for being under age. I'd hung back on the pavement to make it look as if I wasn't trying to get in. 'Do you know who my dad is?' Coates had bleated to the bouncer. 'Do you know what a kick in the face is?' the bouncer had retorted. He should have let me in. I'd have bought him a pint.

Bramerton was offering a quid for the bet. Coates was demanding a fiver. Typical of him: all that money and still he wanted more. Arsehole. But in any event, Norma Geary slept with guys from Ulster Television and was way out of Mark Coates's league.

It was another five minutes before I saw a trio of French Lit students — one boy, two girls — enter through the main door, make their way through the throng of people milling around the tennis table and carve a pathway to the coffee bar. At that, I was out of my seat and straight to the counter on the pretext of buying soup. I wanted news of Andy. The trio were standing to my left, breathing heavily and conversing *sotto voce*. I leaned closer.

'Where's Carrie?' the boy said, turning round as if he'd lost someone. Feeney, I thought. There was a Carrie Feeney who did French.

'She's gone with him,' one of the girls replied.

'In the ambulance?' said the boy. 'They let her?'

'She insisted. She wouldn't let go of him. Aaargh, fuck, she's got blood on her blouse and everything. It's so awful. Poor Carrie.'

'Did you see it happen, Emma?' the second girl asked.

'She's fancied him since fourth form. No, he was sitting

behind me. Right behind Carrie. Did you see her cradling his head? She's going, "I'm here, I'm here . . ." I can't get that out of my mind.'

Whannnggg. I felt a bolt go through me. Oh no . . . Oh God, *no* . . . Lights dazzled my eyes and I clutched the edge of the counter for support. With a sick feeling in my stomach, I pushed away from the coffee bar, barged past the French Lit trio, stumbled out of the side door and down the stairs to daylight and oxygen.

I stared madly at some kids in the quad playing football with a tiny air-flow ball. 'That used to be me,' said a voice in my head, but I shook it away. I was thinking about alphabetical order. Trust a venerable institution like the College to have a passion for alphabetical order. Passionate about rugby, passionate about alphabetical order. I saw the football kids' faces gleam in the sun as I counted back through the examination desks from D to F – this one for Emma Drysdale, that one for Carrie Feeney, and the one right behind Carrie for Andy Finn, also known as Lou, musician, mentor and leader of the Decadents.

Had to decide, quickly. The hospital was west. I ran north.

3
The Decadents

The room was pale blue. It had a bed in one corner by the window, a table by the bed, a sink with a toothbrush in a glass, and an oval rug on which sat a battered armchair with burn holes in both arms. Record sleeves were scattered on the floor, along with books, magazines and two editions of the *Belfast Telegraph*. A bottle of Smirnoff stood on the window-sill. The room smelled of tobacco.

Andy lit two Rothmans and passed one to me. Lying back on his bed, he pushed open the window with his elbow and dangled his cigarette hand out into the June afternoon.

'You looked like you were having a heart attack,' he said. 'Sheila's going to think you're really weird now.'

'She thinks I'm really weird already,' I exhaled.

'She's going to think you're getting weirder. Use that thing under there.' He directed my fingers to a saucer beneath the armchair. It had a squashed fag-butt in it. I placed the saucer on my shaking knees. 'She's going to think you're weirder than ever.'

'I always think she looks at me like she knows something that I don't.'

'Yes, well . . . This time she did.'

Twenty minutes earlier, I had broken with revision proto-
col and telephoned from the call-box outside the school
gates. His mother had answered. I asked her if she had
heard the news. Who is this, she said. I asked her if she
had heard from the school. What news, she said. Who is
this, she repeated. I told her to prepare for a shock. 'Something's happened,' I babbled. 'They've taken him to hospital.' Who's taken who to hospital, she said. Who are you,
she inquired suspiciously.

'Andy! He's gone in an ambulance! Things are wrong!
Sheila, listen! I'm in a phone-box!'

'Andy's in the kitchen,' she replied, then hesitated as if
she were forming a mental picture of someone. 'Are you
. . . a friend of Andy?'

'What kitchen? The kitchen where?'

'The kitchen here. In my house. Where I'm speaking to
you from. Are you the boy who follows Andy's band?'

Follows. What a ridiculous mother word.

'Why did they put him in the kitchen?' I asked, non-
plussed. 'Couldn't they move him?'

There was a pause before she said, 'Hold on. I'll get my
son.'

My ensuing cross-purposes conversation with Andy
hadn't shed any light on the matter, and when the pips
went and I found I had no more change, I put my head
down and sprinted, cursing, all the way up the Malone
Road to the crumbling, dishevelled house in Cranmore Park.
His mother had said not a word to me as she opened the
front door, merely raising her eyebrows and pointing up
the stairs.

'You're looking well,' Andy had greeted me uncertainly.

'Take the armchair, for God's sake. Can I get you a glass of water?'

I'd gasped a Yes Please gasp, sinking into the chair.

'Have you had some kind of attack or something? What was that you told Sheila about an ambulance?'

I'd gasped a Just Give Me a Minute gasp, rocking backwards and forwards in the chair.

'Sorry I didn't make it to the coffee bar,' Andy said, fiddling around with boxes and glasses at the sink. 'But you'll understand why when I tell you what happened. I'm just seeing what I can offer you from the medicine chest. Here, have these. Wait till you can breathe or you'll choke on them. And you'd better have two of these. These ones are painkillers and those ones are aspirin. I just took some before you got here. I had a very nasty shock about half an hour ago – I was just telling Sheila. Drink it in little sips. Honestly, I nearly passed out. I thought I was going to puke.'

I held the glass to my brow. The four tablets felt damp in my other hand.

'Slow *down*. You're making me worried, for God's sake. Take it easy, just take short breaths. Look – I'll tell you *my* melodramatic story first, all right? Yours is obviously too melodramatic to get into just yet. All right. *My* melodramatic story. Here we go. Completely surreal. I'm in the exam about half an hour ago. Everything's fine with the paper, it's not too hard, and we're almost at the end of time. And all of a sudden there's a crash, a huge big crash behind me. Like a shelf falling off the wall or something. I look round and there's Matthew Barr collapsed on the floor. You know skinny Matthew, the athletics guy? The one who goes out with Norma. He's just lying there on the floor looking absolutely dead to the world. So the girls who are sitting near him start screaming, because there's blood coming out of his mouth, out of his nose – it's even coming out of his ears. And this invigilator guy they've brought in from Queen's is running around like a headless chicken. "Keep back! Keep back!" He's absolutely out of his mind, and he's holding his *stopwatch*, because we were all meant to be stopping any minute. There's an unbelievable commotion going on – has Matthew had a brain tumour, or does anyone knows is he an epileptic, or what the hell has happened to him? And everyone's arguing and shouting different things to this invigilator. "Lift his head! I know what to do!" "No, don't move him!" "No, lift his head so he doesn't swallow his tongue!" All this. "Give him the kiss of life!" "I'm not giving him the kiss of life, look at all the blood!" Because the *blood* . . . aucchh. There were streams of it going under the desks, I'm not joking. It was like a horror film.'

Questions were occurring to me. I didn't ask them.

'So *then* – just as I'm thinking, Well, maybe we shouldn't move him till the doctor gets here – then *stupid* Carrie Feeney lifts him up off the floor, and of course what happens but blood pours out of practically every hole in Matthew's head. I really do think there must be something we don't know. I really think there must be a secret love affair going on between him and Carrie. She was acting like she was his *wife*. "Talk to me . . . My beloved! Say something!" I mean, God almighty. And the amount of blood! *Aucchh* . . .

'So *then* . . . She got pulled away, I can't remember who pulled her away. And the invigilator by now has stopped having a nervous breakdown and he says we should just leave our papers and collect our bags and clear off. So . . . no, I think Carrie stayed. Yeah, she stayed actually. She must have been caked in blood. I know Emma Drysdale got some on her too. Emma went off to be sick – as did that Wilson dick, incidentally, so I'll be interested to hear what version *he* puts around. And . . . and then what happened? I think that's it. Alan Owen had already gone to call an ambulance from the staff-room. Someone probably volunteered to tell Norma. No! Alan ran to the sanatorium. "Right, I'm off to the san." Fuck me, what presence of mind. None of us had even thought of it. Because I remember the invigilator looking at Alan as he ran out. "Err . . . what's a san?" Alan just *flew* out the door. We all traipsed out like idiots. A few people went to the Botanic. Can't really blame them. And that was the end of the exam. Thank you and goodbye – pick up your results in August. Absolutely ghastly. Carrie must have stayed with Matthew. And I came home. I hope he's okay.'

Andy had addressed his monologue to the ceiling. Presumably, hearing gasping sounds from the armchair, he had attributed them to my breathless and distressed condition. I was doubled over in the chair with hiccups and convulsions, laughing so hard that my ribs were in agony. I laughed and hiccuped, hiccuped and laughed. I wheezed sheepishly at Andy and gave him a thumbs-up sign. I slapped my thigh again and again with endless unspeakable mirth.

He raises his eyebrows, I thought, just like his mother. The same look of indefatigable patience. The same refined curiosity. Ever such a fleeting hint of pity.

'Take your tablets, Doug,' he said in a monotone. 'I don't know. I hope you don't go to a lot of funerals, that's all. There's just a chance that you'd let the side down.'

*

The first time I'd met Sheila, I had made a highly amusing remark. It was so highly amusing that neither of us had ever forgotten it. Bringing in the dinner plates and cutlery now, she said to me, 'The sharp knife is for the chops. They might be a bit gristly – it's not my regular butcher, I'm afraid. I'll just get the gravy. Oh, and . . .' She did a Lieutenant Columbo turn in the doorway. 'Feel free to stab them if they move.'

'What was that about?' Andy asked me, intrigued.

Andy's group, the Decadents, had played a gig in a Lisburn youth centre. I'd helped them unload their gear from the car – without looking once at the woman in the driver's seat – and had gone off to drink two illicit cans of Tuborg in the caretaker's office with Andy. Sheila had come in wearing an ostentatious fur coat. I thought she was getting the keys to open the soft drinks bar.

'Careful!' I cried. 'That animal may be still alive, madam. Andy, get a knife. Kill it, kill the bastard.'

'Andy, I'm going now,' Sheila said coolly. 'Have a good concert. Phone me later.'

'You've made a friend there,' Andy spluttered when she had gone. 'That coat belonged to my grandmother.'

I'd endeavoured to apologize when she returned later to take the gear home. But by then I'd had two more Tuborgs and she took a dim view of me putting an arm round her shoulder.

'You managed to sort out the misunderstanding, did you?' Sheila asked Andy as she re-entered the dining-room with a gravy-boat and a teapot.

'Eventually,' he nodded, waving his fork at me. 'He thought it was me that keeled over in the exam. He got a bit concerned. He thought I was on a life-support machine in a casualty ward. He was acting on erroneous information.'

'I wish I had friends who were that concerned about *me*,' Sheila said brightly, but something in her eyes told me she was glad she didn't. The three of us ate our dinners looking studiously at three different paintings on three different walls of the room.

When we'd finished, and after I had offered to do the washing-up and been expertly rebuffed, Andy remembered that there was a record he wanted to play me. Up in his bedroom, he told me to look away while he put it on.

'Two points if you can guess who it is. A bonus point if your opinion is the same as mine. Which I'm sure it will be.'

It was *Talk Talk Talk*, the new Psychedelic Furs album – there was no mistaking the heavy-smoker rasp of Butler Rep. All the singers in Belfast tried to sound like him. Andy had the added advantage of looking a bit like him too: punky-bohemian, tousled, beadily intelligent.

'It's so *light*,' I scowled, a minute into the second track. 'This one's just weedy pop. Dave Lee Travis would play this.'

'My thoughts exactly,' Andy said. 'I'm going to take it back and say it's scratched. Terrible disappointment, isn't it? "Pretty in pink", for fuck's sake! He's turned into Steve Strange. Too many cocktails with bits of fruit in them. I'd rather listen to Adam and the Ants.'

He got up to take it off.

'Second album syndrome, you see?' he said over his shoulder. 'What did I say about Gang of Four? These guys should've just split up. Remind me never to make a second Decadents album.'

'You still haven't made the first.'

'Ah,' he said, bending down to find another record. 'Well.'

'Ah well what?'

'Ah well, let's get my A-levels done. Ah well, let's get some money. Ah well, let's find a studio. Or are you suggesting we do it here?'

He put the Psychedelic Furs' debut album on the record-player, turning it up to hear the quiet introduction to 'India'. I wondered if he remembered that this was the first record we'd talked about when he, Noel Johnston and I sat side by side drinking Pernod on the stairs at the party in Finaghy. Probably not. Andy's memory was frightful.

Mind you, I thought with a plummeting heart, he wasn't the one who'd neglected to go back to school after lunch to do his 3 p.m. Latin exam. There would be repercussions from that on Monday, especially if Isobel had happened to mention to Brooke-Taylor that she'd seen me. I'd only realized I was missing an exam when Sheila asked if I was planning to stay for dinner.

'So tell me,' I said quickly, 'was French Lit all right?'

'Yeah, didn't I say? I thought it was just about manageable. Lots of Gide, which was nice of them. If I do as well as that in the oral, I reckon I've a good chance of a B. Queen's want two Bs and a C, and I should get a B in Russian. The only one I'm worried about is Maths. I might have to do some pleading in August.'

'Lou, come on,' I said for the hundredth time. 'It's not too late. Get the College to write you a letter to UCL or Goldsmiths' or somewhere. They'll ask for exactly what Queen's are asking, and you can get yourself out of here. Leave this fucking bomb-site and start living. London's where you belong. Not Belfast.'

'Spoken like a true Dubliner.' He lowered the volume so we could hear each other.

'Go to London,' I said. 'I'll join you next year. We'll get a flat. You can take me to the Marquee and introduce me to all your rock 'n' roll friends.'

'Or take you to my park bench and share my bottle of cider with you. I'm not going to London. You go to London if you want. Come back and visit me. Keep in touch, you know the number.'

'This is a dying country, Andy,' I said sadly.

'Wait till you see England,' he replied, and laughed.

Night was falling. The only skimpy light in the room glimmered from a red bulb in the miniature lamp that lay between us on the bare floorboards. We had moved from the bedroom to the attic where the Decadents stored their equipment and rehearsed once in a blue moon. Looming up in the shadows behind Andy's head was the outline of a sleek UFO balanced adroitly on a slender pole. The rest of Robert's drum-kit was invisible in the darkness.

Andy was going into one of his diatribes about being middle-class. He was a bit drunk. Untwining his legs from the lotus position, he gestured to a guitar that he'd told me many times had cost him £14. 'Not even a copy of a copy,' he said now. 'Oh no. A copy of a *copy* of a copy. Fourteen pounds that cost me, and you hear all these wankers saying, "Oh, it's all right for Andy, he lives in Cranmore Park, he's loaded, he gets a new fucking Fender guitar every Christmas straight from the factory." I mean, look at it. It was only worth five. One of these days I'm gonna be playing it and the neck's gonna fall off.'

He flicked cigarette ash into a dish. 'They're jealous,' he was waiting for me to say. But I said nothing. He had a point – well, a sort of point – but I was too busy reaping the whirlwind of the vodka. I put my head back against Andy's amplifier (£25) and listened to his voice echo. I had never had vodka before. It was like drinking a piece of Ryvita.

'They probably think I've got some kind of trust fund. Limitless cash at my disposal. Just trot along to the bank every few weeks with a sack. Know how much that amp cost? Twenty-five quid. The kids round here get more than that for delivering the *Telegraph*.'

'Laay . . . zeee,' I said with some effort.

'So I don't live in a council house. Big deal. Is that my fault? Would you want to live in one?'

'Bthhh.'

'Do you think I like it when Vance Armstrong and those other dicks take the piss out of me for being in school uniform? "Ooh, look. He's singing in his school uniform." That's right, Vance, I'm singing in my school uniform. They're the only set of clothes I've got that don't have holes in them. But, hey, keep wearing your really nice checked trousers, Vance. Keep looking like a fucking golf player, Vance, the girls love you. Keep getting the words wrong in "Sweet Jane". You dick.'

Nineteen-year-old Vance Armstrong was a topic on which, like the second Psychedelic Furs album, I unreservedly saw eye to eye with Andy. The founder and frontman of the dismal Berlin, Vance was a diehard punk clone who made a big noise with the dilettantes in the east Belfast streets of Braniel. 'He lives in the fockin' Broniel,' Andy would scoff, in a passable imitation of Vance's salty brogue, 'with his brother Doniel and a sponiel called Nathoniel.' And although Andy's and Vance's groups were both inspired by the Velvet Underground, the similarities ended there. Andy had a sincere understanding of the Velvets' music and history. Vance just ripped them off. Berlin were so shameless that they would play 'Sweet Jane' twice at every gig – the second time as an encore, despite no audience ever asking for one. 'Vance, you don't get it,' Andy would shout through cupped hands as Berlin trooped back on. 'They're applauding because you've *left* the stage. They don't want you to come *back*.'

But Vance had a rhino's skin and a duck's back. He also – and I didn't think Andy knew this – had designs on Andy's little sister Denise, whom he'd ogled from across the room when the Decadents and Berlin played on the same bill at the Pound. As far as I was aware, Vance's crush on Denise was the only thing that stopped him from hopping on his motorbike and speeding over to Cranmore Park to beat Andy's smirking face to a pulp. Denise would soon be sixteen, and Vance would be very keen to be at the party. As would we all.

Whereas poor Vance had problems even pronouncing songs (Berlin would occasionally, if the mood took them, perform something entitled 'Shishter Ray'), Andy diligently went to the trouble of writing his own. The urge to compose original material by no means made him unique in Belfast, but it did make him unusual. And Andy's material was the most original in the city by far. The Decadents had a stack of songs that surpassed every one of their rivals' fumbling dirges and carbon copies, putting them comfortably at the head of the pack and enabling Andy to claim, with justifiable pride, that he'd never had to sing a Velvets cover in his life.

Late in April, on the cusp of revision exile, he had played me a new song on his guitar. It had a driving riff, and strange words that he sang with his eyes closed. I was completely stunned.

You finally find your helpless mind is trapped inside your skin
You want to leave but you believe you won't get back again

'Have you any idea how good that is?' I mouthed. 'That is . . . just . . . phenomenal. What's it called?'

'It doesn't have a title yet. Call it "New Song" till I think of one.'

'Play it again!'

This time I'd bashed around on Robert's kit while Andy sang into the microphone. I was dreadful at keeping a beat, but I had a whale of a time smashing at the cymbals. For three minutes, Andy and I were the finest guitar/drums duo in town.

Even the most ambitious bands had their work cut out finding gigs in Belfast, and the Decadents, to my regret, were not the most ambitious of bands. I couldn't see the logic in Andy's idleness; if I had written those songs, I'd have wanted them to be heard by the whole world. Vance and Berlin would periodically play the Harp Bar, but Andy ruled this out as too dangerous. If the crowd hated you at the Harp, they threw their beer glasses at the stage – and they would take extra-careful aim, Andy felt, if the singer in the band were arrogant and sported eyeliner and a school jumper. The Pound was more egalitarian than the Harp, but had a neurotic habit of closing its doors to live music for long stretches without warning. There was the McMordie Hall at Queen's, but you couldn't play there unless you had a record out. The vast majority of Belfast's pubs were hostile to electric music of any kind, scared of being invaded by under-age drinkers. That left two options.

The first was the Ulster Hall, which enlisted young local groups to open for headlining English bands such as the Stranglers and Siouxsie and the Banshees. These concerts were crammed to the rafters, and often thrilling to attend, but cropped up only a few times a year. Ninety-nine per cent of English musicians steered clear of Belfast *in toto*: its venues, its maximum-surveillance airport, its soldier-inhabited streets, its security checkpoints, its tanks, its helicopters and its bomb-damaged hotels. More fool them, because the bands who did play Belfast and survive with limbs intact would always turn up in *NME* or *Sounds* a couple of weeks later, raving about the Ulster Hall having a better atmosphere than any venue over the water. 'Those kids are starved for music,' a well-meaning Jean-Jacques Burnel or Steve Severin would tell the journalist. 'They're not cooler-than-thou or standing there with their arms folded like the people in London.'

However, there were one or two obstacles in the path of the Decadents if they wanted a support slot at the Ulster Hall. Andy was a grammar-school boy from the Malone Road who knew none of the right faces in what passed for the Belfast music business. Terri Hooley at Good Vibrations, who could pull strings in promotion and management, was sceptical of Andy and called him Fauntleroy because of his English accent.

Also, should the Ulster Hall deign to give the Decadents a twenty-minute showcase, there was a risk that the head-liners would be all wrong — a heavy metal band or something worse. 'I'm not putting the Decadents on that stage if we're

51

going to be opening for some creepy sexist shit like Thin
Lizzy or Saxon,' Andy said flatly.

That left the other option: youth clubs. Since forming
the Decadents in June 1980 from the ashes of his previous
band X-Posé, Andy had played just seven gigs in twelve
months, mostly in youth clubs around south Belfast and its
environs, where the audiences were sparse, mystified by the
music and too bashful of each other to jump around.

Andy was less scathing about them than I. 'Don't be so
judgemental,' he'd say. 'Get them young, that's my motto.
No, I had a good time out there.'

'You'd never catch Berlin playing a dump like this, would
you?'

'Well, let's see how many fans Berlin have in six months'
time. A few punks from the Braniel. A couple of Vance's
biker friends if they're not washing their Kawasakis. I call
that fuck all.'

Another excuse that Andy used for the Decadents' intermittent periods of inertia was that he had yet to find the
right blend of musicians – and it was true that the band's
line-up was in a permanent state of flux. Robert had been
the Decadents' drummer since November, but Andy was
always pairing him with incompetent show-offs or kids
from the College who said they were bassists but turned
out to be dicks. Sometimes Andy would sack people for
the most tenuous of reasons. Robert's predecessor on the
drums had been ousted for suggesting that the Decadents
should spell their name with a Z on the end. A rhythm guitarist called Clive Gardiner had lasted one gig before Andy
kicked him out for – officially – stopping in the middle of
'Fast Song' to use his asthma inhaler, but – unofficially –
for being called Clive. 'I'm sorry, but that name's unaccept-

able,' Andy had told me afterwards. 'I can't have Clives playing my songs. I mean, Andy's nothing to write home about, but I've taken steps. I've shortened it to Lou.'

Whatever the Decadents' line-up, wherever the youth club, there were two people guaranteed to be in the audience: myself and Andy's sister Denise. She would always be nicely dressed (no school uniform for her), would always whoop with glee when the Decadents took the stage (assuming there was a stage), and would always scream 'More!' and emit deafening whistles with her fingers in her mouth until Andy led the band back for an encore with a nonchalant wink at his crazed, insatiable fanbase.

Denise was a cherubic fifth-former who had picked up a Belfast accent with uncanny swiftness – possibly at the very moment the wheels of their plane from Heathrow had touched the Aldergrove runway in 1977. She idolized her vain brother, and fell about at his cattier observations, but she herself was an unadulterated sweetheart with no vanity or cattiness in her bones.

'Denise asks Sheila for a rabbit every birthday,' Andy once said to me. 'She sees good in everybody. God knows what she makes of you.'

I'd soon learned what. After many a smile and a nod at youth clubs and in Cranmore Park, the angelic Denise had fluttered up to me on the night in February when the Decadents and Berlin played the Pound. I'd brought Owen Bramerton with me and we were sitting at the bar. Denise came up and assassinated me as comprehensively as if she'd emptied a machine-gun into my body.

'I've just realized who you look like,' she giggled. 'Leo Sayer.'

'Wow. Thanks a lot.'

'He speaks very highly of you,' said Owen to Denise with a laugh.

What a . . . what a *savage* blow that had been. A comparison that insulted not only my face, but my hair, my height and any vestige I might have of self-esteem. Denise hadn't meant it to sound remotely unkind, which was the most humiliating thing about it. I almost wept. But relief was at hand, for Andy had been listening at the bar. He swivelled round to us.

'Ah no, *much* more like Doug Yule, d'you not think?' he said. 'Which in my book makes him an honorary member of the Decs any day. (*To me*) Stand up. No, it's okay, stand up. Right, now – tell me that isn't Doug Yule from the Velvets. It *is*. It's Doug Yule. Watch this. Hi Doug, nice to meet you, what are you doing in Belfast? There – see? Too famous to answer. What more proof do you need? Jesus Christ, imagine thinking Doug Yule was Leo Sayer the disco hamster. "I'm a one man band . . ." Of course you are, Leo. Nobody wants to play with you.'

It had been decent of him to do that. I didn't look like Doug Yule any more than Andy looked like Lou Reed. But an hour later, during the Decadents' set, he had dedicated 'E Minor Song' to 'our friends Denise and Doug', and since that night he had never called me anything else.

'Doug . . . *Doug* . . .'

His voice was beside me in the attic.

'Are you asleep?'

I came back to reality with a start, knocking over my glass and spilling vodka. It would drip through the floorboards, I thought. Stain them like Tipp-Ex.

'Shall I get Sheila to run you home? I'm sure she wouldn't mind.'

'No, no, don't worry. I'll be fine. Actually, yes. Okay. Good idea.'

He was gone several minutes. I thought of Leo Sayer in his clown's uniform, wanting so badly to be tall and suave. And I thought of tall, suave Andy in his College uniform, wanting so badly to be the opposite of his father, that clown who'd divorced Sheila and vanished back to Middlesex. And I thought of the Decadents and the money they would need to break out of Belfast – thousands and thousands of coins and soggy notes, trickling like vodka through floorboards and never being seen again.

4
South Belfast Sting

Extract from the Manuscript, written June 8

The pop songs had numbers. Neat, black, three-digit numbers that said 124 or 133 or 141 or 156. To play a song, you looked at the selection on the rows of cards behind the glass. You kept looking, kept looking — no, not that one — kept looking until you found 'Blockbuster' by Sweet. Then you said the three-digit number to Daddy in a very urgent voice while tugging at his elbow and pointing to the slot where the coins went. That's how you played a song on a jukebox in an amusement arcade or a Wimpy bar.

A Wimpy bar like, say, this one. It's a Saturday afternoon in January 1973 and we are gathered here today in the sight of waitresses, O Lord, that we may marry hamburgers and chips in an everlasting union. There is one squeezy red plastic ketchup squirter on each table, there are charming menus in the windows that show you how your meal will look, and there are families of Dubliners coming through the door at intervals, sizzling from the rain. We used to be a Dublin family ourselves. But now we just come down for weekend visits when the Hillman Imp isn't banjaxed.

I saw the jukebox in the corner of the Wimpy as we were walking in, naturally, but I didn't say anything to my parents because that's not how the plan goes. You have to do everything the way the plan says. Tell them about the jukebox too early and the plan is blown sky-high. 'We're here to eat, aren't we, not chuck money in machines,' they just say crossly, and that's you told good and proper. So you have to be sneaky and pretend there is no jukebox. You don't look in the corner, you only look at the menu, and only at the hamburgers and chips, not the knickerbocker glories and banana boats on the back. Good boy.

When the waitress writes down what everybody's having and goes away to tell the chef, you pretend to listen closely to your parents' conversation about getting rid of the Hillman Imp and buying a Triumph. Stop that. Do not squeeze the squeezy red plastic ketchup squirter – you won't impress anybody and you'll get sauce all over your cardigan. Leave it alone. Now the next part of the plan is the tricky part.

Somebody from one of the Dublin families has to go over to the jukebox and put some money in. The plan doesn't work otherwise. Oh, that's handy – there's someone putting money into the jukebox now. Pretend not to watch them. A clever way of doing this is to tidy up the table by putting the squeezy red plastic ketchup squirter back where it was, next to the salt-cellar, the pepper-pot and the sugar-shaker. And now you just wait for the jukebox to play the song.

It doesn't have to be a song you know. Look pleased whatever it is, and start humming the tune quietly. Not that quietly, dummy, or no one will hear you. And don't bang the salt-cellar and the pepper-pot together in time to the music. You'll ruin everything.

'What on earth is this song?' they will ask.

You can say anything here. Say it's 'Stay with Me' by Blue Mink. They won't know.

'Where did you learn it?'

'It's in the charts,' you reply. 'I've heard it loads of times.'

'How? You haven't got a radio.'

(Yes, well, that's a bit of a sore point. I've been meaning to talk to you about that.)

'No, I know, but I've heard it a lot of times on jukeboxes. You know those things that you can play a song on and it only costs five pee? They have them in some Wimpys, but I don't think there's one . . . Oh yes there is. Over there in the corner, and it's not being used by anybody at the moment.'

We have ignition. Hold on to your hats.

'And it takes five pees, does it?'

Lift-off! 'One five pee. Only one five pee. Or you can play three songs for ten pee, which works out at better value.'

'Well, shall I see if I have a five pee? Is there a song you'd like to play?'

'Yes, there's one in the charts that I quite like.'

Majestically done. Now run to the jukebox (to display gratitude) and find the number for 'Blockbuster' as quickly as you can. Good boy, congratulations.

Now that I'm eight, I am ready for 'Blockbuster'. I am old enough and ready enough. I want Sweet to sing 'Blockbuster' to me out of the jukebox. I know how it starts and what it sounds like and what some of the words are. I've heard 'Blockbuster' before. But although I can remember how it starts and what it sounds like and what some of the words are, I've suddenly forgotten everything about it, so I need to hear it again.

'Well, I'm not hearing anything.'

No, that's normal. There's always a delay after you put the money in. Then there's a clicking and whirring noise, which lets you know that everything's ready, and the clicking and whirring noise changes into another noise that's like the police cars on McCloud. This is the noise that makes me feel embarrassed, hot and happy. It's the noise that tells me 'Blockbuster' is starting.

'*That's the right one, isn't it?*'

It's the right one, yes. This is the one that I like. It's the song that makes the best flavour when you mix it with what makes me.

'*It's a bit loud.*'

A bit loud, yes. That's the sound that I like. Let's do something as soon as 'Blockbuster' is over. I wanna drive the dodgems. I wanna go in a police car. I wanna ride Champion the Wonder Horse. I'm not going to cry once today. No fear.

The rain will still be pelting down outside. It will smack our faces as we go out of the Wimpy, which is the reason we came in. The awnings of the Dublin shops will provide shelter for the people with bare heads, while the ones with umbrellas queue for buses. I will be laughing because I like it when the splashes land on my hood, and because I've remembered that the dodgems aren't open in the winter, you dummy.

At the beginning of the new term in September 1980, Mark Coates had surprised the other Virgins. He had grown an inch and a half since they'd last seen him in June – but that wasn't the surprise. 'And I don't just mean an inch and a half in *height*, ladies,' he added with a chortle – but, revolting as it was to contemplate, that wasn't the surprise either. The surprise was that Coates, shortly after returning from his family's annual August holiday in the Caribbean, had purchased a musical instrument.

Coates was not known to be of a musical disposition, and accounts were legion of the College's Christmas carol service in 1976 that he had sabotaged with his tone-deaf recorder playing. According to witnesses in the orchestra pit, an excruciating 'Hark! The Herald Angels Sing' was the final straw for the conductor Mr Jessop, who, out of eyeshot of the parents' gallery, leaned over and snatched Mark's recorder from his mouth. 'Coates,' he hissed, 'you shall not destroy music of beauty.'

And yet, in August 1980, Coates had bought a Rickenbacker bass guitar. He assured the Virgins that they were looking at a star of the future. Coates would 'learn the hang of' the bass in a fortnight by playing along to Bruce Foxton on *Setting Sons*, and would promptly form the College band to end all College bands. An advertisement duly went up on the sixth-form centre notice-board: 'Talented bassist seeks singer and guitarist. Also drummer. Book your audition now! Influences: Jam, ELO, Vapors.' He had no replies.

'Belfast's no place for a musician,' I heard him say to Owen Bramerton when the ad had been taken down. 'It'll be a different story when I get to Cambridge.' The bass guitar was not mentioned again.

But Coates would not have sold the bass, I knew, because the only transactions that appealed to him were those that made a profit. You couldn't sell a Rickenbacker bass in Belfast for more than £100 – and Coates had bought it new for £210. Besides, I hadn't seen any cunningly worded For Sale advertisements on the notice-board. ('Bruce Foxton's bass. Genuine. Complete with autograph. Only £275.')

No, Coates would still have the bass. He would have four weeks to practise it. I didn't think it was beyond the realms of possibility. Coates would be the new bass player in the Decadents.

My Friday night at Andy's house had given me a pounding headache, so it wasn't until mid-afternoon on Sunday that I was able to phone him. We exchanged pleasantries, discussed hangover cures, very much our usual type of social call. I let Andy repeat and embellish the Matthew Barr story from Friday, without interrupting him. My plan was a complicated one and I had to step carefully at every stage along the route. Andy didn't know he needed help, but I knew. And if he wouldn't help himself . . .

'Oh, speaking of Matthew,' I said airily, 'what would happen if one of the Virgins asked Norma Geary out?'

'Norma? No chance. When? Do you mean hypothetic-ally? Absolutely not a chance. Those kids are out of their depth. They're better off saving up their pocket money for a prostitute in the Europa.'

'What about if one of them asked her out on Friday? Just after she'd heard about Matthew?'

'You jest. You're not serious. Really? Come on, spill the beans. Who was it?'

'I think he thought she was crying because she was worried about her exams.'

'Christ in heaven,' said Andy. 'Well, he'd have been flattened. She'd have kicked the living shit out of him. And I know a lot of people who would've helped her. "The Virgins . . ." Well named.'

'You don't like them?'

'Come on. They're little kids. Puerile little boys and girls.'

I changed the subject. 'By the way, who are you getting to play bass for Denise's party?'

'Funny you should bring that up,' Andy said. 'I was just thinking about that. I had a look in Good Vibrations yesterday and the only bassist I could find a number for lives in Ballynahinch and he likes Crass and the Angelic Upstarts. No thanks, Sid. They may be desperate times but they're not that desperate.'

'You wouldn't be tempted to ask Paul Leckie?'

'Fuck, no, I'm not going through that again. Paul Leckie? "Here, Finno, what's your album of the year? Mine's *Me Myself I* by Joan Armatrading. The lyrics are really meaningful. Would you like me to tape it for youse?" Did I tell you he taped me *Duke* by Genesis and asked me if we could do "Turn It On Again" in the Decs? "It's got great drumming, so it has." Yeah. Goodbye, Paul. Have a nice life.'

I laughed.

'And the only other bassist I can think of is Edwin Fleming, but he's off on a kibbutz for the summer. And I can't put an ad up in Good Vibrations because they'll just take it down. Come on, Doug, who else plays bass? Do you know anybody?'

'Not off the top of my head,' I said slowly. 'Give me a sec, I'm just thinking. Bassists. Do I know of any. Let me see. Bassists.'

I let five seconds tick by on the clock in our hall. Then another five.

'I suppose there's . . . No, hang on, he'd be no good.'

'Who?'

'No, it's all right,' I said. 'I just thought of somebody, but I don't have a number for him. Somebody at school.'

'In the Lower Sixth?'

'Yeaaah, that's the trouble. Lower Sixth. Because you know we've got these frigging exams until the nineteenth, and he's never around when I'm around because he's doing – what is it he's doing? – Politics, Computer Studies and ah . . .' Opening the telephone directory on the hall table, I traced my finger down the column. 'Auto Maintenance.'

'But you'll see him the week after, won't you? When the exams are over?'

'He's hardly ever in the sixth-form centre, unfortunately,'
I said in a rueful voice. 'It's a shame I don't know his
surname, or I could put a note in his pigeon-hole. Then
there's Wimbledon coming up as well, which I know he
really likes watching. Oh, this is so annoying. I might not
see him again before the end of term.'

'So that's him out.'

'Yeah,' I agreed mournfully. 'I mean, unless . . . The thing
is, I've been to his house before. Well, not for years, but I
can vaguely remember where it is. I don't know the address,
but I'd be able to find it. You keep going up Malone Road
and it's one of the roads up there. I'd recognize the house
if I saw it.'

'Bladon Drive? Deramore Drive? Deramore Park?'

'That's what I mean, I don't know the address. I'd have
to walk around until I recognized the house. Let me think.'

Ten more seconds ticked by.

'Who is this guy anyway?' Andy asked abruptly. 'You
haven't told me what kind of music he listens to. You
haven't even told me his name. All I know is he likes tennis.'

'No, he's great. He was in a band last year, now that I
think of it – him and his friends. They were pretty good. I'm
trying to remember what they were called.' The telephone
directory helped me out. 'Axis Industry. They were a bit
like Joy Division, that whole Factory scene. I saw them
practising in the Music block a couple of times, they were
starting to get good. But then the singer left so they jacked
it in.'

'All right, fine. But how do I get hold of the bassist? Do
you want me to walk up and down Bladon Drive singing
Joy Division songs?'

'Well, look,' I said placidly. 'Where are we now – June?

And today's the seventh. We've got a bit of time. Why don't we get our exams out of the way first? This guy won't need more than one rehearsal, he's that good. You could even teach him the songs the day before. As soon as my exams finish, I'll take a wander up Bladon Drive, or wherever he lives, and I promise you I can find the house. I just need to see it from the front.' My hand tightened around the phone. 'I'll keep going back there till I find it. Might take me a few days.'

'And you're absolutely sure he can play bass? Why don't you just get his number from the other kids in Abstract Industry?'

'Axis Industry,' I laughed strenuously. 'Sure, if you think Annadale won't mind me walking in and asking if I can look in all their classrooms for three guys in the sixth form. They're not from the College, Andy. They all go to Annadale, apart from the bassist. And I only saw them practising once or twice and I didn't really get a proper look at them.'

'Why were they practising at the College then? Why didn't they practise at Annadale?'

'*I* don't know. Better facilities. Fewer people around. And of course the bassist would have the run of the Music block at the College, because of his brother playing the oboe. He left last year, though. I think he went to Edinburgh.'

'What's his brother got to do with it?'

'Because,' I said patiently, 'the bassist must have got the keys off him. He must have made a copy. To have somewhere to rehearse.'

I was back on safe ground. Bands in Belfast would do anything for a rehearsal space. Berlin had once broken into a Presbyterian church.

'Okay, okay,' Andy interjected. 'So you reckon you can find him. It sounds a bit convoluted, going looking for a house . . .'

'I literally only have to see the front garden. It's got roses and daffodils and a swing – oh, look, I'll find it.'

I replaced the receiver with a sigh of relief. The plan was afoot. I went back upstairs to my room to do some more writing before dinner. Tomorrow morning I would have a harder task: convincing Mark Samuel Agnew Coates of Deramore Park South that his chariot of destiny had arrived. Andy didn't know it, but Coates was the perfect bass player for the Decadents. He had a bass. And he had money.

Extract from the Manuscript, written June 8

Fear? Oh, you mustn't show it. You have to be brave and keep your eyes peeled. You have to watch out when Blockbuster's about. He's a wicked, evil man who's done something so bad that every police car in the world is on his trail.

For instance, if he gets you, and you've got long black hair, he'll make it go white – it already happened to Sweet's singer. When Sweet are on Top of the Pops *round at the O'Keefes' house, the singer feels his hair with a furious look on his face, holding it out to show everybody. It's his way of saying to us, 'Do you want to know how bad Blockbuster is? Look what he did to my hair. And what's more, if he finds you, and you've got long black hair, he'll do this to you too. That's why we've got to catch him.'*

I know he's not really saying that. It's just a song in the charts. But it's very realistic. It sends a shiver down my spine to think that Blockbuster could be a cut-throat like the pirates in Treasure Island.

He might have a wooden leg and a parrot, and he might know where the pieces of eight are buried. God! He might even be blind like Blind Pew and have a stick that taps on the ground to tell you he's coming. But then, if he's blind, how does he know if you have long black hair? He could be deaf and know that, but not blind.

Sweet will be on Top of the Pops *again on Thursday. Fiona O'Keefe says so, because 'Blockbuster' is at number one now. I'll ask if I can have my tea at the O'Keefes' house. I'm sure the answer will be no. Then I'll ask if I can watch* Top of the Pops *on our television. Don't bother answering that one.*

It's not as if I'm asking to watch The Liver Birds. *If I can play songs on a jukebox, I don't see why I can't watch* Top of the Pops. *It isn't rude or grown-up. Jimmy Osmond's parents let him go on it, and he's not much older than I am.*

I've got to think of a plan. You sometimes have to be crafty about these things. A few lies might have to be told. But lies are not the same as being evil like Blockbuster if they're in a good cause. Jimmy Osmond probably tells his parents a right load of old rubbish sometimes.

At one o'clock on Monday, I finished a three-hour History exam in which I filled one page with everything I knew about the Suez crisis and seven pages reiterating everything I'd said on the first page. I got to the sixth-form centre just as Piers Mawhinney was leaving it.

'Is Coates up there?' I asked him.

'No, he's not. Aren't *you* the wee rebel, though? Not turning up for your Latin exam on Friday, I hear. Bad boy.' He cackled and strode off across the quad.

In the coffee bar, Owen Bramerton and Caroline Howard were sitting together at a table for four, reserving the other two chairs with their blazers and bags. *Sheep Farming in Barnet* was on the stereo, much to the visible satisfaction of Lorraine Dawson and her crimped-haired cronies seated near the counter. Bramerton and Howard, I thought to myself. Not the ideal combination, but it would have to do. I paid for an oxtail Slim-a-Soup at the counter and made as if to walk past their table and sit on my own. Bramerton lifted one leg to block my path.

'Have we got something contagious? Sit down and tell us how your exam went on Friday. Oh, I forgot – you didn't go.'

Caroline gave a whinny. I had a brief glimpse of her crooked teeth and immense gums before she concealed them with her customary mask of disdain. It paid to be wary of Caroline Howard. The vitriol she trained at other girls behind their backs was astonishing, and she wasn't tremendously polite to their faces. The boys were referred to as 'penises' – or, if she was being pejorative, 'wankstains'. She knew words beginning with C that Sven Hassel would have blanched at, and dropped them casually into anecdotes about her family in Newtownbreda and her Saturday job at Boots. The most foul-mouthed virgin in civilized Europe, Caroline despised us all.

'So what was your excuse?' Owen asked me, removing his blazer from the chair beside him. 'Suicide attempt?'

'I left my hockey stick at home,' I said facetiously, but I could see the joke meant nothing to him. Acne-faced Owen had no memory of our second- and third-form friendship, terminated when we chose different O-level subjects. He was affable enough to me now, but only in the present tense, not in the past. Owen's self-confidence did not permit him any recollections of pre-adolescent times. Oh well. I'd been a devout self-reformer like Owen in recent years –

without the confidence – before the memories started worming their way through my defences. Owen's defences never came under threat. No anxiety or existentialist dread for Owen. He didn't even fret about his acne.

'Is the other chair for Coates?' I asked him as I sat down.

'Aye, he'll be in later. Why? Do you need to borrow some money?'

'To buy your Latin teacher a wee present,' Caroline tittered. 'A wee linen handkerchief for sir, to say sorry. Aww.'

'No, it's not important,' I said. 'Just that there's a party in Cranmore Park on July the ninth and I've been told to invite everybody. Come along if you're around. I suppose Coates will be away on holiday.'

'No, Mark will be here,' Owen said. 'They go to Barbados in August, so his mother still has her suntan when the coffee mornings get going again.'

'Oh, that's right,' I said. 'I'd forgotten. Well, if he's going to be around, it's in Cranmore Park on the ninth. He lives up that way, doesn't he?'

'Whose party is it?' Caroline asked. 'Will there be all screwing in the bedrooms and up the stairs? I bet Kelly Farrell's going to be there, screwing. Little anorexic bitch.'

'Well, this is why you probably won't want to go,' I said offhandedly. 'It isn't a Lower Sixth party. It's going to be full of fifth-formers.'

'You can stop right there,' muttered Owen. 'A party's a party, but I've no intention of watching silly wee boys getting drunk. I'll be staying home. I've got shelves to dust.'

'And me,' said Caroline.

'Fair enough,' I conceded. 'Actually, it probably would have been even worse than that, Owen. You'd have been watching a lot of silly little *girls* getting drunk. The place is going to be heaving with them. Can you imagine? Millions of fifth-form girls everywhere, getting drunk and throwing themselves at anyone in trousers. Sounds vile. Apparently there won't even be any adults there to stop them.'

'You're inviting me to a fifth-form *girls'* party?' Caroline snapped. 'The fucking cheek you have. Them wee millies are the biggest whores in the school. I know things about some of them girls that would make you sick.'

Owen's eyes had widened slightly. I decided to press on.

'Well, I did think it was the sort of thing none of us would be seen dead at,' I admitted. 'I probably won't even mention it to Coates, to be honest. I'm only going myself because there's a band playing.'

'A band?' Owen said. 'Who? A fifth-form band?'

'No, it's those guys the Decadents. I've no idea why they're playing. Must be some sort of comeback thing. I thought they'd split up.'

I was depending on Caroline to say the necessary words to Owen. She didn't let me down.

'Ooo-hoo! The Decadents! Wee queer boys wearing their mummies' make-up! Oh, you've *got* to go to that party, Owen. Oh, Owen, take your *NME* with you, and you can sit around talking about all your favourite wee homo bands with the Decadents. All the Spandau Ballet homos. New Romantic. David Bowie in his lovely dress.'

'Shut your yap, Caroline, the Decadents are all right,' Owen retorted. 'They're one of the best bands in Belfast. At least they're doing something original.'

'Oh, that's right, Owen,' I said. 'I'd forgotten you'd seen them.'

He turned to me. 'Did they split up? They were good, though, at the Pound. Are they getting back together?'

'Well,' I said in an apprehensive tone, 'they were hoping to. But unfortunately, from what Andy the singer told me, it's a problem of not being able to find people who can play certain instruments. I mean, he had terrible trouble finding people to play bass in that band. Terrible trouble. In fact, he's still looking for someone to play bass at this party in Cranmore Park on the ninth. He can't find anyone at all. I get the feeling the Decadents probably won't be able to play.' I added under my breath, 'Shame. I'd like to have seen them.'

Caroline hooted.

I went on: 'And the bass is *such* an important instrument in a band, that's the thing. Andy the singer is always saying that. He's always saying things like, "The bass is like the king in a game of chess. He doesn't have to do much, but if he's not there you might as well pack it in. It's bloody typical of Belfast not to have any good bassists. People who know about David Bowie, Lou Reed and the Jam." But there we are. He just can't find anyone. *Au revoir* to the Decadents. Great shame.'

Caroline prodded Owen across the table. 'My brother saw the Decadents play in this youth club last year,' she said. 'Guess how many people were there. Not including the ones in the band.'

'When's the party?' Owen asked me.

'The ninth,' I replied. 'It's in Cranmore Park.'

'Eleven,' said Caroline.

'And it's just a bass guitarist he needs?'

'That was all he needed,' I confirmed. 'Too bad.'

'*Eleven*. And you'd have thought they were playing the Ulster Hall. Dedicating songs to their wee friends in the audience and getting them to shout for an encore. James said they were crap.'

'You know who has a bass?' Owen said.

'Paul Leckie,' I cut in. 'I know, Owen. Nice idea. But he'll be away on holiday.'

'No, no. Mark. Mark has a bass.'

'Mark,' I said, puzzled. 'Oh, Mark McLean? From Carrickfergus?'

'No, Mark Coates. Do you not remember? He bought a bass last year and tried to get a band started.'

'Put a wee ad up on the notice-board,' Caroline said pertly. 'I remember.'

'Oh, that's *right*,' I exclaimed. 'But hold on, that was months ago. He'll have flogged the bass by now.'

'No, he's still got it,' Owen said. 'It was in his bedroom the last time I went round.'

I shrugged noncommittally. Bass guitars in bedrooms, eh? Heigh-ho. You've seen one, you've seen them all. Owen would have to make all the running now.

He began firing questions at me. Would the Decadents play at the party if Mark agreed to join? Would the Decadents want Mark to join? How long would Mark have to learn the songs? What was the date again? I pursed my lips at each question, saying nothing. Owen then began trying to convince me of the suitability of Mark. He led me to understand that Mark was quite the dark horse. He evangelized about Mark's bass-playing astuteness, skill and discipline. He listed all the songs that Mark could play – some of which may even have been true. He wore down my misgivings and ultimately he persuaded me.

'Yes, but Owen,' I said with a fatalistic shake of the head, 'you're forgetting one thing. What did I just tell you about the party? There's going to be a whole load of silly little drunk fifth-form girls who'll be staring at Mark while he's playing, and they'll probably hassle him all night and ask him to' – I laughed joylessly – 'sign their tee-shirts or something. I appreciate you trying to help, Owen. But we're back to square one.'

Caroline saw Coates come through the door before I did, but, crucially, I saw him before Owen.

'I'd better shoot,' I said. 'I've got a Latin teacher to apologize to. Wish me luck. Shame about that party.'

I took my soup mug up to the counter, passing Mark without a word. Usefully, I noticed a hairline fracture in the mug as I set it down, and I stood for a few seconds examining it. From the table I'd just vacated, I heard the voices of two people. The first was Mark growling, 'What's up with him?' The second was Owen saying, 'Coatesy, my son, your wanking days are over.'

5
History Revision

Kitchen sounds had a soothing quality at 4 a.m. Nylon socks on spotless linoleum. The pull of a cord made the fluorescent light purr. The refrigerator opened for business with a soft thunk. Cold water swooshed from tap into kettle spout.

I was used to creeping around the house at night, and it was usually to the kitchen that I came. Soundlessly, weightlessly, I would pad down the first two flights of stairs from my bedroom, pause on the landing outside my parents' door, then continue my descent like a thief in a cartoon tiptoeing to the notes of a xylophone scale.

Do-ti-la-so-fa-mi-re-do. Ground floor: living-room, dining-room, hall, cloakroom and kitchen.

These were the daytime areas, but they hadn't been my daytime areas for almost a year. Since withdrawing from the world into solitude, I had confined myself to the top of the house, sleeping when I could (or wanted to) and slinking down in the small hours to make coffee and rummage in the fridge for things in jars, tin foil or Tupperware. My nocturnal routine was disconcerting to the rest of the family, particularly when it accidentally synchronized with their morning routine and we all found ourselves queueing for the bathroom in our dressing-gowns. I hadn't received a formal complaint from them yet. Maybe they thought my upside-down way of life was a revision strategy.

The fridge tonight contained a carcass of ham, jars of pickles, a lettuce, tomatoes, a small fat cylinder of smoked cheese and a packet of corned beef. I had run out of Vesta curries – the only hot food I knew how to cook – and was too distrait for a salad. I took the cheese and the corned beef, some coffee and the kettle, and stole away upstairs.

The bookcase in my bedroom was cluttered with the booty of previous raids: empty Guinness bottles, dirty cups, plates, spoons, marmalade, a loaf of Slimcea, a box of Frosties. I cleared a space for the kettle by sweeping *The Odessa File*, *Catch-22* and a Dick Francis paperback on to the floor. The cheese was a nightmare to unpeel with my bitten-down fingernails. In the end I used a Guinness bottle-top.

I ate my supper at the window, pulling back the curtains to study the council of birds on the roof of number 91. Why they always chose 91 for their councils, and not 89 or 93, I didn't know. Ninety-one must have been the equivalent of their City Hall. Their agenda each day consisted of chirping for about an hour and buggering off once they'd inconvenienced as many people as possible. They weren't unlike the real Belfast councillors in that respect.

After a few minutes of spying on them, I decided to pick a bird to identify with. 'Find me a bird,' I said, like Rachel Roberts in *O Lucky Man!*. 'Can you sniff him out for me? Can you?'

One bird was chirping away in a highly strung fashion

to a pair of bigger birds on the TV aerial, who were ignoring him and looking towards the Lisburn Road. 'You would appear to have the right credentials,' I said. But then he turned his head in the same direction as them, and was instantly disqualified. 'You blew it,' I said. 'You're not me.'

I became aware of a bird on the guttering who had a distinctive pattern of behaviour. Every time a newcomer landed he would fly away, circle the rooftops of Malone and Eglantine Avenues, and return moments later to perch on a different part of the guttering. I had a winner. 'Superbird,' I pronounced him with a Benny Hill salute. 'Now that cursed Yankee Doodle Pigeon has met his match.'

When I had eaten all the corned beef and sucked the last flakes of cheese out of the wrapper, I plugged my yellow foam headphones into the stereo and listened to side one of Roxy Music's *Flesh + Blood*. I had been playing the album for three days solid. It had some of the dullest middle-of-the-road songs that Roxy had ever recorded, but since Monday no other music could scratch me in the spots where I itched.

My behaviour had been a bit like *Flesh + Blood* in places. Cold. Inscrutable. Professional. As with Roxy, my latest stuff was a good deal more questionable than my earlier stuff. I positively hated deceiving Andy, and I wasn't all that crazy about hoodwinking Mark Coates. In my bedroom I had turned to the Classics in my collection, but every one I put on seemed to be sending me barbed messages. *Rubber Soul* – 'Nowhere Man', 'I'm Looking Through You,' 'Run for Your Life'. *Imagine* – 'Crippled Inside', 'It's So Hard', 'Gimme Some Truth'. Anything whatsoever by Bob Dylan.

In my mind I heard Tinmeer, that great pragmatist,

scorning me for being so conceited. 'But this is not the way to listen to the Classics! Remember, those songs were not written for you. You were how old when the Beatles made *Rubber Soul*? One year? Two? Then it is not your right to monopolize it.'

He'd have loved *Flesh + Blood*, ho ho. ('An effete fiasco! How can you stand it? I give up on you!') Yes, well. I was indifferent to its hi-tech blandness as a matter of fact, but I was grateful not to be frightened out of my wits by the lyrics. There was something about Roxy's decline into awfulness that satisfied my arch-villain soul.

As of now — 4.35 a.m. on Friday — the plan was working and I had Andy and Mark in position. I would keep them apart for four weeks. Andy wouldn't ask any more questions; he imagined I'd be embarking on my Bladon Drive bassist-hunt towards the end of June, coming up trumps with an easygoing Joy Division fan. Instead, on July 8, I would present him with his new bassist, an uncouth arsehole who liked the Vapors and reeked of Blue Stratos. All in a good cause, I reminded myself. You sometimes have to be crafty about these things.

Mark had been deeply suspicious about my involvement, but flattered by the Decadents' interest. He had also been delighted by Andy's matey letter to him (which I had writ-ten) and titillated by the thought of having his clothes torn off him by Denise's fifth-form friends. Mark had made just two stipulations when we spoke in the coffee bar on Thurs-day: he wasn't going to wear eyeliner at the party for any-body, and the Decadents would have to pay his taxi fare both ways. I told him they would be honoured. Meanwhile he accepted my explanation that Andy, Robert and the organ player Dermot were up to their necks in A-levels and would be too busy to rehearse with him until the weekend of July 4–5. I emphasized to Mark that the Decadents' songs were musically straightforward and could be learned even as late as July 8 if the weekend rehearsal fell through, not that there was a serious likelihood of that happening.

'Play along to this every day in your house,' I said, loaning him my copy of *White Light/White Heat*. 'You won't actually be playing any of these songs in the Decadents, but they'll give you an idea of what the Decs sound like. Don't do any fiddly bits, just stay on the thick strings. And skip the ballad.'

'"Lady Godiva's Operation",' he read on the back cover. 'Was that to make her tits bigger?'

'On second thoughts, just play the first song and the last song,' I told him. 'We don't want to be musos.'

I made him swear that he would listen to *White Light/ White Heat* day in, day out for a month, and that he would pop home to Deramore Park South for a play-along-a-Velvets session whenever he had a free morning or afternoon between exams. The Decs would be considerably cheesed off, I intimated, if they knew their hot-shot bassist were drinking coffee with his buddies in the sixth-form centre rather than psyching himself up for the band's momentous comeback show. He followed my reasoning.

I thus eliminated Mark from potentially disastrous chance-meeting-with-Andy scenarios in the coffee bar. Just to be on the safe side, I also warned Andy by phone that word of Denise's party had leaked to Paul Leckie. Leckie was hell-bent on securing a forty-minute support slot for his new group, Fusion Express. 'He's in the coffee bar all day long, waiting for you to walk in,' I notified Andy. 'He's like a man possessed. His quote to me was, "I see Fusion

Express as being Northern Ireland's answer to Weather Report. We can really turn those fifth-formers on to jazz-rock. By force if we have to." You'd better keep a low profile.' Andy sounded alarmed and said he would.

I had to hope that Andy and Mark wouldn't bump into each other on the Malone Road or in the city centre. There was no contingency plan for hazardous encounters outside school. I could hardly monitor their every move, after all. I could only manipulate the ones that occurred to me.

Stirring another coffee with a jittery heart, I reflected that it was all a question of taking responsibility for one's actions. That's what everything came down to. Obviously, I would be faced with certain situations in which taking responsibility for my actions did not apply so much. But these situations could be evaluated with discretion as and when the need arose. School-work, to use one of the more conspicuous examples, would plainly be an area where taking responsibility for my actions was impractical, since an inauspicious performance in an essay or an exam was, as often as not, directly related to sleep deprivation, existentialist disenfranchisement and other factors beyond my control. A recent History essay had been handed back to me with the words 'Random gunfire at an indeterminate target. Slack research or a cry for help?' written underneath in red pen.

But I could begin by taking responsibility for my scheme to plant Mark Coates in the Decadents. And this I was happy to do. Turning to face southwards, I solemnly raised my coffee cup and mentally transmitted my confession to Cranmore Park.

I am sorry for lying to you, Lou. My pattern of behaviour has been treacherous, erratic and unforgiveable. I will have to live with my conscience for the rest of my life. I offer no plea other than Guilty as Charged. I go to the gallows knowing there can be no appeal, no last-minute pardon. There are no extenuating circumstances that could lessen the severity of the crime I have committed.

I will simply bring to your attention the fact that one of us had to take the initiative, and, what a surprise, the initiative fell to me. You were content to procrastinate — which is, let's be honest, not the first time that's happened — whereas I am a man of action. I took action because that's the kind of man I am, and I take responsibility for my actions even though you left me with no choice. I will meet my executioner with a clear conscience, my friend. It would not be stretching a point to say that you, and you alone, brought this mess on yourself. I shall put my faith in Superbird and the appeal system. This is a blatant miscarriage of justice and as infamous a case of mistaken identity as I have ever witnessed.

But each clink of the spoon in the coffee cup only seemed to murmur betrayal.

HISTORY (PAPER 3)
15 June 1981. Duration: 2 hrs

Answer FOUR questions from the list below, writing an essay (no shorter than 400 words) on each one. Read all the questions carefully before starting to write. Do *not* answer a question that is not on the list.

1. Give an account of the events that immediately followed the narrator's move from Dublin to Downburn, County Down in July 1970.

2. How significant was Downburn in the narrator's early development?

3. Describe the effect on the narrator (and on world history as a result) of acquiring his own copy of Sweet's 'Blockbuster' and its concomitant B-side, 'Need a Lot of Lovin''.

4. Sweet were a mildly entertaining transvestite act whose work is of no relevance today. Discuss.

5. Suggest TWO plausible reasons for permission being granted in March 1973 for the narrator to watch *Top of the Pops*.

6. Examine the importance of the bass guitarist in 1970s life, using ONE of the following groups to illustrate your answer: (a) Nazareth, (b) Manfred Mann's Earth Band, (c) Sweet.

7. Summarize the principal socio-political arguments why Lieutenant Pigeon's 'Desperate Dan' can be said to have failed as a consolidation measure in the post-'Mouldy Old Dough' period.

Extracts from candidates' essays, History (Paper 3)

1. Give an account of the events that immediately followed the narrator's move from Dublin to Downburn, County Down in July 1970.
The narrator and his family moved, in July 1970, from Dublin to Downburn in County Down. The move was because of his parents' wishes to live and work in the North. July 1970 was about the time when the World Cup was on, however the narrator had not then known about football. England were beating West Germany 2–0 when Alf Ramsey took off Bobby Charlton and Franz Beckenbauer led the German fight-back along with Gerd

Muller. Brazil went on to win the tournament in a well-known final where they hammered Italy 4–1.

When the narrator and his family moved from Dublin to Downburn, County Down in July 1970, the first thing that he saw was a big party in the street. They turned left off Lough Erne Lane, into Foyle Crescent where they were going to live, but the road was blocked by tables that went all across the road from one side to the other side. Children who were younger and older and about the same age as the narrator, were playing out in the road. Balloons were flying up in the air. The narrator saw the front gardens of the houses, they were full of toys and bikes. He thought the party was to celebrate his family moving there from Dublin. (The narrator sometimes gets things wrong.)

A girl on a bike that had white tyres went over to their car and talked into the window which was rolled down at the time. She asked them all if they were the new family and she told them that number 9 was up on the right. They knew that already from the estate agent. The narrator thought her accent was strange, because he'd never been in Northern Ireland before. We have a different accent to the one in Eire. It is often the subject of a witty column in the *Belfast Telegraph*, which is our city's leading newspaper.

Another thing the narrator noticed that day was a boy dribbling a football in the road, similar to the football used by Pele, Jairzinho, Tostao, Rivelino, Carlos Alberto and all the other players in the World Cup-winning Brazil team of 1970. The boy with the football was however not known by name yet. (He would later be Raymond Adair.) The girl on the bicycle was Fiona O'Keefe and she was having her seventh birthday.

He became friends with the other children after that,

and when it was Fiona O'Keefe's birthday every year, he
would always remember the party that was happening in
the road when he and his family moved from Dublin to
Downburn, County Down in July 1970.

2. How significant was Downburn in the narrator's early development?
The move to Downburn has often been likened by the
narrator to the end of World War II austerity and the
first flushes of utopianism. The analogy, which epitomizes
the narrator's propensity for exaggerating, casts Downburn
in a favourable light that is perhaps more rose-tinted
than he realizes. Recurring phrases such as 'sleepy idyll',
'undying summers' and 'tranquil bungalows' have the effect
of painting Downburn as a toytown fantasy (i.e. a child's
world) impervious to conflict and sectarianism (the adult
world). Yet there are many contemporary descriptions of
Downburn that would seem to dispute the narrator's
sentimental evocation. He writes of 'a gossamer village
. . . hidden from commerce, nestled by a limpid stream'.
This is in stark contrast to verified reports in other texts
depicting Downburn as a conventional Belfast suburb
whose primary function was to house the early-1970s
overspill.

The narrator is no less romantic in his portrayal of the
cul-de-sac Foyle Crescent ('wide as a valley . . . a hill with
ineffable vistas at its summit . . . bonny lawns ascending
like an emerald ladder to paradise'). These passages
are universally adjudged by historians to be unreliable.
Twentieth-century Downburn records make no reference
to a Foyle Crescent, nor to any road with such singular
characteristics. They do, however, mention a Lough Foyle
Lane, one of several cul-de-sacs served by the meandering

thoroughfare Lough Erne Lane, and most scholars now believe that the family lived at 9 (or possibly 11) Lough Foyle Lane. The location bears no resemblance to the breathtaking Eden so extravagantly delineated by the narrator, being, as far as we can gather, a common or garden suburban cul-de-sac comprising bungalows identical to those in the neighbouring cul-de-sacs Lough Moss Lane and Lough Neagh Lane. The 'ineffable vistas' of which the narrator writes have perplexed one or two historians whose expeditions to the 'summit' of Lough Foyle Lane yielded only the prospect of bungalows to the east, north and west, and a farmer's field to the south. Another commentator has propounded that the narrator's expression 'ladder to paradise' may be a subconscious derivation of the Led Zeppelin song title 'Stairway to Heaven'.

It is probable that the role played by Downburn in the narrator's early development was one of ambivalence. The significance of Downburn in his teenage writings must, therefore, be open to question.

5. *Suggest TWO plausible reasons for permission being granted in March 1973 for the narrator to watch* Top of the Pops.
... the O'Keefe family next door (7 Foyle Crescent) were important in that the narrator could see that their experiences differed from his own in regard to what they were allowed and what they were not allowed to do. He used this as a way to blackmail his parents. When Thursday came round and he wasn't allowed to watch *Top of the Pops*, he would go off in a huff. Sometimes he would come back in and put his ear to the wall separating the living-room from the O'Keefes' living-room, so that his parents could

see him trying to hear *Top of the Pops* through the wall. He would shake and, of course, cry. On Friday mornings he would leave his lunch-box at home to show his parents that he was miserable and had no appetite . . .

. . . in March 1973 the preliminary manoeuvres ended and the campaign entered a crucial phase. The attack was two-pronged. Margaret O'Keefe had to go into hospital to have a baby (Stephen), rendering it imperative to find temporary accommodation for the five O'Keefe children. The narrator was able to make the successful suggestion that his family take in Fiona and Conor as they were closest in age to himself. Margaret gave birth on a Tuesday, but her long and painful labour required her to remain in the maternity ward, under observation, until Friday. It was at this critical juncture in the hostilities that the narrator gave the signal for Fiona and Conor to ask if they could watch *Top of the Pops* on Thursday evening. Already suffering heavy losses in this 'propaganda war', the narrator's parents accepted the request. From that day onwards, further compromises were inevitable. Encouraged, the narrator now turned his attention to the so-called 'second front' . . .

. . . was occasionally allowed to listen at weekends to the pop station Radio One on the family's Grundig radio. One Saturday in March, the station played a new song by Dawn called 'Tie a Yellow Ribbon Round the Old Oak Tree'. The narrator formed an instant and lifelong hatred of the song, but had a shrewd inkling that it might find admirers elsewhere in the house. Taking the radio into the kitchen, where his mother was reading the *Daily Mail*, he let the melodious strains of 'Tie a Yellow Ribbon Round

the Old Oak Tree' fill the room while he made pretence
to search for biscuits in the larder . . .

. . . all the more illustrious a success given the demoralizing
failure of his attempts earlier in the year to interest his
mother in Carly Simon's 'You're So Vain', Elvis Presley's
'Always on My Mind' and Harold Melvin & the Bluenotes'
'If You Don't Know Me by Now'; and his father in Olivia
Newton-John's 'Take Me Home Country Roads' and
Strawbs' 'Part of the Union'.

   The outcome was a threefold triumph for the narrator.
His mother rushed out to buy 'Tie a Yellow Ribbon
Round the Old Oak Tree' in a Belfast record shop (and
more importantly a discount-priced 'Blockbuster' by Sweet,
by then slipping out of the Top 20). The narrator was
allowed to watch *Top of the Pops* every Thursday, as his
mother wanted to see Dawn singing her favourite song
(by then climbing towards the Top 10). And the narrator
was promised a transistor radio for his next birthday . . .

. . . had crept up on the blind side and taken the opposing
camp completely unawares. The sleight-of-hand tactics
succeeded so spectacularly that the narrator was convinced
for many years afterwards that music and deception possessed mutual properties . . .

6
Dream Three

Ten years before, the Modern Languages block had symbolized the College's audacious arrival in the space age. No school in Northern Ireland at the turn of the '70s had a more exalted reputation for Modern Languages than the College. No students in Northern Ireland had been given such an avant-garde setting in which to learn them.

The second-floor French language lab was the first place I had ever worn headphones. In September 1975, my fellow first-formers and I had sat in our individual soundproofed audio capsules and obeyed the *écoutez et répétez* instructions from an unseen tape-recorder. Headphones! Silver knobs on the desks! This was a school that really knew how to put its fees to good use. We had all hummed the *Star Trek* theme in our make-believe rockets, twiddling the silver knobs to hear our watery voices at treble their normal volume in the headphones.

The lustre of the language lab had faded through routine and *répétition* as that interminable first year dragged on. By June 1976 I felt as though I had done half a decade at the

College, most of it in the lab, my head sagging and my mind vacant, cosmically hypnotized by the droning in my ears of the French robot-woman. Reading *Nineteen Eighty-Four* that summer, I immediately associated Room 101 with the language lab, and Big Brother with the mechanical intonation of Madame des Headphones. Second-form French was to be a winter in purgatory. I spent day after sluggish day trying to break the silver knobs, wrestling them like Inspector Clouseau with his fist stuck in a vase, mortified by the thought of Mrs McNulty getting the rats out if she caught me. *Alors mon petit, voici les rats . . . écoutez et répétez. Tu aimes bien Big Brother, n'est-ce-pas?*

I didn't do French any more. I'd kicked it into touch (as the Rugbywankers would say) after the O-levels; and had a bash at the old Spanish (as my father would say) instead. The rooms for Spanish were on the third floor of Modern Languages. Most of our lessons were taken in a compact classroom painted vanilla ice-cream white and perfumed with Mrs Idge's cologne. Periodically, we would file into an adjacent language lab – Lab 2 – which had giant windows and was a magnet in September for footsore wasps needing a quiet place to die. And die they did, sooner than they expected. Mrs Idge would squeal and swipe at them with her duster, which was the cue for Douglas Bevan to doff his headphones, emerge from his soundproofed capsule to ironic cheers, and do the honours with a well-aimed slam of a high-velocity dictionary.

The vanilla room was locked when I got there at 10.55 a.m. on June 22 for my penultimate Spanish class of the summer term. It wouldn't be a lesson today as such – more a recapitulation-cum-reckoning. Mrs Idge would read out our exam results and there would be the traditional taunting of those who'd exceeded eighty per cent. I did not anticipate being among them.

The corridor outside the classroom had a broad window-ledge that waiting students could sit on, and I had just pulled that week's *Sounds* out of my bag when somebody clomped up the stairs whistling 'Little April Showers'. I turned to my left and saw Tim Brooke-Taylor coming round the corner. 'The very man I'm looking for. You and I need to have a serious chat.'

Brian Hinney claimed that before applying for the Head of Classics post at the College in 1980, he had run the Latin department at a school in Aberdeen. I was in no doubt that he told this yarn to throw people off the scent, because Hinney was the doppelgänger of Tim Brooke-Taylor from the Goodies. Had the two men ever been seen together? No. And why? Because they were one and the same.

Brooke-Taylor had been teaching me Latin for the past ten months, speaking in a Scottish accent that never quite sounded appropriate. It was my guess that he was hiding out at the College while the Goodies licked their wounds from the lousy series with the John Travolta episode, the one that everybody said was their all-time nadir. I surmised that Brooke-Taylor had freaked out and taken up teaching because he wanted to put something back into society. I knew he would drop the Shughie McFee accent and return to London as soon as Bill Oddie's private detectives tracked him down. And it infuriated me that Isobel Clarke couldn't see any Tim Brooke-Taylor likeness in our teacher – only some David McCallum around the eyes.

'Or what's commonly known as a chin-wag stroke bol-locking. Shift up a bit, son.'

Brooke-Taylor was wearing his warm-weather combo of cream linen jacket, raspberry shirt and burgundy tie. I was still attempting to focus on him when he sat down on the ledge beside me. 'I've been marking your exams, for my sins,' he said, crossing one jade-coloured trouser leg over the other. 'The exams you *did*, I mean. I'll not count the one you were ill for. And I'm afraid to tell you – can you put the music paper down for a minute? – that Ground Control is having a bit of bother with Major Tom.'

This was another reason the Latin students appreciated Hinney. He was young enough to know about rock. The older teachers' knowledge of music started at Gracie Fields and stopped at Slim Whitman. I remembered the Goodies even doing a punk special in '77, and wondered if it had been Hinney's idea.

'Did you hear what I said? You've made a right dog's dinner of the whole show.'

'Did I fail all of them?' I heard myself ask.

'*Fail?*' he laughed. 'Fail would be an accolade, sunshine. I've got your Tacitus paper here, and it's just ... You didnae get enough *marks* to fail it. You're not even on the scoreboard. Same story with every paper, I'm finding.'

I felt suddenly lost. *Failed*. As in `... not passed?

'And from what Leo Duffy and Francesca Idge are saying about you in the staff-room, you're this year's calamity kid. You've gone up in smoke. Duffy's put one of your History essays up on the wall, I was just having a gander. Doesnae make pretty reading over a cup of tea and a digestive, I can tell you.'

My thoughts raced dangerously. *The Calamity Kid*. A western? Had I seen it? Teachers were talking about me in the staff-room? In a bad way? While eating digestives?

Other Lower Sixth-formers were coming up the stairs, followed presently by Mrs Idge, who was carrying two foolscap box-files. She made a *phew!* face to Brooke-Taylor – *phew*, all those stairs, eh, they get me every time. 'Right, Fran?' he said. I had the swimmy sensation that she couldn't see me, that I was too insubstantial. The other students had confident looks – looks that said they'd got eighty per cent in Spanish and they knew it. I'd seen those looks all through May and June but hadn't understood them until now.

'I'll not keep him long, Fran.'

'Have as long as you like,' she replied. 'He's only going to hear the same from me.'

The classroom door closed behind her. I saw my Tacitus essay in Brooke-Taylor's outstretched hand, saw an Ingersoll watch and blond hairs on his arm, and recognized some words that I had written two weeks earlier when I'd believed myself to be substantial. *'Nero was a hell raiser, a star chaser, a trail-blazer, a natural-born raver.'*

I wanted to curl up in a ball. I'd thought I was being inventive. I'd thought he would enjoy my style, put huge ticks over the most outstanding sentences and write 'Bravo!' in the margin. I'd thought he was a music fan.

'It gets worse,' he said, turning the page over. 'Do you want me to show you?'

I shook my head.

'I've a wee rule in life,' he went on. 'My wee rule is that names like – where are we, now – Eddie Jobson and David Cross should not appear in essays about the Roman Empire. I personally don't care to find names of pop musicians when I'm marking an essay, and when I do find them, I get a bit irate. This kind of gear is not on, mister. Do I take it you were making some sort of smart-alec reference to playing the fiddle while Rome burns?'

I nodded.

'Well, you need to wise up. Because if you do anything like that next June, you can fling your UCCA handbook in the bin. Which is what I was tempted to do with this.' He waved the paper at me. 'Now it so happens that I'm partial to Roxy Music, and I do know who Eddie Jobson is. The other character. David Cross. Would you mind clueing me in?'

'King Crimson,' I murmured from a long way away.

'Oh aye,' he said. 'My brother-in-law rates them. Never took the plunge myself. Okay, now we're getting somewhere. King Cr-r-rimson. So are you saying that . . . Where's that pile of shite you wrote here? These "cadences of molten terror". Is that something you've written for me about King Crimson?'

I nodded.

Brooke-Taylor shook his head. Or maybe it was me that shook my head.

'All right, now here's the deal,' he said firmly. 'Can we make this the last time that King Crimson turn up playing their fiddles in 64 AD? In Rome or anywhere else, right? And you'll put a note in your diary for one o'clock tomorrow, because we're going to have a coffee in the sixth-form centre and you're going to tell me why a B-plus Latin student has suddenly started losing his marbles. Fair? And it'll stay between the two of us, okay? Good man. Cheer up, son, it's only life.'

He glanced at *Sounds* as he got up to go. 'If I were you, I'd put the cadences back in the music papers where they belong. That rag must have changed a lot since I used to read it. Aye. Elkie Br-r-rooks and Robert Palmer. Back in the day.'

He disappeared down the stairs in a riot of colour, leaving me to Mrs Idge's Spanish inquisition.

That night I had a dream. It was my first legitimate dream since the memories started, and there was a disturbing, cinematic intensity to it. In the morning I would have a gluey dream hangover throughout Assembly and History. When Mr Duffy gave me back my History exam papers at 10 a.m. and one of them had a pinhole at the top, I didn't know if it was a dream, or déjà vu, or a premonition.

'Worthless,' was all he said.

The dream began with a *Goodies* episode. It was a disappointing one in a new style, and it involved Graeme Garden asking Oddie and Brooke-Taylor to think of another name for igloos. I had the notion that the script was unrehearsed, because all three of them seemed tetchy and uncomfortable. 'We can't call them igloos,' Garden kept saying. 'What are we going to call them?' Every name they thought of was a mispronunciation of a word already in use, which made Garden impatient. But he wasn't being funny-impatient. It was an extremely serious episode of *The Goodies* and he wanted them to stop being childish. I was a member of the audience, but I was standing close to the three performers. I realized that it was their last ever episode.

The dream jumped. The Goodies were watching themselves on a screen to find out what was going to happen in the show. Bill Oddie was George Smiley in *Tinker Tailor Soldier Spy*, looking for 'a very irregular gentleman' in a public school. When he said 'a very irregular gentleman',

Brooke-Taylor and Garden were seized by the urge to find the man for the sake of national security. There were deserted playing fields ahead of them, with big Hs in the grass. Oddie spotted a wheelie-bin at the back of some buildings, falling into it head first after clambering up the outside like a monkey. There was a round of applause that ended abruptly as if someone had pushed a button. Oddie seemed to become more purposeful and I began to have confidence in him. He helped the others climb into the wheelie-bin and they found themselves in an underground meadow. Oddie told them to look for a combine harvester. There was 'a very irregular gentleman' who had to be over-powered before the combine harvester smashed through the fence and reached Red Square. While the Goodies were walking through the meadow in Sherlock Holmes hats, they came upon a beanstalk shaped like an H, and reacted emotionally at the sight of it, laughing and crying. Then they were on the Giant's Causeway, where they agreed that the 'very irregular gentleman' was one of the Goodies. I now reappeared in the dream. I saw that Oddie and Garden had horrific facial injuries. Tim Brooke-Taylor's face was turned towards the sea, so I slid between his legs and looked up at him from below. His face was mean and had a cruel sneer, but the other two hadn't noticed. I tried to shout a warning to them, but they were bounding ahead with magni-fying glasses, looking in the rocks for 'things in three'. Then the Goodies were on their three-seater cycle on a road in barren country, but Brooke-Taylor was trying to pedal backwards without the others seeing. 'It's the three that we want,' said Oddie, pedalling forwards furiously. I could feel Brooke-Taylor's breath on my neck. We pedalled into a tunnel and came out of it sitting on different saddles. I was at the back, looking at the arrows on Brooke-Taylor's prison uniform. Mr Duffy was at the front, agreeing that three was the answer. I asked Brooke-Taylor over his shoulder to tell me if Laurel and Hardy were going to be there when we arrived, but everybody else started thinking of names and saying 'two' in a sing-song voice. 'Abbott and Costello, two-o-o.' 'The Two Ronnies, two-o-o.' I was tired of it. I wanted to think of a name that would make them say 'three-ee-ee'. I tried the Marx Brothers but I couldn't remember what they were called. I tried the Three Musketeers. That was more successful – suddenly we were all musketeers.

The coffee bar in the sixth-form centre was famously off limits to teachers. However, even more famously, they wandered in any time they liked and we were powerless to stop them. We'd know when a teacher was at the counter: the ambience would change and we'd hear conversations dying in mid-air. Doofus or Colin or whoever was on bar duty would fawn over them – coffee on the house, yes sir/miss, coming right up, my word it's frothy today and how about a complimentary Pot Noodle or are you watching the calories, sir/miss? – and the sixth-formers would make small talk, keeping their language clean until the teacher departed and the profanities could recommence.

Although I was dreading my 1 p.m. *compromiso* with Brian Hinney, it amused me, as I surveyed the coffee bar, to think of the double-takes and lowering of voices that would greet his entrance. What the hell is *he* doing here, everybody would think. Why is he sitting with *him*, everybody would ask themselves. Conspiracy theories would fly.

Then again, perhaps they already knew. Hinney might have told Isobel Clarke about my Tacitus paper ('. . . and this will stay between the two of us, Isobel, okay?'), possibly during a clandestine tryst in the park. There was no denying that Isobel was quite a nice-looking girl. If Hinney was young enough to know about rock music, he was young enough to have clandestine trysts with quite nice-looking girls in the park. Maybe he and Isobel were an item. Perhaps they were engaged.

Or Mr Duffy, in a rum-induced rage, could have xeroxed my History essays and posted them to the home addresses of all the sixth-formers, signing them 'A Friend'. The old soak might even have sent my essays to the *Belfast Telegraph*. The *Tele* always liked to make a big fuss about the 'prestige' and 'international renown' of the College. We were one of its parochial clichés, like the 'inimitable Ulster sense of humour'. Jesus! My History essays would ignite an editorial frenzy. ('Alas, this organ is in receipt of documents that will tarnish the worldwide eminence of the College and shock every reader . . . deplorable impertinence more befitting a harlequinade . . . unseemly citations of "glamorous rock" groups . . . despite the laudable ministrations of his pedagogue Brian A. Hinney of the Pictish kingdom . . . vulgarities equal in depravity to those seen at a burlesque or kinema . . .')

When Isobel's hennaed hair danced into view through the coffee bar's side door, I waited for her to buy a Twix and a Coke and thread her way towards the speaker seats. I was at a table near the back, but an artful sneeze made her look round and see me. She came over and sat down.

'Is Hinney not with you?' I asked her.

'Hinney? No. Why would he be?'

She ripped open the Twix. Specks of week-old orange nail varnish lingered on her thumbs and forefingers. The skin under her eyes crinkled as she bit.

'He said something about meeting me here.'

'Oh, why's that?' she inquired. 'Is he still on about you missing the exam?'

'Mmm. Bit worried he might fail me.'

She said through a mouthful, 'Fail *you*? Uh-uh. He loves you. He'll just mark you for the ones you did.'

That was a relief. Isobel didn't know.

She offered the two fingers of Twix to me across the table, one of them amputated at the knuckle. I didn't know which one to take. I chose the amputated one, biting a chunk from it and holding the inch-long chocolate stump out to her. It was obvious from her face that I'd eaten the wrong one.

'Keep it,' she said. 'Have a party.'

Isobel sometimes wore elaborate earrings at school when she was feeling adventurous. They were pearly and sparkly, and she'd been told on a few occasions by teachers to remove them. I'd always thought her rather exotic – a mystical sort of person. When the craze for crimped hair had hit the sixth form the year before, Isobel had smiled knowingly but not been swept along. To those such as Lorraine Dawson who argued that hair-crimpers had made henna obsolete, Isobel would give a quizzical frown and an almost imperceptible moue of reproach, but would never utter a word in her own defence. She would have considered that a waste of breath. In conversation with the Virgins she was the same – an imperturbable girl who put her case with prudence and economy; a subtle inversion of the Cheshire Cat. She wanted to do a degree at Hull and become a travel writer.

'Are you any good at analysing dreams?' I asked her.

'Mark thinks so,' she said. 'He's always telling me his fantasies.'

'Is he now.'

'Mm-hm. I'm in some of them.'

'Really? Is Mark ... I mean, does he ...'

'Want to go to bed with me?' she said evenly. 'Looks that way.'

'And are you ... I mean, do you think you'd ever ...'

She smiled. 'Go to bed with Mark? I think that's my business.'

'Of course. Of course. Well, can I tell you about a dream that you're *not* in? You might be able to help me understand it.'

'If you want.'

I told her the dream. She frowned at certain passages but mostly looked off into space, tapping her nails on the Coke can.

'God, you ...' she said at the end. 'You're always on about Hinney looking like Tim Brooke-Taylor. He's nothing like him.'

'Never mind that. What do you think it means?'

'It might have something to do with numerology,' she suggested. 'Numerologists think that everybody has a number that influences their life. I'm not into it – it sounds too much like horoscopes and all that crap. But let's say your number's three. It might have a big influence on you. You know, in your life. Have you three brothers and sisters? Were you born on the third of a month? Or at three o'clock?'

'No ... no ... no ...'

'You're doing three A-levels,' she pointed out.

'So are you. So's everybody. Where does the combine harvester come into it?'

'Talk of the devil.'

'What?'

'Talk of the devil,' she repeated. 'Your date's here.'

'Right, lads and lasses,' Brian Hinney said behind me, clamping a hand on the back of my chair. 'One of you can stay. Izzy — sorry, love, you're gonnae have to leave us. Another coffee for you, son? Do they do cheese and onion up there, or is someone gonnae offer me the rest of their Twix?'

'I'll think about it, your dream,' Isobel said, rising from her seat. 'I'll think about it.'

She left the chocolate on the table and set off with Hinney to the counter.

Hinney must have been a prog rocker in the past. He began our tête-à-tête, once he had returned carrying two milky coffees, with a pastoral prelude (was I going anywhere interesting in the summer holidays?), warmed up with a lively intermezzo (that Isobel's quite a gal, though, isn't she?) and then kicked in with the main riff after about five minutes.

'How much revision did you do exactly? Be straight with me.'

'Very little,' I admitted. 'I . . . don't know. Finding it difficult to concentrate lately. I suppose that probably comes across in er . . .' I stared at my shoes for five seconds. 'In more ways than one.'

'Well, here's how I read it,' he said, leaning forward. 'It's gonnae be one of three things. Either you've got mixed up in glue-sniffing. Or it's a girl. Or you're having problems at home. Because it's not just a lack of revision. Can I be honest? Your Tacitus gave me the willies. It's the only time I've ever shown someone's essay to my wife – and you know what she said? "This is no joke. Get that boy out of there and get him some help." That's my wife saying that. Do you see why I'm worried?'

'I do, sir, but ... I don't know, I think the holidays might do me some good. Give me a chance to recharge my batteries.'

'Do you get on with your parents?'

'Yeah. They're all right.'

He leaned closer. 'Tell me you're not on glue.'

I laughed. 'I'm not on glue.'

'Have you got a girlfriend?'

'Um ... not at the moment. I wouldn't really say I had a girlfriend, no.'

His eyes were steady. A bit too judicious, I thought. I wasn't the kind to hold eye contact for very long.

'But if you needed someone to talk to ...' he prompted me.

'I'm not sure I'd go to anyone. Who did you have in mind?'

'I'm not sure. Who's your housemaster?'

I grimaced. 'I'm not in a house any more,' I said truthfully. 'I used to be in Churchill, but they turfed me out a couple of years ago because I wouldn't swim in the inter-house heats. They said I had no motivation. I don't like swimming if that's what they mean.'

'Scared of losing?'

'Scared of drowning.'

He threw some quick-fire questions at me. 'So what *can* you do? What do you like doing?'

'Oh . . . not much. Writing. Sort of. Talking about music – sometimes. Drinking coffee. I'm pretty good at that.'

'Ever touch the hard stuff?'

'Nope.'

'Not even a beer?'

'The pubs won't let me in.'

'What kind of things do you write? Poetry?'

'Nah, not really. Pretty random stuff. Nothing earth-shattering. I wouldn't call it poetry.'

'Ever shown it to anybody?'

'Absolutely not,' I bristled.

'Have you got many friends? Apart from Isobel?'

'One or two. They're more mates than friends, I suppose.'

'What university are you going to?'

'I haven't decided. It'll be in England.'

'To do what?'

'I've no idea. It's all up in the air at the moment. Would you laugh if I said Latin?'

He did laugh. 'Latin in Rock Music? Latin in Post-war Contemporary Culture, majoring in King Crimson and Eddie Jobson? I don't think there'll be many takers. What do you want to be? What do you want to do with your life?'

'I don't know. Maybe write for some sort of newspaper.'

'Any particular sort of newspaper?'

'Not really.'

'Did you feel okay when you did the exams?' he asked.

'Um . . . *yes*. I wasn't feeling bad or anything. I can't really remember.'

'You cannae remember? It was only the other week.'

I affected catatonia. I shouldn't have. 'Seems . . . so long ago . . . somehow.' Now he would think I was out to lunch.

The next question-and-response would be the clincher. Look into his eyes. Take control.

'How did it go with Francesca Idge?' he asked.

'So-so. She told me to do the exams again over the summer. She's going to mark them in September. And she told me never to take the piss out of her again.'

'Oh aye? She say that in Spanish?'

'No, English.'

There was a pause.

'Right,' said Hinney, getting serious again. 'So you're not on glue, and there's no girlfriend, and you're not having problems at home. And nobody's forcing you to do any swimming you don't want to do. Okay. Well, as things stand, this is a headmaster issue. I don't mean in a punish-ment way, but I do mean counselling, advice, all that gear. Now, I can be talked out of going to the headmaster – which is what we call a deferral – but you'll be on probation as of today, in my custody. I'm sorry if all these words sound heavy, but next year is going to be the most important year of your life and it seems to me you need a push in the right direction. Look at me. I want you write me an essay for Friday – so you've got three days – and I want it to be a proper Tacitus essay, the one that you should have written the first time. And I don't care if you haven't revised the Annals, because you're starting tonight. You have one chance to rescue this situation. One chance. It's not every teacher that would give you that chance.'

'I appreciate that, sir.'

'So I'm getting an essay on Friday?'

'You are. Absolutely.'

We discussed terms. Three days to revise the Annals sounded a bit on the demanding side from where I sat, but

Hinney wasn't in the mood for negotiating the deadline, and in any case I was strangely awed by the numerical connotations. Three days. *Three-ee-ee*.

'Anything you'd like to ask me?' Hinney said as he drained his coffee. 'Don't be shy now.'

'No, sir. I think everything's fine.'

'So you're into your music, are you?'

'I suppose I am.'

'Ever hear of a band called Cream?'

'Of course,' I nodded. 'Eric Clapton was in them.'

'Aye, and Jack Bruce and Ginger Baker. I saw them play in Manchester when I was at teacher training college. Three guys — but man, what a noise. They made a ginormous racket. Good music, too.'

'Actually, there is something I'd like to ask you, sir,' I said. 'If you don't mind. I was wondering if people ever tell you that you look a bit like Tim Brooke-Taylor from the Goodies.'

'Naw,' Hinney guffawed. 'I never get that. Tim Brooke-Taylor, the guy in the Union Jack vest? Afraid not. But there's an actor that I'm told I look a bit like. He was in *The Man from UNCLE*. Turned up again a while back in *Colditz*. Scottish surname.'

'David McCallum,' I sighed and Hinney snapped his fingers.

'Come and see me on Friday,' he said as we made our way to the main exit. 'Make it around three. And for God's sake bring me something to put me in a good mood.' He stopped. 'Where are you off to now? Are you getting chips?'

'No, I'm going to look for somebody.' A needle in a haystack, I thought. 'I'll see you on Friday.'

There was a note on my bedroom door when I got home

that evening. My mother had written the first message and my father had added the other two underneath.

'Please put the kettle back in the kitchen when you're not using it. Other people have to live here too.'

'Phone Andy. Urgent.'

'Vance Armstrong rang, 6.20 p.m. Needs to know about a party in Berlin. Will call you tomorrow.'

7
The Rivalries

Extract from the Manuscript, written June 26

'Tie a Yellow Ribbon Round the Old Oak Tree' by Dawn was as immovable as the tree that's standing by the waw-ter-siiide. In the spring of 1973, Dawn's hit resisted all attempts to dislodge it from the top of the charts. It may have been at number one for nine weeks. Or it could have been twenty — who but a masochist was keeping score? The Tuesday announcement of the new Top 30 became a grey formality, a weekly exercise in disillusionment. 'Surely,' I thought, experiencing a feeling that was new to me, 'things used to be better than this.'

Sung to a bouncy tune that would have made a useful sitcom theme, 'Tie a Yellow Ribbon Round the Old Oak Tree' is about a man being released from prison who fears that the woman he used to go out with will have forgotten him. More in hope than expectation, he wonders if she has seen fit to tie a yellow ribbon round the old oak tree, as requested by him in a letter, to indicate to him that she is still his beloved. Approaching the oak tree on a bus, he observes that she has tied not one but a hundred yellow ribbons round it, in order that he may find it easier to notice. There is jubilation on the bus as the other passengers share in his good fortune. The end.

But that's me remembering it in 1981. Now here's me talking about it to Raymond Adair in 1973: 'What a load of puke. Puke, puke, puke. I hate "Tie a Yellow Ribbon Round the Old Oak Tree".'

'Turn the radio off, then. Let's play Wembley at your house.'

'I don't want to play Wembley at my house. I'm upset now. All the fun's gone out of life.'

'Don't be stupid. Here you go again, thinking too much about that song. He's not harming anyone, you know. There's no need to be Mr Bring-Back-Hanging.'

'He's been in prison, Raymond. He's a criminal.'

'Yes, and he's paid for it. Isn't a prison sentence enough for you? Anyway, you liked Blockbuster and he was a criminal. You said he was "a fiendish mastermind".'

'That's completely different. Blockbuster wasn't happy. Listen to the last verse of "Tie a Yellow Ribbon Round the Old Oak Tree". All the people on the bus are cheering. How do they know he won't murder again?'

'Where does it say he murdered anybody? He probably just stole some grub from a supermarket.'

'Oh, well in that case let's just knock down all the prisons. Let's just not have any law and order at all! Bloody socialists. I'm going home.'

McCloud would have had something to say about a convicted murderer being released from prison without so much as a by-your-leave. 'Save the yellow ribbons for your victims,' McCloud would have said, dragging him off the bus and punching him. 'You're going back to the can.'

Darn right, McCloud. And if Cannon had been there — well, that song would have had a very satisfying outcome. 'Save the yellow ribbons for the DA,' Cannon would have said, pushing him off the bus with his stomach. 'You got yourself an appointment with the chair.' There was never any nonsense with Cannon. He'd have strapped him to Old

Sparky, yanked the lever and told that communist Raymond Adair to put it in his pipe and smoke it.

But that's me thinking about Raymond in 1973. In 1981, Raymond is a person from the past who no longer exists. (There you go, Ray, I thought of something we have in common.)

I'm sure there are singles nowadays that spend long periods at number one in the charts — Adam and the Ants' 'Stand and Deliver' seemed to be up there for a while; maybe it still is, I haven't looked — but because I'm not a pop kid now (or a raving Nazi for that matter) they don't have the ability to close down me and my world as confoundedly and as totally as 'Tie a Yellow Ribbon Round the Old Oak Tree' did all those years ago. Dawn's immovable tree stopped the motion in me too, shutting off my engines and bringing my childhood machine to a standstill. I began to realize that music had the power to stunt as well as expand. There would be no more growth, no more evolution in my world, until the old oak tree had fallen. Even my mother was bored sick of it, and talked of pop-swopping with someone at work for 'Amazing Grace'.

Every Tuesday lunchtime on the Radio One Top 30 rundown, Johnnie Walker would say to us, 'It's another week at the top for . . . you've guessed it.' Dawn's tiresome bouncy tune would start up behind him, sounding more tiresome and more bouncy than ever, as though it were jumping up and down and flicking V-signs and gloating. Oh not again *I'd think. Not* another *action replay of the week we've just lived through. Not another week at the top for you've guessed it.*

And in between jumping up and down, flicking V-signs and gloating, Dawn would honk at me from inside the radio: 'Yoo-hoo! Hard cheese, Sorluza. Better luck next time!'

But I knew Sorluza. I was familiar with the finer details of Sorluza. And he never had better luck next time.

Sorluza was a competitor invented by Raymond for the Foyle Crescent Olympics. He was a 400-metres runner from Argentina who always complained bitterly about being cheated. ('Issa not fair. I wassa not ready.') All of us in the cul-de-sac took turns to play him, a task that entailed acting in a shifty manner, complaining and making sinister comments to the other athletes about what would happen to them when the Olympics were held in Buenos Aires. After a judges' inquiry, Sorluza would be escorted from the cul-de-sac in a half nelson, still complaining, and Raymond would say to all the viewers at home: 'This is a side of sport that no one wants to see.'

The Top 30 was the Olympics of pop. Every Tuesday lunchtime, after a judges' inquiry, Johnnie Walker cheated me out of a gold medal and gave it to Dawn. This, I thought, was a side of pop that no one wanted to see. And in my stunted and embittered state, Sorluza became a character I found difficult to shake off.

Johnnie Walker: 'It's another week at the top for . . .'

Me: 'I've guessed it.'

JW: 'Hasta la vista, Sorluza. Better luck next time!'

Me: 'That's easy for you to say. I'm the one who's grown no inches in height since April. Look at the notches on the door-frame if you don't believe me.'

JW: 'Ha ha. Adios, midget.'

Me: 'Issa disgrace.'

But at last there came a Tuesday — a gold-medal Tuesday for one frustrated amigo. On the horizon, a group of lumberjacks appeared, armed with heap big axes from the fires of hell. To fallen oak trees! To growth! To our future!

Vance Armstrong was too cool for school. The Berlin frontman liked to boast to the Decadents that he had left the education system at the first available opportunity ('the day after his eleven-plus', Andy said cynically) and become a postman. Vance had subsequently repaired televisions for a living, and later driven an Interflora van, with the result that he now knew not only the whereabouts of every street in Belfast but in many cases the names of the people in the houses.

'You live next door to the Hammonds, don't you?' he'd said to me on the phone in mid-week. 'I killed a blackbird in her kitchen once. It flew in the window and got stuck to the toaster. Fuckin' terrible.'

Fuckin' terrible just about described how I was feeling that day. I'd been reading Tacitus when Vance rang – what joy: from one migraine straight into another – and I had Andy on my back demanding a progress report on our Bladon Drive bassist. He wanted me to go record-shopping with him on Saturday. Sure, why not? As long as Brian Hinney hadn't had me carted off to the board of governors on Friday.

When Vance had finished explaining how to wring a bird's neck the humane way, I put the receiver back to my ear and said tersely, 'What's up?'

'I've been hearing about this gig in the Maleown Reowd,' he said in a preposterous upper-class accent. 'The poof's getting his band back together, is he? Did he not have the decency to tell me? I'm his biggest fan. I worship him.'

I didn't like Vance's tone. I told him I didn't know what he was talking about.

'I've been on sleeping tablets since their last gig,' he continued tearfully. 'The doctor says I've manic depression. Please tell me they're getting back together. Please tell me it's true.'

I could hear his flatmate laughing in the background. Her name was Alison something, or Alice. She sang Nico-esque vocals for Berlin, usually in a leopardskin mini-skirt and the wrong key.

'Ah, I'm only kidding you on,' Vance said. 'It'll be good to have some opposition again — we were getting lonely, so we were. Tell the boy I'm glad to hear he's back. And I mean that most sincerely, folks. So this gig in his house: is it a private orgy or can anybody come?'

'It's not a gig, it's a party,' I retorted. 'And how did you hear about it?'

'I have my sources,' he simpered. 'Will they be playing in the *drawing*-room? Will his butler be serving Cointreau?'

I refused to descend to Vance's level. I said nothing.

'Oh, I've something for you to tell the boy. We're going to be in the *NME*.'

'Yeah,' I yawned. 'Sure you are.'

'Aye! A wee lad out in Bangor writes for them. He says he's going to do Berlin when we play the Harp.'

'You're lying, Vance. I get the *NME* every week. There's no one from Bangor writing for them. No one from Northern Ireland, even. There hasn't been for years.'

'No, there is. He's just started. You'll see it tomorrow, he's done a review of Pragmatic Control at the Pound. I didn't believe it either. That's why I'm ringing you. They've put a kid from Bangor on the *NME* — tell the boy — we're all going to be fuckin' legends!'

I'd heard of a little test that you could do to check if Vance Armstrong was telling the truth. I knew he wasn't, but it wouldn't hurt to make sure. There was one thing that Vance never, ever joked about. Andy found it hilarious.

'Swear on your motorbike,' I said.

Vance sighed. 'I swear on my motorbike. Now do you believe me?'

'Bloody hell, Vance!' He was telling the truth.

'That's why I'm ringing you,' he said excitedly. 'I could

put a wee word in for the Decadents with this kid from Bangor.'

I was suspicious again. The Vance I knew would never help the Decs; the only words he'd put in for Andy would be libellous and homophobic. But he seemed to read my thoughts. 'A nice word,' he stressed. 'I'd do the boy a favour. He scratches my back, I scratch his. What's the matter with that?'

Then I suddenly remembered why Vance wanted to go to the party. I saw the angelic face of Denise Finn in my mind, and I thought to myself: how many innocent people must I trample and betray for this monstrous plan of mine to work? And without taking a breath, I added Denise's name to the list.

'So you want to come to the party?' I said warily.

'Fuck that, pal. We want to *play* at the party. Tell the boy. We'll go on first and do half an hour.'

'That might not be possible,' I warned.

'Make it possible,' Vance shot back. 'Put your grammar school education to good use. Tell him he's getting a word put in at the *NME* and he should be fuckin' grateful.'

'What if he says no?'

'Well,' Vance replied, clicking at a cigarette lighter. 'I'll tell you what. We'll send him a postcard when we get to America: weather lovely, wish you were here, blah blah blah. And he'll still be playing "Wank Song" and "Shite Song" every night in some fuckin' youth club in Lisburn.'

There was no way round it. Berlin had to perform at the party. And now my plan had to become even more complicated.

Extract from the Manuscript, written June 26

A miraculous new 45, cola-fresh and overwhelming, lipsmackingly pumping pride and panic to my heart. 'Oh,' I said, 'Lordy. It's them. I'd know that feeling anywhere.'

The name of the feeling was 'Hell Raiser' by Sweet. A song beatier than 'Blockbuster', kind of not really the same only sort of much much more so, because a hell raiser is different to a blockbuster, and must start with an explosion.

Yonder! Out of the radio, the thundering hooves of rapture's horses.

'Hell Raiser' burst into the charts high — number four or five — and Sweet dressed up as superheroes when they sang it on Top of the Pops. *There was great importance to this because superheroes, of course, would have no trouble chopping down an oak tree. During the song, Sweet's white-haired singer Brian Connolly broke a microphone stand over his knee, looking so tough that I got a thrill imagining what he'd do to the convicted mass-murderer in 'Tie a Yellow Ribbon' when he dragged him off the bus.*

Oh boy.

'Geronimo!' (Thwack.) 'We'll go to number one now, thank you.'

Darn right they would.

Brooke-Taylor had a woman with him when I delivered my essay on Friday. She was about forty-five or fifty, with black hair tied back in a red chiffon scarf and a string of pearls hanging loosely down the front of her white blouse. There was a confidential atmosphere in the room as I entered, and when the woman looked up at me it was with a graveness and a slowness that alluded to bad news confirmed. It wasn't a look that said *This is a bolt from the blue, Mr Hinney*. It was a look that said *I've had my doubts for some time*.

'Leave it there,' Hinney said curtly, pointing to an empty spot on his desk. 'I'll talk to you on Monday.' I placed the essay down and left the Classics block with a feeling of foreboding. It occurred to me that the woman might be on the board of governors.

Although the holidays didn't officially start until four o'clock on Tuesday, Friday afternoon at the College felt as amiable as a last day of term. My one-time Geography teacher Mr Vettle said hello to me as I was walking towards the quad. He called me by my Christian name; I hadn't even been aware that he knew it. Mrs Idge held the door of Modern Languages open for me with her foot, and chuckled an affectionate 'oh, sorry!' when she realized I wasn't coming in. Everyone seemed relaxed. Everyone looked optimistic. Even *Lord of the Flies* has a happy ending.

In the quad, small boys in shirtsleeves were taking advantage of end-of-term laissez-faire by wearing their ties as headbands and playing five-a-side football with a shuttle-cock. They were most likely second-formers – if not, first-formers. It was hard to tell them apart as you got older.

Attendance was not compulsory for the Lower Sixth in these final few days, but some of us came in nevertheless to empty our lockers and pigeon-holes, or (and I wished I could have been among them) to go to the Botanic in posses and arrive back drunk. The Middle Sixth were all gone now: they'd cleared out for good. The only ones I would see again were Andy and whoever else got into Queen's.

The sixth-form centre was silent, the counter in the coffee bar closed off by a metal grille. No more Toyah and Rainbow to cringe to, no more Slim-a-Soup until September. All gone. Owen Bramerton was sitting under a speaker with a tissue to his nose, looking engrossed in the

NME. I had already bought it on Thursday: it made interesting reading.

'Are we still on for the party?' Owen asked me through his tissue. 'Bark's big dight?'

'Mark's big night,' I echoed. 'Yeah, we're still on. No hassle.'

They all wanted to come now. Cranmore Park would be a Virgins' convention. Piers had been disgusting, bragging to Caroline about 'liking them young' and incessantly singing the Stranglers' 'Bring on the Nubiles'. Caroline was going to be squired on the night by 'an obscene wee penis' from her German class who wanted to do things to her that I frankly didn't like to think about. Coates was holed up in his mansion for the time being, playing bass guitar and drooling. I wondered what the hell I had started.

'Haven't seen Isobel, have you?' I asked Owen.

'Dot id today. She bight be id od Bunday.'

'Monday. Ah.' I was disappointed. The Goodies dream still troubled me, and Isobel was the one person I trusted to interpret it correctly.

To our left sat a table full of Bigots arguing about the recent increase in civilian tit-for-tat killings. Owen folded the *NME* in two and started to read the album reviews. One of the Bigots was saying that tit-for-tats were necessary to preserve the balance in the population, but a Bigot named Florence Seawright was contending that a shoot-to-kill policy by the army would be far more effective. 'It's the best way to stop people dying,' she remarked.

'Are you listening to this garbage?' I said dejectedly.

'Just ignore them,' Owen sniffed. 'They've been at it all afterdood. They'll lighten up when another hugger-striker goes.'

He dabbed his nose carefully with the tissue. Then he said, 'Aw, Jesus' and blew it violently, peering into the tissue and wincing. 'Acne *and* hay fever,' he groaned. 'Nice going, God. Thanks a fuckid billion.'

'Acne, hay fever and hockey,' I said, touched. 'It's been a hard life, Bram.'

There was a flicker of a smile as he put the tissue away. His devastated nose throbbed purplishly like Rumpole of the Bailey's. 'Hasn't even begun, my son. Hasn't even begun.'

'Is Mark suffering too?' I asked. I had a vision of Coates dripping copious liquids all over Andy's attic and short-circuiting the Decadents' equipment.

'Not as bad as me. Urr . . . urr . . . *hang on* . . .' A sneeze was advancing and Owen couldn't get the tissue out in time. He gave a puppy whine and expelled a Herculean *raaashhew!* into the reviews pages of the *NME*.

'Now if only,' I probed at him, 'you could have done that in the winter. Just think, Bram: hundred per cent immunity from games. "This child's not well. How dare you make him play hockey?"'

No flicker of a smile from Owen this time. He got up, taking the *NME* by the tips of his fingers, and trotted away to find a bin. Isolated and with nothing to read, I overheard Florence Seawright declaring to my left, 'Catholics are going to outnumber us in ten years if we don't stand up for ourselves.' It was time to go home.

Later that night, as I sat up writing the Manuscript and brooding over oak trees, I remembered something that Raymond — my apologies — something that *Ray* had said to me on Tuesday evening. After thinking about him for weeks, I'd tracked him down to a pub where Queen's students drank. Big mistake. He harangued me for embarrassing him with 'anecdotes' of Downburn in front of his Law course colleagues, and told me we had nothing at all in common. What he said was, 'Them two there – they're the ones that know me. You *knew* me. Your dad knew my dad, but they don't *know* each other. Not in their heads.'

I shouldn't have gone looking for old friends. It was too speculative and I would only find shadows. I didn't know Raymond Adair or Owen Bramerton in their heads – only in my head, and that was the trouble.

Extract from the Manuscript, written June 27 (morning)

I'm sure I've mentioned Clare Beattie somewhere. Sure I have. The bowl-haired satirist of Downburn Primary? Oh yes, nobody could forget Clare.

This was the era when Clare came to the fore. The era of 'Hell Raiser', Sweet and me. Henceforth known herein and thereafter as the era of Sweet, me and Clare. Out of my absent mind and into my eyeline she moved, never to be half-seen or overlooked again. I can run her like a film reel. She walks, she talks. She lies. Always she lies.

Clare was a Slade fan. She bore a grudge against Sweet on principle. The two groups were rivals in the charts, and Clare, whose father sometimes went out at night wearing a balaclava, knew a thing or two about rivalries. The war in Northern Ireland often seemed a faraway concern to me in my cosy cul-de-sac, but it was close enough to Clare for her to be unusually coy when the Downburn branch of the UDA came up in conversation; let's just say that old man Beattie was more than the local fishmonger. Whatever it was that he did in the UDA, the fact that he did it gave Clare an aura of secrecy around our school, and she exploited it to the hilt. More knowledgeable about music than the rest of us, she operated her own little Ministry of Pop Information all through

1973 and 1974. Only it wasn't information: Clare, you Lied to us. If I was a liar, Clare, and at times I was, you were a Liar.

I remember thinking it odd that the two ladies in the New Seekers had both lived in Downburn's Woodland Road — as Clare revealed when 'Pinball Wizard' made the Top 30 — and had once owned Mackeys the newsagent's. But then a lot of what Clare said sounded odd, owing to the frenetic, gabbling way she talked. Clare was a model of the '. . . oh, and another thing' school of oratory, and she'd quite often have a piece of semi-chewed Wagon Wheel in her mouth while she was orating. She sounded a bit like the cement mixer outside Jack Lemmon's house in How to Murder Your Wife: *gabbledy-gabbledy, gloppity-gloppity.* 'And you know the two ladies in the New Seekers? Gloppity-gloppity used to own Mackeys, so they did.'

Mackeys where I got my Beano and Topper every week? Mackeys where Mrs Mackey knew not to put any all-black liquorice allsorts in my Lucky Dip because they tasted like puke? 'Yes,' said Clare. 'That Mackeys. Gloppity.'

How strange.

Not as strange, mind you, as Dave Hill in Slade being the nephew of the Reverend Ian Paisley — which Clare had divulged to us when 'Cum on Feel the Noize' was at number one in March. Nor as strange as David Cassidy being a lollipop man's son from Belvoir. Indeed, it surprised us to learn that many of the stars we'd seen on Top of the Pops had a Downburn or County Down connection. Rod Stewart came from up Saintfield way. Marc Bolan had a caravan on Newcastle beach. Dave Edmunds was from Killynure and his mummy went to the same church as Clare's aunt Maureen.

The Marc Bolan who was in T. Rex? Yes, said Clare. That Marc Bolan. Halfway up the beach, on bricks. A caravan with 'T. Rex are the Best' painted on it and all their song-words written all around. You could see it from the road. And sometimes he came out with his bucket and spade and made sandcastles. Gloppity.

But should the subject ever turn to Sweet, Clare, do you remember what would happen? Your face would cloud over and the gloppity sounds would decelerate with revulsion. Sweet, you said, had no right living in Northern Ireland and taking food out of the mouths of good honest hard-working Protestant people. Sweet were Fenians and papists, which was why they had been forcibly evicted from their Dundonald council house and warned not to come back.

I knew it wasn't true. I had read in Pop Star *that Sweet came from Middlesex. But I wasn't brave enough to confront Clare. And, as Angus Massey pointed out, nobody else in school had that kind of information.*

Clare brought her transistor radio in on Tuesdays, enabling her to lie to us about the new Top 30. She would mooch off into a corner of the playground, taking her friend Esme Walsh and a couple of Wagon Wheels with her, and she would shout out the bulletins as Johnnie Walker announced them. 'Three new entries . . . Two non-movers . . .' Then the lie: 'There's a new number one!*'*

'Can you not turn the radio up?' somebody would ask her.

'No. Shut up. It's my radio. Get back over there or I won't tell you who's in the charts.' If we moved towards her, she would throw a tantrum and turn the radio down, or off, until we backed away. So we all formed a line together, like tiny defenders at a free-kick.

Some of the chart positions she would shout to us would be correct. 'Chicory Tip up two . . . Argent down four . . .' But then there'd be a curious drop for a group she didn't like ('Hot Chocolate down nineteen') and we'd find out that it was a lie when we watched Top of the Pops *two days later. 'Hot Chocolate went up three,' I would mutter to Angus Massey or Michael 'Goofy' Greer in assembly on Friday.*

'I know, Clare's a lying cow,' they would whisper back. 'And she said there was a new number one and there wasn't.'

'Somebody should go and tell her.'

'We can't. She's the only one with a radio.'

For most of the spring of 1973, Clare, like all of us in Class 5, heartily despised 'Tie a Yellow Ribbon Round the Old Oak Tree' by Dawn. And she was, like all of us, crestfallen that 'Hello Hello I'm Back Again' by Gary Glitter was repeatedly unsuccessful in shifting Dawn from the number one spot, even though she told us three weeks running that it had. These were rare examples of Clare's lies having good intentions. We all dreamed of a Top 30 without Dawn at number one: Clare briefly gave our dream life.

Sunlight would bathe the playground and we would rejoice like munchkins; then out from her corner would mooch Clare, turning up the radio, and we would hear 'Tie a Yellow Ribbon Round the Old Oak Tree', still bouncing away at number one, and Clare would look angry, smug and sympathetic all at the same time.

However, on the Tuesday that 'Hell Raiser' by Sweet appeared in the charts, Clare's opinion of 'Tie a Yellow Ribbon Round the Old Oak Tree' executed a mammoth about-turn. It became her favourite song overnight, and she even bought it, bringing it in to school to show us. As the sole Sweet fan in Class 5, I was now a sitting duck, for the Slade—Sweet rivalry was a civil war to Clare in all but name, and it called for her to put on her balaclava and get very nasty.

I'm from the South. I didn't understand about the rivalries. I wasn't prepared for what was coming.

I stayed up all night writing the Manuscript, then went to meet Andy on Saturday morning.

Gone were the grey school uniform shirt and trousers. Standing outside the post office by the College gates, Andy wore new black drainpipes, a new psychedelic-looking shirt and new sunglasses. He had done a serious amount of work on his image since I'd last seen him on the Matthew Barr Friday.

'Where did all that come from?' I said, suddenly inadequate in my Undertones tee-shirt and faded jeans.

'Can't a man buy clothes occasionally?' he answered with a pout. 'Do the working-class mafia not allow it?' He ran a hand foppishly through his hair.

'You've had that cut, too,' I said.

'"Styled" is the word, I think you'll find. A very reasonable coiffure if I say so myself.'

We hung around idly on the pavement. I was unsettled by this brand-new Andy, this chic innovation before me. But irritated by him as well – intensely irritated – because he had clearly cost money. I thought he didn't have any money. That was one of the frigging reasons for concocting my plan in the first place. Frigging Andy was supposed to be frigging skint.

'Well, this is nice,' he said at length.

The deceitful bastard.

'Standing here next to the letter-box and so on. Great.'

I've been a complete fool. Oh my God, are those are new winkle-pickers?

'So where do you want to go?' I inquired, none too cordially.

'Um . . . tff . . . doot-doot-doot . . . Knights,' he decided. 'Let's see how many people have sold the Exploited album.'

I've been so blind. I've been as blind as Blind Pew.

Requiring a five-minute walk through the Queen's district – a walk that in turn required Andy to admire his reflection in the window of every parked car in University Road and Mount Charles – Knights in Botanic Avenue was a shop where, like Good Vibrations a bit further down, you could buy LPs both new and second-hand.

The next time I do this walk, I'll have a fucking guide-dog with me.

But Knights was also a record library, and in the '70s

I'd been on its membership books for several years, borrowing used albums of the calibre of Uriah Heep's *The Magician's Birthday* at ten pence a go. Duggie and Paul Knight had on certain occasions substantially increased the size of the library in one fell swoop by buying my record collection off me. This would happen when I changed my allegiance from one musical style to another — say from Yes to Devo — which sometimes involved taking records back to Duggie and Paul that I'd purchased from them only a week earlier. They would look at me, then at my records, then at me again, and shake their heads sadly at the fickleness of their young customer. So young. So clueless.

'Can you imagine anybody actually *listening* to the Exploited?' said Andy loudly, searching for second-hand copies of *Punk's Not Dead* in the E section at the rear of the shop. 'How much pleasure do you think there would be in a situation like that? I mean, Jesus Christ ... I'd rather be nailed to a lamp-post and shafted by Gloria Hunniford.'

'Have you found one?' I asked coldly.

'There aren't any. Incredible. All the little punks must fucking love it. "Ooh, it's like a return to the good old days." Sitting there with a big hard-on. You know who probably bought it? In fact he probably got it the day it came out.'

But I wanted to avoid Vance-baiting for the moment, so I distracted Andy by reaching past him and pulling out a tattered ELO album, *Face the Music*. Ten pence to borrow it, or it had a sticker offering it for one pound seventy to buy. I tried to appear fascinated by the album — or at least by the sticker — but I'd never been into ELO even as a prog kid. Those plodding choruses just weren't symphonic enough, my friend. However, I had been a twelve-year-old fan of the Eagles, whose *Desperado* was right behind *Face the Music* in the rack. I sensed an Andy tirade.

'Bands beginning with E are always shit, aren't they?' he said. 'I mean, here we have a perfect example: the Eagles. You probably had this, didn't you? *Yes* you did, this is probably your copy. I bet it still has your name on it. "Property of Doug Yule, aged three." Come on, where have you written it? "The Eagles are my bestest, most fave band. *Desperado* is super." Fuck! Will you *look* at the moustache on this guy. Hubba hubba hubba! Excuse me, sir, do you have a licence for that moustache? What a fucking sad indictment of American manhood. Is there any woman *anywhere* who would be impressed by that moustache? "Hi, baby, wanna go for a ride in the 'tache? Hey, hop in." You could get an entire Ethiopian village in it. "Let's cruise, baby. Wanna hear some shit music? Hey, I'll play you our new album. Don't mind the Ethiopians in the back, they live there." Whoah, watch yourselves, everybody – he's got a rifle. Nobody make any more 'tache jokes or he'll blow our heads off. What a spanner. If he had any intelligence he'd shoot the other Eagles, wouldn't he? Save the world from *Hotel California*.'

'Hmm,' I said.

'Here, have your copy back. Don't go sneaking it out the door while I'm not looking.'

The racks of new albums were at the front of the shop, and Andy went off to smirk at them while I stayed to see if the second-hand section had any American records from the '60s. It wasn't a territory I knew too much about – the Velvet Underground and Dylan aside – but Andy was a proselytizer and he maintained that American '60s music was some of the most wonderful ever created.

And he'll be able to buy all the '60s records he wants with his new-found wealth, the two-faced bastard. 'Eoww, Dad left us in saach a tangle. You've neow idea . . .'

Not that Andy would have been very keen on the '60s groups that Tinmeer had guided me towards in the fourth form – Jefferson Airplane, the Grateful Dead, Buffalo Springfield – the 'seminal West Coast outfits' as Tinmeer called them. He'd been another con-merchant. There was obviously something about me that attracted them. Something in my demeanour that said, 'Ahoy there, supercilious bullshit artist. Come and lead me up the garden path.'

In February or March 1979, at Tinmeer's behest, I had borrowed from Knights a triple album by the Grateful Dead. The statistics alone should have been a sufficient deterrent. Six whole sides of music – with the Grateful Dead playing on all six of them. The rental fee was an exorbitant thirty pence, and I grumbled to Tinmeer that it had better be worth it. 'Money well spent,' he commended me. '*Europe '72* is an acknowledged classic.' When I put on side one at home, I practically fell into a coma.

'Four packets of Wotsits I could have got for that,' I sulked. 'You stupid bugger.'

'An acknowledged classic,' he repeated. 'Seminal.'

'Listen to it – it's just country and western. Does "seminal" mean useless?'

'Money well spent.'

Tinmeer had other ways of tricking me into frittering away my pennies. He persuaded me to borrow a Jefferson Airplane LP from Knights by showing me a picture of their violin player. 'Exemplary musician,' he said. All I saw was a bald old man who looked like Errol Brown's grandfather. 'Blues-trained,' Tinmeer insisted. 'He added considerably to the overall performance.' It went without saying that the LP was crap. Then there was Love, the apples of Tinmeer's eye. Their album *Forever Changes* was acknowledged as seminal, surprise surprise. 'Robert Plant used to be a teenage Love fan,' Tinmeer pontificated, implying that I'd stick my head in an oven if Led Zeppelin said it was okay.

As it transpired, Knights's library never contained any albums by Love during all my years of membership. But it contained one now, and I had just found it. Available for borrowing (10p), or for buying second-hand (£3).

The cover of the album was a gold frame with a photograph inside of six — no, wait — seven men standing around some kind of tower or monument. One of the men resembled the Incredible Hulk. Another was blond and cool, like a male Marianne Faithfull. Some men were white and some were black. I couldn't hypothesize a music — not even a bar or a note — that could be produced by the seven together.

The words on the gold frame said *Da Capo*, which doubtless explained why someone in Knights had misfiled it in the D rack. I remembered Tinmeer mentioning that it had an extremely long track on the second side, and yes, here it was in the credits — 'Revelation'. I was intrigued by its biblical-sounding title and its fearless, nineteen-minute vastness. It reminded me of Green Regent's 1975 concept album *Pentateuch*, with its epic side two, 'Deuteronomy'.

'Deuteronomy' (Hempridge–Beaufort–Dexter, 21:49) . . . a suite of music so epic and symphonic that the Regent needed an 84-piece orchestra to play it live . . . but just the once, only the once . . . Wembley Stadium, '77 . . . Hempridge weeping and soloing, soloing and weeping . . .

Poor old Hemp.

Three pounds for Love's *Da Capo* — and I had a fiver on

me to last all weekend. I read some more song-titles: 'Steph-anie Knows Who', 'Orange Skies', 'Que Vida!' Three pounds and I could have them. One more title: 'Seven And Seven Is'. Seven and seven is three pounds; elementary record-shopping maths.

I flipped the album cover back and forth. Three-fifths of my fiver for a rocket-trip in Stephanie's orange skies. Or alternatively, three quid squandered on a tour of Stephanie's industrial estates. Which was it to be? I'd baulked at Love's hippy name at fourteen. Now they looked like my kind of band.

Someone had come up behind me. I felt absurd and intruded upon, and hoped that I hadn't been thinking out loud. The intruder said in an English accent, 'Naked . . . men's . . . buttocks.'

I turned. 'You'll rip that,' I warned him.

Andy had wedged his head into an album sleeve and was wearing it like a dunce's cap. He said again, 'Naked men's buttocks.'

'I heard you.'

He took the sleeve off his head – it was now horribly creased and twisted. He made the sound of a trumpet as he squeezed it open and shut.

'*Mwaap-mwaah* . . . Naked men's buttocks. *Mwaap*. What've you got there? *Mwaah* . . . Oh, *Da Capo*. You should get that. I wouldn't bother with side two, though – it's an abortion. I really am desperately excited by my naked men's buttocks.'

He waved the ruined sleeve at me. It was *To Each . . .*, by A Certain Ratio, and there were some naked men in the bottom right-hand corner, walking in single file.

'Buttocks,' Andy said. 'Naked men's buttocks.'

I pushed the sleeve away. 'Are you buying that?'

'Like hell. These Factory fucking Third Reich bands bore the shit out of me. They shouldn't allow people in Manchester to make records, don't you think? Except the Fall, we'd allow them ... and Magazine. And I suppose my fabulous bassist who I still haven't met yet would want to add New Order to that, would he not, Mr Yule?'

So Andy had remembered. Well, to hell with him – the plan was kaput now anyway. I might as well ring Coates and tell him to unplug his bass and sod off to Barbados. The Decadents wouldn't be needing him after all.

These pompous dictators. Pontificating about what I should and shouldn't do. If it's not the sage of Hamelin, it's the Earl of Cranmore. Behold him in his finery – to the manor born, he is, and rich as Croesus.

'I'll just pay for this,' I said, putting *Da Capo* under my arm and feeling in my pocket for the fiver. 'Unless you have a spare fifty-pound note you can lend me. And is it all right if I make my own mind up about side two? I do like to think for myself occasionally. I do actually have a mind of my own.'

Whether he reacted or not, I didn't look to see.

Extract from the Manuscript, written June 27 (morning)

It was from Angus Massey's brother Gordon that I learned I had VD. 'Hell Raiser' had climbed to number two on Tuesday, but was being held back by Dawn, so it had been one of those equivocal weeks.

'You've got VD,' Gordon told me as we sat in our socks on the varnished wood floor of the school's assembly room. 'Everyone says so.'

'What's VD?' I asked, picking at a sock.

Gordon wasn't sure. But I had it, and everyone was saying so.

If VD were anything like my psoriasis the year before, I knew I could expect the unwanted re-emergence of the calamine lotion bottle. As it was, I had psoriasis to thank for being the only boy in Class 5 wearing long trousers. Now that I had VD, they would surely rig me out in sackcloth, measure me for callipers and put a paper bag over my head.

'Have I really got VD?' I asked someone who I thought would know.

'Where-did-you-pick-that-word-up! Of-course-you-haven't!' my mother gesticulated furiously. 'And don't ever use language like that again.'

Sent instantly to bed, I passed a restless night, I recall, tossing and turning for almost a minute before the slumber farmer came to collect me in Tootles, his pink tractor. At assembly the following morning, I took Gordon into my confidence.

'I don't think I have got VD, you know. Do you mean psoriasis? I get that sometimes, but it's nearly gone away.'

'All I know,' replied Gordon, 'is that Angus says it's VD all right.'

Angus was sitting in the row ahead of us. As soon as 'Onward Christian Soldiers' had finished, I called over to him and asked why he'd told Gordon that I had VD. Angus gave me the name of a third party. Seconds later, I was turning round to speak to Goofy Greer in the row behind, who, in the brief lull before 'The Lord is My Shepherd', informed me that he'd heard it from Buck-toothed Rosemary White. En route to our classroom after assembly, I managed to elicit from Buck-toothed Rosemary the suggestion that I should really be talking to Esme Walsh. Which told me that it had come from Clare Beattie.

Clare and Esme sat beside each other in Class 5 on the girls' side. The girls' desks faced the boys' desks (mine faced Buck-toothed Rosemary's, though Buck-toothed Rosemary usually looked diagonally across at Goofy Greer, presumably to compare teeth), and the desks stretched around the walls in a rectangle, except for a gap that Mr Wyatt could walk through if he wanted to teach us from the middle of the room.

To see Clare, I had to look to my right, to where Mr Wyatt had moved her and Esme in January. They had been chewing, and he said that people who chewed had to sit next to the blackboard. Clare still chewed every day (slowly), but Esme had stopped.

This particular morning, Mr Wyatt was teaching us about the past, and about the boring jobs that everybody in Ulster had to do to afford sweets in the old days before Mackeys was built. There were lots of unappealing words to memorize, such as 'flax' and 'workhouse', and Mr Wyatt asked us all to say them in unison.

'Flax,' everybody said, with mouths opened wide. 'Workhouse. Linen. Flaaaax. Loooom.'

But one person wasn't obeying. As I looked to my right, Clare was staring straight at me and silently mouthing, 'Pay-pist. Fee-nian. Vee Dee.'

'Sir,' I put my hand up. 'Clare Beattie's saying bad words when she should be saying flax.'

I put my hand down. Angus Massey seemed to have gone stiff beside me.

'Clare Beattie,' Mr Wyatt said sternly to her. 'What have I said to you before about bad words in class?'

She looked daggers at me. 'Sir, he's a lying Jap. I never gloppity bad words, so I never.'

'Are you chewing, Clare Beattie?' he barked at her. She was really glaring at me now. 'I asked you a question, madam. Are you chewing?'

Clare shook her head.

'Don't you tell fibs to me, Clare Beattie. And you can stop trying to swallow it, for I know it's there. Open your mouth. Open . . . your . . . mouth.'

Clare reluctantly opened her mouth. There was a grey lump on her tongue.

'Spit it into your hand. I said spit . . . it . . . into your hand.
Now away outside and put that in the bin, you filthy child. And when
you come back in, you can say you're sorry.'

It was a heavenly moment. Clare scraped back her chair and left
the room with a face that could have sliced bacon. She returned wiping
her hand on her navy-blue tunic, sat down, scraped her chair forward,
took a deep breath and apologized to Mr Wyatt very softly.

'Good. Now go into the middle of the room and say sorry to all
the boys and girls one by one. Say "I'm very sorry" to all of them,
and don't leave anyone out.'

There were gasps. Incredulity fizzed through Class 5.

Clare looked horrified. Even I was dumbfounded by the harshness
of the punishment, and I was generally in favour of people being
punished harshly. Beetroot with indignation, Clare scraped back her
chair again and got to her feet. Mr Wyatt pointed her towards the gap
in the desks, following her in.

'She won't like this,' said Angus quietly.

Clare went first to Esme. 'Horry,' she mumbled.

'Say "I'm very sorry,"' Mr Wyatt rebuked her. 'Do it again.'

'I'm very sorry,' said Clare to a stunned Esme.

And off she went on her humiliating circuit of the room, Mr Wyatt
constantly by her side. Clare's voice grew fainter as she moved towards
the desks in the corner. Soon it was inaudible. She had twenty-eight of
us to apologize to.

I was starting to feel uneasy. Angus had got into the spirit of it,
and was whisper-singing 'She'll be Coming Round the Mountain When
She Comes'. But I wished that Mr Wyatt would call a halt to the
punishment before Clare came round the mountain to me.

It was too late, and her voice was getting louder again. Before I
knew it, there she was. 'I'm very sorry,' she said to Gordon. 'I'm very
sorry,' she said to his twin brother. She had four to go.

'I'm very sorry,' she said to me, and on she passed.

But I didn't hear the other three apologies. I didn't see Clare sit down, or see Mr Wyatt pick up the chalk, or see him write 'flax' and 'loom' on the blackboard. I only noticed that later.

'I'm very sorry,' I kept hearing Clare say to me. 'I'm very sorry. I'm very sorry.'

That was it. That was how she'd said it.

'I'm very sorry . . . that I had to do . . . what I am going to do . . . to you.'

'What *is* that song?' Andy said. 'The one you keep whistling.'

I laid my Knights record bag on the curved leather of the window-seat and sat down next to it with my back to the bar.

'Sorry.' I smiled. '"Tie a Yellow Ribbon Round the Old Oak Tree". No excuse, is there?'

'Listen, if it makes you . . .' he started to say. 'Just sit there and fondle your LP. I'll get the drinks.'

It was just gone twelve and we had found a city-centre pub. An upstairs haven behind C&A, it seemed to be called Killane's on the door and the Black Bell on the windows. It had rosy-red decor and little alcoves, a buttered toast smell and a dense cigarette fog that wasn't quite dense enough to conceal an under-age sixteen-year-old. I hoped the staff wouldn't see me and sling me out, but with my back to the bar it was feasible they'd leave me alone. If challenged, I could show them a Youth Hostels Association card with a false date of birth. Sometimes it worked and sometimes it didn't.

I bowed my head, yawning into my chest. What a day.

My right shoe skidded on a betting slip that had been dropped under the table, but I was too tired to kick it even a centimetre. My all-night Manuscript marathon had been snack-free, so as well as feeling tingly from fatigue I was also amazingly hungry. I estimated I had been awake for forty-one hours.

In the alcove opposite me, an obese ginger-haired man with enormous sideburns and a furtive Bobby Charlton lookalike in a donkey jacket were gazing at something over my head. I assumed it was a lunch menu on the wall.

Yes, I'll have a Vesta curry on a bed of fluffy rice, please, to eat and sleep in simultaneously. Luxurious aromatic diced beef and downy rice beckoning to me from a voluptuous pillow of feathery sauce. The bloke in the psychedelic shirt is paying.

'You had it there, you had it,' said the Bobby Charlton lookalike. 'Back, back.'

'BBC1, big man,' his fat companion chipped in.

'Here's BBC1 here,' said a Scottish voice. 'There's no sound.'

An instant later, the sky erupted. Crowds cheered and roared above me, and a commentator exclaimed, 'Aw-ho-ho, in she *goes* . . .' The volume was quickly turned down. 'Master Garfield,' murmured the commentator politely. 'Well I never.'

I was sitting under a bloody television. Could someone not have told me? Shrinking into my seat, I waited for the men in the alcove to shout for the manager and protest that their view of *Grandstand* was being obscured by an eleven-year-old.

'There's Crenshaw,' the fat one announced. 'Always the bridesmaid.'

'Three under?' said the Bobby Charlton lookalike. 'Should have had a shilling on him.'

Derision. 'Not at all.'

130

'Three under?' He had horizontal streaks of angrily brushed hair going from ear to ear, but there were intermittent islands of white like the bunkers at the Open. I imagined ants with minuscule golf clubs playing on his head.

'Not at all,' the fat man insisted. 'Seve's the boy.'

'Seve? Not at all. Too far back.'

'Seve? Not at all.'

The fat man lowered his eyes suddenly, meeting mine. I responded with one of those matey, adult-like nods of the head that I knew you did when people looked at you in pubs. The fat man nodded. I did the same. Then the Bobby Charlton lookalike nodded at me and I nodded, and I wondered if I should make an adult-like, well-informed observation about the golf. ('It's never too far back for Seve in actual fact. His putting skills are irrefutable.')

A Guinness arrived on my beer mat. 'For you,' said Andy. The barman had drawn a shamrock in the creamy head. 'And . . . for me.' He placed a pint of lager next to a spirit glass with ice in it, and went away again.

'Your friend likes a drink,' the fat man remarked, with another nod to me.

'He unquestionably does right enough,' I said in as deep a voice as I could muster, nodding vigorously. Neither of them nodded back.

A packet of Tayto cheese and onion crisps flew past my shoulder and landed on the table. I had torn them open and eaten the top ones by the time Andy fell into his seat in a flurry of bony limbs. Lighting up a Rothmans, he took a sip from his lager, poured half a bottle of tonic water into his other glass and sighed.

'Well, here we are. Got the fags and the booze and the

crisps, and we're putting the world to rights. Cheers, boy.' He clinked my Guinness. 'So when do I meet him?'

'The day before. He gets back from Donegal in the morning.' I worked my way through the next layer of crisps.

Andy took a long swig of lager. 'Ten days' fishing in Donegal. I think the phrase "it takes all sorts" would be the one that comes to mind. At least he won't have a suntan.'

'And learning the songs will be no problem. He says one rehearsal on Wednesday will be fine.'

Andy gave me a dubious look. 'Fine for him, he means. Dermot and Rob'll be having heart attacks.'

'No, it'll be great, you'll see. And I've told him you don't allow curly leads. He's going to bring a straight one.'

'Good,' Andy said. 'I could never get Paul Leckie to understand that. Thanks. And obviously no sunburst plectrums, tell him.'

I stuffed more crisps down me and asked how Dermot and Robert were.

'Dermot's staying in Belfast, has he told you?' Andy said. 'He's not going to Aberystwyth any more. I don't think his A-levels went too well. Haven't talked to Rob lately.' He made rapid drumming motions, crossing and uncrossing his hands. 'Denise likes Rob. What's the bassist's name, by the way? Dermot says he might know him.'

'Johnny,' I replied. 'But everyone just calls him Hemp. Short for Hempridge.'

'Oh? I thought you said you didn't know his surname. Wasn't that why you couldn't find him in the phone book or something?'

The smoke from Andy's cigarette made me sneeze. Rather startling us both, I sneezed again and felt in my pocket for a tissue while holding up my other hand to warn Andy that further sneezes were not inconceivable. After waiting for thirty seconds, I let my hand fall to the empty crisp packet, scrunched it up, threw it at the ashtray and missed. Two more throws were needed to hit the target. By then Andy had completely forgotten what we were talking about.

I took a conspiratorial look around the pub. Andy did likewise.

'What?' he said.

'So does Sheila know?'

'Who? Oh, about these?' he said, peering downwards at his new shirt, trousers and boots. 'Yeah, of course. I've been wearing them all week.'

'No, but I mean, does she know where they came from?'

Andy grew evasive. He shook his Rothmans packet from side to side. 'Well, yes, but we haven't quite done the introductions yet. Sheila can be a tad funny sometimes about the people I bring home. As I believe you know.'

'This new relationship is fantastic news, Lou, I really mean it. It'll be a huge inspiration for your songwriting.'

He shook the Rothmans packet up and down. 'Well . . . yeah . . . relationships. Got to write about 'em eventually, I suppose.'

'And you still won't say who it is?'

A firm shake of the head. 'No, wouldn't be fair. People could get hurt.'

That was exactly what he'd said half an hour earlier when he caught up with me in Great Victoria Street. Now I knew the truth: well, most of the truth. I knew about the gifts, I knew about the relationship, I knew that it wouldn't be fair to name the other person because people could get hurt. He was probably a teacher, perhaps a married man with a family, someone who must on no account be exposed.

'I know how delicate these things are,' I'd said in Great Victoria Street. 'There's just so much ignorance around here, unfortunately.'

Andy had grinned. 'Ignorance is precisely what I want there to be. The more ignorance the better.'

'I just think it's despicable the way people have to keep these things secret.'

'Well . . . I dunno . . . there are worse things, aren't there? Come on, let's go for a drink. I'll try and get you into that upstairs place round the back of C&A. They won't have anyone on the door on a Saturday.'

I'd started whistling a tune as we walked into the city centre. It made me smile to think of Andy being showered with presents by an older man (possibly a head of department). We had never talked openly about his sexual leanings, but they hadn't been too hard to guess. It wasn't as though he went out of his way to chase girls.

'Incidentally,' I'd said as we turned the corner into Wellington Place, 'I had a stroke of luck with that bass player last night. Found the house first time. He says there's absolutely no problem with the ninth — "Count me in for definite," those were his words — but he's away off on a fishing holiday today and he doesn't get back for ten days. It's him and his dad. They do it every year, so he can't get out of it.'

'A *fishing* holiday? For fuck's sake . . . Ten fucking days?'
'Yeah, in Donegal.'

'I'm going to have a word with this guy. I fucking mean it.'

We'd strolled along Donegall Square North, me whistling, Andy swearing, past the bus-stops on the left and the City Hall on the right, then into Donegall Place and up to the security barrier to be frisked for guns and ammunition. Panic over. Everything exactly as it always was when life in Belfast was normal.

DOUG'S PLAN
June 7, 1981

The Plan will run as follows.

1. Andy is the premier songwriter and band-leader in Belfast by a mile. He knows it and I know it. We've both said it many times.

2. However, the idea of getting off his rectum and pursuing a wider audience for his music is for some reason anathema to him. He denies it but I can prove it.

3. (i) For instance: the Decadents showed early promise with two excellent concerts in the summer of 1980, one in a church hall in Malone (prior to Andy and me being introduced) and one in Finaghy (after we had met at Noel Johnston's party). I was immediately enthusiastic about the Decadents – some would say that they were one of the few things in my life that warranted enthusiasm – and I was also, as a frequent reader of the *New Musical Express* and other publications of a weekly nature, full of good advice for Andy about what the band should do next.

(ii) Conversation in attic of Cranmore Park, September 1980.

D: The first thing, obviously, is getting an album out. Don't go to EMI or CBS, they're idiots. I know the Furs are on CBS but that's a fluke, they probably signed them without hearing them. Your best bet is to avoid major labels completely.

A: Avoid major labels completely.

D: Now, I've been reading in the *NME* about these independent labels that are starting up all over the place. They have them in Liverpool, they have them in Manchester – and there's tons of them in London. And what they do is put out records on their own. I mean, that's why they're called independent, because they're nothing to do with EMI or CBS. They haven't got much money – you know, not millions of pounds – but they care more about the music and they're run by real fans.

A: Go on.

D: Now, the interesting thing about independent labels is that the *NME* think they're the future of music, and they prefer them to major labels. Look at it this way. The *NME* want to write about new bands – that's what the *NME*'s there for – and all the good new bands are on independent labels these days.

A: Except the Psychedelic Furs. No, I'm listening, go on.

D: Now, another interesting thing about independent labels is that there's one in Scotland now. It's in Glasgow. The *NME* are saying – and *Sounds* as well – they're saying that the best new bands are in Glasgow now, not Manchester or Liverpool, and they're giving them tons and tons of coverage in the *NME* and *Sounds*. Do you see what that means?

A: The coverage is moving north.

D: And? Where's the obvious place the *NME* and *Sounds* will look for new bands next? Ta-daaa.

A: What – here? They'll have a fucking fruitless search, won't they?

D: (*ironically*) Ah . . . only, I seem to remember seeing a pretty good band playing in Finaghy the other night.

A: You're fucking crazy. First of all you tell me to slam the phone down on CBS when they ring up to offer me a million pounds. And now you're having me doing interviews tomorrow with the *NME*, who never come to Belfast anyway. One small point I feel I ought to make: we've done two gigs. Two. *Deux*. Shall we take it one step at a time before we start thinking about what we're going to wear on *Top of the Pops*?

4. My initial efforts thus ended in ridicule.

5. (i) Yet in the ensuing weeks of that autumn season, I strove to impress on Andy the need to record a cassette of the Decadents in rehearsal, which we would mail to the *NME*, *Sounds*, John Peel at Radio One, and some of the independent labels in London, Liverpool, Manchester and Glasgow.

(ii) Précis of conversations in attic of Cranmore Park, October–November 1980.

A: No. Out of the question.

D: But Peel plays new bands every night! You know he does. If we send him a tape of the Decadents, he'll put it on the radio.

A: And it'll sound dreadful. We've done three gigs, all right? The songs are still in complete chaos. Let me get the band ready before you start writing to Tony Blackburn and Terry Wogan about us. Oh, and before I forget, I've sacked the bass player. But don't say anything to him, we're still using his amp.

6. In December, I asked Andy to at least provide me with a Decadents cassette that could be played in the sixth-form centre to raise awareness of the band locally. He answered in the negative.

7. My attempts throughout January and February 1981 to exhort Andy to enter a cheap Belfast recording studio and make a Decadents 45 (suggested A-side, 'Strange Song') met with total failure.

8. In almost every discussion *vis-à-vis* the possibility of recording any Decadents music or Andy Finn composition of any kind, the same two excuses have tended to be omnipresent: (i) the band has a severe shortcoming in the bass guitarist department, and (ii) the Finns have money problems, Andy's father having left them in a tangle. Sheila is the breadwinner in the family, and deems Denise's education to be of more importance than the Decadents' career.

9. I must confess myself troubled by Andy's procrastination. Perhaps he in some way lacks assurance. Perhaps, as Vance Armstrong believes, he simply has no ambition in the sphere of music. But why, then, compose such ambitious material as 'Fast Song', 'Drone Song' and, most recently, 'New Song'? And why make lavish claims for his own ability, such as 'I can piss a better tune than Elvis Costello can write.'

10. (i) If indeed it is in the area of assurance that Andy finds himself deficient, then that is an area in which his deficiencies have my commiseration and my empathy. For it was my own deficiencies in that area that occasioned my post-Easter psychological tribulations – mercifully transient and inconspicuous to most outsiders – which culminated in my unprecedented hour of clear-headedness during the morning of today, Sunday June 7.

(ii) Recalling words and images from the afternoon and evening of the previous Friday, I succeeded this morning in devising a Plan. This Plan is the solution not only to the Decadents' two problems outlined in 8 (i) and (ii), but also to some other problems that relate to my own personal circumstances. These shall be set aside for the moment.

11. (i) I increasingly feel that the solution to the Decadents' problems lies in the shape and person of Mark Coates. Whilst a list of Coates's deficiencies would be long indeed, his attributes include financial wealth, a bass guitar and amplifier, a profiteering outlook and exceptional gullibility.

(ii) I believe that Coates will finance the recording of a debut single by an up-and-coming Belfast band (a) if there is a chance that he will make some money out of it, and (b) if he is in that band and playing on that record himself. Via chicanery, I will make Coates a member of the Decadents in time for Denise Finn's birthday party on July 9. By arranging for the party guests to comprise several of Coates's closest friends, I will ensure that his musicianship receives a warm ovation. Thus enthused, Coates will consider it his duty to contribute to the furthering of the Decadents' career in a fiscal manner of speaking.

(iii) Andy, after a period of disbelief and unhappiness, will recognize the logic of having an affluent, greedy cretin playing in the band. Spurious guarantees will be made by Andy and myself to Coates, to the effect of cutting him in on a percentage of the Decadents' record sales, which will almost certainly be in the high tens of thousands once John Peel and the *NME* get behind the band. The patronage of Peel and the music press is a tried and tested route to success used by all the best bands like Joy Division and the Fall. If everything goes to plan, I foresee the Decadents being on the cover of the *NME* – and in the lower reaches of the Top 40 – before Andy has finished his first year at Queen's.

APPENDIX TO THE PLAN
June 28, 1981

Within the last few days, developments have arisen that would seem to make the Decadents' imminent appearance in the *NME* a certainty. The existence has been revealed of a journalist in Bangor named Karl Marks, who has written the following review in the current issue of the aforementioned organ:

PRAGMATIC CONTROL
Belfast
A brave new city or the same old theatre of hate? Every dissipated/dislocated punker in town has dressed up in last year's jackets and badges to frug and bop to Pragmatic Control's abstract spastic pop. And to see if Belfast can do a Postcard with the expertise that it can do a letter-bomb. Formerly two-chord no-hopers Verbal Crusade, the Prags are in thrall to Fire Engines' lubricated shinypop groove thang, hurtling into the cluttered funk of 'Shadow-boxing with God' as though it will one day be the Belfast post-punk anthem that sinewy vox man Fergus seems to think it already is. Such dance-chancers are thick on the ground over here, y'see, tirelessly restyling/remodelling their out-dated numskullery to fit the new scenes and new heroes (Joy Div, K. Joke, Josef K) as fast as the *NME* can discover them. Will Belfast ever rival Glasgow *et al.*? Not while the top-selling albums in the city are by Crass and the Exploited. For now, Pragmatic Control are purveying only pose when we demand (deserve!) poise. Me? I say phooey to this *cabaret vulgaire*.
Karl Marks

I truly feel that Andy will find a kindred spirit in Karl Marks. Moreover, I have no doubt that Marks is a genuine music fan who knows the difference between real talent and the usual old Belfast charlatans, as is evident from the enjoyable hatchet job quoted above. I will therefore engineer, via chicanery, a meeting between Andy and Marks. If at all possible, I will arrange for Marks to see the Decadents perform on July 9, and suggest to him that he express his ardour for the band in a lengthy *NME* review (possibly spread over two pages), parts of which I will offer to co-write.

On or around the day of Marks's interview with Andy for the cover story of the *NME*, I will mention in passing that Coates is not a full-time member of the Decadents and should accordingly not be visible in any of the photographs.

Once Andy and I are established in London, we will oversee a 50,000-copy re-pressing of the commercially successful 'Strange Song', this time excluding Coates's name from the typed Decadents line-up on the back cover.

We will then discuss plans for breaking the Decadents in America, mainland Europe and other continents.

8
Glue

NME, *July 4, 1981 (on sale in Belfast July 2)*

STRATEGIC ELEMENT/BERLIN

Belfast

Someone save my life tonight — please. The death disco
has come to this ill-starred/thrill-starved city, and just
look at all the punkers trying to pogo and gob like it was
'78 again. Am I perchance at a Cockney Rejects gig (rally?)
— no, siree, I'm watching just about the most hotly tipped
Belfast band in yonks, and I'm in hysterics. But I'm not
laughing. Strategic Element, formerly thuggish also-rans
Negative Justice, have mutated into some tepid, fetid, atro-
phied white boy dance hybrid of ACR and *Sandinista!*,
hectically purloining their contorted/distorted Fac-funk
cacophony and dishing it out with the preening pretension
of Strummer, Jones and Simonon. Local big-shot Ronnie
McSweeney is SE's singer, a veteran of at least 14 woeful
bands who were better than the one he's in now. Forced to
endure Ronnie's referee-whistle solo on the execrable 'Urban
Police Patrol', I almost pine for the return of support band

Berlin, whose dunderheaded sub-Velvets dirges (including, ahem, 'Candy's Wrists') suggest that Reed, Cale *et al.* have much to answer for in these parts. More than ever Belfast needs bands that can stimulate, not simulate.
Karl Marks

On Friday Owen Bramerton phoned to give me the name of the stationers in Newtownabbey where Isobel Clarke was working for the summer. Abernethies — I jotted it down — Abernethies of Newtownabbey. Owen enunciated the name and number perkily, like an announcer saying at the end of a TV programme, 'Felicity Kendal is currently appearing in *Wedded Bliss* at the Theatre Royal, Haymarket.' Owen, however, was being sarcastic. He did not recommend that I contact Abernethies or have any dealings whatsoever with Isobel Clarke.

'You do velly excerrent thing, Blamerton,' I thanked him in an Oriental falsetto.

'Bollocks,' he said, and hung up.

Isobel had become elusive of late. She hadn't come to school on the last few days of term, and Caroline Howard had had no joy phoning her house. Owen, who lived close to her, had called round on Monday evening and talked to her on the doorstep, but she hadn't invited him in. She had been vague about her plans and a bit weird with Owen. Even Brooke-Taylor, earlier the same day, had seemed a bit vague and a bit weird about Isobel.

'Good to see you back in the land of the living,' he first complimented me during our Monday-morning chin-wag stroke chat. He'd awarded my Tacitus essay sixty-three per cent with an exclamation mark.

'The land of the living?' I said. Sixty-three per cent. I could breathe again.

'Correct. Now try and stay in it.'

'What was the average? How did I do compared to Isobel Clarke?'

'The average was sixty and never you mind how Isobel Clarke did. You're not to ask me how Isobel did. We're all gonnae have a nice holiday and hopefully we'll all come back from it in one piece. Any other questions or can the Nosy Parker start minding his own business?'

I would have liked to ask him about the woman in his room on Friday. (Have she and the other school governors now been notified through the proper channels that I'm back in the land of the living, sir?) But I didn't want to end the term on a *faux pas*.

Only Owen, Mark Coates and myself had the energy to go in to school on Tuesday, the final day. Coates had kept away from the sixth-form centre for two weeks: I hoped he'd been plunking along to *White Light/White Heat* on his bass as instructed. Looking like a corpulent Kid Jensen in badminton whites, Coates was chauffeured on Tuesday by his brother Jeremy, a College old boy bulging out of a tweed suit that ponged of wet labrador. In an unoccupied coffee bar, Jeremy aimed blasé recollections of the school's Dramatics Society at me and Owen while Mark emptied his locker downstairs.

'Yerse . . . *The Lion, the Witch and the Wardrobe*, ah yerse, the incorrigible C. S. Lewis. Yours truly played the wardrobe, haugh haugh. And what was the one with the weavers? Two chaps from the third form, decked out as weavers – haugh! – they were the real McCoy, too, looked just like a pair of weavers, tape measures and whatnot. That was a treat. Till

Deborah whatsername's brother pissed his pants upstage and we all got the brunt of it – haugh! *pssssss* – mind where you're walking, boys! Splish splosh and what have you.'

His accent was like Billy Bingham doing an after-dinner impersonation of Terry-Thomas and forgetting to stop. 'Term before, made quite a decent stab at Badger in whojim-maflip. *Toad of Toad Hall.* Oh yerse. Toadie to the rescue, beep beep. His infernal contraption. Ratty! Another partner in crime.'

College old boys were always a pain in the neck. They turned up to every ceremony – Prize Day, Poppy Day, the unveiling of a newly painted wall – and made nuisances of themselves by saying 'hear, hear' in the speeches and bawling the polysyllabic Latin words of the school song with puffy eyes and moist cheeks. Jeremy couldn't have been much older than twenty-six but he already had the fogeyish old-boy drawl off to a T, and he patronized Owen and myself as if he were marvelling at two precocious infants.

'Got the Spanish, eh? Good for you. Well done. Bit like our friend Manuel on the box. "He's from Barcelona." Good for *you.*' And to Owen: 'More of a mathematician, are you? All that two-plus-two lark? Johnny algebra right up your street? I thought as much.'

Tediously, Jeremy quizzed us about whether such-and-such a teacher was still in residence (yes), whether *Collegian*, the school magazine, was still published annually (yes), whether we liked rugger (no) – what? you mean you chaps don't like rugger (no); and behaved for the most part like a whiskery colonel who hadn't set foot in his Alma Mater since the 1920s. It was the old boys' disease: nostalgic dementia. They all had it. I knew that I would be different – that I wouldn't degrade myself by becoming an old boy of the College. I was looking forward to leaving, and leaving meant Goodbye, not I'll Be Right Back. Leaving was a verb – a doing word – and it conjugated: *I am leaving, You won't see me for dust, He/she/it can parade about in a tweed suit on Poppy Day if it please them, but We are not like You or They.*

'The prodigal son returns,' Jeremy Coates noted jovially as his brother struggled into the coffee bar with a heavy Adidas bag, a couple of badminton racquets and an assortment of folders. 'Need a hand with your bumf, Mark, or can you make it to the jalopy? Fun talking to you chaps, must say. Cheerio.'

'Toodle-pip,' said Owen, earning a malevolent look from Mark. Brother followed brother towards the exit. Between them they had left the air around our table pickled with a compound odour of Blue Stratos and damp dog.

'What's the deal there?' I asked Owen. 'Is he in the RAF?'

'Jeremy? Car crash,' Owen said apathetically. 'He's got a metal plate in his head. Technically he shouldn't be driving.'

'Christ . . . yeah . . . I remember now.' Mark had been called out of French by the headmaster's secretary. 'Rat Trap' had been number one at the time. 'Wasn't it in Australia?'

'He hit a kangaroo. He was doing a hundred and forty in the outback, pissed out of his mind, some kind of government field trip. When he came round in hospital, the nurses told him he'd run over Skippy. They were only kidding him on, like.'

'He does seem like a nutcase, even for an old boy,' I said.

'Oh, he's a loony. But he knows he's a loony so he's smarter than he lets on. It's been said that he's the brains of the family.'

'Christ.'

'Brainier than Mark anyway. And not as lethal behind the wheel.'

'Can't Mark drive?' I asked.

'Can he fuck. He's failed his test fifteen times. One time the guy failed him before he started the car. But Jeremy's a dead careful driver since the accident.' Owen tapped his forehead. 'Plus he can listen to Downtown in the car without turning the radio on.'

The coffee bar was oppressive in its silence – a property condemned to a desolate summer – so I suggested a wander down to Good Vibrations. It was bearable outside weather-wise and Owen's hay fever wasn't too bad. We figured a ten-minute stroll wouldn't kill him.

'See you in September, you bastards,' Owen celebrated with a clenched fist when we were out of the gates. 'Or not as the case may be.'

'We've no choice,' I reminded him. 'We haven't anywhere else to go.'

I looked back at the top-floor windows of the glowering mansion, where the boarders in the dormitories would be tidying their bunk-beds for the last time. Then off to Alder-grove in the morning to begin their journeys to Africa and the Middle East. Flying home to mums and dads who paid whopping fees to get rid of them for nine months of the year. What must those family holidays be like. Sheer ecstasy, uh-huh.

Owen gossiped about Mark, Piers and Isobel as we walked down University Road. It was mostly superficial tittle-tattle about this and that, him and her, what she'd said to them – but any Isobel gossip interested me. I wanted to hear more.

'She's a funny girl, Isobel,' I ventured.

'She is indeed,' Owen said drily. 'She'd give Billy Connolly a run for his money any day.'

'No, but . . . she's quite singular.'

'You mean as opposed to quite plural?' he said. 'Aye. She's one in a million.'

'No, but I mean . . . something fascinates me about her.'

Fascinates is far too strong, I scolded myself. *You should have said 'captures the imagination'.*

Owen's reply was unexpected. 'Have you ever heard the expression, "Don't be a fucking fool to yourself"?'

'No, why? What about it?'

'Don't go near her. Understand? You'd only be a fucking fool to yourself.'

I was taken aback. 'Why? Is she . . . ?'

Don't use 'sleeping with' or 'screwing'. 'Is she in an established relationship? Is that what you're saying?'

Owen's sceptical look told me that he was unwilling to go into detail, but that he would endeavour to make certain things clear.

'Take a word of advice,' he said. 'Isobel's not the cute wee petal you think she is.'

'Well, I'm sure there've been boyfriends,' I shrugged. 'That stands to reason.'

'I'm not talking about that,' Owen said testily.

'What, then?' I was bewildered. '*Girlfriends?*'

'*No,*' he snapped. 'Think.'

'What do you mean "think"? Think of what?'

'God, you really are naïve, aren't you?' Owen said. 'All this "I'm so deep and existentialist" shit that you talk – and there's kids in Sunday school more sussed than you. And not just about the Bible either. Everything under the sun.'

Owen wouldn't elaborate. He was hinting to me – I

could recognize the hint, even if I couldn't take it – about a dark secret in Isobel's world; something that, in the documentary film of her life, would be accompanied by spooky music like *Picnic at Hanging Rock*. But what secret?

'Anyway, I know what I'm doing,' I said.

Owen stopped outside a barber's in Bradbury Place to blow his nose. 'You? You haven't a fucking clue. I sat next to you in class for two years, in case you've forgotten.'

'No,' I said thoughtfully, 'I haven't forgotten.'

'And while you were sitting playing Prog Hangman with yourself, some of us were learning one or two things about the ways of the world.'

'So it *is* about boyfriends?' I said eagerly.

Owen rolled his eyes. 'Ohh . . . See when we're in Good Vibes, can you do me a favour? Pretend you don't know me.'

I bought *Forever Changes* by Love for £3.99 that afternoon. I fell in love with its eleven gorgeous songs immediately and played them non-stop for days. They more than compensated, I felt, for side two of *Da Capo* being such an abortion. I intended not to bother with side two when I taped *Da Capo* for Isobel. I would leave that part of the cassette blank, to denote words and feelings unspoken.

Letter to NME, *written July 3*

Congratulations on your new Belfast correspondent Karl Marks. His reviews of Pragmatic Control and Strategic Element articulated/formulated opinions that many people in this city have been thinking for years. If I have one reservation, he was too charitable to the abysmal Berlin

who, in addition to being abysmal, are typical of the head-in-the-sand attitude that prevails among Belfast bands – an attitude that's all the more sickening when it leads to true originals such as the Decadents being ignored. Would that flowers could grow in concrete! Keep up the good work.
Genuine Music Fan, south Belfast

Friday the third of July. Denise's party was less than a week away. Pretexts, pretexts, my kingdom for a pretext.

I could say to Isobel that I'd cracked the Goodies dream, which would give me a pretext to take her aside after the Decs had played, and present her with her *Da Capo/Forever Changes* C-90 (inscription inside). But first I needed to check that she would be at the party. Butterflies, butterflies.

How did people know when it was make-their-move time? In what way did they phrase it? How did Jeremy do it? 'By Jove, I see the clock has struck nine-thirty. I wonder if you would care to have some of my Tuborg. Might I call you darling?' I couldn't talk to Andy about girls. I couldn't talk to girls about boys. Who could I talk to about boy–girl stuff?

Isobel wasn't working in Abernethies when I rang. They said she didn't start her job till Monday. *Did I want to leave a wee message for her, honey?* No I did not.

I called the Clarkes' house. Her brother Julian grunted that she was out: no idea where, no idea how long. *Who did I say my name was again, mate?* But I hadn't said a name, mate. 'I'll catch her later or at another time in that case,' I blabbered quickly. 'Thanks mate.'

There was no one to see me blushing in the hall – my family were playing tennis somewhere up the Malone Road

– but I hid my face all the same. The butterflies were kicking like eight-month-old babies in my stomach.

The next number I dialled was the home of Mark Coates. We were now entering the final stages of the plan and only a few more lies remained to be told. Everything was fixed for zero-hour on Wednesday, when I would make my breathless phone-call to Andy to report a catastrophe in Donegal – (but Lou, *listen* to me Lou, the show must go on. No, it's *not* being callous, Lou. No, it's not being sacrilegious in the slightest . . . Listen to me Lou, it's what he would have wanted).

Although the Coateses had been ex-directory since the '70s, their number was one of the easiest in Belfast to remember: Satan's ambulance. Six-six-six nine-nine-nine. *So you've been known to fantasize about Isobel, have you,* I thought as I dialled the three nines. My finger spun the third with venomous force.

'Please hold the line, young man,' said an elderly house-keeper or cook. 'I'll just transfer you to his room.'

There was a long silence that ended in a loud click.

'Mark Coates speaking. To whom am I talking?'

'I don't hear any music,' I said. 'Why is there no music?'

'Hello?' said the old woman.

'It's all right, Granny,' Mark cut in. 'I've got it. You can put it down now.'

'Can I put it down?' she said.

'Aye, put it down, Granny.' There was another click. 'Mark Coates speaking. To whom am I talking?'

'I don't hear any music in that room you're in. I hope you're not slacking on your practising.'

'Oh!' he said. 'Right . . . you. No, everything's fine. I've got the hang of it no bother.'

'And you've been playing along to *White Light/White Heat* whenever you can?'

'Aye, but wait till I tell you — I've learned "Walking on the Moon" and "Turning Japanese" too. Are you still there? So I don't know if Andy fancies doing either of them on Thursday. Like, I realize he's into the Velvet Underground and all that, but I think it would be good to have variety. Doing "Turning Japanese" would be genius.' Mark's voice dropped to a whisper. 'You know what it's about?'

'Yes, I know what it's about,' I sighed, 'and the Decadents won't be playing it. Like I told you. Nine songs. All written by Andy, all dead-easy bass lines to learn. A chimpanzee could play them.' (And will be, I thought darkly.)

'Well, as long as they're not like that "Sister Ray",' he said in a huff. '"Sister Rubbish" more like. I reckon they're just jamming away for badness.' His voice fell to a whisper again. 'So is he singing about getting a blow-job?'

'Now you're all right for rehearsing on Wednesday afternoon?'

'Aye, dead on.'

'Just one thing I forgot to ask you. The lead that goes into your bass — is it curly or straight?'

It was curly. I asked him to pop into town and buy a straight one, and get some black plectrums while he was there. He agreed on condition the Decadents would reimburse him.

'I'll take you over to Andy's house on Wednesday, so be ready about half-four. Yes, you can still have a taxi — we'll go in it together. There's just one other thing I don't know if I've mentioned. Andy's worried he might have fucked up his A-levels. He's usually fine, but some days he's a bit peculiar. Don't be upset by it. I mean if he doesn't say much to you, or if he starts talking about death or whatever. It's just his A-levels.'

'Aye,' said Mark doubtfully. 'Dead on.'

After I had spoken to Coates, I pulled the phone into the lounge, drank a two-spooner mug of black coffee and steeled myself for an unpleasant squabble with Vance Armstrong. Twice I got halfway through his number and stopped, battling against caffeine and nerves. The Berlin part of the plan was proving to be the trickiest part of all.

Following a heart-to-heart in the attic of Cranmore Park the previous Tuesday, and as a result of much to-ing and fro-ing, Andy and Denise had consented to a twenty-minute performance from Berlin at the party, provided that Andy could choose which songs they would play. I had not relayed this proviso to Vance, partly because I knew what his response would be and partly because Andy kept changing the set-list as he thought of more and more ludicrous hits from the Top 20s of yesteryear. I profoundly hoped that when Berlin heard on Wednesday about the Decadents' bereavement, they would want to give the party a miss. But if they didn't, I'd have to tell Vance that Berlin would be starting their set with Bonnie Tyler's 'It's a Heartache', then going into 'Night Boat to Cairo', 'Davy's on the Road Again', 'Pearl's a Singer', 'Y Viva España' and 'What You're Proposing'. The performance was to conclude with a medley of 'When You're in Love with a Beautiful Woman', 'Army Dreamers' and 'Boogie Oogie Oogie'.

'And Vance has got to be word-perfect on all of them,' Andy had commanded. 'None of that slurring he does. I want to hear every word and I want to be moved by them.'

'You're wicked, Andrew,' Denise had reproved him in a fit of giggles. 'Vance will be so cross.'

I tried to calculate how much of Berlin's set-list I could safely read out to Vance over the phone before he threatened to come round and break my legs. Probably not very much. Probably not even as far as 'Night Boat to Cairo'.

But there was sensational news when I got through and spoke to Vance's flatmate Alison or Alice. Denise's party would have to go ahead without Berlin, because all their gigs had been cancelled by Vance until further notice. I flopped back on the settee, relieved, and listened with mounting excitement as Alison or Alice told me the story.

Vance was on the warpath. He had read Karl Marks's review in the *NME* of Berlin at the Harp, and he had hit the roof. And who wouldn't have hit the roof? (This was Alison or Alice talking.) A joke was a joke but that review had gone too far. Vance didn't mind criticism when it was constructive, but that review had been just plain and simple abuse. And Vance drew the line at abuse, which was why he and Berlin's drummer Luke were going to find Karl Marks and batter his head in.

They would not be alone. In Lavery's bar on Thursday, Vance and Luke had run into Niall and Fergus from Pragmatic Control – who also didn't mind constructive criticism, but not when it was abuse. The vigilantes were now four strong. And within an hour they were seven, for in the back bar of the Crown who should Vance, Luke, Niall and Fergus meet but Ronnie, Wee Ronnie and Macker from Strategic Element.

By getting on the wrong side of Strategic Element (this was still Alison or Alice talking), Karl Marks had made a serious misjudgement. Them boys were hard as nails. Nobody with any intelligence wrote snide remarks about Ronnie's referee-whistle solos, or about the fact that he'd been in fourteen different bands. It might interest Karl Marks to learn that Ronnie had done time in the Maze for GBH.

I didn't know that. Oh yes, said Alison or Alice – and Ronnie sorely resented the critique of his referee-whistle solo on 'Urban Police Patrol'. Which, for Karl Marks's information, was in fact called 'Urban Beat Patrol' so he was going to get another battering for being deaf as well as disrespectful.

After Ronnie had been at him, Vance and Luke would pile in and teach Karl Marks not to call Berlin's songs dirges just because some of them happened to be slow. What was left of Karl Marks after Vance and Luke had finished with him would be kicked fucking senseless by Niall from the Prags, and did I want to know why? Because Niall had a kid sister with spina bifida, that was why, and Karl Marks had written that the Prags were spastics.

My excitement had passed and I felt suddenly scared for Karl Marks. His reviews had been just what Belfast needed, and now Belfast was going to retaliate. But against whom? Whose identity did that pithy pseudonym hide? Some teen-ager out in Bangor who'd merely put into print what we'd all been saying in private? For that they would lynch him?

I thought of pock-marked Ronnie McSweeney onstage with Negative Justice a year earlier, in an abject and short-lived venue round the corner from the Grand Opera House. 'This one's for all you cunts not dancing. It's called "Fuckin' Start Dancing, You Cunts".' McSweeney had been a seeth-ing torpedo of a man, incensed about everything. He was the type who would lynch a duck for quacking.

'Who is Karl Marks?' I asked Alison or Alice, who was ministering to some sort of animal at the other end of the phone. 'What's his real name?'

'We don't know,' she said dull-wittedly. 'Vance never asked him.'

'Oh, you've met him?'

'Vance has. *No*, Billy! Play with your snake. Go and get the snake. Ronnie and Fergus and them ones never met him or heard of him.'

'Did Vance meet him at the Harp?'

'Oh aye, and he phoned us the other week too, and we don't know how he got our number. But Vance didn't have his specs on at the Harp. He just said a wee lad came up to him in the bogs and went, "I'm Karl Marks and can I just say your band were unbelievable."'

Yes. Yes, I could imagine somebody saying that about Berlin. Andy and I had often said it ourselves. I wondered if the snake was a real one or a rubber one. Could be a real one, knowing Vance.

'So Vance just saw – what? A blurred outline?'

'Well, he won't wear his specs 'cause they're National Health and they look like Buddy Holly. He was having a slash in the bogs and the wee lad just came up behind him. They didn't have a big discussion or anything.'

'What did he say to Vance on the phone? Why did he ring?'

'He said he was Karl Marks and he was going to write about us in the *NME*. He said he knew Luke and he'd make sure everybody in England heard about us. But Luke's been racking his brains and he can't think who it is.' Alison's or Alice's tone hardened. 'Vance thought it might be one of youse.'

'The Decadents? I promise you it isn't. But what'll happen now?'

'Get the snake, Billy . . . Oh, they'll find him. They're

thinking of getting the train out to Bangor. And he deserves everything that's coming to him, the evil wee fucker.'

'Yes, but Alice . . . Alison . . . Al –'

'Alex.'

'But Alex. Couldn't they just shove him around a bit and give him a friendly warning?' I said helplessly.

'Friendly?' she retorted. 'What's friendly about him slagging the fuck out of the three best bands in Belfast? What's friendly about destroying our livelihoods? You tell me that. How are we going to face people in London? We were getting set to do a gig over there with the Prags; Vance was all dead excited about it. We were told by the *NME* our band was unbelievable. Now look at us. *Get the fucking snake, I said.* Friendly? You've a strange definition of friendly.'

'It's just a little review, though,' I pointed out. 'Most people wouldn't have read it.'

'Was it friendly to take the piss out of "Candy's Wrists"? You tell me that. That song's a true story, so it is. It's no laughing matter. And how did he even know what it was called, when Vance never said the name of it at the Harp?'

'Candy's Wrists' was low on laughs, certainly. A ballad based on the tempo of the Velvets' 'Femme Fatale', and also on its chords and melody, it was sung by Alison or Alice or Alex, with backing vocals from Vance on the choruses:

Candy's seventeen
She feels just like a trampoline
She prays to Jesus on the phone
All alone

Candy starts to cry
Now she just wants to die
And she knows she's going to just take the knife
End her life

(CHORUS)
Oh Candy, little girl (tell me it ain't so)
Such a cruel, cruel world (the truth I have to know)
Oh Candy, I am here (why d'you have to go)
Your wrists they had to bleed
Although there was no need . . .

The night time's getting late
But Candy don't hesitate
And now the blade just cuts teenage skin
It's a sin

The angels all will cry
Candy, little angel in the sky
We'll never know why you live no more
Or what for

(repeat CHORUS twice)

Berlin had debuted 'Candy's Wrists' at the Pound in the summer of 1980. Andy, whom I hadn't known well at the time, had been standing beside me in an audience of about thirty. I'd felt a nudge in my ribs after the first chorus.

'I know it's an awful song and it would be unfair to single out individual lines, but did she just sing "the night time's getting late"?'

'I think so.'

'Thank you.' Then he had shouted 'dicks' at the stage.

So . . . no more airings of 'Candy's Wrists' or forthcoming Berlin gigs, by order of Vance. Andy would be most amused. I decided to tell him on Thursday when the *NME* came out. What with my letter namechecking the Decs, and the three-page Sterling Morrison interview in April, the *NME* was really improving.

I'll make sure everybody in England hears about you. Who would say something like that to Vance?

And what had Vance said to me? 'A wee lad out in Bangor writes for them . . . I didn't believe it either.' Something troubled me about that. Or was it something else? My conversation with Alison/Alice/Alex?

Or maybe it was just the idea of a local writer making an improbable reputation for himself in little over a fortnight, despite having no name, no face and no known address. Who was Karl Marks? Where was Karl Marks?

July was marching month for the Orangemen. If I walked down to the Lisburn Road on a windless evening, I could hear pipe-and-drum bands practising in the distance for the time-honoured march of the Orange Lodges on July 12. The twelfth was the day when Protestants in Northern Ireland commemorated their greatest ever Cup win, William of Orange's giant-killing victory over James II's strongly fancied Catholic army at the Battle of the Boyne. That battle, for the Jules Rimet Trophy and Control of Ireland and Scotland, had been fought in 1690. Quite a long time ago, but memories in the North were not the kind that faded. Many people remembered the battle well, including people who hadn't been born until 1957. Hence the popular joke about the aeroplane pilot saying to his passengers, 'We will shortly be landing in Belfast. If you'd all like to put your watches back two hundred and ninety-one years.'

I loathed Irish jokes normally. I loathed English comedians telling Irish jokes. I loathed Irish comedians telling Irish jokes. No matter how clever an Irish joke was, I loathed the joke and the person who told it. And if it was funny, that was worse. I loathed funny Irish jokes, especially clever ones. But '. . . put your watches back two hundred and ninety-one years' was a *brilliant* joke, the funniest and cleverest yet. I just wished all those loathsome comedians would stop telling it.

The July 12 marches were broadcast live every year on BBC1 Northern Ireland, giving atheists such as myself the option of mocking the bowler-hatted berks from the comfort of our living-rooms should we be unable to sleep through all the noise on the Lisburn Road. But in 1980, just before I got to know him, Andy had elected to watch the parade from a bus-stop at the bottom of Cranmore Park. He was on the lookout for a drummer and, as he later said, 'some of those Orange Lodge kids are as good as Keith Moon'. Espying a school-age virtuoso marching along and whacking away at a snare, Andy fell into step with him and asked if he would be interested in joining an androgynous post-punk group influenced by the Velvet Underground and the Psychedelic Furs. 'We're called the De—.' That was as far as he got.

'You know when people say "your feet won't touch"? Well, mine really didn't. I was lifted up by two guys with bowler hats and dumped at the side of the road. They thought I was some kind of horrendous Republican pervert. Old women were screaming at me, it was absolutely remarkable.'

We were drinking lukewarm cider in Botanic Gardens. 'You're mad,' I said, gawping at him. 'You don't do things like that on the twelfth!'

'It was an amazing sight, though, the parade. I'm glad I went. They really care so passionately about it, don't they? You could almost see the blood in their eyes.'

'Yeah – *your* blood. What an incredibly stupid thing to do.'

'Ah!' He winked. 'Ulster boy defends his people. I get the picture. Loyalty to the Loyalists.'

'You're so far wide of the mark,' I said hotly. 'If you don't understand something, don't fucking talk about it.' I'd stormed out of the park and left him there.

Andy had a detached way of looking at Northern Ireland, which came from being an uprooted Hounslow boy and a cynic. He didn't feel he belonged in Belfast – but now that he was here, he wasn't going to move back. I was the opposite. I was desperate for departure, never to return to the city where I belonged. Why stay in a place because you belong there? What was so good about belonging? In September 1982 I would leave for England, to live among the English and among the music. To see where the music had been made and to watch it being made still. As far as I was concerned, if other people wanted to stay in Belfast and die, that was their funeral. *Just don't come running to me when your legs are blown off.* Another popular Irish joke.

It annoyed me that Andy couldn't see this. 'I feel a lot safer here than I did in Middlesex,' he once said. 'It was no fun being chased by gangs of ten-year-olds on my way to piano lessons. Or being beaten up at school for not supporting Arsenal. Or Tottenham Athletic, or whatever fucking team it was. Belfast's much more civilized.'

Civilized! 'Andy, it's got two cinemas. It's a capital city, for Christ's sake, and it's got two cinemas.'

'Well, we only had one. And that closed down. And we lived in a shoebox. Poor but happy, we were. Happy and suicidal.'

'Yeah, but didn't you ever go to London?'

'Oh, sure . . .' he allowed. 'Horrible fucking place. Yes, I went to London. What a wonderful experience that was.'

'And how many cinemas does London have? About a million.'

'Yes,' he said, 'and I hear if you don't like the film, the actors come down off the screen and give you your money back. And then sometimes they take you out to dinner in one of London's two million restaurants. I believe that actually happens.'

Cynical, always cynical. He was probably just prejudiced against London because Arsenal played there. At Highbury, they played. Highbury in London. Highbury. High-bury. Sublime, enigmatic-sounding word.

On the black-and-white TV in my bedroom, I saw every English film I could. Surrounded by English records and English literature, I read the UCCA handbook from Aston University to York, and the *NME* and *Sounds* gig guides from Aldershot to Yeovil, learning about towns and cities, venues and bands, campuses and halls of residence. 'This is England,' they said, collectively. 'Come and see.' Only one more year of school and I could go and see. In the new year, I would fill out my UCCA form and list my five choices of university. The thought of writing ENGLAND, PLEASE in foot-high red marker had crossed my mind.

And in my mind, the Anglophile was virtually in England already. My body was the only part that still lived in Belfast, and my body had never had much relevance to the rest of me. Somewhere in Bangor – or wherever Karl Marks called home – there was an Anglophile mind like my own, dreaming and waiting. I knew when my wait would end; I hoped Karl Marks did too. Perhaps, when I took the ferry ride from Larne in 445 days' time, I would lug my suitcase and bags of records out on deck, and there I would spot a pale, frail youth with a notebook, leaning over the rails and staring down at the disappearing water. We might just exchange a glance, he and I, as our vessel travelled full steam ahead, onward, away.

'I'm Genuine Music Fan,' I would say shyly.

'I'm Karl,' he would reply. 'You don't know how encouraging your letters were. They really kept me going through the hard times.'

'The hard times . . .' I would nod. 'I dunno, Karl. Sometimes they all seem like hard times.'

'They do, Genuine, they do. Put it there.'

We might even find that we were going to the same university.

QUIZMASTER: *What is your name?*
CONTESTANT: [indistinct]
Q: *Your occupation?*
C: [muffled]
Q: *And your specialist subject?*
C: *Idealizations and Misconceptions of English Student Life.*
Q: *You have two minutes on Idealizations and Misconceptions of English Student Life, starting . . . now. From which three films, shown recently on BBC2, has the narrator gleaned most of his facts about life in England?*

163

C: O Lucky Man!, Here We Go Round the Mulberry Bush and The Rebel.

Q: *Correct. How much separation exists in his mind between the England portrayed in those films and the England of the present day?*

C: *No separation.*

Q: *Correct. What is the narrator's view of the term 'Swinging London'?*

C: *That it continues to be a factual description.*

Q: *Correct. Which two things, according to the narrator, always occur at student parties in England?*

C: *People take LSD and have sex with a girl who is walking around twirling a white umbrella.*

Q: *Correct. Which three-word phrase is used by the narrator to describe what he believes to be the effects of an LSD trip?*

C: *'Surreal, magical kaleidoscope.'*

Q: *Correct. In many of his idealized party scenes, the narrator encounters a pop musician who is 'trying to get a band together'. Who is he?*

C: *Brian Jones?*

Q: *No, Syd Barrett. In which English county do the majority of these idealized parties take place, and why?*

C: *Hampshire, because he supported Hampshire cricket team as a boy.*

Q: *Correct. Complete the line in the narrator's* Tribute to Hampshire: *'A domain where a man might reasonably . . .'*

C: *'Attain transcendence.'*

Q: *Correct. What is the key difference cited by the narrator between a party in England and a party in Belfast?*

C: *Oh . . . glue . . . er, the . . . People sniff glue at parties in Belfast.*

Q: *I'll accept that, yes. What is the cryptic statement often made by a girl with black lipstick at student parties in England, and how does the narrator reply?*

C: *'The secret of everything is nothing.' 'Nothing and yet everything.'*

Q: *Correct. The girl with the white umbrella, Jemima, bears a facial resemblance to which contemporary school-friend of the narrator?*

C: *Pass.*

Q: *How does the narrator take his leave of these student parties?*

C: *He has a friend from London who comes to pick him up in an E-type Jaguar.*

Q: *Correct. What are the narrator's parting words to Jemima?*

C: *'This is Archie, he's going to be my publisher. Must dash. Nice doing LSD with you.'*

Q: *Correct. What does Jemima then do?*

C: *She jumps in the car and laughs gaily all the way to Devon.*

Q: *Correct. Which two adjectives describe Jemima's earrings?*

C: *Pass.*

A-WHEEP-WHEEP-WHEEP

Q: *And in that round, [name drowned out by applause], you scored twelve correct answers. You passed on two. The facial resemblance of Jemima is to the narrator's school-friend Isobel Clarke. And the adjectives that describe her earrings are 'pearly' and 'sparkly'. Can we have the next contestant, please.*

I awake, fully clothed, on the carpet. The other occupants of the room – half a dozen eighteen-year-olds in leather jackets and combat trousers – are sniffing from little white plastic bags. *Closer* by Joy Division is playing on the turntable, for the fifth time tonight. The effects of the Tuborg have not cleared, making my head feel torpid and violated.

Gagging from the stench of glue and unwashed combat trousers, I get up and walk to the toilet. There is a queue of people I don't know. Where is Andy? Why did I come here? How will I get home?

'Look at him, trying to see into the toilet at all the wee girls,' Caroline Howard tut-tuts. 'You vile wankstain.'

There is a bang at the door. Someone says the police are here, but it's only a bunch of hooligans from the pub down the road who want to come in and wreck the house. In the front room, side one of *Closer* gets under way for the sixth time.

I'm bored with these Belfast parties. I want to go to England and see what real life is like.

In the attic, Dermot Moffatt and Robert Tait were standing up and lying down respectively. Sci-fi fanatic Dermot, a College peer of Andy's who'd been a Decadent since March, was biting on a finger and looking despondently at a card-board box on the floor crammed with pedals, leads, adaptors and screwdrivers. As Coates and I entered the attic, Dermot turned away and said, 'He's gone to get smokes.'

Robert, a sixth-former at Belfast Royal Academic Insti-tute, woke up, looked at us and yawned. The drummer had a penchant for spontaneous naps and could lie flat on any surface, his shaggy whitish-blond hair becalmed behind him, and be out like a light in a second.

'How's it hanging?' he asked.

'This is Mark,' I explained.

'Aye,' he said.

I helped Coates bring in his amplifier, which we put next to Andy's cabinet beneath the poster of the Beatles from *The White Album*. Coates was feeling awkward, I could tell, and I hoped he wouldn't attempt one of his *double entendre* ice-breakers. Dermot could be a sensitive soul. In the kitchen, cups of tea were being made by Sheila, who was still piqued about paying the minicab driver. The ambience of the house was frosty and Andy — frostiness personified — wasn't even in.

My breathless phone-call re: the catastrophe in Donegal

had been something of a shambles. I now suspected that Andy suspected my whole bass player saga had been highly suspect. He'd gone very quiet, which wasn't like him, and had agreed to my suggestion that Mark Coates of the Lower Sixth should step into the breach ('a real arsehole, but he lives just up the road and he's always talking about how much he loves the Velvets') without swearing at me. To sugar the pill, I'd brought forward by twenty-four hours my disclosure of the conversation with Alison/Alice/Alex and Berlin's retirement from the Belfast stage – but Andy had said only, 'That's a shame for music lovers' with no emotion in his voice. I was beginning to fear that the game might be up.

'Should be a good party tomorrow,' I remarked to Dermot and Robert. 'Wonder what everyone'll make of "New Song".'

When neither of them answered, Coates said cheerfully, 'What's that, then?'

'A song,' Dermot replied dourly. 'It's new.'

'It's also fantastic,' I leapt in. 'I envy you, Mark, being able to play bass on a song like that. Wait till you hear it, you'll be completely bowled over. It speeds up and up and up. Faster and faster and faster.'

'That's 'cause we've got a shit drummer,' said Dermot, taking a screwdriver out of the cardboard box. I looked to see if Robert was smiling, but he was asleep.

'Er ... so, Dermot,' Coates asked before I could stop him, 'will you be wearing women's make-up tomorrow night, like?'

Dermot seemed to notice Coates for the first time. He looked him up and down and said, 'Why? Do you need a lend of some false eyelashes? Talk to the singer.' He turned his back on us again. 'I'm a musician ... somebody has to be.'

'A-levels,' I mouthed at Coates, making a thumbs-down sign. Below us, a door slammed and feet came bounding up the stairs.

I looked nervously around the room, seeing only paralysis. Dermot clutching his screwdriver, stone-faced. Robert stretched out on two chairs, exposed navel squinting like Popeye. Coates in a green corduroy jacket, grinning daftly. In the cab, I had advised him what to say to Andy: four words, then shut up.

The door burst open. Lou had arrived.

'Andy, I'm sure you remember Mark Coates . . .' I began.

Andy stared at Coates. 'We've met.' He scowled, tearing off his black pullover and slapping twenty Rothmans on his amp. He flung another twenty over to Dermot, who caught them by his ear.

'Take my eye out, why don't you?' the organist bristled.

'Rob,' Andy snarled. 'Up.'

'It's a terrible business,' said Mark. I exhaled slowly. *That should cover it*, I thought.

'Rob, are you just going to lie there and sleep,' Andy shouted, 'or will you actually be playing the drums at some point? Because if not, you can fuck off home.'

'A-levels,' I mouthed again to Mark, who was staring at me in some consternation. I ran an illustrative finger across my throat.

'It's a terrible business,' Mark reiterated.

Robert got to his feet, lifted back his right leg, sent one of the two chairs skidding over the floorboards towards Andy, and sat down on his drum-stool. Dermot was slumped over the organ, an unlit Rothmans between his lips, beating

out a deliberate tattoo with his palms on the instrument's
side panels.

'I'm told you can play bass guitar,' said Andy, tilting his
head to look down his nostrils at Mark. 'That true?'

'Oh aye,' Mark chirped. 'And I'm told your songs are
fantastic. I can't wait to hear them all.'

Still tilting his head, Andy moved it forty-five degrees
to the left so that his nostrils were pointing at me.

'You were told that by him, were you?' he said.

'Oh aye.'

The nostrils twitched slightly and moved round again to
face Mark.

'Might be as well to get a second opinion,' Andy said
in a monotone, reaching for his £14 guitar.

Mark Samuel Agnew Coates may have been an arsehole,
but he was an industrious arsehole. He studied hard at
school, turning in homework that was both accurate and
neat, and his dream of being accepted by Cambridge University in 1982 was by no means a ridiculous delusion. Though
the gulf between our personalities would never permit me
to like him, I had once or twice come close to tolerating him
and forgiving his gross lecherousness and hateful avarice.

What was that flower that you picked bits off and said,
'She loves me . . . she loves me not . . . she loves me . . .
she loves me not . . .'? Since our first meeting at a Churchill
house pep talk in 1975, my viewpoint on Mark had been
rather like that flower. 'I despise him . . . I despise him not
. . . I can't stand him . . . I can stand him up to a point . . .
I fucking detest him . . .'

Mark no doubt made use of similar flowers himself in

his fantasies about Isobel ('she's wearing a bra . . . she's not wearing a bra'), and not the least vital of my manoeuvres at the party would be to confide in Isobel a tenable fantasy that outclassed Mark's yet stopped short of being nauseating to her. I had been making notes on a sheet of A4 all morning: a French kiss here, a bikini there. But where was Isobel's nausea cut-off point?

'Yeah, I'm going,' she'd said on the phone from Abernethies. 'You going?'

'I'm going, yeah.'

'Then we're both going,' she deduced level-headedly.

'I may have something for you,' I added. But she'd gone.

I.C. FANTASY CHECK-LIST 8/7/81

1. FRENCH KISS

2. BIKINIS, GENERAL BEACHWEAR

3. PARTIAL NUDITY/BINOCULARS

4. SCHOOL LATIN CLASS, BENDING OVER DESK WITH ME THERE

5. BACK OF VAN/BLANKETS/CANOODLING cf. HELEN MIRREN IN *O LUCKY MAN!*

6. SHE DOES IT TO ME AND I DO IT TO HER

7. IN THE LOO AT PARTY

8. FLASHING IN S.F.C.

9. HER AND C.H. GETTING READY TO GO OUT ???

Meanwhile, in Andy's attic, it was becoming apparent that the Decadents, far from collapsing in a feckless musical heap, were sounding surprisingly okay. Andy, Dermot and Robert were still in appalling moods, but the arsehole on bass was a veritable eye-opener. He wasn't the most nimble of musicians, nor the most supple of movers, but no one was asking him to be either. In an Andy Finn composition, the bassist only had three notes to play anyway, and he could often get away with two. Rooted woodenly to his spot beside Andy, Mark fell back on the instincts that had served him well for six years of grammar school. Hear something once and do it badly. Hear it again and do it better. Do it a third time and get it right. He learned the Decadents' nine-song set in three and a half hours.

'These songs are class,' he said to Andy several times, until at last the iceman thawed and made a comment about it being a pleasant change to meet a bassist who kept his tongue in his mouth while he was playing. I stifled a laugh. Blue Stratos Boy had made the grade.

'We thought you were going to be a wank-artist,' Robert said, scratching his belly, after an unblemished run-through of 'E Minor Song'.

'It's been a problem with us in the past,' Andy told Mark. 'We get these wank-artists in and they always fuck us up. You know, Genesis fans . . .'

'Paul Leckie,' Robert nodded. 'Or do you remember that kid who played with us in Dunmurry? God, the shit he listened to. Bad Manners, Secret Affair . . .'

'We even had a corpse in the band for a while,' Andy said equably. 'Can't quite recall what that was all about.'

'I gave that kid a hiding in Dunmurry,' Robert sniggered. '"Don't you go hitting my cymbals with your guitar, thinking it looks cool. *Boff!*" "What? What have I done?" Here's Andy to him: "Consider yourself out of the band." It was a sketch. There was me, jumping over the drums at him like the guy in Golden Earring.'

'Ah-ha,' Andy reflected. 'Youthful high spirits.'

'"Radar Love", did they do?' said Dermot with a droopy

smile. 'I saw that on *Top of the Pops*. Dook-dook-dook-dook, dook-dook-dook-*kooh*.' He and Robert began to sing misremembered lines about driving all day with Jerry Lee on the radio.

I would have corrected them – indeed, I would have named the 1973 Golden Earring line-up for them – but something in my brain had just made a connection with something else. I shut my eyes and tried to think back. *The night time's getting late . . . but Candy don't hesitate.*

Berlin at the Pound. Luke climbing out from behind his drum-kit. No . . . I couldn't quite remember.

'No offence,' Andy addressed Coates. 'But consider yourself in the band for tomorrow night, wank-artist.'

And with a cymbal crash from Robert, Mark was inducted into the Decs. Just after nine o'clock, when it was clear that everyone knew the songs, Andy put down his guitar and declared the rehearsal over. He had not spoken to me, or looked at me, since a quarter past five.

'Sheila will run you home,' he told the others blithely. 'Back here at eight tomorrow. We'll be down in the telly room.'

'Andy's mum,' I enlightened Mark, who had turned to the wall and was investigating the Beatles poster. 'He calls her Sheila.' My first words since ten to five, they rasped like sandpaper.

'And we know what she calls you,' Andy said suddenly, kneeling over his fuzz pedal and looking at Dermot. There was an uncomfortable pause.

'Well,' I hesitated. 'Yes . . . we did get off on the wrong foot. These things can happen. Well played, by the way.'

But no one responded. It wasn't obvious any more who was talking to whom.

✳

Sheila ran me home. Neither of us had much to say during the five-minute journey. The news on Downtown had announced the death of another hunger-striker, and Sheila was concerned about Denise and her friend Roberta being out late at the pictures and not phoning.

'Fifteen-year-olds are more mature than you think,' I reassured her. 'They've probably just gone off with some boys.'

She dropped me off at the Northern Bank on the Malone Road rather than drive into Malone Avenue. That was okay, I needed the exercise. Rolling down the passenger window, I got out of the car, reached in through the window and handed her a Basildon Bond envelope marked THE ONLY SOLUTION.

'Could you give this to Andy? Tell him it explains everything.'

'Oh?' Sheila said, blinking at the envelope and putting it on the dashboard. 'Won't we be seeing you again?'

'No, you will, don't worry,' I laughed. 'Thanks for the lift. God, let's hope Denise is all right, though.'

The car sped off into town.

Two minutes later I was climbing the thirty-nine steps to my bedroom. I was thinking not about Denise, but about animosity and provocation. I was thinking about scuffles and insults, and a boy who had waited twelve months to take his revenge on Berlin. *Luke, what did you do to him?*

'Andy,' I had implored, waiting in the hall for Sheila to get off the phone. 'You can have the whole story in due course. He's not bad, is he – Mark – I mean it sounded great up there. But Andy, this is really important. Cast your mind back to when Berlin played the Pound last summer. When they did that song about Candy.'

173

'Cast my mind back,' Andy mimicked me. 'Cast my mind back to getting a phone-call about some dead bass player being washed up on the coast of . . . fucking . . . "Oh, but *Andy*, I think I may know a suitable *replacement*. Shall I go and *fetch* him?" What the fuck are you playing at, you sick little dildo?'

'Well, he is suitable, isn't he? Look, I know there's a certain amount of explaining to be done and I'll be happy to do it. But please, try and remember. There was another band playing that night, wasn't there? And some trouble broke out.'

'Really?' said Andy witheringly. 'Did someone die? Was he a bass player? Because these things can happen.'

'It was something to do with Luke. He came out from his drum-kit and hit somebody. What were the band called? It was something to do with the *other band*.'

'Ohh . . .' Andy looked around the hall irritably. 'Yeah . . . I can't remember. I remember there being a fight, but not who started it. Ask Luke.'

I was about to say that it might be a matter of life and death, but I stopped myself in time. I might have known old Sieve Memory would be hopeless. Christ on a moped, he would have forgotten the dead bassist controversy in a couple of weeks, if not sooner. He already seemed to forget that he abhorred Mark Coates. ("'Bye, Mark, thanks. Wow – taxi. I see we travel in style.')

In my room, I switched on the television and the stereo. Putting *Flesh + Blood* on my headphones, I watched the end of the news with the sound down. Someone had come in while I was out and taken back the *Radio Times* and *TV Times*, which I could expect to receive a note about, so I didn't know if there were any good films on. Wednesdays tended to be American thrillers. Sunday nights and Saturday afternoons were usually best for English films: *Passport to Pimlico, The Titfield Thunderbolt,* that sort of thing. *The Lavender Hill Mob, Loot, Georgy Girl.* The Comedy Realism school, I supposed you'd call it.

Side one of *Flesh + Blood* drifted by without me paying attention. I was starving now, but I was going to wait until midnight when the house was dark before eating. That's when I would go down — when there was no one else around. Andy would have read the letter by then. He would take it and hold it, and he would read all the things I'd told him ... In the hall, some expression in his eyes had taken me by surprise. Did he have a relative who had drowned? Or was he just being temperamental because he thought I'd foisted Coates on him? What a hypocrite: Andy had bantered with Coates, shaken hands with Coates, practically proposed marriage to Coates. And what about me, the one who had organized everything, treated like *persona non grata.* In our lighter moments (though there had been precious few of those), hadn't Andy specifically said that the Decs would only start to turn the corner if and when they found the right person to play bass? *Earth calling Lou. Testing, testing. Anyone there?* Now you've found the right person, jackass! Or to be more precise, *I* found him (admittedly presenting him to the Decs in a roundabout way).

But these and other issues would be clarified by my letter. With luck Andy would be all smiles tomorrow, our differences forgotten. And just wait till he read the bit about the Coateses being made of money! Book that recording studio now, my son! 'Strange Song' here we come ... Decs on 45!

Side one of *Roxy* was coming to an end. Grabbing a

Pentel, I took *One Flew Over the Cuckoo's Nest* from the book-case, skipped to pages 194–5 and pulled out the folded check-list.

10. I HENNA HER HAIR WHILE BOTH UNDRESSED

As I mulled over numbers eleven and twelve, I began to draw a drum-kit in the left-hand margin. It took me back to being a kid and drawing Mick Tucker of Sweet in my school books, which I must have done hundreds of times. Most of the time Mick Tucker would be bashing his drums like a madman, but some of the time he would just be holding his sticks in the air and looking pleased. Mick Tucker was pleased to be the drummer in Sweet all of the time. He knew it was a better job than being Archimedes, Handel Oratorio or Dr Livingstone-I-Presume. 'Yippeeee,' the speech bubble coming out of Mick Tucker's mouth used to say, from time to time.

When you were drawing a drum-kit, you always had to start with the big round drum at the front. Next came the two drums that balanced on the big round one and angled inwards, and you had to make sure to get those angles right. Then the schick-schick cymbals – opened just a fraction. Next, the drum on the floor at the side. More cymbals to the right and left. And finally you wrote the band's name in capitals on the big round drum.

BERLIN.

Luke, I thought. *What did you do to him?*

Berlin had just begun playing 'Baby Satellite', the first song in their set. 'Bow, bow, bow, baby satelli-ite . . .' it went, identical to 'Satellite of Love' by Lou Reed. Andy called it 'The Great Minds Think Alike Song'.

I was waiting to be served at the bar, sucking my cheeks in acrobatically and trying to pass for eighteen. I had managed to pass for about seventeen and a quarter when there was an anguished cry from the stage and the music ground to a halt. 'Where's that wee shite?' Luke roared, blundering out from behind his kit. Elbowing Vance to one side, he scoured the faces of the thirty people in the crowd.

'You! It was you!'

The boy was something to do with the other band. I had arrived late and missed them, but I had an idea Andy knew one of them to say hello to. They were called Jive something . . . or Bop something . . . or Jive Bop something.

'Son, you are *dead*,' Luke hollered, springing off the stage and throwing a punch. Too many heads were in the way for me to see the boy face-on, but he had red hair – dyed red, not ginger, and spiked on top – and a tee-shirt with writing on the back. Luke manhandled him into the toilets, where friends of Berlin stood guard at the door. I never saw the boy after that. 'Baby Satellite' had eventually restarted and I'd resumed my exertions at the bar.

Everything now hinged on whether Luke Corrigan had a good memory for names and faces, or – like Andy – a rusting sieve with a dent in it. By rights Luke shouldn't have had a memory at all, for he and his Braniel dole-pals were into glue. I'd seen them at a Berlin/Pragmatic Control party in Shandon Park, sitting on the floor of a blacked-out room with a white plastic bag each and *Lust for Life* (ironically) on the stereo. They had been scary to look at. Heads lolling, no part of them moving, not a great advertisement for the DHSS.

But if Luke's memory hadn't totally been nullified by the glue, he might possibly be reminded of a red-haired boy at the Pound in July 1980. And Vance would remember him too — yes, Luke, it's all coming back; now what was the name of that band — and they would look at each other in awe like Pixie and Dixie splitting the atom.

Radical Jive. That was their name.

What happened in the toilets, Luke? What did you do to Karl Marks?

Two copies of the *NME* traditionally hauled themselves every Thursday from England to the newsagent's beside the Co-op on the Lisburn Road. I always bought mine in the morning; the other copy would always be gone by lunchtime.

At 10.15 a.m. on Thursday, after another night without sleep, I bought the *NME* with a keen sense of anticipation. Crossing back over the pelican crossing, I read the letters page as I walked up Malone Avenue. It had no letters from Belfast, only idiots moaning about Brixton and Toxteth. The bloody Northern Ireland postal service had cocked it up again. However, a week late would be better than nothing.

I dozed and listened to *Flesh + Blood* throughout the afternoon, making a few notes, before ceremoniously putting on my red mohair jumper at eight o'clock and setting off for Cranmore Park. I took the Malone Road to avoid the sound of pipe-and-drum bands. When I got to the house, Dexy's Midnight Runners were blaring out of the ground-floor window. Their album was a favourite of Denise's.

She opened the door herself.

'Happy birthday,' I said. 'I'm afraid I didn't have time to buy you a present.'

'Mind where you're walking,' she replied with a pert smile. 'There's a kitten loose in the hoose.'

'A kitten?' I grinned, slamming a foot down on the hall mat. 'Squash the kitten.'

Denise's face fell. 'You mustn't squash him. He's beautiful.'

In the front room, six or seven girls were dancing and shouting along to Dexy's while a lone boy sipped a can of Carlsberg and smoked a cigarette. All the furniture in the room had been cleared out, save for the record-player and the coffee table. In the corner where a TV and a lamp normally stood were Robert's drum-kit, Dermot's organ, a microphone and some amplifiers. Against these were propped a Rickenbacker bass and a £14 guitar.

I met Sheila on the way up to the attic. She was bringing down a tray of dinner plates and she had to stand sideways to let me get by. I told her to be careful where she trod – some moron downstairs had let a kitten loose.

'Gentlemen,' I saluted, entering the attic. 'As I live and breathe.'

There was a smell of spaghetti Bolognese and the four Decadents had cans of beer. Everybody stopped talking. Feeling thirsty myself, I borrowed Mark's can and took a slurp from it. I wiped the mouth-hole with my sleeve, as you were supposed to, and gave it back to him.

'How's the sleep deprivation going, Rob?' Andy asked evenly.

'Yeah, Rob, how's the existentialist paranoia?' Dermot piped up.

'Ah, not too bad,' said Robert. 'I wish I could say the same for the pressures of overwork.'

As they were talking, I noticed that Paul McCartney's face on the Beatles poster had been covered up with a sheet of A4. I didn't need to read it to know what it was.

Dear Lou,

This has not been an easy letter to write. May I say firstly and without further ado . . .

'That was nice of you,' I murmured to Andy, who was looking down at his winkle-pickers.

'Thank you,' he said. 'I thought it was for the best.'

Dermot and Robert laughed. Robert had a high-pitched, hyak-hyak-hyak laugh that I'd never much cared for.

'Consider yourself an ex-fan of the Decadents,' Andy added.

'Without further ado,' said Coates, speaking for the first time.

I felt myself redden. 'All right . . . I see. If that's the way you want it, fine. Okay, be like that. But can I just say . . .'

'Existentialist paranoia,' Coates jeered. 'Oh, wait till Mawhinney and Caroline hear that. We're going to read your letter out downstairs.'

'It's our new song,' said Robert. 'We're hoping to release it as a *day-byoo* single.'

They all laughed except Andy. I tried to get him to look at me, but he was finding his winkle-pickers fascinating. The situation seemed to have deteriorated to my disadvantage. Bastards. Livid, I rushed over to the poster and ripped the letter down. Then I ran out of the attic and raced down the stairs two at a time.

There is something sad about leaving a party before it begins. No one apprehended me or called after me, or even saw me go. I'd never missed a Decadents gig before, but I knew in my heart that I would not be witnessing another.

I was trying to save your stupid fucking band, I thought miserably as I walked home. *Save it and help it and give it a real chance.*

In a hedge at the bottom of Adelaide Park I deposited Isobel's Love C-90. Inscription inside . . . and no longer relevant. Word would get around the Virgins that I had offended the modesty and self-respect of Mark Coates, which would mean summary excommunication by Isobel and Owen. Middle Sixth year at the College was already destined to be agony. Coates's parents might even sue me for what I'd written about them in the letter. *Bastards*. I went back to the hedge and fished out the cassette. I would listen to it tonight, alone.

It wasn't until I was safely in my bedroom with the curtains drawn that I looked at the letter again. It was my letter, and yet it wasn't. It took me a while to come to terms with it — what was in it, and more importantly what was not. It was a clumsy and incriminating piece of writing, that was for sure; the work of a sleep-deprived mind. But it was not the letter I had written. The handwriting was Andy's.

PART TWO

9
Summer Excerpts

July 13: A sixth Republican prisoner in the Maze, Martin Hurson, dies after forty-six days on hunger-strike.

Conversation. Members of Sweet in the RCA factory, England, early 1974

Brian Connolly: Are you ready, fellers?
Andy Scott, Steve Priest and Mick Tucker: Yeah; uh-huh; okay, etc.
BC: Now today we are going to be making a new single called 'Teenage Rampage'. Nicky Chinn and Mike Chapman, the two men who make up our songs for us, have made this one up specially and I think you're going to like it.
AS, SP, MT: Uh-huh; okay; yeah.
BC: It goes like this. *Raaaaaaayyyy*, we want Sweet, we want Sweet, we want *dooooov*, der-ner, *dooooov*, der-ner, *dooooov*, der-ner, all over the land the kids, *a-tamp-a-tamp-a*, you'll be doing this bit Steve Priest, at thirteen they were foolin', *neow-neow-neow-neow*, come join the revolution, *dan-da-dan-da-dan*,

there's somethin' in the air, *yeah*, yeah, *yeah*, yeah, teee-naaaage raaampaaage now, now, now, now, now, *raaaaaaay*.

AS, SP, MT: Okay! Yeah! Uh-huh!

BC: Need I remind you that we've had some disappointing chart numbers lately. I'm thinking particularly of 'The Ballroom Blitz' only going to number two last September instead of number one. But this is a new year, so I hope you've all remembered to write 1974 in your jotters, and now let's make 'Teenage Rampage' and show everybody we're still the best band out. Then we'll listen to Johnnie Walker telling us we've gone to number one next Tuesday. That way we can be on *Top of the Pops* at the end, not the beginning or in the middle.

The Manuscript, July 14

Mahood, the shuffling janitor, set the milk crate down with a clang on Esme Walsh's desk, rubbed his back and shuffled out of the classroom. The invalids and rejects of Class 6 made anxious little movements in their chairs, trying to get closer to the milk but knowing not to take a bottle without permission. Over the rim of the crate, the brown eyes of Esme peeped out plaintively like a dormouse in a toast rack.

Sounds of enviable activity carried through the window from the football pitch, where Mr MacLelland was conducting trials for the Class 6 and Class 7 Downburn Dynamos. Gordon Massey, the non-sporting twin, had his head out of the window and was studying the miniature Peter Lorimers and Kevin Keegans below.

'Hack-pthoo,' he spat.

I turned the pages of the Pop Star *annual, finding the one that had the info about Geordie. Two of the men in Geordie were called Brian, the most attractive of all pop star names. The lead guitarist* was called Vic, which was more of a football name. Pop star names differed completely from football names. If you were a pop star, you could be called Rod, Rick, Mick, Nick, Noddy or Brian. But if your name was Rodney, Gary, Stewart, Dennis or Kevin, you had to play football. Some names were common to pop and football, such as Jimmy, Brian, Dave, Steve and Kenny. But Norman was football only, just as Marc was definitely pop.

'Hhheeeek-pthoo,' spat Gordon. 'Nearly.'

'You'll get into trouble,' I told him, turning to the page with the info about 10cc. Lol Creme (gtr, kbds, vcls; b. September 19, 1947), Graham Gouldman (bs gtr, vcls; b. May 10, 1946), Eric Stewart (ld gtr, vcls; b. January 20, 1945), Kevin Godley (dms, vcls; b. October 7, 1945).

10cc was where my formula for pop star names and football names came a bit unstuck. There was no way you would have called Lol Creme a pop star name. And Graham, Eric and Kevin were about as football as you could get. But 10cc had very old dates of birth — they had been born years and years before the men in Sweet — so it was possible they'd been footballers for one of the fourth division clubs and then changed their minds and become pop stars. Raymond's collection of football annuals might have some info about them, if I looked at the pages on Rochdale, Hartlepool or Southport. But not Accrington Stanley; they had died of old age and become ghosts.

There was no chance of me and Gordon ever being footballers, sadly, even though Gordon had a good name for one. Our trial for the Class 6 Dynamos had been brief. My legs had buckled on contact with the ball, making me fall over, while Gordon, after almost wetting himself laughing at me, had mistimed a tackle and taken a boot-full of Desmond Semple's studs up his thigh. That was the end of Gordon.

'Am I in the Dynamos, sir?' he asked Mr MacLelland pathetically. Mr MacLelland told him he could be a reserve. I was also a reserve, as were all the other boys who hadn't made the teams.

'Can the reserves go up to their classrooms and read quietly till Miss Calcross and I get back,' Mr MacLelland ordered. 'There's too many cowboys on the prairie and not enough Indians.' He took hold of Goofy Greer who was waving goodbye to us sarcastically. 'You. Upstairs. Read.'

Esme Walsh, too microscopic to be anything but a reserve in any team, had got tired of sitting behind the milk crate and had moved to another desk. Now that I could see her, I observed that she was reading the Magpie annual she had got for Christmas. We had all got annuals for Christmas. Our parents must have had a Christmas presents meeting one night when we were in bed, and decided to buy us annuals. No one in Class 6 had got the same annual as anyone else.

'Slade?' said Gordon by my side.

'Mmm, it tells you how they make up their songs,' I showed him. 'Noddy Holder goes round to Jim Lea's and they make them up together.'

'Liar. Do they? That single's fab, though, isn't it? It's a deaker single so it is.'

He was talking about 'Merry Xmas Everybody'. It was more fab and more deaker than 'My Friend Stan', sure, but it would have been hard for a single to be less fab or less deaker than 'My Friend Stan'. That had been wick.

'Have you heard the new Sweet single?' I asked Gordon.

'Aye! No, I haven't. What's it like?'

'Fab,' I raved. 'It's going to be number one on Tuesday. I'm bringing my radio in.'

Gordon ambled over to the crate and took a bottle of milk. Peeling the top off, he drank half of it and put it back. 'Aaaaaaaah,' he said. Esme looked at him inquisitively. He flicked the bottle-top away and it landed on a chair. Esme's eyes followed it.

Esme was obsessed with Shetland ponies these days and had become quite a likeable person since the scandal. But neither Gordon nor I liked girls or Shetland ponies, so we never had a great deal to do with

Esme. Gordon left the lovey-dovey side of things to Angus, who did kissing in the cloakroom with his fiancées.

The Class 6 Dynamos returned, muddy and panting. Angus sat down at his desk, very purposefully ignoring us. We weren't all friends with each other any more, mainly because Angus had changed so much and now did kissing as well as football.

'Did he make you captain?' Gordon asked him across the desks.

'Naw . . . vice-captain.'

Gordon and I traded satisfied looks. To the new, stuck-up Angus, being vice-captain was as discreditable as being a reserve. What would the fiancées in the cloakroom think of that?

'Oh! The lovely sound of hush!' said Miss Calcross, beaming, as she came in with the netball team. 'Goodness me, I thought I'd find nothing but dead bodies. Who wants milk?'

Clare Beattie waddled past the back of my chair, just close enough for me to hear the two words she uttered under her breath, and, contemptuously brushing the bottle-top from her seat, lowered her fat bottom on to creaking wood. Then, chewing slowly, she set about ogling her vice-captain lover for the rest of the day.

Letter to Owen Bramerton, July 18

Dear Owen,

I haven't been well lately, so I was wondering. Would it be possible to tell me what happened at Denise Finn's party the other night? I don't mean literally everything that happened, but if you could give me the edited highlights.

I would have phoned, but I've lost my voice unfortunately. So maybe it would be better if you wrote back, because I don't know if I'd be able to make sense on the phone or if I would just be croaking like a frog.

I'm not going away anywhere, so write any time. Please write as soon as you can. Looking forward to receiving your reply by return of post.

Yours,

Hockey Fan

Phone-call to Abernethies of Newtownabbey, Monday, July 20

AoN: Abernethies.

Member of the Public: Good morning. Would it be possible to speak to Isobel please?

AoN: And who might you be?

MoP: I beg your pardon?

AoN: Are you a friend of hers?

MoP: Oh. Is she not allowed to take personal calls during working hours? I mean, not that it's a personal call in the sense of being . . . I mean, is she busy with a customer?

AoN: (*to someone else in shop*) There's a lad here wants to speak to Isobel. Do you want to talk to him?

MoP: Hello? I'd like to talk to Isobel if that's possible.

AoN: Isobel doesn't work here, son. Can you just hang on a wee second? The manager needs a word with you.

MoP: The manager?

AoN: Yeah, the manager. (*To manager*) I think it's from England.

MoP: Oh, wait, I'm losing my voice. I'm terribly sorry, I'll have to go.

NME, *July 25 (on sale in Belfast, July 23)*

COALITION OF GLASS

Belfast

The modern dance has come to this blighted/benighted morass of a city, and one band at least is tripping the light fantastic. Only days old, yet already with a glowing sheen of justified confidence, north Belfast quartet Coalition of Glass walk on to the stage of this grim(y) venue unannounced but leave it as undisputed champions of scorched earth post-punk replete with cerebral nous. If the Pop Group had made *Boy*, if Howard Devoto fronted the Bunnymen, if the Slits had been the Supremes . . . So many ifs, so little time. Formed by ex-members of the underrated, much-missed Radical Jive, COG (who are as cogent as they are cognitive) have no fewer than 12 authentic classics in their flawless 40-minute set. I'm on tenterhooks during 'Landscape of the Damned' and 'Fallout' – am I dreaming or are these the most monumental songs of fear and loss since *Unknown Pleasures*? And can this really be happening in the same city that spawned all those pig-ignorant Arthur Mullards like Strategic Excrement, Berlin *et al*.? Wild-eyed COG vox man Richard assures me there'll be more incandescent gigs to come, plus an EP ('we wrote four new songs today without even trying'), and world domination *naturally*. Belfast is burning. Watch this space.

Karl Marks

Conversation. Members of Sweet in the RCA factory, England, mid-1974

Brian Connolly: The reason I have asked you all here today is because we have a new single to make. This time Nicky Chinn and Mike Chapman have come up with something a little different. I know you were as disappointed as I was that 'Teenage Rampage' only got to number two in January instead of number one, but may I just repeat, fellers, that there was no disgrace in coming second to such a fab and deaker single as 'Tiger Feet'.

Andy Scott, Steve Priest and Mick Tucker: Okay; uh-huh; yeah.

BC: Now, our new single will be 'The Six Teens', which is about all the people we knew in 1968 before we made 'Blockbuster' and became the best band out. People like Bobby and Billy, for example. You remember Bobby and Billy, don't you?

AS, SP, MT: (*uncertainly*) Uh-huh . . . yeah . . . okay . . .

BC: Well, I hope you do because Nicky Chinn and Mike Chapman have gone to a lot of trouble over this. And they've written a very strange tune which everyone will think is rubbish until they've heard it four or five times. 'The Six Teens' is a new kind of Sweet single — it's looking back at life and it makes you think about things that have happened to you, and things that are still to come — and it's ideal for people who have only one more year of primary school left before they do their eleven-plus. And it's also got some good drumming in it, so it has.

MT: Okay.

The Manuscript, July 24

Was it really seven years ago that I lay on my bed in Foyle Crescent on a sweltering July day — while cricket matches were being played on the television, in the cul-de-sac, in our back garden — and heard Johnnie Walker say that the new Sweet single had gone into the charts at number eighteen? Eighteen??

Eighteen. It was the sort of number that Clifford T. Ward went in at. My age times two: the age when you have to leave home and find a pretty girl to marry you in church. Eighteen.

'Oh . . .' I mewed. 'Help.'

I had been hoping that Sweet might — oh, I don't know — go to number one and make me feel successful for a change; make me strut around for seven days with my chest out; whatever that feeling was that I got when music and happiness came together. But that feeling was absent from 'The Six Teens' — it was the first Sweet single not to have it.

'Where's Hampshire?' inquired Yorkshire in the garden.

'Hampshire's browned off,' said Somerset. 'I don't think he wants to be in the Gillette Cup. We'll put Leicestershire through to the semis, shall we, and fix his wagon.'

'The Six Teens' was sung by a grown-up who became sad when he thought about how much fun life had been when he was younger. Oh dear . . . I wished Sweet would stop thinking about things like that. And we could all go looking for Blockbuster in a great big gang like we used to.

'I'm not browned off,' I objected. 'It's not the be-all and end-all, you know, only getting to number eighteen.'

A certain Argentinian 400-metres runner might have disagreed with me. 'Issan outrage!' he would have howled, demanding a rerun. But Sorluza was another of those 1973 mainstays who hadn't survived to the summer of '74. Raymond Adair didn't play the Olympics now.

Belfast Grammar was changing him into a serious person: he would walk past our house in the mornings with the straps of his rucksack trailing on the ground, because his shoulders had enough trouble carrying the weight of the world. He told my brother I was a pest for always knocking on his door and asking if Pushova was coming out. Reluctantly, he did agree to play the World Cup with me and the O'Keefes in the cul-de-sac, but when I asked him to make up funny names for the Poles and the Bulgarians, he said I was being childish. Well, if I was being childish, he was being serious.

Music was being serious too. I didn't notice at first, but it was. There were singles that had people dying in them, for instance. 'Seasons in the Sun' was sung by a dead man, and 'Billy Don't be a Hero' was sung by a dead man's wife. Women bought those singles because they liked a good cry — or so I read in some info about 'Billy Don't be a Hero' in Pop Star *— but oh dear, dear, dear . . . Music was being too serious.*

And when they weren't dying, the people in some singles were living on a desert island with no books or electricity, like the man in 'The Air that I Breathe'. Then all the groups started making ballads like 'The Air that I Breathe', even Slade. There was one Top of the Pops *where everything was either a ballad, or a single about somebody dying, or a single about a grown-up thinking about how much fun life had been when he was younger. It was like watching* Match of the Day *when both games end nil–nil, and I've already seen the scores on* Grandstand, *so it's a complete waste of time and I've had a completely ruined weekend. 'Thanks for completely ruining* Top of the Pops,' *I wanted to say to all the groups that night. 'Not one of you sang a rocker, or went to Devil Gate Drive, or looked as if you were having any fun at all. This has been a complete waste of time.'*

In Class 6, Miss Calcross used to tell us to be thankful for the good things in life. The good things in life happened when God, pottering around Heaven and watering his plants, remembered that he loved his little sunbeams in Downburn and decided to give us a nice surprise.

Hands up if we could think of some examples of God's nice surprises.

'Miss, a new brother or sister.'

'Very good example, Rosemary, well done.'

'Miss, the World Cup.'

'Yes, that could be a nice surprise, Desmond, if the World Cup makes you feel thankful to God, then, yes.'

'Miss, beating the Comber Crusaders.'

'Yes, Desmond, but don't forget that God loves the Comber Crusaders too. What else apart from football would be an example of a nice surprise by God?'

Well, Miss Calcross, good question.

Peace in Northern Ireland? A visit from the Wombles? Clare Beattie being decapitated in a netball accident?

But no, those were dreams not surprises. A nice surprise would be a key to turn the clock back from 1974 to 1973, when Raymond had come out to play and Sweet had been successful, and I'd had that feeling I got when music and happiness came together. Goodbye Raymond, goodbye Sweet, goodbye 1973. The feeling was absent from 'The Six Teens' because the feeling was gone.

August 1–2: Republican prisoners Kevin Lynch and Kieran Doherty die after seventy-one and seventy-three days on hunger-strike respectively.

August 8: Republican prisoner Thomas McElwee dies after sixty-two days on hunger-strike.

England v. Australia, Fifth Test, Old Trafford. BBC Radio 3 commentary, August 14.

Commentator 1: Very woebegone chap, isn't he?

Commentator 2: He should try working down the mines. No time for pop music there.

Commentator 1: No indeed. There speaks the voice of experience. Allott again from the Warwick Road End, here he comes, he's in past umpire Constant, he bowls and Dyson goes back and looks to force the ball away on the off side, and there's no run. Yes, he's rather good at imagining other people having fun and rather less good at having it himself, if you see what I mean. Problems with the fairer sex I dare say.

Commentator 2: And I will wager you a pound to a shilling that if someone was to give him some friendly advice about where he's going wrong, he would tell them to get knotted. He wouldn't listen to them. He wouldn't.

Commentator 1: One does sense that it will all end in tears.

Commentator 2: Oh, there's no doubt about it.

Commentator 1: He's been rather in the doldrums this summer. Allott running in, he's there, he bowls to Dyson who drives. Allott fields off his own bowling and there's no run.

Commentator 2: Serves him right for playing silly buggers.

Commentator 1: Would you say that was the crux of the matter?

Commentator 2: I would. He's handled the situation in so far as I can see in a very shoddy fashion and in my view he's alienated them as should be treated better.

Commentator 3: The seventh time that's happened since 1979.

Commentator 1: Good heavens. Allott with three slips and a gully, he's in now, he bowls and Dyson with a lot of bottom hand driving right across the line of a half-volley. Rather an ungainly stroke and they get no run.

Letter received from Owen Bramerton, August 17

Dear Student,

We regret to inform you that Existentialism is not, and has never been taught as a BA course at the University of Coleraine and it has been necessary for us to reject your application. Try the Poly.

I was away in Scotland when your letter arrived, so apologies for the late reply and I hope you haven't topped yourself in the meantime. I tried phoning you yesterday.

Was it laryngitis that you had? Or did you come down with one of your 'mystery' illnesses e.g. Winter Limping Disease. I know there was nothing wrong with you, the only place you're ill is in the head, you poser.

You missed an interesting party. Hardly any of the L. Sixth were there, just Isobel, me and that freaky guy Paul Leckie who knows Andy. Mark was there of course, but I'll get to him/the band/music in a minute.

Have you said something to Andy's sister? She really has it in for you. I was asking where you were and she said you'd gone, 'Good riddance'. The mother doesn't seem to like you either. The only ones sticking up for you were Andy and me. (This was in the kitchen.) I thought you were getting on fine with his sister when we went to the gig at the Pound. Shows you what I know.

I won't say too much about Isobel but her behaviour was not respectable. She didn't even have the decency to do it where there were no fifth-formers around. I told her she needs to catch herself on before next year. It was lucky Sheila (Andy's mother) had gone over the road to a friend's.

The Decadents were excellent, you should have been there. Mark Coates in good musician shock! Well, as good as he needed to be. He seemed to have the right idea. They were really good.

What happened to you anyway? Andy said you had to rush home for something and never came back. Coatesy tried getting off with one of Denise's friends upstairs but I don't think he got very far. That drummer Robert's an animal though. He had a tee-shirt on that said SICK OF SELF-ABUSE . . . COME AND DO IT FOR ME. Coatesy offered to buy it off him for five quid. I think Robert ended up with Denise. He was asleep in her arms when I left.

I'm sure some of this is old news you'll have got from Andy and Coatesy by now. Coatesy's having a start-of-term party in September and the band are going to play. But I'll see you before then.

All the best,

Owen

August 20: A tenth Republican prisoner in the Maze, Michael Devine, dies after sixty days on hunger-strike.

Advertisement on sixth-form centre notice-board, September 1

World-class guitarist, synth, horns and percussionist needed for Finaghy/S. Belfast band. Influences: Genesis, early Steve Hillage, Mahavishnu Orchestra. Contact Paul Leckie, lunchtimes.

10
Transmogrification

The night before the new term, my entry into the Middle Sixth. A time for intricate scheming. And this I did.

This I did, sir, drinking several pints of ferocious black coffee through the night as I mapped out my movements and facial expressions for the coming three months. What I would say. How I would look. How I would look when I said what I was saying.

Pints and pints of coffee and intricate overnight scheming, sir. And that's why I'm asleep in your History class at the moment.

About ten and a half hours ago, sir, at 4.45 a.m., I remember pulling back the curtains. 'Superbird,' I vowed, 'this term people are going to see a new me. What's happened here is there's been a transmogrification.' Waves of caffeine pulsed giddily between my window and Superbird's roof, making him vibrate like a clockwork toy. The coffee mug jitterbugged in my trembling hand. 'This coffee won't keep still, my feathered friend. Look, it's trying to fly away. But I won't let it.'

Hours must have passed, sir. The next time I looked, I

was on the bed and the curtains were drawn again. The kettle on top of the bookcase had gone. I heard someone having a shower downstairs.

For an hour after that, my heart pounded in an apprehensive, last-thoughts-in-the-prison-cell-before-being-led-outside-and-publicly-hanged way. It's called going back to school, sir, and don't tell me you don't fear it too. I couldn't decide which was the more grisly to think about — the summer I'd just had, or the autumn I was about to walk into. I dreaded the inevitable collisions with Virgins, Bigots and Rugbywankers, and even wondered if I should try to stay out of the sixth-form centre for the entire year. But no, I would have to face them all. I was now in the Middle Sixth and the final countdown — to my A-levels, to my escape, to my destruction or whatever it would be — had begun.

Do you know what I did yesterday, sir? I listened to records from noon till nightfall. Not to pass the time or to perk myself up, for those would be shallow pursuits to a transmogrified heathen existentialist virgin unrequited depressive Anglophile, sir, as I trust you will concur. I mean you might as well go kite-flying, mightn't you, if all you want out of life is fun? Let's face it, sir, fun is for morons. The real reason that I listen to records is because I've been doing it for half my life and I don't know how the hell to stop. Do you think Stalin was the same, sir, when it came to being a tyrant? Was he a tyrant for fun, or had he just been doing it for half his life and didn't know how the hell to stop? Notice how my mind instinctively makes an analogy between listening to music and tyranny in the USSR, sir. I may be fast asleep but I'm still thinking like a History student.

You're a bit old to understand, sir — in fact, gossip has it you're pushing seventy and really you need sleep more than I do — but I've been protected and damaged by music since I was eight years old. Currently I cannot listen to a single record in my collection without either sucking my thumb or bursting into tears. There's a song from 1974 that I dearly wish I could sing to you: I used to think it was a song about other people's pasts, but now I realize it was a premonition of my future. And I know that if I heard 'The Six Teens' today, two boys would merge together — the one that has suffered the damage and the one to whom the damage was done.

I envy my classmates. They do a fine job, sir. You're looking at the much-vaunted Northern Ireland brain drain right here in this room. Companies in England, Scotland and America will get the benefit of their academic excellence and ambition. With super-qualified geniuses like them around, I'll be lucky to find a job selling hot-dogs. What have you been doing for the last eight years, the companies will ask me? Listening to records, I will say. Then do you mind if we curtail this interview and show you the door, they will ask? That's all right, I will say — if there's one thing they taught me at that venerable institution Belfast Grammar it's how to recognize a door.

Mrs Idge thinks I'm weird, sir. In my oral exam last term, I read out the names of all the songs on Japan's *Gentlemen Take Polaroids* album in a Spanish accent. Mrs Idge is going through my translation papers this week, and if I don't get sixty-three per cent with an exclamation mark I'll be up in front of the board of governors. *Me siento mareado. No puedo respirar y tengo un dolor en el pecho.*

At any rate, sir, I've just spent an unprosperous summer

with the Manuscript attempting to exorcize the ghosts of 1974 on the off-chance that it will make your incredibly tedious History lessons easier to bear in 1981, and here we are on the first day of term and it hasn't worked. So I've put my Manuscript away in a drawer where I cannot see it (much as you did with my essays last term, sir, after you had appended your waspish verdicts to them). The Manuscript has become nothing more than a depot of bad memories, so I am taking a well-earned breather, sir, which is why I do not appear to be moving at the present time.

My school uniform felt clammy against my skin this morning, a result of my being overheated by the coffee and also my decision, which incidentally I now regret, sir, to get dressed at 2 a.m. Leaving the house and feeling air hit me, I was tempted to lie down in the road and doze off.

Have you ever heard of Green Regent? No, of course you wouldn't have. I made them up in the third form. I became quite good at making up groups, sir. From the age of twelve to about fourteen, I doubt whether I ever knew the disappointment of real music. There was nothing disappointing about Green Regent, only success after success. You may be interested to learn, sir, that *Fol de Rol* was the best-selling British album in 1976. And that Green Regent's tragic star Johnny Hempridge — may he rest in peace, sir — won the *NME* and *Melody Maker* Best Guitarist polls for three years running. And that *Fol de Rol*'s follow-up, *A Quorum of Kings*, sold quintuple platinum in the winter of 1977. I'll write you an essay about the Regent for my mock A-level, sir, and you'll see what a phenomenon they were.

You taught me History in 1977, do you recall, when I was younger and smaller? I looked for Owen in the coffee bar before coming here today — Owen was the boy who sat next to me in 1977, but now he has acne and sends me curious letters that keep me up all night with anxiety — which is another thing I now regret because I bumped into Paul Leckie outside the coffee bar, who was putting an advertisement up on the notice-board, and he insisted on having a conversation about 'Abacab', the Genesis single, which put paid to any hopes I might have had of staying awake for the afternoon, sir.

I seem to have been transmogrified into a very sleepy cat, sir. I don't know if it's even worth bothering with the UCCA form — I'll be much too tired to fill it out. I'm just going to sit here at this desk, the same desk I sat at in 1977, and you can waffle on about History until June.

I don't suppose you know how Andy Finn got on in his A-levels, do you? We're no longer on speaking terms, unfortunately. That, too, has been keeping me up all night with anxiety. I have so many things I want to say to Andy, but you know what friends are like — there one minute, gone the next. *Plus ça change*, would you not say, sir? Did I ever hand in that essay I wrote about Raymond Adair? *Plus ça change* . . .

Sixth-form centre, 11.20 a.m. Thursday, September 3

I put down the *NME*. It had nothing by Karl Marks again.

What on earth was going on in London? First the *NME* had contrived to lose my letter, and now they were printing review after review about New York jazz groups. Had someone mad been put in charge? You heard these New York jazz groups on John Peel some nights and you asked yourself if the Velvet Underground had struggled for nothing. I was glad I'd be long gone before the New York jazz trend made it to Belfast – imagine all the neanderthals like Ronnie McSweeney and Fergus Matchett wearing berets and playing alto saxophones. Some time in mid-1985.

If Karl Marks was, as I now believed him to be, the drummer in Coalition of Glass (formerly Radical Jive), he would be easy enough to track down. Paul Leckie would know where their next gig was taking place. Paul had his ear to the ground and always knew about upcoming concerts before anyone else. I wasn't surprised he had been at Denise's party; once he'd heard the Decadents were playing, it would never have occurred to him not to go. He would have stood watching Mark Coates, privately lamenting the lack of bass-guitar solos, and afterwards he would have collared Andy and said, 'Yon Coatesy's no Jaco Pastorius, is he, Finno? I should never have left the band.' 'You didn't leave the band, Paul,' Andy would have smirked. 'You were sacked from the band. I sacked you. Sacked you, Paul, sacked. Paul, you were sacked. Sacked by me from the band.' Poor Paul Leckie. He lived in a world of fantasy.

My transmogrification now allowed me to talk to freaky-deaks like Paul, and even to approach them openly. He was sitting at a table by the counter with a chicken-and-mushroom Pot Noodle, the first of two that he ate every day. I joined him.

'Did you buy it yet?' he asked.

'No, I didn't buy it,' I said crossly. 'I don't like Genesis.'

'Bad attitude, mate. Shouldn't be so snobby. It's the best single in years.'

'I don't like singles any more. They're just a commercial ploy to get people to buy albums, and I'm not going to buy a Genesis album.'

'You should get *The Lamb Lies Down on Broadway*,' Paul said. 'Masterpiece. Came out in '74.'

I didn't want to be reminded about '74. I didn't want to be reminded about the £5.75 I had paid for *The Lamb Lies Down on Broadway* in Knights as a third-former, or about the £1.90 I had received for selling it back to them in the fourth form. Love of Genesis was the most shameful of all loves, and by God I had loved Genesis. I'd loved them so much I had made them the support band to Green Regent at Wembley Stadium. *Hempridge soloing and weeping . . . his final rhapsody before the illness claimed him . . . gone so young . . . if our heroes won't die for us, we owe it to ourselves to kill them.*

'So what are you listening to?' Paul asked. 'Have you got the new George Harrison album?'

'Oh, you know . . .' I said airily. 'Everything from Love to Syd. It's got to be '67 or '68, though. Music's dead, Paul. If you took out the Birthday Party and the Teardrops there'd be nothing. And the Fall.'

Paul looked cautiously at me from under his frizzy fair hair as though I had spouted something in Sanskrit. I stared back at him. I could not believe he had bought the new George Harrison album.

'And I'm quite intrigued by what I've been hearing about this band Coalition of Glass,' I added.

'Ah, well,' Paul said, tapping the side of his nose, 'you know there's a rumour about them?'

For a second I thought he was going to tell me that Kark Marks's cover had been blown. But he carried on: 'A few people reckon they're doing a Midwife.'

'Oh *really*?' I said. This was interesting.

'Seemingly they got given a great write-up off one of the comics. When was the last time that happened to anyone from here? So people are putting two and two together. Them boys are doing a Midwife, mark my words.'

It had been — what? — three years since I'd last seen the guitarist from Midwife on the Lisburn Road. He had lived two streets away from me in Derryvolgie Avenue, a lanky goon with waist-length Scott Gorham hair, platform boots and aviator sunglasses. I'd been rather impressed by him at thirteen. But within months he and his band-mates had gone into hiding and Midwife had become a stigma on the cadaver of Northern Irish rock.

Midwife's heavy metal music came along on the cusp of the punk revolution in 1977, but still, for every reborn Belfast punk kid who deemed heavy metal to be *passé* and embarrassing, there were ten others who identified with 'Whole Lotta Rosie' and 'Black Dog' much more than with the risqué anarchy stance of the Pistols and the Clash. Anarchy was always a non-starter in such a controlled city as Belfast, and I knew a lot of teenagers who bought *Never Mind the Bollocks* at the end of '77 only to drift back to heavy metal when *Van Halen* and AC/DC's *Powerage* came out the following May. Teenagers like me.

Midwife were our local stars. I wasn't old enough to see their gigs, but I wore one of their badges for a couple of months. It had their logo — 'Midwif' scribbled in slanting letters with a tiny 'e' coming out of the cross in the 'f' — and a head-shot of a leering nurse in a surgical mask. In the spring term of 1978, much talk was heard of Midwife supporting AC/DC at the Ulster Hall and going on to be famous.

Their guitarist was responsible for writing the songs, which were said to be as good as any English band's. But there was something he hadn't told the others. The truth emerged when the singer, Malcolm, sent a tape to *Sounds*. Malcolm boasted in his letter of Midwife's 'stunningly original material . . . our lead guitarist and musical composer is, we feel, the natural heir to Page, Blackmore and the like'. *Sounds* wrote a postcard to Malcolm thanking him for the most exquisite comedy to have entertained the office in weeks. They had been playing Midwife's tape to death, shouting 'stunningly original material!' and 'we feel!' as they did so.

Midwife's guitarist had thought he was being clever. A man with not an original idea in his head, he had stolen every one of the songs from obscure heavy rock albums he'd bought in London. But an obscure heavy rock album in Northern Ireland was not necessarily an obscure heavy rock album in the offices of *Sounds*, a paper that knew about heavy rock. The postcard to Malcolm listed the bands and albums that the natural heir to Blackmore and Page had filched his songs from: *Paper Money* by Montrose, *Squawk* by Budgie, *Rocka Rolla* by Judas Priest . . . *Sounds* concluded, 'You should, we feel, look for a new musical composer.' In the next issue, they ran Malcolm's letter under the headline YOU COULDN'T MAKE IT UP (BUT THESE BOZOS DID).

Malcolm, fair play to him, pinned *Sounds*' postcard up in a city-centre record shop. Midwife split and none of the members appeared on a Belfast stage again. Malcolm's younger brother Ivan disbanded his Annadale school punk group, the Seditionaries, too upset to continue. And every long-haired band in Belfast thereafter fastidiously made a point of announcing to the audience when they were playing a cover. 'This one's called "Shanghai'd in Shanghai" – and before you fucking say anything, yes, we know it was written by Nazareth.'

If Paul was right and Coalition of Glass were indeed doing a Midwife, they were playing a dangerous game. *NME* reader Owen Bramerton had seen the rave review and was suggesting we go together to their next 'incandescent' gig. Vance Armstrong – who had himself been doing a would-be Midwife for years, but Vance was only plagiarizing Lou Reed and *everybody* plagiarized Lou Reed, so it wasn't really classed as stealing – would most certainly want to check out his new opposition. Strategic Element and Pragmatic Control would surely be there too, if only to look for Karl Marks in the audience. The Decadents might even wander in. And, between us, someone would be bound to know the obscure songs that Coalition of Glass were passing off as their own.

However, that was *if* Paul was right. A big if.

I tended to think not. I thought that Coalition of Glass were probably the victims of a bitching campaign by other bands jealous of the *NME* review, and that their songs were self-written. But there was also the possibility that those songs could be total garbage or a massive let-down – especially if, like the *NME* review, they had been written by the drummer. One way or another, Coalition of Glass risked being found out. I wondered if Karl Marks had thought of that.

'When are they playing next?' I asked Paul.

'Uh . . . the twelfth.'

'Whereabouts?'

'A youth club in Lisburn. And you know what cracks me up? When Andy Finn persuaded me to join the Decadents–.'

'Finish your Pot Noodle, Paul,' I said.

Friday, September 4

I hadn't for the life of me been able to come up with a theory to explain why Andy had rewritten my apology letter in his own hand before showing it to the Decadents. Specifically, I couldn't work out why he'd omitted the four paragraphs about Mark Coates and his family. For the last two months I had been exhausting every avenue of second-guessing. Maybe Andy really had got fucked up about his A-levels. Maybe he'd had a gay crisis of some kind – his relationship with the teacher might have turned nasty. Maybe I wasn't completely out of favour after all. Or maybe I had never been in.

Doubling my predicament was the memory of the Clare Beattie love-letter in 1973 which had caused a scandal at Downburn Primary. But that was a letter that *I* had rewritten – painstakingly, over the course of several days until the spelling mistakes were just right and the sentiments oh-so-damning – and my motive had been basic self-preservation. Clare had fumed, and Angus had cut me off without a word, but the letter had achieved its aim. She had stopped telling heinous lies about me. She had left me alone.

But why Andy would go to the trouble of rewriting my apology, taking out the central paragraphs that established the grounds for the deception . . . and then consign me to a painful summer of tears and transmogrification, cricket and morbid visions, the Ashes and the ashes-to-ashes. I could not sleep for worrying. What was that word the hippies used? Karma. Was it karma? Are these my chickens – I thought – coming home to roost? Is this why I'm always thinking backwards these days? Because there isn't going to be a forwards?

I had hoped Andy might phone me on results day. But there was not a peep. All I could do was reread what Owen had written ('the only ones sticking up for you were Andy and me'), but each time my heart leapt with pleasure at that, my eyes fell inexorably to the cataclysmic paragraph below, in which Isobel did it at Denise's party while there were fifth-formers around.

I had attended the party two hundred times in my dreams and nightmares. It had replaced *O Lucky Man!* as my favourite film, despite the torture it put me through. For the camera, however much I begged it not to, always averted its gaze when Isobel did it while there were fifth-formers around. The camera would let me see the fifth-formers, but it would never let me see Isobel doing it.

Owen and I could not discuss this. He didn't want to, and I had resolved not to talk about myself until I was out of Belfast. And I couldn't very well talk about Isobel without talking about myself. Neither of which Owen or I wanted to do.

Isobel had missed the first three days of term. At Latin on Wednesday morning, where I would normally have sat beside her, I arrived early in order to bag a desk on the other side of the room. 'Bit of a cold,' I was intending to say to Brooke-Taylor. 'Brrr . . . radiator . . . might be warmer . . . well, any-way.' But he didn't question me and Isobel didn't show up. Nor on Thursday. Then, on Friday, somebody came in and sat down at Isobel's desk — and I honestly looked at that girl three times before I realized it was Isobel herself.

She had changed the way only girls can change in the summer holidays. Boys can will themselves to undergo a transmogrification, but girls just metamorphose. They can take a new form. And there was simply no physical or formal similarity between the girl sitting at Isobel's desk and the person I had last spoken to in June.

'Fucking hell,' whispered my new desk-mate Ian Bailey. 'The state of her.'

Her hair was long and had reverted to its natural black, but looked greasy and abandoned. It was tied in an unflattering pony-tail. She had lost weight and her head sagged. She fidgeted constantly with her ear lobes. When Brooke-Taylor left the room to quieten down a rowdy Greek lesson next door, she turned to face us with her back against the wall, looking over my head towards the window and biting her lip. She was blinking hard and appearing to have difficulty focusing. Mark Coates would have noticed the lovebites just above the collar of her shirt.

'Don't,' I warned Bailey, who was about to say something. 'Don't.'

Oh Isobel, I thought. *Don't.*

But she did and she had and she would. I didn't know for certain what she was up to, but I understood why Owen had been disgusted and why Abernethies had been so churlish on the phone. I wasn't the only one who'd had a bad summer.

'She's scary,' said Bailey. 'Tell her to fuckin' turn round.'

Voices echoed from a distant, innocent June. *Never you mind how Isobel did . . . Isobel's not the cute wee petal you think she is . . . We're all gonnae have a nice holiday and hopefully we'll all come back from it in one piece.*

Isobel didn't come to the coffee bar with us after Latin; she just sloped off across the quad. The holiday must have changed her personality, I thought. She hated pony-tails. She'd once told me there was no moral or lawful justification for having one.

Piers Mawhinney and Caroline Howard were at the counter buying Kit Kats. They had come from Maths and wouldn't have seen Isobel yet. What disastrous friends to have at a time when she badly needed friendship: that pair would skin her alive.

'Mark's having a party,' said Piers. 'So is he really in this band or is he just lying out of his arse?'

'He's really in them,' I confirmed. 'Has he said anything about — you know, who he's going to invite?'

'Not that I've heard,' Piers shrugged. 'Just that you're not coming because you're a cunt.'

Caroline whinnied with mirth, but it was nothing new. Mark had been saying that for six years. Six years of me being a cunt and Mark being an arsehole. Six years of schooling in a nutshell. *Plus ça change.*

11
Coalition of Glass

Owen and I met at seven outside the College's western gate and caught the bus to Lisburn. Paul Leckie, who had passed his test in July, was driving there. We'd told him not to expect a fusion band, but the truth was that none of us had the faintest idea what we were likely to see. Only Owen was anything approaching sanguine.

For various reasons – the disinclination of pubs to let me in; my reluctance to scream in the faces of pot-bellied bouncers, 'Look, shit-for-brains, this forged Youth Hostels Association card clearly states that I was born in December 1962' – my Saturday evenings had a tradition of being spent at home playing albums in the dark and waiting for *Match of the Day*. It felt odd to be going somewhere on a bus, to be shivering into a coat and have coins jangling in my pocket, and I was aware of the other passengers sizing me up and down and thinking *Not like him to be out on a night like this*. I could see their admonishment reflected in the window and wondered if my jumpiness were the prelude to a mild agoraphobia period. Or even a severe agoraphobia period with hallucinatory side-effects, fear of buses and a dose of pneumonia.

'Guess what I found the other day,' said Owen next to me, 'when Dad and I were mucking about in the garage.'

'God, I don't know.'

'Well, you've been talking about nothing else lately. Take a wild guess.'

'Oh! No – Joey? You found Joey?'

'It was like holding a wooden spoon in a bandage, and it was *stinking*. It's just a dead titchy wee thing now. I remember when it came up to my chin.'

'What about mine? Came up to my eyes.' I laughed.

'Dad took a picture of me holding it. He goes, "Owen, to think that hockey stick was once bigger than you were. You may shake my hand, son." A very moving occasion in our household, so it was.'

'It must have been.'

Owen tutted philosophically. 'Ah, Joey. A man never had a more faithful wooden friend than you . . . So go on then, memory boy. How many weeks did we get out of doing hockey that time?'

'Four,' I replied without hesitation. 'Every Tuesday, if "Don't Give Up On Us Baby" by David Soul was at number one, it pissed down with rain all day and games were cancelled. Four weeks of euphoria. I haven't loved a God-awful ballad so much in my life.'

'Four weeks,' Owen chuckled. 'I think I even went out and bought it, just to keep it at number one.'

'You did buy it. I lent you half the money.'

'That's right. I remember going in Sounds Alive. "The David Soul single, please, mister." And he looked at me like something crawling out from under a stone. I think I kept it till Christmas and gave it to my mum.'

'But then came the day . . .' I prompted him.

'Aye, and we couldn't understand what went wrong — there was something else at number one . . .'

'"Don't Cry For Me Argentina" by Julie Covington.'

'. . . and then the rain stopped.'

The stopping of the rain in February 1977. It had seemed so irrational. What was life in Northern Ireland if not kneecappings on the news and rain? I hadn't even brought my hockey stick into school, so confident was I that David Soul and the rain would be a marriage of permanence. Why the need for change? Why profane a sacred union?

'I had to borrow Mr Malahide's emergency stick,' I groaned. 'That was the day I got hit by the ball.'

'*I* got hit by the ball,' Owen cried. 'It was me. You never got hit by the ball. You never went near enough to it to get hit. You were a scaredy little coward bastard. I had to have stitches in my head.'

'You did . . .' I nodded dreamily. 'Malahide took you to the hospital. That's weird, I wonder why I thought it was me.'

'Because you lived in cloud-cuckoo-land,' said Owen, looking out of the window. 'With your imaginary friends in your imaginary village.'

'Mmm.' The bus was slowing down. 'So was I never hit by the ball ever?'

'Ach, no,' scoffed Owen, getting up. 'Nothing ever touched you. Nothing nor nobody. You just *acted* brain-damaged.'

He pulled me quickly to my feet and shooed me towards the exit doors. We had to leap on to the pavement to avoid a puddle. 'Thank you, driver,' I called out as the doors closed. Owen socked me on my upper left arm, narrowly missing the tender zone where I'd bled buckets from the BCG injection in the first form. Owen would probably tell

MUSIC FOR BOYS

me it was *his* BCG injection that had bled. Hay fever sufferers could be terrible hypochondriacs.

The youth club was on the first floor of a music school
that farmed out its high-ceilinged rooms by night to language classes, pottery courses, flower arrangers, OAPs with
a sociable hobby or interest. When the Decadents had
played there in 1980, an under-twelves boxing tournament
had been going on over our heads. It was a cavernous
building where even a plimsoll echoed on the stairs.

Owen and I paid the woman at the entrance twenty
pence and became youth club members for the night. Paul
Leckie was already inside, lurking near the refreshments bar
with a bottle of Pepsi and a straw. There were a couple of
dozen people in the place. Straight ahead of us, a rostrum had
been set up for the band – possibly as much as a foot off the
ground. While Owen brushed raindrops from his waterproof,
I ran an eye over the equipment. Only one microphone for
vocals; a Beatles fan on bass; a guitarist who liked FX pedals
(because he'd seen U2 at the McMordie Hall, I presumed);
and a drummer with a very small kit.

'Nifty-looking Hofner bass he's got there,' Paul noted.
'Of course the tricky bit's knowing how to play it.'

I became conscious that I was being stared at by strangers.
There seemed no sign of familiar faces from Strategic
Element or the Prags, but I didn't like to look at faces for
more than a split second and those bands would never
acknowledge a College boy anyway. Nor was it obvious
from everybody's leather jackets and Outcasts and Killing
Joke tee-shirts who the Coalition of Glass foursome might
be. They were probably downstairs in the caretaker's office,
swigging smuggled-in four-packs of lager for Dutch courage.

'Let's get some drinks in, Bram, the fuck sake,' I said

216

loudly, lest any Lisburn Hell's Angels be listening. 'I've got a thirst on me like a mule.'

'It's Pepsi or Pepsi,' Leckie told us. 'You can have any colour you like as long as it's black.'

'We can pretend it's Guinness then, can't we?' reasoned Owen, leading the way. At least this was one bar that couldn't refuse to serve us.

'Have you had any replies to your advert yet, Paul?' Owen asked once we had purchased our bottles and moved closer to the stage.

'Have I bollocks,' said Leckie gloomily. 'That dump's a wasteland for the music I'm trying to play.'

'What music are you trying to play?' I asked him as two six-foot youths appeared from nowhere and stood directly in front of us.

'Music that's pushing the frontiers of exploration and improvisation but it can still be melodic and accessible,' said Paul as we changed our positions. 'You know like the way Vangelis and Mark Knopfler are melodic and accessible but they're geniuses as well? The thing about you punkers is you've made muso a dirty word. You're like Hitler with the Jews – let's round up all the musos and have a big holocaust. Youse are prejudicial, and what's more youse are philistines. Can musicians not take pride in their musicality? I always have, sure. I'm thinking of calling us Maestro Calculus, or else the Maestro Litmus Orchestra, or else Litmus Criterion. I want to really experiment with seeing how far us and the audience can go.'

'And who have you got in the band besides you?' asked Owen.

'Aw, it's just me at the moment, like,' Paul admitted. 'Early days.'

The club filled up gradually while we talked. Karl Marks's review had evidently been widely read in the neighbourhood. I looked again at the meagre drum-kit on the rostrum: in my experience that seemed to indicate that Marks would hold down a no-frills beat like Mo Tucker of the Velvets. Andy was forever telling Robert in the Decs to 'play less . . . make it sound primal'. This meant using the floor drum instead of the cymbals to bash out the rhythm. 'Not the hardest thing in the world to do,' Andy had often said. 'Try explaining it to a drummer, though. If they were any stupider we'd be keeping them as pets.'

As the room continued to fill, I detected something anomalous for a local band's gig – there was an atmosphere of real excitement and expectancy in the audience. We were having to shout to hear ourselves. Some seventy or eighty people were now jostling for a view of the low stage; another ten or fifteen and the barmaid would be coming among us with a loud hailer saying we'd beaten the Northern Ireland youth club record.

Suddenly Owen nudged me. 'Get a load of the crash helmets behind us,' he murmured. 'Do you reckon that's the new Lisburn fashion statement?'

'Crash helmets . . . where . . . oh no . . .'

I knew even before turning who it would be. Yes indeed. There they were, clad in his-and-hers motorcycle clobber, surreptitiously passing a half-bottle of Gordon's between them. Vance, seeing me, raised the bottle and cackled evilly. Alison or Alice or Alex curled her lip, took the bottle off Vance and secreted it in her tiger-striped handbag.

'Could be trouble,' I said to Owen.

Vance came forward. He had his crash helmet under one arm and his peroxide mop was matted and sweaty.

'Haven't you boys got *diplomas* to be doing?' he taunted us. 'Shouldn't you be in your *library* reading your *prospectus*? Writing your *syllabus*?'

'They let us out on parole,' I smiled nervously. 'Time off for good behaviour.'

'Haven't had the pleasure — Paul Leckie,' said Leckie, holding out his hand.

'Fuck off,' said Vance, ignoring it. 'So what brings the Higher Fifth out to Lisburn tonight? Have you been reading the music papers when you should have been revising your *discourse*?'

'Vance Armstrong,' I explained to Paul and Owen. 'Vance sings in that band Berlin.'

'Oh, you're in Berlin — me and him saw you when you played the Pound,' Owen enthused, to my horror. 'You did a great version of "Satellite of Love".'

Vance shot me a where-did-you-find-this-pinhead look. 'My band doesn't do "Satellite of Love", son,' he said icily. 'Next time get your fuckin' ears sponged out.'

Hastily, I asked Vance if he anticipated Coalition of Glass posing any sort of threat to Berlin's dominance of the Belfast music scene. His head rolled back and he grimaced.

'What do *you* think? When they've only been going since the weekend? It takes *years* for a band to get good. You can't just put a brilliant band together when you feel like it. Fuckin' I'd be the first to admit we weren't that brilliant when we started out. Hard work and practice, wee lad. That's what gives us our edge. Just like you and Spotty Muldoon and this Hair Bear cunt, learning your *question-naires*.'

Leckie swiped a stray lock of frizzy hair out of his eyes. 'Couldn't agree with you more, Vince,' he said warmly. 'I've just been telling these boys the same thing. Sure even Dire Straits had to pay their dues. In fact if you listen to the lyrics of "Sultans of Swing" . . .'

I blanched. 'Will you give over about paying the Jews. It's all right, Vance, he's been writing a dissertation about Hitler. Actually, Paul, what were you telling me earlier about Coalition of Glass? I found it quite interesting what you were saying.'

Leckie looked blankly at me.

'About them . . . you know . . . there was that other band who did it too . . .'

Vance interrupted. 'You mean doing a Midwife? Fuck me, have you only just worked that out? We've known for ages – we heard it from Wee Ronnie and Macker. Fuckin' why do you think I'm here? I'm going to get up on stage and slap the sly wee hallions. See what they said in the *NME*? "We've wrote four songs today without even fuckin' trying. Ooh, we are so talented." Wanna know the truth? They've nicked everything off the Psychedelic Furs. They're going to be playing the whole of that first album *and thinking we won't know.*'

Vance cackled gleefully and belched.

'You never told me that, Paul,' said Owen.

Jesus, I thought, how could Karl Marks be so bloody *dim*? Nicking everything from the first Furs album? It was an acknowledged classic . . .

'And see that bottle we've brought with us?' Vance added. 'I know a journalist in this room who's getting that on the back of the head. Wee fucker. *Come to Vance, Karl!*' Vance was cackling and bellowing, and it struck me for the first time that he was extremely drunk. '*Vancie wants a word with you, Karl!*'

Seconds after Vance had staggered away, the four

members of Coalition of Glass came out of a door at the rear of the club, cigarettes in mouths, and took up their instruments. The drummer had a black tee-shirt, red hair and glasses.

'This one's for Karl,' said the singer into the microphone. 'We wrote it this morning.'

NME, *September 26, 1981*

COALITION OF GLASS
Lisburn
The disciples came by bus, by car, by foot and by motor-bike. Like the Sex Pistols at the 100 Club, two years from now 10,000 people will be claiming they were here tonight. Coalition of Glass are officially the most stupendous spectacle to grace Northern Ireland since Georgie knew Best. I've seen them twice now and I'm frightened. Oh yes. Frightened to think of the carnage in *your* town when this band tour Britain next year. Frightened of being deafened by the din of all those posers/losers like the Au Pairs and Modern English throwing down their instruments and giving up. Cos right now, if you're not in Coalition of Glass you belong to the past. Prowling the stage with murderous *élan*, flamboyant vox man Richard dedicates the first song to 'our great friend Karl' (my blushes!) and it's like hearing Iggy duet with the ghost of Jim. Eight new tunes follow, all astounding. Drummer Alastair is a mini-malist machine, primitively producing a brutal beat that begs for comparison with the VU's Mo. But COG are no lurid Lou Reed counterfeit. The sepulchrally opaque intro to 'Everything Will Be Known When We Get There'

may be redolent of 'Heroin', but the band tell me that's intentional — it's 'inverse homage', no less, because the sprawling 14 minutes of 'EWBKWWGT' proceed to lay waste to the cartoon culture of leather-jacketed Lou-alikes who've been infuriatingly prevalent in this neck of the woods going back to ye darke ages of '79. Returning to the stage for an encore (to cheers not heard here since St Patrick banished the snakes) and some clod in the crowd heckles, 'Do "Sister Europe".' But Richard just fixes him with one of his drop-dead glares and says, 'This one's "Mushroom Cloud". We wrote it an hour ago.' And you know what I can't get over? They really did.

Karl Marks

The caretaker's office was on the ground floor of the building, down a corridor, third room on the left. Owen's gloved knuckles thrummed out a steady rhythm on my back as we walked. Leckie, close behind, had timed the penultimate song at seventeen minutes. Even he was saying it was astonishing.

'This one,' I said.

I rapped on the door, opened it and put my head round. My eyes met the fishnet tights of a punk girl who'd been dancing windmill-style during the last few numbers. She was sitting on the guitarist's knee, feeding him puffs from a ciggie. There were another two girls in the room, one of them squeezed into a corner with the bare-chested singer, who was voraciously kissing her and feeling her up. I had rehearsed on the stairs what I was going to say, but the rampant orgy scenes disconcerted me and I forgot my words.

'Come in or get out,' said the singer, ducking his head

and coiling his shoulders free of the girl's embracing arms, 'but shut the fucking door.'

I beckoned to Owen and Paul and we entered the smoky office. There was nowhere for us to sit.

'Can we um . . . is it okay if we er . . .'

Owen saved me. 'One word, lads. In-fucking-credible.'

The drummer had taken off his glasses and was sitting on a green filing cabinet just inside the door with his legs drawn up and his hands clasped tightly around his shins. 'Why, thank you,' he said.

'Where are you all from – Belfast?' Owen asked him.

'We never reveal information like that,' the singer cut in. 'Security reasons.'

The drummer looked at us. 'Do you live round here yourselves?'

'No, I live in Holywood,' replied Owen, 'he lives in Finaghy and he lives on the Malone Road.'

'Well, the Lisburn Road really,' I corrected him. 'Near a Chinese takeaway. The Malone Road's just full of doctors and bloody rich people, isn't it?'

The Hofner bassist, squatting below me with a cigarette in his cupped palm, seemed amused. His Pretenders quiff had collapsed in the maelstrom of the seventeen-minute song and was now a dank pudding of clumps and tangles, like my hair just after I washed it.

'That wouldn't be the sound of middle-class repentance I'm hearing?' he said drily. 'We know a few people like that. Do . . . we . . . not.'

Shifting forward on the filing cabinet, the drummer sniffed. 'There is only one thing worse than being middle-class,' he quoted in an aristocratic English accent, 'and that is *not* being middle-class.'

'I never said that,' protested the bassist in the same voice.

'It was one of Wilde's,' said the drummer.

'Have you been playing the bass long?' Leckie asked the bassist. 'Haven't had the pleasure, by the way,' he added, offering down a hand. 'Paul Leckie.'

Transferring the cigarette to his mouth, the bassist reached up and shook Leckie's hand limply. He didn't, however, answer the question. I tried to remember how the Monty Python cheese shop sketch went. I might be able to take a chance with it if they were Python fans. *Do you have some Wensleydale? No, but Wensleydale is my name.* Unfortunately it was a while since I'd heard it.

'You are . . . a *star*,' the girl in the singer's arms giggled, her finger gently tapping out each word on his nose.

'I know,' he said into her neck. 'I can't help it.'

'I think I saw you lads at the Pound actually,' I ventured, 'when you were Radical Jive. I seem to remember you supporting those wankers Berlin.'

Did I imagine a flash of eye contact between the bassist and the drummer? A look of momentary concern? But it was the singer who spoke.

'Wankers would be an understatement,' he said, uncoiling himself again. 'Excuse my language ladies, but cunts would be a better description.'

Two of the girls tittered in harmony and the singer looked pleased with himself.

'The only description,' the guitarist added. 'Can't think of a better one.'

'Do you know Berlin?' the bassist asked me abruptly.

'Yeah, worse luck.' I rolled my eyes. 'What have I done to deserve that? A couple of them are upstairs now. That wanker of a singer and his cunt of a flatmate.'

All three girls in the room stared at me censoriously.

'We knew they were there,' the drummer said. 'We heard them heckling us. They were trying to get us to play Psychedelic Furs songs. Richard, did he say anything to you as we were coming off?'

'He said we were shit,' the singer replied, snuggling deep into female neck once more. 'Incorrect.'

'You know what I think they're here for?' I said to the drummer. 'They were looking for Karl Marks.'

I wanted to see how his eyes reacted. They didn't.

'Is Karl Marks up there?' Owen asked the bassist. 'Or did he leave?'

The bassist did not answer. It felt as if everyone in the room was waiting for somebody else to make a speech. I kept watching the drummer, but there was no emotion in his face at all.

'Karl Marx?' said Leckie, misunderstanding. 'Why would he be here?'

'Well exactly ...' the drummer agreed vaguely. 'Why here ... why there. To be or not to be. That is two questions.'

'Is he going to be writing about you in the *NME* again?' Owen asked.

'Well ... he *might* be,' said the drummer even more vaguely. 'If we can find him. But that's the thing about Karl, he's ... kind of hard to find.'

Everyone laughed, including the girls. But whatever the joke was, I didn't think the girls were in on it.

'Well, you're certainly a better drummer than that wanker Luke in Berlin,' I remarked, watching the boy on the filing cabinet like a hawk. 'He couldn't hit his way out of a paper bag.'

And now came the reaction. Very slowly he turned his head to me, looked into my eyes and said mistily, 'Ah . . . is that his name? I don't think I remember him introducing himself. So I never knew what his name was. Luke?'

'Luke Corrigan,' I elaborated. My cheeks stung. I was being observed by at least half the room.

'He has a lot of cymbals,' the drummer went on, smiling at the memory. 'A *big* drum-kit. Nice guy — lets you use it. Now I've never gone in for a lot of cymbals myself. I've got a pretty small kit compared to most people. Luke . . . Luke . . .'

He paused and I thought he'd stopped altogether. But he hadn't.

'Doesn't like other drummers putting a crack in his ride cymbal. Oh no no no no. He's really proud of his ride cymbal.'

'You weren't to know,' the bassist said softly.

'But at the same time . . . it's got to be said . . .' The drummer's expression had changed and he looked agitated. 'When you've never used one before . . . you tend to whack the fucking thing as hard as you can.'

'You're okay,' the bassist hushed him. 'We're all okay.'

'Well done, dickhead.' The singer glared at me. 'Give yourself a fucking Rolo.'

'Whack,' repeated the drummer, rocking back and forth on the filing cabinet. 'Whack. Whack. Whack.'

12
Downfall

Letter to Status Quo, c/o Vertigo Records, May 1975

Dear Francis, Rick, Alan and John,

I hope you are keeping well and having pleasant weather in England. We have had rain here this week, but yesterday was a bit more sunny so I walked home without my duffel-coat on. I only put it on at the corner of Lough Erne Lane and Foyle Crescent because my mum doesn't appreciate me walking home without my duffel-coat on, so I put it on at the corner of Lough Erne Lane and Foyle Crescent to fool her. Some of the other boys have mums who don't bloody well care if they wear their duffel-coats walking home or not. My mum says she's not interested in what other boys' mums do or don't do, all that matters is me having my duffel-coat on when I'm walking home. The woman drives me *mad*.

This is just a short note to say that I am listening to 'Roll Over Lay Down', which we went into town and bought on Wednesday. I stayed in the car with my dad while my mum went into the record shop. As I told you in the other letter, you have to have someone sitting in the car or the army blow it up. They think you're the IRA and you've left a bomb in the car so they come and do a controlled explosion. It's like a normal explosion only no one gets killed (unless there is someone hiding in the boot of the car, hee hee).

It's nice to be writing to you again. I wrote to you before to say how much I bloody well liked 'Down Down' and I was keeping my fingers crossed that it would stay at number one. I'm sorry it went down to number five. I hope you don't think my letter was a jinx. Well, here I am again and this is just to say that I am playing 'Roll Over Lay Down' now. I think I like it even more than I liked 'Down Down' if that's possible. Status Quo is the best group there is, which is saying something!!!

Clare Beattie thinks Slade are still the best, but I know she doesn't really think that because now Slade only do ballads. If you don't know about Slade, they are the group with the singer called Noddy Holder. They used to be quite good about five years ago but now all they ever do is ballads. They did 'How Does It Feel' before the Easter holidays. If you didn't hear it you didn't miss anything!!

I've still got the love-letter that I made up from Clare. I'm waiting for her to have me murdered by her father but so far he hasn't done it, touch wood. I don't think he'll murder me now, I hope not anyway. I don't want to be murdered in the fish van. Clare said he would drive the fish van up Foyle Crescent when I was playing outside and he would bung me in the back and drive off at a hundred miles an hour and then later he would murder me when it was quiet and dark. So I wrote the love-letter in her handwriting to make her leave me alone. I told her I would write more love-letters if she didn't. Otherwise she would have kept telling lies about me and her father would have murdered me and the last thing I would have seen was the eyes of the fish looking at me in the back of the van. He sells plaice, cod, haddock, whiting, Dover sole and ray.

You didn't write back to say when you will be playing a concert in Northern Ireland, but I told everybody at school that you are grateful for your Northern Ireland fans because Status Quo is one band that really is grateful for fans. When I heard your songs I bloody well went off my rocker. They are incredible!!! 'Roll Over Lay Down' is your best song, followed by 'Down Down'.

I won't be at primary school much longer because I've done my eleven-plus and if I pass it I'm going to grammar school in September. I hope there are Status Quo fans at grammar school because if there aren't it will be incredible. What I don't want is to go to grammar school and find there are just Bay City Rollers fans or Kenny fans. If they like Queen those people can be quite decent, but if they only like the Bay City Rollers or Kenny those people can be so boring. Anyway I'll let you know if I pass my eleven-plus (wish me luck).

Well I must go now, but if you do write back this time can I have your autographs and some pix of you to show my friends Gordon and Esme? Can you send me some pix of you when you're singing 'Roll Over Lay Down' (or 'Down Down')?

Another thing I should tell you is that Clare says you're a gang of papists. She is the world's biggest liar. She said her brother Stanley had to be circumcised at Easter and the doctor stuck sellotape to Stanley's willy and pulled the sellotape off, and then he stuck the sellotape back on and pulled it off again, and then he kept doing it until Stanley's willy didn't have a hat. That shows you what a big liar Clare is. She's never going to pass her eleven-plus but she might win a Wagon Wheel-eating contest if there was one.

Well I'll go now, but if you do write back please please please send me all your other singles, and tickets for your concerts in England. I was on an aeroplane last year that went to Luton. And please put all your albums in as well.

Yours sincerely,

Status Quo's biggest fan in Northern Ireland (me!!!)

Every day at 9.20 a.m., when assembly ended and the quad became a criss-cross of rucksacked pupils on the move, Owen, Paul Leckie and I would rendezvous at the side entrance to the sixth-form centre. Coalition of Glass had not told us when we would be receiving our manifestos, but I knew I would have mine first because I left for school in the mornings at 8.45 a.m. just after the Malone Avenue postman had delivered.

'Did you get anything?'

'Nothing.'

'Jesus, what's keeping them?'

'Search me.'

It had only been five days since Lisburn, but Owen was as besotted by them as I was. He needed to hear their music again and I needed to know everything about the musicians. He wanted to lose himself in the mystery but I wanted to unravel the riddles. It wasn't relevant to him who wrote what, but for me the writing was paramount and the vexed questions of the songs' origins and Karl Marks's identity required clear-cut answers. Yet when I had pressed them for these answers, they had sucked on their cigarettes or groped their girlfriends and said, 'Sorry, pal. Security reasons.'

'Did Karl Marks write any of the manifesto?' I'd asked.

'He was there at the time,' said the singer. 'I don't remember him contributing.'

'Is Karl in the room with us?'

'It depends which room you're in,' the bassist replied. At which point the singer snapped at the drummer to stop rocking back and forth on the filing cabinet and the moment was lost.

'We have your addresses,' the bassist concluded. 'We'll be in touch.'

Leckie's impression of them, clouded as it was by pro-virtuosity bias, allowed that they were perhaps not Midwifing material from English sources – Owen and I had failed to recognize any of the songs, if they were – but that their arrogance made the Decadents look like Ottawan and would do them no favours in the long run. I disagreed. I thought the arrogance was legitimate, and I knew that Andy Finn had a genuine fight on his hands.

'They're better,' I told Leckie that night. 'I never thought I'd say this about anyone, but you saw them – they're better than the Decs.'

'Better singer,' Leckie accepted. 'He can hit a note.'

'They're better. Better all round.' The admission almost brought tears to my eyes. 'And I think Andy would like them.'

'Aye, he'd say he wouldn't, like, but he probably would. It's just that he wouldn't say it.'

'Well, you know Andy.'

The expedition to Lisburn had created a bond between Leckie, Owen and myself, and all things considered life in

the Middle Sixth was going well. We would team up to
discuss College affairs, Owen's neurotic Computer Studies
teacher and Paul's one-man band, and when we'd gone as
far as we could with those topics we would discuss hi-fi tips,
CND, Dave Allen, snooker versus darts, police brutality,
graffiti on Finaghy kindergarten outbuildings, good films
beginning with P, Bovril versus Marmite, College life again,
Rugbywankers we would like to see the back of and the
amusing ways that they could die. Whichever topic was
under discussion, Owen, with trademark moderation, would
generally say that it could be worse and might conceivably
get better. Paul, whose debating style was alternately lugubri-
ous and table-thumping, tended to argue that it ought to
be getting better by now, but was in reality getting worse.
Both viewpoints had a lot going for them, and I, who argued
last and least, relished our seminars. Mostly we held them
in the coffee bar, sometimes in corridors. Once we had one
in the University Café, where Paul ordered a beef-and-
tomato Pot Noodle and was told they didn't do Chinese.

Besides boosting my spirits, the seminars effectively spelt
the end of the Virgins. Owen's defection to our triumvirate,
coinciding with the absenteeism of Isobel and the frequent
no-shows by stardom-sidetracked Mark Coates, had sent
Caroline Howard scurrying into the clutches of Bigots for
her daily fix of malignant tumour humour. Agnostic Piers
Mawhinney was left high and dry. The Famous Five's
empire had crumbled – and not before time.

'How could someone with your intelligence ever call
yourself a Virgin?' I asked Owen one day.

'That was Piers,' he said dismissively. 'He's all right to
hang around with, but you wouldn't want to spend any
time with him.'

'It's funny, isn't it, how friends come and go. You think they're for life, but . . .'

'*You* might,' he shut me off.

In Brooke-Taylor's Latin classes I maintained surveillance over Isobel, watching with Ian Bailey from across the ancient rotting red wood desks as her lovebites faded day by day. I hated to think who had put them there. Still she declined to follow me to the sixth-form centre after class (though it was perfectly apparent where I was going), merely doing her usual disappearing act as soon as the bell rang. She was ostracizing herself, but she couldn't run from Caroline and her new Presbyterian sidekicks for ever. The College was not the place for Isobel to find sanctuary from sociopaths. As Bailey was fond of saying, you can only so stay so long in a bike shed before some prick asks you for a ride.

There was no word from Andy.

The 1981–82 generation of sixth-form prefects and coffee bar staff was appointed on September 21. In a major shock, Owen polled enough votes from the Middle Sixth to earn himself two hours of bar duty on Tuesday and Friday mornings. 'Power at last,' he exulted. I made him promise to outlaw the Bible, encourage Satanists to make themselves known to the management, spurn all requests for Rush LPs and govern in accordance with a South American formula of corruption and extortion. The acne-ravaged boy took to politics like an old hand.

'Let me test you,' I said. 'How much is a Bounty?'

'Nine pence to some customers, no pence to others. There will be a special rates tariff with respect to sixth-formers in a higher tax bracket, which I will be implementing ruthlessly.'

'How much is coffee?'

233

'Ten pence to some customers, no pence to others. I refer you to my previous statement.'

'My name is Caroline Howard. How will I be served?'

'Rudely, and after I've served everyone else who's waiting.'

Later that day, Leckie found us conferring on a window-ledge in the History block and thought we might be freezing him out of the triumvirate. We explained that we were compiling a list of records for Owen to play on Tuesday morning.

'Bowie — where do you want to start?' Owen said. '*Ziggy. Aladdin. Hunky. Station.* Basically everything. Lou Reed — *Transformer, Coney Island Baby, Street Hassle.*'

'This is is just a rough guide,' I told Leckie. 'Obviously things may change.'

'Kraftwerk,' Owen read out. '*Computer World, Trans-Europe Express, The Man Machine.*'

'Put down Jean-Luc Ponty,' Leckie suggested. 'There's a live album he did that redefines the phrase "mind-blowing".'

'The Stones — basically everything,' I said. 'The Byrds — greatest hits up to the point where they went country. Dylan — up to and including *Desire.* Love — *Forever Changes* and the first side of *Da Capo.*'

'Talking Heads,' Owen took over. '*Remain in Light, Fear of Music, More Songs About Buildings and Food.* The Undertones — everything. The Human League — "Love Action". Teardrop Explodes — *Kilimanjaro* and "Passionate Friend" if we can find it in Good Vibrations. The Tom Tom Club — "Wordy Rappinghood". Squeeze — everything. Elvis Costello — everything.'

'Billy Cobham,' said Leckie. 'Double bass drums. I'll bring you in a live album he did.'

In the event Tuesday morning was here and gone so quick that Owen had time to play only three and a half records from our finished list. All the same, drinking on-the-house coffees to a soundtrack of *Armed Forces*, *Aladdin Sane*, *Transformer* and side one of the new George Harrison album made Leckie and me feel like lords, and although neither of us said it, I knew we were both thinking that the sixth-form centre was much the better for being a corrupt democracy in which he and I finally had a vote.

It was into this improved environment that suntanned Mark Coates came slouching on September 25 after Friday-morning Biology. Owen, who'd been dispensing randomly priced food and drink behind the counter since nine-thirty, greeted him politely but guardedly. Paul and I were listening to Carlos Devadip Santana and Mahavishnu John McLaughlin's *Love, Devotion, Surrender* on the speaker above our heads, and arguing that it was a *tour de force*, a pile of muso shit, an album that redefined the phrase 'landmark collaboration' and a pile of muso shit.

At the counter I saw Coates make a salacious gesture to Owen from his groin area. His twice-postponed party was now confirmed for Saturday night, when this time his parents were absolutely definitely going to be out. And just to rub our noses in the fact that we were not invited, he now wended his way, a Cup-a-Soup in one hand and a Toffee Crisp in the other, over to me and Leckie.

'Seen the price of these things?' he complained. 'Fifteen pee for a piece of chocolate? Outrageous. And these have gone up to twenty.'

He seemed undecided about whether or not to sit down. In their formative years Mark had been sadistic to Leckie, nicknaming him Stabilizers for his lumbering gait and – during break-times – pelting him with confectionery to make him overbalance. These were violations it was difficult to apologize for in later life, even if Mark had wanted to. And so, like the pylon-esque eleven-year-old Leckie in the face of a midget gem bombardment, Mark remained standing.

'I suppose you know I'm having a party tomorrow,' he said in my direction.

I feigned disinterest. 'Oh it's on, is it?'

'Aye, it's on.'

'Yeah. I wondered if it was on.'

'Aye, it's on. I'm having it tomorrow.'

'Is that so.'

'It is.'

Unaware of the subtlety of the situation, Leckie produced a diary from the pocket of his blazer. 'What time do you want us there, Mark? I don't think you ever gave me your address, by the way.' He flipped to the back pages. 'I'll put you under M, that's what I'll do. Fire on.'

With only a moment's hesitation Coates nodded to me and said, 'He knows it. Don't park in the driveway and don't bring any Finaghy wank-dogs into my house. Decadents on at ten.'

Then he marched out of the coffee bar with his Cup-a-Soup and his Toffee Crisp, turning left up the stairs. *Well well well*, I thought.

'An invitation,' said Leckie, putting his diary away.

'Sounded like one to me,' I had to admit.

That afternoon, as I headed back to the sixth-form centre after History, I met Coates again in the quad. He was off to the Science block and surprised me by stopping for a word.

'Listen, I don't know if I said this to you,' he began stiffly, 'but thanks for what you did – getting us in the band and everything. I know I took the mickey out of you for that letter, but I mean . . . aw, well. Thanks.'

'Any time,' I said, confused.

'Right. Good man yourself.'

'Don't mention it.'

'Thanks anyway.'

'Pleasure.'

'And you know about the party tomorrow, so *yeah* . . . come on lads . . . *rock-and-fucking-roll,*' he chanted, swaying from side to side. 'Oh yes. Mark has a nice wee girlie from the Boat Club lined up for his carnal delectation. All shipshape and Bristol fashion. Up periscope, unless I'm very much mistaken.'

'I did it for the Decs, though, not for you,' I said curtly.

'You did it because you're into the band,' he agreed, ceasing his swaying. 'That's fair enough. You can't have a band without a bass guitar, can you, fucking not even Showaddywaddy. You know that and I know that. I just couldn't understand why you wrote your letter. But fair enough, you had your reasons. I know that.'

I answered carefully, remembering my reasons. 'I've always liked writing letters. You can say more in them.'

'And fair enough,' Mark stressed. 'You know that.'

He was being very conciliatory all of a sudden. At his suggestion I consented to walk with him to the Physics labs and have a wee natter. It transpired that he was in a quandary.

'See when I was away in Barbados?' he said as we passed under the canopy which would take us into the Music block and lead us through long westbound corridors to Science. 'Something must have happened with the band. Everything's been different since I got back. I was only away for two weeks.'

'Nice tan, before I forget.'

'Do you like it?' He lifted his profile and I noticed a faint mark at the throat. 'Andy's not too keen. He told me I look like Barry Manilow.'

237

'Andy can be quite vindictive when it comes to suntans,' I said sympathetically. *Surely that is not a lovebite*, I was thinking. 'He styles himself as an anaemic androgyne,' I went on, 'being very thin and pale for an English person as you know. Although in my opinion he's more of a foppish bohemian. I suppose it comes down to skin tones.'

Mark held a door open for me with his elbow and now we were in the bicameral Corridor D, a pair of gigantic gymnasiums to either side.

'I hope the two of you haven't fallen out?' I said.

'Well, see . . . I don't know. I'm sort of baffled. All he does is blank me or act funny since I got back. We never practise or get together with Dermot and Rob or nothing. You know the last time we ever played? That party. Not a phone-call from him to say, "Oh, let's do a practice" or "Oh, let's get together with Dermot and Rob".'

'He's never seen practising as being important,' I affirmed. 'For him it's the performance that counts.'

We advanced into Corridor E – cloakrooms and Art – where I held a fire door open for Mark with my knee.

He grumbled on: 'I know he has the phone number because I gave it to him. I said to him, "We're not in the book but it's easy to remember, it's only two fucking numbers to get right." And he rang me on the Saturday to go out so I know he's got it written down. But he won't call me any more and I went round there last week – I said, "Listen, the party's definitely on for the twenty-sixth" – and he went, "Oh, right" and just shut the door in my face. Right in my face. *Goodbye*, clunk. It was wild. You said he goes a bit depressed or a bit moody – so is that normal?'

I reflected. 'Not as such. I suppose he might be depressed about his A-levels. Did he not get into Queen's?'

'He starts there in a week. He got three Bs.'

'Three Bs,' I said under my breath. 'Gosh . . . good for him.'

Suddenly Mark put out an arm as a barrier, stopping me in my tracks. From a cloakroom at the end of Corridor E a trio of girls had emerged in shorts and netball bibs. They pranced towards us, a little Gail Tilsley-faced third- or fourth-former flanked by two dark-haired Amazonian giraffes who looked about twenty-five. I was afraid that Mark would wolf-whistle his appreciation or do the hideous thing with his pocket where he pretended to have become erect.

'Mind how you go, ladies,' he said unctuously.

'Get to fuck,' the little one replied.

We resumed our journey, soon reaching a fork at which we made a right turn into Corridor F. Instantly, a black Dracula wing-span of billowing cloak bore down on us – a head of department flying back to base – but Mark's step did not falter and the old man swept by without comment. Corridor F led us through fire doors into Corridor F2.

'I haven't been down this way in years,' I said with some distaste. The wall to my left was lined with animal cages; I realized we were smack in the middle of Biology. 'Science was never my forte. It wasn't even my thirté.'

'Gerbils,' Mark observed humourlessly. 'Bastards shit everywhere. You can smell them a mile away.'

Walking briskly, he looked pensive in profile and still there was that unidentified blemish at his throat. *Surely not a lovebite. Not from the teeth of a sentient human being.* I'd heard you could self-inflict them with a vacuum cleaner in desperation. In desperation Mark would do that. And in desperation I wondered how Isobel had inflicted hers.

'There's something else,' Mark said as we came to yet more fire doors which opened into Corridor GI. 'His love

239

life's a disaster. I went into town with him in the holidays and he was in a phone-box in Great Victoria Street just screaming at this girl down the phone. "You can fuck right off . . . don't you come near me again . . . consider this your last warning." Who was he going out with?'

I looked back to make sure we were alone. 'I'm not actually at liberty to reveal that information,' I said quietly. 'Security reasons.'

'Oh what!' Mark exclaimed. 'Is she a *peeler*? Was he screwing a peeler?'

'*No* . . . for God's sake,' I winced. 'Andy wouldn't screw . . . wouldn't have a relationship of that kind with the police. Give the fellow some credit.'

'Well, who then?'

Corridor G1 ended. We were briefly in the open air for the first time since meeting in the quad. At the entrance to Corridor G2 there was a toilet for male Physics teachers. Mark said, 'Let's go in here' and we ducked inside. I assumed we were going to talk, but Mark immediately unzipped his flies and stood at the urinal.

'Aaaaaaaaaaah,' he said, splashing noisily. 'Well, whoever she is I pity her. Because I wouldn't want to be screamed at like that, if it was me. He was going – you know what he did? He took his boots off in the phone-box and he was screaming at her, "Want them back? I'll stuff them down the fucking phone to you right now." He was wild.'

Mark stopped splashing and zipped himself back up. Then he turned to me with a look of chagrin. 'But there's another aspect to this that I haven't told you.'

'Oh . . . ?'

'Aye. I've been lending him money.'

'*Eh?*'

'I've been a fucking mug, I know. It started the night of that party and it's all been adding up. Fags, records, fuck knows what. I'm not sure what to do.'

'How much money?' I asked warily. 'A tenner? Less? More? Two figures?'

'Double.'

'Double a tenner?' I said. 'Twenty?'

'No, double two figures. Eighty-eight pound seventy-five.'

'Jesus Christ.'

Mark sighed. 'He was going to pay me back out of his grant but now he won't even let me in his house.'

'I see.'

I did not. Andy had borrowed eighty-eight quid off Coates – in the space of two months. Andy had borrowed eighty-eight quid off Coates – in the space of two months.

'And that's in the space of two months?' I said.

'Not even that, six weeks. Eighty-eight pound seventy-five he's had off me. Booze, tapes, fuck knows what.'

I swallowed with difficulty. 'Jesus Christ. Hang on, I need to think.'

But Andy, come on, we were only going to fleece him for the money to make a record in a studio. To make a single, Andy, because his family's loaded. Just like I told you in the letter.

'Go back to the beginning,' I said to Mark. 'Tell me what happened at the party.'

MARK'S STORY

Mark is 17. He lives with his parents in south Belfast. His hobbies include the bass guitar, the ladies (for whom he has a roving eye) and money. Heroes: Bruce Foxton, James Hunt. Favourite food: chips in

curry sauce. Hates: self-righteous people (they know who they are).
Would like to be remembered as: someone who lived each day to the
maximum.

Well, what happened was, I left my bass and my amplifier
at his house after the practice and I went home in the
minicab. You told me he'd give me the money back for
that, I remember you saying that, in fact I made a note of
that – so the next day, when I got to his house at eight
o'clock, I sort of casually told him that he owed me the
money for the minicab and for buying a new lead for my
bass. I didn't charge him for the money for the plectrums.
He says to me, 'I am absolutely buggered if I know what
you're talking about,' or whatever it was that he said. So
I told him about you saying I could charge for my expenses.
Rob and Dermot were upstairs in the attic, right, and I
was standing with Andy in the hall. He goes, 'Come up
to my room, I want to show you something.' We're going
upstairs and he says, 'How well do you know him?' Meaning you. 'How well do you know him?' 'Well,' says I, 'I
do and I don't. I wouldn't say he was a mate.' Here's
Andy: 'No. Nor would I.' I'm just telling you the truth.
So we're in his bedroom and he shows me a letter – 'Read
this.' He said you'd given it to his mother. 'Read that and
all will become clear. The kid is fucking mental.' It really
was a mental letter, you know. But like I said, you had
your reasons – fair enough. He says, 'That kid has been
following me and pestering me since I formed this band.'
He says to me, 'Mark, that kid is skating on thin ice.' He
goes, 'Mark, I want rid of him. I cannot have people
writing letters like that to me.' So I'm sort of agreeing
with him because it really was a fucking mental letter. And

he says, 'I know he put you forward for the band – let's not take that away from him – but you must disregard everything else that he tells you. That letter was not written by someone who has any grip on reality. As to where he gets this idea that I can refund your expenses, I simply don't know. The fact is, Mark, I am flat broke and always have been. That guitar I play cost fourteen quid. It's not even a copy of a copy. Oh no. It's a copy of a *copy* of a copy.' Then he tells me that if he gets into Queen's he'll be on the full grant because his family's got fuck-all dough. He goes, 'It'll be the first time I've had more than two pound notes to rub together in my life.' And he starts explaining that his dad walked out the door one day and him and his mum and his sister have been eating sardines on toast for the last four years. He's keeping his voice down so his mum and his sister can't hear, because he doesn't want them getting upset on his sister's birthday. He says, 'Mark, I'll tell you as a friend. I've occasionally had to go shoplifting just to put food on the table.' I'm looking round his bedroom thinking, well, your house doesn't look too bad, and he catches me looking and he says, 'Friends can be so kind. Lending me records, books . . . but it's no use. I can't go on being a burden to them. And of course I won't see most of them again once they go off to university in England.' He tells me not to say any of this to Rob and Dermot, they'd leave the band if they knew he was telling me about all the records and books they've been lending him. He goes, 'They insisted on complete confidentiality. Can you believe it, Mark? They wanted to spare my feelings. That's the character of those boys for you.' Then he takes your letter back off me and he goes, 'And now this kid, who has the audacity to call himself a friend of mine, who knows fine well that every day is a struggle for me and my family, writes me a letter about how difficult *his* life is – *his* life, not mine – and then he fucking twists the knife by offering you money that he knows I am not able to give you. And this bit . . .' He's reading out the letter. '"When we are established in London, we will discuss plans for breaking the Decadents in America, mainland Europe and other continents."' He goes, 'Is he doing that deliberately, Mark? Poking fun at my family's financial problems and having a great laugh at our expense? Is that his idea of friendship?'

So then he says, 'And you know what makes me really angry? That kid is going to be here later on. Watching. Gloating. Bringing everybody down. Oh, he won't even mention the letter – no, he'll be too cunning for that. He'll pretend that he didn't write a letter. He will say nothing about a letter.' And I have to be honest here, it was me that said to him, 'Why don't you put it up on the wall? For the kid to see. And you can read bits of it out during the set, in between the songs.' So Andy, like, punches me in the chest and goes, 'You mean I should put this letter up on the wall in the attic, so that he sees it when he comes up to gloat at us? And then we'll tell him we're going to read bits of it out downstairs during the gig? Could we do that? Wouldn't that be rather cruel?' 'Would it fuck,' says I. 'The kid's got to be taught a lesson.' I'm just telling you the truth, you know? So Andy says, 'You're right. I hadn't thought of it like that, but you're right.'

Anyway, we go up to the attic and Andy shows the letter to Rob and Dermot, saying you had the audacity to write this letter about how you were going to take over managing the Decadents and how you were probably going to kick Rob and Dermot out of the band. So they're furious and they're calling you a cunt. Then Andy says, 'Let's not tell him we know that. Let's be as cunning as him. Let's be really obnoxious to him but not tell him why.' So we all agree that's what we'll do.

Anyway, you know what happened. We had our dinner, which was spaghetti because Andy said it was a special occasion, and Dermot ran out and bought beer, and then you turned up. So then you tore down the letter and you fucked off and it was just the four of us. Andy goes, 'How annoying. He's taken the letter, so now we can't read it out during the gig. I didn't realize he'd be that cunning.'

So we go downstairs and get up and play. Fucking great laugh it was – I forgot one of the songs and just played the same note over and over again. Andy said it was inspired and could I do it that way all the time? It was a shame that Piers and Caroline weren't there, but anyway. Isobel was there but that's another story. And . . . so then Andy asked me to lend him a fiver. After the gig. I said, 'What for?' He said, 'To pay Dermot back for the beer. Or else Dermot's going to be out of pocket, and he has to get back to Saintfield. But don't say anything to Dermot or he'll know I told you.' I didn't really understand what he meant but I lent him the fiver. I'm going, 'So am I lending this to you or giving it to you?' Andy goes, 'Mark, what did I say upstairs? About being on the full grant? Have you any idea how much money I'm going to have in October?' So I thought fair enough, and I lent him the fiver thinking I'd get it back in October.

That's how it started. Then on the Saturday he phoned me up and said, 'Oh, let's go record-shopping.' I met him on the Malone Road and we went to Good Vibrations, and to Knights – ah! he did a really strange thing in Knights I'll tell you about in a minute – and then we went to a few places in the city centre. This was the first time I went record-shopping with him. The second time was the time he made the phone-call to his girlfriend, that was a Saturday near the end of July. The first time, we were shopping and he wanted to buy an album in Good Vibrations. I think the band were called the Fall. He goes to me, 'Oh, that's quite cheap. Lend us a fiver.' So that's two fivers he wants off me. And I'm going, 'I hate to do this to you again, but am I lending this to you or giving it to you?' And he says, 'Mark, October. Think of October.' So I lent him the other fiver.

I'm going to be really late for Physics. Fuck it, I'll say I was puking up blood and I went to the san.

But let me tell you what happened in Knights. You know they do second-hand albums there? So he's standing beside me while I'm pulling out these albums and looking at them, and he's going, you know, 'pitiful . . . dreadful . . . abysmal'. Every album, he just slags the hell out of it. 'Oh, don't buy that, for God's sake.' Then I pull out this album with a really good cover, they were called the Elevators or something. No, the Thirteen Elevators. No, wait, I've got it. The Thirteenth Floor Elevators. Really strange-looking album, like they were a . . . I don't know, fucking mental cases or whatever. I just wanted it for the cover, you know? I was going to have it as like a painting up in my room. I'm quite artistic in that sense, to be fair. So Andy – and so I've put the album under my arm – and Andy rips it out from under my arm and throws it back in the . . . in the . . . in the, you know, back with all the other albums. The racks, aye. So I go, 'What did you do that for?' And he goes, 'I thought for a terrible moment you were going to buy that.' I go, 'I *am* going to buy it.' He goes, 'Oh no you're not. Not if you want to be in my band.' So I just thought fair enough, it must be a shit album and he doesn't want me listening to it. But see later on? After I'd lent him more money so we could go for a pint in a wee pub round the back of C&A? We had two pints and I said goodbye to him and he said goodbye to me. He said he was going to meet someone and could I lend him another three quid? So I did, thinking ... October. Then I went back up to Knights because I wanted to buy the album by the Thirteenth Floor Elevators that has the nice cover that I want for my wall. I don't want the album, I want the cover. So I'm walking up Botanic Avenue and who do you think's up ahead of me, going into Knights? Andy. Fuck knows where he came from, but there he was. So I just stayed outside and went a few doors down to look in windows, because I didn't want him to see me in Knights getting that album he doesn't want me to get. A minute later he comes out and I think, right, I'll go in – he's off up towards Queen's, he won't see me. So I go in and I look for the album, but it's gone. It's not there any more. And I'm looking every-where for it – in all the racks, aye – and I ask this guy who's working there, 'What happened to that Thirteenth Floor Elevators album I saw in here about three hours ago?' He says, 'I sold it just now. The guy who just went out the door.' I says, 'What? The kid with the dark glasses? Him? Just now?' He goes, 'Aye, that's him.'

So the cheeky bastard told me not to get the album because he wanted to go back and get it himself. And I'm a fucking mug for lending him the money to get it. God, look at the time. Listen, I'd better head off. I'm going to tell Dinsmore I was knocked down by a car in Chlorine Gardens, okay, and you were a witness. Back me up if he goes and asks you am I lying. Look, definitely come to the party tomorrow and see us. But don't say anything to Andy about the money or I might never get any of it back. Oh, and don't talk to Rob or he might take a bottle to you. He's okay really but he'll probably call you a cunt.

The Coalition of Glass manifesto dropped through the letter-box on Saturday morning. There was no envelope – just a typed sheet of paper with my name and the number 00019 written at the top. My father, who picked it up and left it for me on the hall table, wanted to know what the deuce or dickens Coalition of Glass was.

'Band,' I explained, racing back upstairs.

'Lovely chatting with you,' he called out after me.

In my room with the curtains drawn and the TV on, I deliberated my seating options for precisely one second (bed? armchair? bed?) and chose armchair. Now make decision about TV. Off? On? If on, how loud? Hurry up quick make decision about off or on and if on how loud.

Off.

I would read the Coalition of Glass manifesto in silence – yes, that was a logical thought – so as not to miss the significance of any of it. But I'd need to make a mental realignment to absorb the significance of new data, for my head had been seething all night with Andy and Mark and old data. So an equally logical thought was that interference from the TV could just as easily be welcome as not, particularly in realignment terms.

On.

'I mean, you've only got to hear the roar when you walk out on to the park to know that with them behind you giving us that support, it's more than a football match, it's in the blood up here. This is their cup final and we have to respect that.'

Unbelievable thing. I'd lost the manifesto. How could that have – I had it a minute ago – where could it have – I had it in my hand – where had the bloody manifesto gone? Ah, there it was in my hand. That was a relief.

'I take it passions run high on a day like today?'

'Well, what I say to the players is get out there and feel it. Get a taste of it. We have the grit and the determination. Do we then have the patience is another matter.'

From now on, seven mugs of coffees, absolute limit. Seven and no more. Absolute limit. Eight's too many – never again. Scary scary heartbeat. Stop at seven in future. Learning all the time. Nothing to worry about. That's the boy. Get a taste of it.

'Nine points between you in the table. Is that going to be a factor?'

'I don't see it being a factor. Local derbies are never about the form book, they're about who can cope with the pressure on the day. There's been a lot of nil–nils here, one–nils over the years, the odd goal deciding it. I see it being an even contest with the odd goal possibly being the decider.'

What a mess this place is. Somebody should come in and do some tidying up round here. Sheets of A4 just strewn on the carpet around the armchair. I could make a start, though. I could gather the sheets of A4 up, put them in order and slide them into the purple folder – this one that says THE PLAN on the front. I could seal the folder with a rubber band. That took longer than I thought. Had a spot of trouble with the rubber band.

'And one final question. Anderlecht on Wednesday?'

'*Again, if we go there and believe, I see no reason why not. I've said all along that we're there on merit, so let's go out there and play like we know we can do.*'

Now we're back in business. Now we're open all hours. Just move the coffee mug here, and there's the rewritten apology letter on the carpet. Neatly covered in red biro where I made my queries and underlinings last night. Fold the letter. Oh, it's already folded. Get *Billy Liar* out of the bookcase. Place the letter between the pages. *Billy Liar* goes back in the bookcase, like so. That didn't take too long.

I know a Billy Liar. He doesn't want to go to London either. He'd rather live in the provinces and die never knowing. Seven's his absolute limit. Personally I'm different. Personally I'm an eight man. Personally I'd handcuff myself to Julie Christie the minute we're on the train, and then we'd maybe see about some coffees.

'*And these headlines in the papers this morning. Do you think he really means to pay the money back in October?*'

'*If that's what he's saying, then I have to take his word for it. The lad's been adjudged to have borrowed the money in good faith, so he's innocent until proven guilty in my eyes.*'

Eighty-eight pounds seventy-five. That's a four-figure sum. Ha ha ha ha ha.

'*But people will be asking how you explain the phone-call in Great Victoria Street. They're bound to speculate on the identity of the person he was having the relationship with, surely?*'

Yes . . . I'm still no closer to the truth there. Mark must have got his wires crossed. He doesn't know what I know. But as much as I know, I'm still no closer to the truth there.

'*People will always speculate. It's human nature to say, "Oh, X has happened so therefore Y and Z." But until we get a comment from the lad, I think we owe it to him to sit these rumours out and not jump in with any accusations. We don't want another wild-goose chase like we had with the lad Karl Marks, where everybody was pointing the finger.'*

Well, that's nonsense for a start. I know who Karl Marks is. He's the drummer that got beaten up by Luke. Whack whack whack. Vengeance is mine said the Lord.

'So best to play it nice and easy at the party tonight?'

'Best to play it nice and easy, and I'm sure we'll find there's not a shred of evidence. I've known the lad a long time and he's always been straight down the line.'

Not a shred of evidence. Self-confessed shoplifter, embezzler and small-town deceiver. Not a shred of evidence.

'Would you even bring up the subject of the Thirteenth Floor Elevators album? That's had a few people wondering.'

Self-confessed shoplifter, shirt-lifter and cheeky bastard. Him with the dark glasses.

'Like I say, until we get a comment from the lad I don't think there's any sense in speculating. Let's wait for the lad to comment. That's his prerogative and he's entitled to a fair hearing.'

Do you irritate your players too, may I ask? Because you're beginning to irritate me.

Off.

I'll read the manifesto in silence. That would be the logical thing.

I was looking in my record collection for instrumental albums. I didn't want silence after all, I wanted a comforting ambience for manifesto reading. I searched my collection for harps, piccolos, chimes, glockenspiels, uillean pipes, mandolins . . .

Couldn't even find a fucking clarinet.

There seemed to be no instrumental albums in my collection. This was a serious oversight, because you never knew when you were going to need an instrumental album.

Ah . . . I remembered how the error had arisen. It had been a day of April showers and ponderous Doris Lessing; a typical skirmish in the Great Record Collection Purge of 1979. After school I paid a visit to Knights with a bulging carrier bag of records.

'They are all in there?' a German acquaintance of mine sought to reassure himself. '*Tubular Bells*? *Hergest Ridge*? That Chieftains one, I hope? Deep Purple's *Concerto for Group and Orchestra* — such asinine hubris. It is in there?'

'They're all in here. Every instrumental album I own.'

'Good. Now, with the money they give you, you buy Derek and the Dominos, Traffic, Dave Mason, Neil Young, Stephen Stills. Okay?'

'Okay.'

'Classic albums, critically acclaimed. Not music for boys.'

'I still think you're being hard on *Tubular Bells*, Tinmeer. The bit with the caveman is amazing.'

'Overrated exhibitionism,' he spat. 'You have outgrown these follies. You are fourteen. I want you now to be a student of lyrics.'

Oh! how Tinmeer adored lyrics. You'd never seen such adoration of the rock lyric form. And what Tinmeer adored, I too had to adore, whether I liked it or not. For a guru so peremptory and elliptical, it was curious that he found joy in the words of others: Dylan, Joni Mitchell, Van Morrison, Robbie Robertson. I'd never taken much notice of lyrics before I met Tinmeer, except to check that they rhymed and sounded reasonably poetic. Tinmeer, however, shot all my poetic lyricists down in flames.

'Jon Anderson. *Jon Anderson.* Are you making fun of me? He just gets out a dictionary and writes down words that he thinks look interesting.'

'Jon Anderson's a prophet,' I argued. 'Bob Dylan couldn't have come out with "Siberian Khatru". It's like a poem because it lets you use your imagination, but it also fits in really well with the music. Talk about skill.'

Tinmeer snorted. 'How many Yes albums do you have?'

'Six.'

'Put them in the carrier bag. We sell them tomorrow after school. Who else do you say is a poet?'

'Well . . . Peter Gabriel, obviously.'

'*Peter Gabriel?* Peter Gabriel could not write a phone number. We sell the Genesis albums too. Who else?'

'Ian Anderson from Jethro Tull,' I said categorically. 'At least three of their albums are concept albums, and *Aqualung* is all about how we shouldn't just be religious without asking a few damn good questions first. You can't sit there and tell me that Ian Anderson isn't a genius.'

'Get the Jethro Tull albums and put them in the carrier bag.'

Tinmeer won the day. By December 1979 I had no instrumental albums in my collection, and no prog rock albums either. I had known him just a year and he had cleaned me out. On his instructions I had bought more Dylan and Van Morrison LPs than I knew what to do with. Tinmeer said he was proud of me.

Oh, but I do have some instrumental music, Tinmeer. I've just remembered. How remiss of a Bowie fan to overlook side two of Low. *Even you liked side two of* Low, *my Germanic friend. Even you.*

The trouble with side two of *Low* was that it was not comforting ambience. It was nightmare ambience. With side two of *Low*, I was liable to have my head filled with visions of Poland in 1939, and Wojtek, and me and Andrzej practising the secret knock. I couldn't read the manifesto listening to side two of *Low*. Side one of *Low*, yes, but not side two.

I had to have instrumentals. The manifesto demanded them. Should I scamper downstairs to the lounge and ransack the light classical repertoire? But that would be an insane move on only three glasses of water. I'd get dragged into an interrogation about mock A-levels and UCCA handbooks and revision strategies, and in which sort of area — *sit back and relax, we're just attaching these electrodes to you as a purely routine precaution* — I felt that my future profession or indeed vocation might lie in a manner of speaking.

Fuck that.

I put on side two of *Low*. In minutes the room resounded to panzer synthesizers and cellos in jackboots. I was Jan the orphan. The manifesto would have to wait for the danger to pass.

Andrzej and his tubercular brother Wojtek had hidden themselves in the cellar, as usual. I had a shawl for the winter ahead. Wrap myself tight and the blithering thugs would mistake me for an old woman. Andrzej and I had been practising the secret knock since dawn: two raps, a pause and a rat-a-tat-tat.

Now they were coming. Here was the crunch of a heel on debris. Crunch, crunch, crunch . . .

Oh, if only Wojtek would stop coughing.

Fifth glass of water. Tee-shirt damp at the base of my spine. Side two of Low *almost over.*

The manifesto was typed on a grey background that could have been a photograph of four-day-old snow. The more the drifting, formless shapes of side two's closer 'Subterraneans' folded themselves around me, the more subversive the manifesto's typography looked. I had the sense that it was an underground communiqué that had already put many of its readers in grave peril.

Coalition of Glass

We are the Coalition of Glass.
Shatter-proof. Crystalline. A mirror.
Your mirror.
   We are the Coalition of Glass.
Allies in art. Nations coexisting. Belfast the new Phnom Penh. Paramilitaries = Pol Pot. Sectarianism is a war crime.
   Sloth = individualist nonintervention. Suicide = ignorance. Death to glue. Death to glue-sniffers. We are the Coalition of Glass.
   We are the Coalition of Glass. *Viva* the writer, the typewriter, the written word. *Viva* Wilde Blake Kafka Kesey Pinter Beckett Fitzgerald Hemingway. *Viva* images (but not image). *Viva* Dali Buñuel Godard Roeg Russell Fassbinder Herzog.
   Death to J. M. Synge and Planxty. Death to the *bodhran*. Death to phoney warriors. Green Rock = the regurgitated panacea. Anti-Lynott guerrilla music coalition. We are the Coalition of Glass . . .

The manifesto continued in this style for several paragraphs. Then came the personnel:

```
Richard - vox
Keith - guitars etc.
Lawrence - bass guitar
Alastair - the beat
```

Parts of the manifesto were restated towards the bottom of the page. Death to . . . *viva* . . . we are a coalition . . . we are a mirror . . . your mirror. It ended:

```
We are all in it together. The type-
writer. The word. The Coalition of
Glass.
```

I was puzzled and disappointed. They had explained nothing about their songs or their musical influences, or their previous incarnation as Radical Jive. They'd put in nothing about Karl Marks. Nothing about how they had met each other or where they lived. No mention of upcoming gigs. No surnames or birthdates.

They hadn't included enough info.

Saturday, 3.40 p.m.

Foetal position on the carpet. Tired. TV back on. No sound.

I'd known for some time that I would have to resolve the fatigue problem if I were ever to stand a chance of escaping. Insomnia had plagued me for too long, and depriving myself of sleep until I keeled over in History was not the solution. In recent days a note had appeared on the bedroom door sarcastically requesting my presence at dinner one of these nights, 'or breakfast if you prefer'. It was the first sign of my family having the ill grace to impugn my nocturnal revision strategy.

But Owen said I'd been shaking awfully in the coffee bar, so maybe the *Sarcastistas* were right. Mrs Idge, too, had told me I looked 'done in', and advised me to heed my biorhythms and retire after Benny Hill – as she herself did – with a hot drink and a Ngaio Marsh. 'Every hour we sleep before midnight is worth two after. I tell all my nephews and nieces that.' (Yes, but presumably she didn't set her nephews and nieces a hundred pages of homework in the evenings. In any case, I could never face homework before I a.m. The fear was too great.) 'You'll feel more healthy, full of the beans. Why do you think they shut the television off at night? Because nobody is supposed to be up! Yes? *¿Comprende usted?* Thinking about it?'

And then she read me the solemn judgement of the Spanish examination tribunal. 'Your composition was indifferent. Translation passable but no firework displays. You are not out of the woods yet, Diego.'

'*Gracias, Señora.*'

'*De nada.* Here's another hundred pages of homework.'

Diego couldn't say he enjoyed sleep *per se*, but there were times when he found it infinitely better than being awake. Sleep was a cordon keeping life at bay – which was exactly where Diego thought it should be kept. For instance, if the poor *muchacho* was feeling under the weather – so sleep. If he was angst-ridden because his voice hadn't fully broken

– so sleep. If his transmogrification was wearing off like a transfer, revealing his puny nakedness to outsiders – so sleep. Or if he had allowed a backlog of homework to build up and had no intention of confronting it – sleep. Confront what: Diego's own academic uselessness? Imagine the harm that would do his morale. 'Confront shit,' says Diego. 'So sleep.'

With a weary thumb, I rolled up the TV volume for the half-time football scores. There had been a sending-off in the local derby, but no goalmouth action so far. Anderlecht would demolish them on Wednesday.

Wednesday, I thought haplessly. *Spanish and Latin. Who cares if I live to see it?*

At White Hart Lane, a Tottenham full-back had scored at both ends, turning from hero to villain in sixteen minutes. At Loftus Road, QPR had thrown away a two-goal lead and were now in total disarray. 'It's been Jekyll and Hyde stuff here,' the reporter blared. 'I don't know about Hoops, we've seen plenty of "Whoops". There'll be some choice words in that dressing-room.'

I would have been excited by the half-times in Downburn. I would have run into the kitchen and told everybody the scores. Not all of them would have been true, but you don't go to war with a liar like Clare without becoming a liar yourself. Any football lover knows that seven–four sounds more evocative than two–one. Just as any netball captain knows that 'my dad's in the UDA' sounds more evocative than 'my dad drives a fish van'. The lies we tell as children are a mere rehearsal for the lies we hide behind as adults. I wonder if Clare's married yet, lying to her husband, lying to her kid. 'A sweet princess, I was. Always minded my Ps and Qs, and thin as a rake to boot.'

At the Dell, Southampton had missed a penalty. 'Second week in a row he's skied one over the bar, can you believe it? Tell you what, this crowd can't – we've had invasions, we've had all sorts.' I visualized the red-and-white-shirted culprit on bended knee in the six-yard box, submitting to his agony. Cocking the revolver, holding it to his ear, thinking back to the bungalow and going *bang bang bang bang fucking fucking bang.*

Ohhh Clare. Tinmeer. Andy. Me. Children of Ulster, Hamelin, Hounslow, Dublin. The children of deceit.

I was in the tunnel now, a long way in. I should have been getting into the party spirit for an evening at Coates Towers, but I was in the tunnel.

Saturday, 4.08 p.m.

> So am I a manic depressive?
> That might seem a trifle excessive
> Moody, lovelorn and dark
> Would perhaps be nearer the mark
> Falling and floundering wildly
> Is unquestionably putting it mildly
> Still, my partner in the suicide pact
> In truth and in point of fact
> Appears as yet too inexact
> So alone I must act
>
> Bitter is the void
> Implacable is the crowd
> But the leper walks unbowed
> Downwards, downwards
> To the cross and the shroud
> And a kingdom come destroyed

Fuck this.

Saturday, 7.53 p.m.

My nose was blocked, my mouth parched from airless sleep. I had sweated eight coffees, six waters and three hours of psychotic dreams into my clothes. Only when I was sure that no assassins were near did I rise slowly from the bed and switch on the light.

A change of tee-shirt later, I called in at the lounge to announce that I was 'going for a walk'.

'A walk where? (*Suspiciously*) Where are you going?'

'How do I know? I haven't been there yet. Probably to a friend's house.'

'Well, when you arrive – phone. And be back by eleven.'

'Oh, come on. The party doesn't even . . . I'll try and be back by twelve.' *And out.*

I caught a Malone Road bus and took my pick of thirty free seats, selecting one at the back. Deramore Park South was about a mile away, something like the sixteenth turning on the left. Cranmore Park was the ninth or tenth on the right. To my rear – the College. Six miles due south – Downburn. A bus passed us on its way into town: it was standing-room only.

I'll try and be back by twelve. Yeah, yeah, yeah.

Hardly likely, my friends. Belfast was a city of self-imposed curfews and streets that emptied on the stroke of half-eleven. For the young person who didn't drive and wasn't much good in a fight, going home could be a journey into the abyss. Even on the Malone Road – yes, even with all that leafy prosperity around – gangs came out of the bushes and attacked single girls, duos of boys and boy–girl trios alike. And then darted back into the bushes to wait for the next lot. Some of the attacks were sectarian-related, of course, but many of them were just attack-related; related to the fact that gangs in the Malone Road bushes had appearances to keep up. I'd never been attacked in Belfast myself, but — what was it, September? There was still plenty of time.

I hoped Coates would let me crash at his place. If you were in someone else's house at twenty-five to twelve, your best bet was to stay there all night. Belfast after curfew was full of people sleeping in other people's houses, so nervous were they of the streets that led back to their own. And since I hadn't any cab fare, and since the days had gone when there would have been hospitality for me at the Finns' . . . and since, and since . . .

A cloakroom in Corridor E, March 1978.

'You can't come in.'

'But I need to get changed for PE.'

Andrew Finn, the English boy from the fourth form, had his back pressed against the door. He was much too strong for me. 'I said you can't come in. Bugger off.'

'But I'm late. I just need to get changed!'

'What *you* need is neither here nor there. Bugger off, insect.'

I took a good run at the door and shoved. It opened a crack, letting me see his tousled brown hair, the blue fog halo, the cigarette. 'Oh, you're *smoking* . . . Golly. But look, I won't tell anyone.'

Finn's unnerving eyes peered round at me. They were the kind of eyes that ring a bell with a third-former who's just got to the warpaint bits in *Lord of the Flies*. 'I know you won't. Because you know what'll happen if you do, you lice-ridden pipsqueak. Okay, come in and get changed. Show me some prepubescent arse. Give me some full-frontal nudity.'

'I beg your pardon?'

'*Joke*. Fucking hell. Come in before this thing sets the bloody fire-alarm off.'

Would he recall that encounter? Not a chance. He couldn't even remember Noel Johnston's party in the summer of 1980, where we officially first met. Irksome engagements, dentist appointments — nothing slipped his mind quite as I did. For the past eight months he had been calling me Doug, and I knew it was because he'd forgotten my actual name.

These memories were vivid, like a film I could rewind and re-view but never edit or expurgate, and when back in the here and now I saw his sister through the bus window at Cleaver Avenue, the film was so dazzling that the real-life contours of Denise did not register at once. She was crossing over the road towards Cadogan Park in a state of some distress. Her friend Roberta had both arms around her, pulling her close, and the girls stumbled as though two of their four shoes had lost a heel. Whatever had upset Denise, she was inconsolable. From my window I watched them hobble into Cadogan Park and out of sight.

But Denise, no, I thought, perplexed. *The party's this way. You'll miss the Decadents if you go that way. You'll miss your brother dedicating 'E Minor Song' to you. Turn back. Come this way.*

The Malone Road was the meridian of my life, and it was a night for incongruous spottings along the co-ordinates. I made my second one a few hundred yards to the south, at the junction with Stranmillis Road. The bus slowed to allow a white Volvo out into the main road, but didn't quite stop. The Volvo braked violently, as did the bus, resulting in a volley of horn-beeping from the car driver, a woman with a blonde beehive. I hadn't seen many hairstyles like it in Northern Ireland, and was just starting to wonder if she'd copied it from the B-52s when I noticed the man in the passenger seat. He, too, had prominent hair. With his jet-black rock 'n' roller's quiff he could have signed autographs as the bass guitarist in the Pretenders. But I'd seen that jet-black quiff (and witnessed its soggy collapse) at a Lisburn youth club a fortnight earlier. The man was Lawrence — bass guitar, from Coalition of Glass.

Poor Denise. At that moment I couldn't have cared less about her.

The Volvo pulled out uproariously, streaking away up the Malone Road and disappearing around a bend. 'They're all out tonight, aren't they, love?' said the bus driver to a girl in an anorak sitting near the front. She agreed that they were. 'All the nut-jobs,' he added, and we began to move again.

In a matter of seconds I created a scenario. The Volvo was fleeing an enraged Kawasaki which had chased it all the way up the Castlereagh Road from the Braniel. 'Stop! Vancie wants a word with you!' the helmeted Kawasaki rider had cackled. The beehive had put her foot down, losing Vance at Central Station, doubling back up the Ormeau Road and then taking the embankment. Now she and Lawrence were going to hole up in Belvoir for the night — at her aunt's house — and respray the Volvo green in the morning. 'That's what reality is like for Coalition of Glass,' I whispered to my reflection in the window. 'They're walking a knife-edge.'

The beehive hadn't been at the Lisburn gig, my reflection reminded me. No, because Lawrence had met her only this evening. He had met her this evening and he would ditch her in the morning, because that was what reality was like for Coalition of Glass. They walked a knife-edge and women of all hair-styles flocked to them.

By the time the road straightened, the Volvo was nowhere to be seen. We passed Bladon Drive on the left, my signal to get up from my seat. There were playing-fields hereabouts where I had dodged hockey balls and rugby tackles as a first- and second-former. On Tuesday afternoons in 1976 this part of the Malone Road had been thick with games-hating eleven-year-olds like me, shuffling off chilly mini-buses and dawdling in single file past lush Deramore gardens to their doom. Tonight, though, the playing-fields were quiescent and harmless, and the only pedestrian on either footpath was Isobel Clarke.

She was waiting for a bus into town. I clambered back to my seat and banged hard on the window. Surprised, she managed to look in every direction – to her left, to her right, upwards – apart from mine. Her bedraggled pony-tail put years on her, but . . . well . . . she was still Isobel. And whose teeth would be biting her neck later? No one that I knew. The Middle Sixth had all but disowned her. But if Isobel wasn't going to Mark's party, what was she doing in Malone?

I got off at the next stop. A bus trundled up the road on the other side. At least she would be safe.

Deramore Park South was the longest of the three Deramores – and, Mark had often claimed, the most expensive to buy a house in. There were no prizes for guessing which house was having the party. I hadn't heard 'Hit Me With Your Rhythm Stick' at such ear-splitting volume in all my born days. The neighbours would be apoplectic – unless Mark had given them twenty quid to go out to the Boat Club, which was not unthinkable, though he'd prob-

ably require change from them tomorrow. But maybe Mark
didn't have many £20 notes to go round these days. Maybe
his wealth had been redistributed to an A. W. Finn savings
account at the Allied Irish, or a cardboard box in Cranmore
Park.

I followed the bass line of '. . . Rhythm Stick' along the
row of gardens. None of the other houses had its lights
on. Mark's, however, was lit up like the Stranraer ferry: he
had talked to Owen of hiring in a load of disco gear to
make the party go with a swing, *know what I mean Brammo*,
hur hur. The garage wall of the house next door was aflame
with wheels of pink and orange fire from the Coateses'
open landing window, the rotations of which seemed to
synchronize perfectly not only with the drumbeat of Ian
Dury's famous hit, but also with the hazard lights that had
accidentally been left on in the white Volvo parked outside.

Caroline Howard let me in.

'The toilets are upstairs, or there's another one down the
hall,' she said maliciously. 'I'll be having a piss in about
fifteen minutes if you're interested.'

'Good. You can finish putting on your make-up while
you're in there.'

I jinked past her and pushed through a cluster of hall-
hoggers, remembering the layout immediately. The pristine
kitchen, assembled in silver to Mona's specifications and
appearing somehow capacious despite being filled with all
the Breville and Moulinex time-savers on the market, had
been designated a lonely hearts' zone. So I gathered, anyway,
from the half-dozen morose faces dotted around its per-
imeter. Leaning on the indispensable dishwasher was a boy

in a fur-trimmed parka. Standing by the irreplaceable freezer was Edward Tomelty from Mark's Physics class, a can of Fanta to his lips. Smoking grimly over the resplendent parallelogram of a sink was a woman with a blonde beehive. And slumped against the futuristic and no doubt solar-powered cooker, hugging a bottle of Blue Nun under the watchful eyes of two denim-clad urchins who clearly hoped he would offer them some of it, was Dermot from the Decadents.

'Dermot,' I said hesitantly.

'You like writing things,' he slurred. 'Write me a sick-note. Say I can't play tonight. Say anything.'

'Problem?' I asked solicitously – but my attention was drawn to the beehive's fingers splayed on the draining-board. Bony, near-skeletal, they weren't much wider than her cigarette.

'*Pshhhh.*' Dermot tottered forward. 'Life is a problem.' He reeled backwards, steadying himself. 'See the singer? Cunt. See the drummer? Another cunt. See muggins here?' He thrust the Blue Nun at me like a relay baton. 'I shouldn't even be in Belfast. I should be away to Aberstrythwyth . . . Absterythwyth . . .'

'Bad luck on the A-levels,' I sympathized. 'What did you get, three Fs? No thanks, I can see some Tuborgs in the oven, I'll grab one in a sec. Can you not retake them next June?'

'And stay in this band another year?' he smarted blearily. 'With that cunt? That would be a face worth than debt.'

The beehive was listening to us.

'Was Denise here earlier?' I asked Dermot. 'Is Andy here?'

'Er . . . yes . . . and yes. He's up in Mark's bedroom.

Don't go up there — I really would exercise discretion. I'm not kidding.'

'Has something happened?'

'Oh yes,' he nodded dismally, 'a lot of things have happened. Do you want me to tell you them in chrolojonical order?'

The beehive ran the cold tap and extinguished her fag with a *tisss*.

'The first thing that happened was I got incredibly drunk in the pub with Rob,' Dermot began. 'Then the next thing that happened was Rob got incredibly drunk at the same time as me, because we were in Kelly's getting drunk together. Then what happened after that was . . . we got a carry-out and came here. I can't remember how we got here. I think we walked, 'cause my legs are all stiff. Then Andy and Denise got here. And Andy shouted at me and Rob and said we were a pair of fuckers for being pissed. Then Rob tipped his wine over Andy. Then Denise started crying 'cause some of it went on her. Then Rob hoicked Denise's tee-shirt up off of her and asked if he could wear her bra while he played the drums tonight.'

The beehive raised her eyebrows.

'Bloody hell,' I said. 'Bloody hell . . .'

'That's when Andy kicked Rob in the balls. Denise went off in tears with her mate Roberta to Roberta's house. Rob had Andy on his back punching his head. Then he sacked him out of the band. And he sacked me as well, but then he told me I was back in. It's only going to be me, Andy and Mark playing tonight. And I can barely see this bottle never mind the Yamaha.'

'Where's Robert?' I asked.

'Don't know,' said Dermot miserably. 'He went.'

'And where's the band going to play? Or what's left of the band?'

'The "family room", it's called. You passed it on your way in. It's about the size of Strangford Lough. We set all the stuff up this morning and Andy goes, "We better do a sound check, hadn't we? This is like being at Woodstock." Rob's kit's still there, but he said not ... Hey, do you know this guy or something?'

I'd seen the beehive waggle her bony fingers reproachfully at someone in the doorway. I turned and found Lawrence grinning by my side.

'It's you, isn't it?' he said. 'The wee lad in Lisburn the other night? You live in a Chinese restaurant.'

'Oh hello. I saw your car outside. You left your lights on.'

'A fan,' Lawrence explained to the beehive, who was gliding over to join us. 'He seen us when we were Radical Jive. Says you left the lights on in the car. Can I just get those cans out of the oven, son? Sorry I took so long, there's a mile-long queue up there. This is Michelle.'

'Are you going to be singing some songs for us?' she inquired of Dermot. 'This lad's in a band, sugar.'

I introduced Dermot to them. Lawrence was affable and curious – he had heard about the Decadents from 'the brothers'. He didn't say which brothers, or what they had told him.

'It's not the best night to catch the Decs by all accounts,' I remarked. 'The singer's lost his rag and fired the drummer. They're down to a three-piece temporarily.'

'And they'll be a two-piece after tonight,' Dermot declared with a scowl. 'He can shove his band up his hole sideways. If there's one thing I really object to, it's violence.

268

I thought we were supposed to be against all that punk gang-warfare mentality. Art-school retro with a suburban resonance — that's what I was told we were. And there he is punching Rob like a skinhead. That's me out, well.'

Lawrence twisted three cans from the Tuborg four-pack, passing one to Michelle and one to me. 'Who is this singer, Dermot? He sounds lively.'

'Andy Finn,' I intruded. 'He styles himself as an androgynous frontman in the tradition of Bowie's "Queen Bitch" or Lou Reed circa *White Light/White Heat*. But the songs are quite psychedelic in their structure.'

'Are they? Dead on. I'm into the psychedelia myself.'

'Aye — you listen to all them American groups I can't stand a bit,' Michelle teased him. 'Like the Electric what-are-they-called?'

'Prunes,' smiled Lawrence. 'Great band. "I Had Too Much To Dream Last Night". Know that? Wild song, so it is.'

I wished we could have heard it. In the makeshift disco-thèque overhead, Lene Lovich's 'Lucky Number' was skipping uncontrollably on a turntable under the strain of stamping feet. Someone took it off after the second chorus and put on 'Message in a Bottle' instead. Ah, I thought — one of those '79 nostalgia parties. I'd been to a few. Any minute now, we'd hear the staccato intro to 'My Sharona' and the ceiling would cave in.

'I'll go out and turn the lights off,' decided Michelle, planting her Tuborg on an ornate spice rack. 'Don't anybody start dancing without me. I mean it.'

Turmeric, oregano, cayenne pepper. I wanted to probe Lawrence about the manifesto, but not with Dermot eavesdropping. Paprika, ginger, cloves. And it would be rude to ask what had brought Lawrence and Michelle to Mark's party. Flashing lights and music, you idiot — what else? Mace, sage, chilli powder. If they had gatecrashed, it was no business of mine.

'Do you like the Wah! Heat album?' I asked Lawrence.

'Haven't got it,' he said pleasantly. 'What's it like?'

How the hell did I know? I hadn't got it either. 'Quite varied,' I bluffed. 'They've gone for diversity, but not at the expense of consistency. There are some tracks which benefit from the production side of things, although one or two could have done with less emphasis on commercialism.'

'Are you serious? Wah! Heat have gone commercial? I thought they were really opposed to that kind of thing.'

'Just on one or two tracks,' I reiterated. 'Fortunately the majority aren't commercial in any way at all.'

'I'll give it a listen,' Lawrence mused.

'Do. I've lent my copy to a friend, annoyingly, otherwise you could have borrowed it. They've done a good job of presenting their musical strong points in the best way possible.'

Michelle returned to find myself and Lawrence scrutinizing spice jars. 'So do you need a drummer for tonight, Dermot?' Lawrence piped up. 'Does he have to be any good?'

'Not really,' Dermot shrugged. 'The last one wasn't.'

'Were you thinking about getting hold of Alastair, Lawrence?' I asked, sensing the use of Christian names would impress him.

'Alastair's working tonight,' Michelle said thoughtfully.

'No, Alastair doesn't get off till eleven,' Lawrence agreed. 'No . . . I was thinking about me. I can keep a beat, can't I, kiddo? You've seen me on the kit. I can drum as well as him up there, sure.' He pointed to the ceiling.

'As well as Stewart Copeland?' I exclaimed, startled.

'Oh — is that the Police? Oh, no, I can't then. I was thinking it was fuckin' "Back of My Hand" by the Jags.'

Stick around, I thought. *It soon will be.*

'What do you reckon?' I canvassed Dermot. 'Would Andy be amenable to Lawrence drumming? If Robert's kit is still in the family room and he won't be coming back? And it's not as though the gig's being televised, is it — or reviewed in the *NME*. It could be fun.'

'Let everybody cool down first,' the organist suggested. 'There's been so much shit going on today ... And for God's sake I need to sober up. I'll talk to Andy in a while.'

Lawrence had exchanged a wry look with Michelle when I mentioned the *NME*.

Dermot repeated his warning that I shouldn't disturb Andy and Mark, but I rehearsed a casual greeting in my head and had confidence it would work. I would barge into the bedroom pretending to be looking for Owen, applaud spontaneously at the sight of Andy and congratulate him on getting into Queen's, and then simply wait for Mark to invite me to sit down and make myself at home.

Once settled on the couch or divan, I would let Mark take charge of the repartee, only interjecting observations and/or murmurs of endorsement if and when Andy made an astute comment about some band being shit, or Denise being an angel, or Robert being a dick. Before long Andy would have left the room to patch things up with Dermot downstairs, enabling me to quiz Mark on the latest developments regarding what we'd talked about in the Corridor G2 loos yesterday. Whilst my troubles with Andy appeared insurmountable — given that there was now too big a divide between us — they needn't prevent me from playing a mediator's role in the troubles between Andy and Mark. Not that much could be done at the party. But further down the line.

So up the shag-pile staircase I proceeded, admiring the chandelier, the trophy cases, the framed certificates of Mark's and Jeremy's GCE results on the walls, and — facing intrepid climbers as they gained the mezzanine — the six-foot-by-three-foot oil-painting of the Coates family dated Sept. '75, with Cambridge graduate Jeremy sporting Victorian mutton chops and Mark spruce and carefree in his new College uniform.

The queue for the bathroom tailed back to the topmost stair. No, hold on — that was the queue for the toilet. I continued my ascent. *This* was the queue for the bathroom: remember the heated towel-rails. In 1977, after a cheerless hockey match up the road was truncated by a downpour, I had sprinted here with Piers Mawhinney to dry out and guzzle tumblers of Cidona. We'd been staggered by the Coateses' quality of hygiene. The sons had a bathroom to themselves — which Mark later became sole possessor of when Jeremy toddled off to work Down Under — and his parents luxuriated in an en suite bathroom with jacuzzi and bidet. Mark took extraordinary pleasure in telling Piers what a bidet was.

Up to the first-floor bedrooms. What had been Jeremy's lair was now a coruscating disco that pumped out 'Cool for Cats' to a floor-load of sixth-form louts bent on bawling out the lyrics in Cockney accents to arouse credulous females. And amazingly they were succeeding. At the end of each verse, the girls trilled back the high parts. 'Coooool . . . *for* caaaaaats . . .'

There seemed no point knocking. I cranked Mark's door-knob and swanned in.

Oh Lord.

More people in the bedroom than I'd expected. Roughly eighteen more, in fact. The two inside the door parted for me, frowning at my apology. I recognized one as Malachi O'Neill from Ballynafeigh, with whom I'd had a hugely embarrassing one-minute conversation soon after I started going to parties in May 1980. Left alone with Malachi in a kitchen, I'd panicked and asked him what school he went to. He told me. It had a saint's name. He asked me what school *I* went to. I told him. 'Oh ... right.' Awkward fifteen-year-olds with nothing else to say, we'd stood motionless until he remembered he needed a slash, and the issue of religion mercifully went away with him. In kitchens with strangers now, I always asked them about music. Even if they liked the Piranhas, you could say they were crap and get a dialogue going.

'Cool for Cats' was so muffled with the door closed that I thought the bedroom must be soundproofed. I did a speedy recce. Jesus, where was the host? Beneath a plume of smoke to the left, a group of people reclined on Mark's bed or on the rust-coloured carpet around it. Deep in debate, not one of them looked up. Seconds before I picked out his head amongst all the bodies, I heard Owen evangelizing about a concert he'd been to.

'Honestly, God's absolute truth – it was excellent. For a youth club in Lisburn, it was more like being at some dead important gig in London or Manchester. Packed solid.'

Unable to see Mark or Andy in the throng, I hung back on the outskirts, inclining my head to read book spines on the shelves. 'You should really investigate them, Andy,'

273

Owen urged. 'The singer's almost as big a star as you. I reckon he could be the new Bob Geldof. His moves, I mean . . . the whole attitude of him. Just does not give a shit.'

Mark owned the complete Leon Uris and Douglas Reeman collections. He was also rather an aficionado of James Herriot – there were hardback and paperback editions of *If Only They Could Talk*. He'd probably had them both signed by the author. ('To Mark. If only you could read. Jim.') On the shelf below were Leslie Charteris, Ian Fleming, Len Deighton, Alistair Maclean . . . oh yes, and *Murder on the Orient Express*, which had been the subject of Mark's book-talk in English one drowsy mid-'70s afternoon. ('So if you like Poirot, which I do, he's another reason to read it. But the most magic thing has to be the ending, for me, and well worth waiting for. It's the whole lot of them. They all went in in turns!')

I heard Andy clear his throat, and all at once the harsh rattle acted as a reminder. I was not here to proffer the olive branch; nor for that matter was I guaranteed to receive it. *You're enemies now, you idiot, not friends.*

'Well, frankly, I don't like the sound of this character one little bit. If you want my opinion, I think he and his stooges should sling their hook.'

'Ah, come on, Andy,' remonstrated Owen. 'Honest, the *NME*'s got it absolutely right. These lads are dead political. Here, look – they sent me this in the post.'

A glacial pause ensued as Andy digested the manifesto. I couldn't see him, but I could see the eagerness in Owen. Presently Andy made a contemptuous sound with his teeth.

'Richard! Is this the Richard who has the dopey brother? And the pair of them were in that band with the ridiculous name that played with Berlin? I haven't heard a *word* about them lately — I didn't even know they were still in Belfast. Well, now . . . so those two are back again, calling themselves something else.'

'Do you not like them?' Owen asked, a bit subdued.

'They're like a couple of catatonic animals that somebody's experimented on,' Andy laughed. 'If you think *my* drummer was subhuman you should have seen *their* one. He had the IQ of something you'd see running around a barnyard. I'd like to know who wrote this for them . . . It's a fuck sight too advanced for the brothers. When I knew those two, they weren't allowed to have pencils.'

'Well, we met them after the gig,' Owen pointed out, 'and they seemed fine.'

Don't look at me, Owen. Don't alert the enemy.

Most of Andy's scorn, I could tell from his lexicon, was exaggerated musical jealousy. From Vance Armstrong to Feargal Sharkey, Andy would not countenance the idea that there was anybody in Northern Ireland remotely as original as him. And the best that could be said for Owen's reference to Bob Geldof was that it had been supremely ill-advised. 'What a gormless tosser you can be sometimes,' Andy had fulminated when I bought the Boomtown Rats' *Mondo Bongo* LP in January. 'Take a bow, doughnut.'

But I was galvanized by his expression 'the brothers'. Now I understood who Lawrence had been alluding to in the kitchen — yet I would never have guessed that the narcissistic singer and the diffident, bespectacled drummer were related. Richard was Alastair's brother, and had been looking on helplessly in the Pound the night Alastair was bashed up by Luke Corrigan. I realized I had been wrong. *Both* of them were Karl Marks. A fraternal pact. Retaliation by sibling pen-power. *Viva the written word. Death to the glue-sniffer.*

'Yeah, you see . . . this is the give-away bit,' Andy jeered. 'Where they mention Dali and Buñuel . . . Yeah, this is Richard. It's obviously the same one.'

'Why's it a give-away?' I heard Mark Coates ask. For some reason I felt relieved to know that he was nearby.

'Because about a year and a half ago, I met Richard in the Club Bar when I was going out with Liz. This kid with mad staring eyes sat down at our table and started talking about Salvador Dali and nuclear rhythms. I didn't know what he was on about – but he said he was in a band so we got talking to him. There's some Buñuel film that he did with Salvador Dali that starts with an eyeball being cut open with a razor, and Richard was telling us about what a revolutionary thing it was in the annals of surrealist history. Me and Liz were just laughing at the foolishness of this, and I think we pissed Richard off. Suddenly he whipped out a penknife and held it really close to his eye. He was joking, right, *obviously* – and I knew that Liz knew that – and I just thought if the silly fucker wants to carve his eyeball open, then live and let live. That's his funeral. Anyway, he chickened out of course. He put the knife away and – ha! ha! – he said . . . he said . . .'

'What? *What?*' Owen and Mark were laughing.

'"I am the Peeping Tom. A wink and a blink and I'm gone." Said with a really, really mad stare, I might add. To which Liz and I just sort of looked at each other and thought: finish your drink right now and let's go. This boy is not at all healthy.'

Liz?

'What were the band like?' Owen asked. 'The one he had with his brother?'

Who the fuck is Liz?

'Oh, I can't remember. I think I only saw them once . . . Average. Predictable in that Bunnymen way. A certain amount of intensity. Not a lot of ability.'

Before Owen could pose another question, I stepped forward into the light and said loud enough for everyone to hear, 'That's strange, you know, Andy. They sounded pretty *able* the other night, from what I saw. Is it possible you and *Liz* didn't have the *ability* to make an independent judgement that evening?'

Not one of the all-time great speeches, but it did at least command his attention. In the cluttered bedside alley of legs, arms and beer cans, a head of tousled brown hair bent forward and turned my way. 'Look who it is,' he said wryly. 'The former Mr Yule.'

Though I couldn't repulse the inevitable blush, my instincts told me to go all out for irony. 'Yeah, hi Andy – I've been hearing a lot of good things about your band. They say you're doing a world tour of Lisburn. Will you be playing tracks off all your albums or just the last two?'

He contemplated me with disdain. *This could be vicious*, my instincts counselled. *Take it on the chin, then go for irony again.* 'That's quite a long sentence for you – well done,' he gibed. 'You normally hold forth in squeaks of one syllable, isn't that right? For a minute I thought there was a cat in here.'

A girl sniggered. I noticed Andy's eyes narrowing slightly with satisfaction.

'It probably came in looking for a *mouse*,' I retorted. 'Or maybe it wanted to borrow some *money*. Say about eighty-eight quid – to go and get *cat-food*.'

'Aww, Jesus!' I heard Coates explode. 'Round of applause for the wanker . . .'

'Oi, bass player,' Andy said, turning to Mark indignantly.

'I hope you don't think I'm casting aspersions, but you've invited some extremely undesirable playmates along tonight. And I must say I find your betrayal of my confidence terribly disappointing for a Decadent. It looks as if I'm going to have to do some fine-tuning to the band's line-up over the next few days. You can consider yourself notified of the situation.'

'I want that money back, mate,' Coates said. 'Eighty-eight seventy-five. Owen's a witness to this.'

'Witness?' Andy sneered. 'What is this — Sooty and Sweep do *Crown Court*? Sit down and drink your lager, you little dicks. Fucking virgins. Fucking trying to tell me what bands I should be scared of. This is Belfast, kids — it ain't New York. If either of you want to take me on, you'll get what the drummer got downstairs.'

Owen, juggling the manifesto in one hand and a Tuborg in the other, looked shocked. But then I remembered that Owen was like that. He was always trying to see the good in people, even when there wasn't any to see.

That night in the family room, Andy Finn's performance was at its most mechanical. 'This is "Dream Song" . . . this one's "New Song" . . . that last one was — oh, what do any of you fuckin' know?'

None of the musicians wanted to be there — or ever see each other again — with the exception of Lawrence on the drums, who knew nothing of the scenes in Mark's bedroom and beat out the rhythm with a squint of fierce concentration. Occasionally he looked quizzically at Michelle, who was nodding earnestly next to me, as though he were saying to her: *These songs have got something, kiddo . . . I don't know what it is . . . there's just something about them.*

And there was, it was true. It was also true that I didn't care if I never heard them again. 'He's a good drummer, that bloke,' I grinned at Michelle after 'Drone Song'. But my voice was cracking from the heartbreak. Andy had donned neither glitter nor foundation for the gig, so what were we to perceive, any of us, but a handsome university fresher strumming a cheap guitar and singing without conviction? When Malachi O'Neill and some other party-goers drifted back to the disco to stomp their feet to the Stranglers' 'Duchess', steely-eyed Lou was drowned out and upstaged. He could not even muster the effort to turn up his amplifier.

I left before the end. Owen had gone home in confusion without saying goodbye to me, and as for Paul Leckie — he had never arrived. *Could I not be part of a triumvirate, for the love of God, let alone a faction?* It seemed not. *Who was Liz?* I didn't know. Some naïve girl who'd been generous enough to buy him boots and a new psychedelic shirt, and been screamed at down a Great Victoria Street pay-phone for her trouble. It was only subsequently — in Botanic Gardens first of all, and then much later in the reviews section of a music paper I seldom bothered to read — that the full story fell into place of why Isobel Clarke was in Malone that night, and why a small-town deceiver named Andy Finn was destined never to leave the safety of Belfast.

13
Winter Excerpts

Epistle from Clare Beattie, October 22, 1973

You are dead. My Daddy out the UDA is going to mudrer
you in the fish van because you are a Fenain Sweet lover
who dose'nt go to Church. Slade rule. Sweet are wick and
you are thier boyfreind. When my Daddy mudrers you I
will lagh and lagh and lagh. If you show aybody this I
will have you mudrered tomorrow. He will take you somewhere its queit and dark. He sells place, cod, hadock,
whitting, Dover, sole and ray.

Epistle purporting to be from Clare Beattie, October 25, 1973

I love you. Keep it a secret and do'nt show this to aybody.
I do'nt love Angus anymore only you. I do'nt know if you
are a Fenain but I hope you are because I love Fenains
becase they get maried and have lovey babys that make
me smile. Please mary me and we can have lovey Fenain
babys that make us smile. I want you to skweeze me and

pleeze me. When we are maried we will live in England and be freinds with Sweet and Mott the Hople. I like the man in Sweet who's has white hair but he is'nt as lovey as you. Be my true love until the twelfth of never. XXXXXXX Clare

P.S. Do'nt show this to Angus.

History essay, weekend October 31 to November 1, 1981

How successful was Britain's inter-war economy compared to other countries in Europe?

It was very successful. Compared to other countries in Europe, it was better, superior and more successful. The inter-war success of Britain, economically, was something that left other countries in Europe trailing in its wake. This fact was never more apparent than during the years 1919 to 1938, when the economy in Britain far exceeded that of other European countries. In a France or a Netherlands, for example, the economy fell considerably short of Britain's, while the Belgiums of this world lagged behind the British economy in a way that seems almost impossible to believe nowadays.

But I would not want you to get the idea that Green Regent were the first rock band I ever invented. Do not make that mistake whatever you do. They were not even the fifth. Thumper came first, in 1974, during a fallow week for the Top 30 in which my usual favourites (Sweet, Mott the Hoople, Roxy Music) found themselves without a hit. Seeking to create my own entertainment – cf. the 19th century; *How We Used to Live*; rural Donegal and Fermanagh today – I made Thumper a new entry at number 15 with a song called 'Snap-a-Crackle Mandy', which climbed to 12 the following week. As there was little chance of seeing the song performed on *Top of the Pops*, I invented the BBC1 music programme *It's Thumper Time* (Wednesday, 4.25 p.m.), a weekly opportunity for Thumper and their friends to sing songs, host quizzes and participate in food fights. I myself became a regular contributor to *It's Thumper Time*, sitting in the Pop Hot Seat and answering questions about the Top 30 put to me by members of the audience.

Thumper had a nondescript image, a charge that could not have been levelled at Wiseguy. Formed in 1975 after an episode of *Wacky Races*, Wiseguy were a rock 'n' roll revivalist sextet whose stubbled faces corresponded to the unshaven Ant Hill Mob. The gimmick was popular. Wiseguy had three Top 20 hits in 1975, including 'Comin' to Getcha', a David Hamilton single of the week.

The more proletarian Hobnail, who combined Rod Stewart haircuts with boisterous Glitter Band tempos, were my first mythical band to release a long-player. I had become a devotee of the LP in August 1975, having discovered to my intense delight that they contained 37 minutes' more music than a single. I could listen to music for much longer periods: two LPs, as opposed to two singles, lasted for 80 minutes rather than six. It became my ambition to own 36 LPs and play music for 24 hours consecutively. Hobnail's *Give It Some Welly*, while not as renowned as so-called 'real' albums in 1975 such as *Physical Graffiti*, *Atlantic Crossing* and *Wish You Were Here*, was far from an anti-climax, boasting as it did four Top 20 hits and a creditable version of Elton John's 'Saturday Night's Alright for Fighting'.

By now a first-form pupil at Belfast Grammar, may the Lord have pity on me, I began meeting other music fans of similar age who shared my interest in Status Quo, Queen, Bad Company and Led Zeppelin. Yet it was my irritation at being outclassed by these knowledgeable music pedants, who in some cases owned more records than I did, that led me to invent a series of internationally famous rock colossi in the months ahead. Much the most important was Triptych.

Responsible for the 'lunar landing' concept album *One Giant Leap*, Triptych were a name often heard on Alan Freeman's Radio One Saturday afternoon show in 1976, their stirring 'Apollo 11 Fandango' being especially heavily requested by one listener in Northern Ireland. My plea for 'more Quo, more Zep and what about some Triptych, Fluff?' was read out on the air in January, forcing the presenter to admit that he was unfamiliar with Triptych but would play Led Zeppelin's 'Trampled Under Foot' more than willingly. In April, my suggestion that the show should feature 'more Tull, more Sabbath and by the way, Fluff, it's been too long since we heard "Apollo 11 Fandango" by Triptych . . .' moved Freeman to respond 'Not 'arf' and play Black Sabbath's 'Iron Man' for my benefit.

Achieving a degree of hard rock and prog rock erudition via the Freeman show and the music papers *NME* and *Sounds*, I invented Tempus (high-selling prog with twin keyboards) and Royal Swan Motif (two-guitar hard rock with a 'no singles' policy) in the opening weeks of the second form. My ardour for Status Quo, Led Zeppelin and other, as it were, 'tangible' groups began to wane. Judging from my unanswered letters, their ardour for me had never been substantial.

A key year was 1977. Bored and unhappy at school —
I cannot think why — I came to associate major albums
by the likes of Pink Floyd and ELP with the rigours
of homework, the dread of morning and the unremitting
awfulness of wasting my young life away listening to some
90-year-old History teacher banging on and on and on
about Clement Attlee and Sir Stafford Cripps and frigging
William Beveridge when anyone with even the slightest bit
of intelligence could see that the world wasn't worth living
in and people were no better than barbarians and all they
ever did was kill and bomb and maim each other because
they thought this version of the Bible was more accurate
than that version of the Bible and therefore these people
should have more rights than those people and so it was
pointless learning about the history of the world around
us when the world around us clearly wasn't going to have
a future.

And what was I supposed to do, listen to *Animals* by
Pink Floyd and become even more depressed listening to
Roger Waters with his stupid bunged-up nose trying to
sing about society being banal and our existences all being
futile and pretending that I really enjoyed the guitar solos
when actually I found them really boring and it didn't
matter because the guitar solo would end in a minute and
Roger Waters would be back sounding as though as he
had a stinking cold and banging on and on about the
senselessness of being alive and other things that I already
knew.

And even moving to England wouldn't have made any
difference no matter how much I wanted to move to
England because all the kids there would have hated me
and not been interested in Royal Swan Motif and Triptych

and they would have said 'naff off, you nerk' every time I tried to talk to them because that's how English kids talked and they were all football hooligans anyway and just as bad as the kids over here.

And ELP's *Works Volume 1* was no fun because it cost a bloody fortune and then when you got it home it only had ELP playing on one side and the other three sides were really long and tedious solo concertos and symphonies for bloody drum-kit and when I took it to Knights they only gave me a third of what I paid for it.

And when punk bands started getting into the charts everybody said oh hurrah look punk music has come along to save us and now we won't ever have to listen to tedious double-albums by ELP and we'll all listen to punk bands instead even though half of them are garbage and the other half will only let us down and become rubbish because that's what always happens in music if you know anything about it and the next thing you know you're buying bloody useless albums that you didn't want anyway.

I wanted a band that wouldn't let me down. I invented Green Regent, the ultimate in hypothetical 1970s UK rock phenomena.

GREEN REGENT (1969–79)
Formed in Surrey by ex-members of Blues Railroad and Clarissa's Vermilion Pigge.
Robert Louis Beaufort (vocals, flute, Alvarez 12-string, illumination & choreography)
Johnny Hempridge (lead and rhythm electric & acoustic guitars, mandolins, lutes)
Quintin Dexter (grand piano, el. piano, organ, harpsi-chord, Mellotron & synths)

Wim Van Krootmeijer (4-, 6- and 8-string electric basses, bass pedals, celli)
Steve Hudd (drums, cymbals, tuned percussion and tympani)

A chance meeting at the Speakeasy between psychedelia-immersed singer-songwriter Beaufort (b. Robert Hayes, Carshalton, 14 May 1947) and 21-year-old blues guitar wizard Hempridge (b. John Hempridge-Smith, Cranleigh, 22 February 1948) led to the dissolution of their respective combos Clarissa's Vermilion Pigge (who had formed in 1967 as the Absent Mynd) and Blues Railroad (ex-Big Jim Lockhart's Blues Railroad Chain-Gang). April 1969 saw the recruitment of organist Dexter (b. Peter Quentin, Guildford, 8 October 1947) and Dutch bassist Van Krootmeijer (b. Eindhoven, 18 August 1945). The drummer's stool was filled by teenage firebrand Hudd (b. Newcastle), already a veteran of several Tyneside R&B outfits. Debuting in July 1969 in front of 250,000 people at the Rolling Stones' free concert in Hyde Park, Green Regent (having rejected names such as Hoggthwacker, Original Sin and Tobacco Road) were an immediate sensation and sold a respectable 600,000 copies of their eponymous debut *Green Regent* in November. Chiefly blues-based, the album was dominated by Hempridge's guitar playing, which critics unanimously agreed to be better than Page, Clapton and Beck combined. *Green Regent II* (1970), backed up by strenuous touring in America, launched the classics 'Tapestry of Your Love' and 'Backstage Lady' on an overwhelmed public, securing the album multi-platinum sales and legendary status. The more

folk-inflected *How Green was My Regent* (1970), the bulk
of which was written by 21-year-old guitar prodigy
Hempridge (b. 1949), showed the band to be as versa-
tile as they were prolific. Though touring regularly in
their personalized Boeing airplane 'Green I', they nevertheless maintained a frenetic recording schedule, releas-
ing in 1971 the magnificent *Regent IV* and *The Fifth
Amendment*. The latter garnered sextuple-platinum sales
despite not having the name of the band on the cover
(or even on the label of the record). By 1972, so much
of the world had been conquered that Green Regent
considered splitting up. Instead, under the guidance of
21-year-old guitar paragon Hempridge (b. 1951), they
moved from hard rock into prog rock, a genre in which
they effortlessly became pre-eminent. 'It was something
we had to do,' Beaufort told *Melody Maker* that year, 'and
Johnny being Johnny, he sort of instinctively pushed us
in the right direction.' The result was *Epoch*, a majestic
set that ranged in styles from Dexter's pile-driving 'No
More as It Ever Shall be Intended (In 15/8)' to Hempridge's acoustic *pièce de résistance* 'Figments'. 'Hearing
Epoch was like knowing the game was up – one was
aware that one couldn't compete with that,' a member
of Genesis was quoted as saying at the time. The recep-
tion from the critics was just as complimentary; one
music paper printed as its review an entirely blank page,
so lost for words was the journalist. In the year following the septuple-platinum *Pentateuch* (1975), Green
Regent scattered to their island retreats amid rumours
that all five were planning solo albums. The silence was
broken in the spring of 1976 by Beaufort's *Repose of
the Laird*, Hempridge's *Hemp*, Dexter's much-maligned

ragtime-jazz piano showcase *On Reflection 1 May Have been Too Tasty* and Van Krootmeijer and Hudd's *Van Krootmeijer & Hudd*, all of which were released on the same day by Green Regent's own record label Centaur. The solo albums charted in the Top 5, but only Hempridge's won widespread approval ('the lyricism of a Segovia ... breathtaking mastery for a 21-year old'), while Beaufort, stung by criticism of his lyrics ('it's glaringly obvious that *sans* Hempridge this guy has little or nothing to say'), refused to have anything to do with the press for the rest of his career. Even the ebullient and outgoing and widely liked though admittedly sensitive and retiring Hempridge, interviewed that summer on his Shetland farm, sounded circumspect and rambling though admittedly eloquent as he described the making of Green Regent's next (and for many, best) album, *Fol de Rol*. 'The project was embarked on in May, once the deal with all the solo albums had been dealt with. I've written all the songs on my own again. But I don't know, man ... A lot's happened in the world. Will we still be the biggest thing internationally and musically? You tell me.' It was evident from the moment *Fol de Rol* reached the world's hi-fis that Hempridge need not have worried. Released in December 1976, it became the year's highest-selling UK album in only a week. 'Just when you think Green Regent are down, they come back with something like that,' an exasperated member of Yes commented. 'You have to hand it to Hemp, I suppose, for instinctively knowing what to do.' The 21-year-old guitar idol, however, fell tragically ill in mysterious circumstances in 1977. 'Hemp Quits on Eve of Knebworth!' cried the front-page headlines in

Sounds, *NME*, the *Washington Post* and other publications. 'Green Regent may have to nix live work for the foreseeable future after band-leader and Byronic guitar Christ-figure Johnny "Hemp" Hempridge, 21, fell tragically ill last week in mysterious circumstances. A concerned Robert Louis Beaufort told our news desk, "We don't know the exact cause of the tragically mysterious illness, but the idea of doing Knebworth without Johnny is not something we wanna even think about."' From his hospital bed, Hempridge wrote all the material for 1977's *A Quorum of Kings*, skilfully recording his guitar parts despite being connected to a life-support machine. A miraculous recovery saw him join the band for dates at Wembley Stadium in September (known among fans as the 'He is Risen' tour), but the recovery was all too brief and the tragically mysterious illness set in again. A changing musical climate was encouraging people with not even a fraction of Hempridge's talent to form punk bands; with names like the Stranglers and the Vibrators, they denigrated Green Regent as 'dull prog twats' but none of them sold any records. 'My problem with the punk scene,' said Beaufort in a rare interview, 'is that, number one, these cats can't play, and (b) they haven't paid their dues like me and Hemp have.' Interpreted by many as their response to punk, Green Regent's next album *The Audipus Complex* was to be their last with Hempridge. 'It's all about a young kid from the country who moves to the city and has problems at school and so on,' the guitarist explained between blood transfusions. 'He lives in his imagination, which let's face it is not a bad place to be, and he's giving his whole life and soul to music. Music really is his sanctuary, but it's also a double-edged sword because he's obsessing about music to the exclusion of everything else. Parents, you know, school-work, the world around him – he uses music to blot it all out. I kind of see him coming from Northern Ireland, but it could be anywhere.' *The Audipus Complex*, complete with notorious 'frightened boy' artwork, topped the album charts and inspired one leading punk musician to remark, 'I wish I'd never started a punk band. When you hear Hemp soloing like that, and those incredible songs like "All Alone in Sound" and "The Leaving of Downburn", you realize just how fantastic Green Regent and the prog thing in general really are.' In December 1978, Johnny Hempridge died. He was just 21. An ill-starred attempt to carry on without him yielded the final Green Regent album, *When One Door Closes . . .*, but the Beaufort-penned set was dismissed by one American critic as 'presumptuous verging on the downright blasphemous'.

I loved Hemp and I killed him. And when I told Tinmeer what I had done, he said . . . Well, first he asked me who Hemp was. '*Who voss ziss Hemp?*' That was how Tinmeer talked until I softened his accent a bit in 1979. 'He was my mythical lead guitar idol,' I explained. 'He was in Green Regent. Dammit, he *was* Green Regent.'

'And ziss is how you spend your life?' Tinmeer gesticulated. 'Inventing ze groups because you feel that music is not good enough for you? Let me tell you something. Music is *too* good for you.'

I shan't be handing this essay in, sir. A mythical idol may have been a necessity, but a mythical guru could be seen as self-indulgence.

Advertisement on sixth-form centre notice-board, November 4

For sale. Rickenbacker bass and H/H amplifier. Both in excellent condition. Serious offers only to Mark Coates (coffee bar Thurs. and Fri. 1 p.m.–1.30 p.m.), or tel: 666999 (evening).

Belfast Telegraph; *November 9*

GROUP BIDS FOR 'SMASH' HIT
by Graham Mickerson
If you follow local pop as I do, you cannot have missed hearing about Coalition of Glass. A Mickerson tip-for-the-top, the boys have been around for only a few months but are already turning heads with their infectious brand of thinking man's rock. Early days maybe, but they could soon be joining famous names like Bruce Springsteen, Heaven 17 and Paul Brady in the hit parade.

I caught up with the band's lead vocalist Richard Pirrie, a Queen's medical student, to get the low-down on what's been a-brewing. Pirrie, 20, put together Coalition of Glass in the summer with his brother Alastair, 19, and two pals from Malone and Finaghy. The personable singer first took my point that aside from Stiff Little Fingers and the Undertones, bands from these parts have traditionally failed to make headway over the water.

'However, I think we're different,' Pirrie confided.

I put it to the talkative vocalist that homegrown rock has never been so vibrant — with Pragmatic Control, Strategic Element and Berlin all striking a blow for musical enterprise on this side of the Irish Sea.

291

'Where we have the advantage over those bands is in our songwriting,' Pirrie mulled. 'We're not afraid to take inspiration from the greats.'

The boys' ready way with a tune seems certain to kindle interest from record company bigwigs in England. There are plans afoot to release a disc next year, 'which will probably be a song we wrote for a friend of ours, Carl, who has moved to London to become a journalist'. University and other commitments prevent the band from following Carl across the pond at this juncture, but they hope to make music a priority in 1982.

'There is no rush, Graham,' Pirrie emphasized to me. 'A good song in 1981 will still be a good song in ten years' time.'

I'll raise a glass to that!

Conversation. Isobel Clarke and myself in Botanic Gardens, November 12

It is lunchtime. Isobel has a bottle of blackcurrant cordial and a piece of tissue containing an unspecified number of antihistamine tablets. I have a bottle of Pernod (the smallest we could get, though it's looking incriminatingly large to me) and two polystyrene cups from the sixth-form centre.

Me: Should we grab that bench?

Isobel: Yerse.

Me: Or we could keep going and see if it's quieter behind those trees . . . ? I'm just thinking of the bottle. Whichever you prefer.

Isobel: Nah, let's sit here. We're nearly eighteen, aren't we?

Me: You might be. Okay, as you wish. The defendant may be seated.

Isobel: Yeah . . . that's it . . . 'I have asked you here today . . .'

Me: That you shall be found guilty of treason and witchcraft and sentenced to be hanged by the neck. Guards, take her away.

Isobel: I think Owen would enjoy that. I think he'd pay to watch.

Me: No . . . not true.

Isobel: Do you want me to open that for you?

Me: I can manage.

Isobel: Mister barman.

Me: What'll you have? We've got . . . er . . . Pernod and black, or we do a very nice blackcurrant with Pernod.

Isobel: Pernod and black will do me very nicely.

Me: I hope these things don't leak. That's my only worry at the moment. We'd better not clink glasses, they might disintegrate. I don't think Japanese ingenuity went into making these somehow.

Isobel: I used to come here in September when there were leaves everywhere. Now look at it.

Me: A barren winter's scene.

Isobel: I used to sit over there where that dog is.

Me: Is this where you used to come? What did you do?

Isobel: Don't know. Not much. Sit and think. Cry. Hide . . .

Me: I haven't cried for years.

Isobel: Haven't you? I cry all the time. I think it's really important to cry.

Me: I cry sometimes.

Isobel: I cry all the time. Just endlessly. I can't remember the last time I didn't feel like crying.

Me: I'm the same. I'm just relentless when it comes to crying.

Isobel: God . . . some people might accuse you of overdoing the Pernod. Nice, though. Get my breath smelling wonderfully of aniseed.

Me: Really? Will that lead to problems later?

Isobel: I shouldn't think so. I'm not expecting any problems in that area later.

Me: Really? Are there any areas where you are expecting problems?

Isobel: I'm sure there are. I can probably think of a few hundred . . . So cheers. How've you been?

Me: Terrible.

Isobel: Brrrr . . . I no like this weather, it's too cold. So much for your al fresco lunch suggestion, mister Eskimo. Maybe the woolly tights would have been a good idea.

Me: I know. I wish I'd worn them.

Isobel: These are laddered all over the place. Look . . . here. And this one.

Me: Oh yeah . . .

Isobel: And look at this. You could get your fist in that. Brrrr . . . cold legs.

Me: How are things at home?

Isobel: Oh, chaos. They're thinking of selling me and getting a new one. They're going to take me back to the shop where they bought me. 'This one's *crap* . . .'

Me: I think parents have a lot to learn.

Isobel: Do you? About what?

Me: Well, they don't understand what it's like to be us. I was reading somewhere recently that life gets a hundred per cent harder for every generation of seventeen-year-olds every year.

Isobel: What did you read that in?

Me: I can't remember. Or maybe I didn't read it, but I'm sure it's absolutely true. It's the sort of thing I could easily believe.

Isobel: You know there's only two years and a bit to go till 1984? Big Brother is watching you.

Me: Yeah . . . I bet Orwell didn't know how true-to-life that bloody book was. Every sentence in it is like a premonition of now. Scary.

Isobel: Can you imagine being alive in the year 2000?

Me: I'd be . . . what . . . thirty . . .

Isobel: Thirty-seven. Thirty-six.

Me: Thirty-six. No, thirty-five for most of it, then thirty-six in December.

Isobel: Why are so young, then? Did you skip a year?

Me: Mmm. Back in primary school, when we were down South.

Isobel: You'll regret that in the year 2000. When we're all thirty-six and you're only thirty-five. We'll all be laughing openly at you.

Me: You all laugh openly at me now.

Isobel: I know . . . We don't mean anything by it, though. We just find you laughable. It's nothing personal.

Me: There isn't going to be a year 2000 anyway. We'll all have gone up in a big mushroom cloud. Ka-boom.

Isobel: It'll be like *The War Game* . . . diving under tables. Did you see that last year when they showed it at school?

Me: Yeah. I had to go out to be sick.

Isobel: Me and Caroline just sat there holding on to each other and sobbing. If that's the world that we're growing up for . . .

Me: Precisely. You think you'll be thirty-six but really you'll be dead.

Isobel: Are you still having nightmares about the Goodies? Or have you started having nuclear trauma nightmares instead?

Me: No, I don't have Goodies nightmares. I have nightmares about castles now and again. There's always somebody at the door telling me I can't come in. I'm always left standing outside feeling like a moron.

Isobel: Sexual.

Me: No . . .

Isobel: Sexual. Trust me.

Me: Well now, Miss Freud, this is all very sudden. I can remember when it was numerological.

Isobel: I didn't want to traumatize you. I had this pathetic idea in the back of my mind that you might be sitting next to me and I didn't want you being traumatized in Latin and getting traumatic all over my desk. Thanks for deserting me, by the way, traitor.

Me: I wasn't deserting you.

Isobel: Traitor.

Me: I wasn't deserting you. I was alarmed by you.

Isobel: Oh, *alarmed* . . .

Me: I was alarmed by you. Miss Pony-tail with the lovebites. You were enough to alarm anybody.

Isobel: Thank you, mister deserter. Mister traitor. Now I know who not to ring when I need a friend, don't I? And we don't talk about lovebites in polite company. They were um . . . teeth-prints.

Me: So who was the lucky dentist?

Isobel: Just a . . . fuck off. You're only thirty-five. If you were thirty-six I might tell you.

Me: Mark Coates by any chance?

Isobel: Mark Coates! You're obsessed with Mark Coates. I'm going to tell him he's got a secret thirty-five-year-old admirer. I'm going to tell him not to be *alarmed*. No, it wasn't Mark Coates. God . . . They may be desperate times but they're not that desperate. Even in my worst moments of bad Isobel, I'm never that bad.

296

Me: Aren't you? That's a pity.

Isobel: Well, there you go. I've disappointed you.

Me: This stuff is actually horrible. I don't know why we're drinking it. I blame you.

Isobel: Blame me. Put all the blame on me.

Me: God . . . *life*. An unreasonable and endless list of demands and impossible conditions and terrible drawbacks weighted against us at every turn.

Isobel: Very well. I accept.

Me: We haven't left school yet and already we're doomed.

Isobel: I accept. You've talked me into it.

Me: Oh, I wish . . . I wish that . . . The problem is . . .

Isobel: How are things between you and Hinney?

Me: Hinney? Good. Can't complain. Why?

Isobel: It may have come to your attention that he doesn't rate my chances in June.

Me: It's never too late, though, you know, to catch up. I fucked up last term and now he says I'm back on course. You just need to do a lot of reading over Christmas.

Isobel: I tried that. I think it's too late. There's such a lot . . . I'm just worried that I fucked everything up over the summer and it's too late to come back. No, really. He's even had my mum in. He's had her in twice.

Me: I know. I saw her once, actually. She had a red scarf on. I didn't know who she was at first.

Isobel: She hates me with a passion. She can't believe her rotten luck, having a daughter like me that's let the family down. 'What have I done? Am I not a good Protestant? Where have I gone wrong? Raising a daughter who brings shame on my house? Where have I sinned, Lord? Speak to me, Lord.'

Me: I'm sure she doesn't think that.

Isobel: You haven't met her. And she doesn't just think it, she says it. 'I gave you life . . . and all you give me is embarrassment and shame. You bitch-daughter, I should have thrown you in the reservoir when I had the chance.'

Me: Hey . . .

Isobel: Don't look at me for a minute.

Me: Oh dear . . . Do you want to borrow a disgusting hand-kerchief or will you be all right?

Isobel: Oh God! Isobel . . . Isobel . . . you silly silly silly *cow*.

Me: Silly silly silly . . . Here . . . Oh, can't I look at you? Come on . . . When did you start doing it?

Isobel: Don't you dare look at me. Wait a minute. Where's my tissues . . . oh God, where are they . . . Hang on. Look away and count to ten. Right, hang on. Wait a minute . . . Eight, nine, ten. Okay. What? When did I what?

Me: When did you start doing it?

Isobel: Doing what? Glue?

Me: Yeah.

Isobel: February.

Me: February? What was so bad about February?

Isobel: Nothing. It was no worse than January or December.

Me: Then why did you do it?

Isobel: No reason. I just did it.

Me: What, you just thought: I am going to sniff glue because it's February and oh, look, there just happens to be a bag of glue here . . .

Isobel: I was at a party. A *party*. You know – *fun*?

Me: All right. Don't bite my head off.

Isobel: You don't smoke, do you? I should have got ciggies at the post office. You don't smoke.

Me: What's it like, glue? I've often wondered.

Isobel: Ffffff . . . take a look at me. It's the most glamorous thing in the world, obviously. Says Miss spotty-fucked-up-shit-looking-alarming complexion.

Me: No, really. What does it actually do to you?

Isobel: Oh, just . . . What, you mean when you're . . . ? Just . . . I don't know. Bliss, I suppose. Bliss and oblivion. I don't know.

Me: Really? You completely lose your bearings?

Isobel: Oh yeah . . . I did anyway. But, you know, there were other things going on as well.

Me: I think Owen knew.

Isobel: Owen knew because he saw me at that party. But Owen didn't know I was doing it until that party.

Me: He seemed to think there was some boyfriend in the picture. I can't quite remember what he said . . .

Isobel: Owen? Owen didn't know anything about it. No one did. No one knew. I mean – did you?

Me: No, I didn't know. So what happened first – boyfriend or glue?

Isobel: Fffff . . . be a bit more direct. 'What happened first, evil person? You fell in love or you sniffed glue? Talk! Answer!'

Me: Well . . . you've never really said much about your life. I don't know what to ask.

Isobel: I need more of that . . . Thanks. Fill her up, barman. Um . . . what happened first? I sniffed glue. At a party with someone that I fancied. Well, more than fancied by that stage, really. He didn't like glue but I did. Then I fell in love with him. Both things happened in February. *Satisfied?*

Me: I'm not torturing you, evil person. You're not going to have your fingernails pulled out.

Isobel: Oh. Well, you wouldn't be able to . . . They're not

299

great nails at the moment, are they? They used to be longer.

Me: Don't pick at them. Who was he?

Isobel: Who, the . . . boy? The love of my life . . . bless him.
Can't say. Someone you know.

Me: And are you still on glue? Answer! Talk!

Isobel: Believe it or not, I stopped a month ago exactly. It's
my anniversary today. One month to the day. Although
obviously we're still left with the drink problem and the
antihistamine problem. But you know, one step at a time.
As I keep telling my probation officer.

Me: You have a probation officer!

Isobel: No, dear. Just a joke.

Me: God . . .

Isobel: I nearly did have, though. I got into some trouble in
the summer. To do with the person that I can't talk about.

Me: Whoever he is.

Isobel: Uh-huh. Mystery man. We must not even whisper his
. . . infamous . . .

Me: So much secrecy! It's the love that dare not speak its
name!

Isobel: It certainly is, m'dear. But I nicked quite a lot of
money from a shop I was working in. About a hundred
quid out of the till. I thieved it good and proper, I did.
Blimey, guv'nor. And the shop asked my mum and dad if
they wouldn't mind paying it all back or their little girl
would get put in prison. Honest. Honest, guv'nor. Weren't
my fault — society was to blame. Ooh, it was looking bad
for Isobel . . . She was looking at a long stretch . . . You're
the first person I've told that, incidentally. I'd be grateful
if you didn't spread it around.

Me: I'll put it in the school magazine.

Isobel: That'll be lovely.

Me: So the guy you were going out with doesn't know you stole the money?

Isobel: Oh, *he* knows. Yeah, of course. I mean, I did it . . .

Me: Why did you do it? To buy glue?

Isobel: No! You troglodyte. Where are you from? Glue's not that expensive.

Me: Well, to finance some East European arms deal, then? To spring your mad brother out of a Siberian labour camp? What?

Isobel: No. Nice Isobel doesn't get involved in wicked things. Nice Isobel buys presents.

Me: You bought presents? Who for?

Isobel: The person I can't tell you about. Nice Isobel is also discreet.

Me: How many of those have you just taken?

Isobel: Well, there are . . . six left in the tissue. So . . . six. Pour me some more liquor, barman.

Me: And your mum and dad paid the money back to Abernethies?

Isobel: Aaah . . . so you know the name. Yes, they did. And I had to pay my mum and dad back – which I'm doing, bit by bit. I just got some money to pay the last bit back. Then I have to start paying my mum back the money I've been nicking from her purse since June. What a palaver, guv'nor.

Me: And so the person you can't talk about . . . the person you were in love with and you stole the money to buy presents for . . . and this is someone I know?

Isobel: Oh yes.

Me: From the College?

Isobel: Oh . . . well . . . at one time. Yes.

Me: Someone who was at the College but isn't any more?

301

Isobel: Very little gets past you, I see.

Me: And when did this start?

Isobel: I told you. February.

Me: And how did it start? Without telling me who it started with, if you like . . .

Isobel: Ooh. 'Twas a moonlit night. I was all a-quiver on me own in the Club Bar. He was all on his own in the Club Bar. Eyes met across a crowded Club Bar. 'Fancy a drink?' 'Yeah, and the rest.' Sex at first sight. Blah blah blah. You know how these things work.

Me: I don't, actually. You're a shocking hussy.

Isobel: Yes, well, certain people have said this. But I like it, so screw them.

Me: And he was at the College then?

Isobel: He was at the College then, at that time, during the period of which we are speaking, yes. Brilliant deduction.

Me: And you continued seeing a bit of each other?

Isobel: We continued seeing all of each other. Oh . . . bad Isobel.

Me: Until he left the College?

Isobel: And after. Until Isobel's heart broke and she couldn't take it any more. And prison cells loomed for the bad, bad girl. Big iron bars and big cakes with files in them. 'Isobel Anne Clarke, you are a habitual criminal who sees arrest as an occupational hazard . . . I sentence you to twenty years in the slammer with Fletcher and Godber. Good night.'

Me: Why did you go to Denise Finn's birthday party?

Isobel: Well, now you're asking.

Me: When do those tablets start working?

Isobel: In a few minutes. If I were you, I'd get all your important questions in quick, pal. You might have to carry me back to school. Think you can manage that? Think you're man enough?

Me: I'm glad you're putting henna in your hair again. It looks so much nicer than when you had it in the pony-tail.

Isobel: Thank you . . . I'll take that insult as a compliment. Why didn't *you* go to Denise's birthday party?

Me: I did. I was there, but I left early. I fell out with her brother.

Isobel: Aaaaah.

Me: Not as badly as I fell out with him a few weeks ago, but still pretty badly. The recent one was terminal, so I suppose that makes the other one . . .

Isobel: Provisional.

Me: Yeah. Do you know Andy well?

Isobel: Errrr . . .

Me: He quite likes you, I think. As a friend.

Isobel: Fffffff . . .

Me: I think out of all the Virgins you were his favourite.

Isobel: Hmmmm.

Me: Unfortunately there's no two-way traffic with Andy. The guy's just a bastard and that's that.

Isobel: Yep.

Me: It took me a year to realize it, but he's a very cold and unfeeling person.

Isobel: Yep.

Me: We were never really close. I thought we were, but he was just stringing me along. He seemed to get some pleasure out of that.

Isobel: Yep.

Me: He was the one who got me interested in a lot of the music I listen to today. He was a great person to know, really funny . . . Until I outlived my usefulness and he got rid of me.

303

Isobel: Mm-hm. This is sounding familiar.

Me: Which actually happened the other week at Mark's party.

Isobel: Yep.

Me: Where, funnily enough, I saw you waiting at a bus-stop on the Malone Road.

Isobel: You did. Ah.

Me: Almost as if you'd been to Mark's house and decided to leave for some reason. Weird.

Isobel: Or decided not to go in. For some reason.

Me: Very weird. Is the person you were in love with the same person that I'm thinking of?

Isobel: What makes you think I'm not in love with the person you're thinking of any more?

Me: Are you?

Isobel: Possibly.

Me: The person that I'm thinking of was going out with someone called Liz who bought him clothes, and the person that I'm thinking of got pissed off with Liz and screamed horrible abuse at her from a phone-box in Great Victoria Street.

Isobel: Oh – is that where the person that you're thinking of was phoning from? I didn't know that.

Me: Did you know about the phone-call?

Isobel: Oh yes. When phone-calls are made to my house, I tend to know about them.

Me: But you're not Liz.

Isobel: Nope.

Me: So . . .

Isobel: Elizabeth Reilly. She's Liz.

Me: Elizabeth Reilly?

Isobel: My predecessor. You don't know Elizabeth Reilly? All right, the quick bitchy version: looks like a troll, no tits, arse as big as a hovercraft, personality of a sheep. She's a gorgeous human being.

Me: That's a very unbecoming thing for you to say, Isobel. Whereas you, of course, are perfect in every way. An absolute goddess. A consummate specimen of womankind.

Isobel: Well, I don't look like a troll.

Me: And you have . . . tits.

Isobel: And a proper-sized arse that doesn't take passengers.

Me: Well, I'm glad to hear it. And a nice personality, if I may say so.

Isobel: None of my gentlemen have complained, sir.

Me: But if the person that I'm thinking of was going to be at Mark's party, and if you were in love with the person that I'm thinking of, why didn't you go in?

Isobel: Maybe I was about to go in, but then maybe I saw the sister of the person that you're thinking of coming out in hysterics, and maybe I thought I'd better not go in because the person that you're thinking of might not want to see me anyway.

Me: Why not?

Isobel: Because maybe at a previous party he'd told me I was a glue-sniffing whore and he wanted me out of his house and out of his life.

Me: No.

Isobel: Yeah . . . That's made you go a bit quiet, hasn't it?

Me: Why would he say that?

Isobel: Er . . . 'cold, unfeeling'. I think you said it a minute ago?

Me: Oh, Isobel . . . *Isobel* . . .

Isobel: Poor Isobel.

Me: Jesus Christ. Did you break up at Denise's party?

Isobel: No, troglodyte. People don't usually get out of their heads on glue if they're still going out with people who they're head over heels in love with and desperately trying to impress. No . . . He'd told me it was over in May.

Me: Oh, of course, because he was revising for his A-levels and couldn't see you?

Isobel: Excuse me, troglodyte. In May, we were out every single night in the Club Bar or the Botanic. Revising for your A-levels is not in the same league as going out with me.

Me: So you broke up at the end of May?

Isobel: Yeah. But there were a lot of secret assignations after that. I just couldn't keep away, I'm afraid. And my itchy fingers saw the purse open . . . and the till open . . . and I thought: let's buy some nice things for my cold, unfeeling lover. Silly cow.

Me: Is that why his mother . . .

Isobel: His mother hates me. She should meet *my* mother, they'd get on wonderfully. His mother banned me from their house, you know. 'I'm not 'avin' 'er in 'ere! I'm tellin' yer now!' I got a bit tipsy, m'dear.

Me: I always say the wrong thing around his mother.

Isobel: Oh yeah? 'Forget your mother for once in your life. Take me up to bed and fuck me rigid.' Did you ever say that? I did.

Me: Oh my God.

Isobel: 'Get 'er out of the 'ouse now! I'm not 'avin that kind of language in 'ere!'

Me: She doesn't talk like that, Isobel.

Isobel: How do you know she doesn't? How do you know who I'm talking about?

Me: And . . . so you broke up . . . He told you it was over at the end of May. But you refused to accept it?

Isobel: Yes, troglodyte. I, like a fool, believed there was still a torch there flickering for me. Fucking bastard.

Me: Even though he'd called you a glue-sniffing old whore?

Isobel: Thank you. You really should join the diplomatic service when you grow up. He didn't say that till later. Oh . . . oh, *bloody* hell . . . I mean, what did I do to him that was so bad? I was really in love with him . . . Do more barman stuff quick before I cry.

Me: I don't know why my hands are shaking . . . It's strange, though. There was a time when I thought he must be gay. I really got that impression.

Isobel: Who? Who must be gay?

Me: The person I'm thinking about.

Isobel: Did you? I can assure you that the person I'm thinking about isn't anything of the sort. Why did you think that?

Me: The make-up, the way he talks. The way he was. Sort of camp.

Isobel: Camp compared to Piers Mawhinney, yeah! Well noticed, darling. But not camp like Larry Grayson or . . . But . . . yeah . . . I see what you mean. He has very attractive eyelashes. He only wore make-up when he played his music. He was just the best musician, wasn't he?

Me: Yes.

Isobel: He played his guitar for me. And we used to listen to Joy Division round at my house. 'The Eternal', 'Decades' . . . Oh . . . I can't listen to those songs now without crying. So I listen to them now on my own, and I cry.

Me: I thought he didn't like Joy Division.

Isobel: We'd lie there in bed, listening to them in the dark.

Me: Right . . . really? He's a nasty person, though, isn't he? I'm not surprised you . . .

Isobel: No ... he's not nasty, he's nice. He's just got a lot of problems. Poor little boy.

Me: Why? Like what?

Isobel: Dunno. Doesn't like weak people. He's very strong, or he thinks he is. 'I am strong. I am more strong than you, weak bitch. Fuck off. I am a strong person.' No, I'm joking ... It wasn't like that.

Me: You think he has problems?

Isobel: Of course. He's had a fucked-up life. The army background – his father fucked him up. His mother kicking his father out fucked him up, and him seeing them fighting all through his childhood fucked him up even before that. And that English upper-lip, stiff self-control thing he's got. He's a bit of a mess, the person I'm thinking about, he really is.

Me: I didn't know his father was in the army.

Isobel: Aaah.

Me: Does that explain why he's so ... I don't know.

Isobel: How could you be his friend and not know his father was in the army? It's all he ever talks about. 'My father, my father ...' Club Bar, the two of us are in there – let's go back to my place, baby. 'No, wait, I want to say some more things about my father, my father, my father.' Oh, okay, I'm listening ... I don't mind.

Me: Supercilious? Is that the right word?

Isobel: Ffffff. Yes, if you want. Supercalifragelistic. Super-fucking-duper ...

Me: So why did you two keep it a secret from everybody? Why did you pretend you weren't going out?

Isobel: That was him ... He had some friend who was really keen on me. I don't know who. But he said we had to be careful.

Me: What? What's this?

Isobel: He said he had a friend who'd told him one night when they were drunk that he was in love with me.

Me: He said that?

Isobel: I asked him why it mattered if it was only said as a drunk thing, but he said we had to be careful because he didn't want his friend getting upset, or feeling left out or really hurt, because he thought he might end up doing something stupid.

Me: He said that?

Isobel: He talked about him a bit. He said he was a good friend. And he was worried about what this person might do if he knew about us.

Me: But why would he say that?

Isobel: Because he's sweet. I thought it was a really sweet thing for him to be saying.

Me: Why did he say his friend would do something stupid?

Isobel: He said *might*. It was a possibility. It was somebody to do with the band. He wouldn't tell me his name.

Me: I wonder who it was . . . then . . .

Isobel: Listen. I'd like to know who it was. I've got a lot of free evenings these days, m'dear. I've been thinking of holding boyfriend auditions in the coffee bar. On the tennis table might be good. 'One at a time, boys . . . line up.'

Me: Form an orderly queue . . . yeah . . . who knows? Maybe this person will turn up for an audition.

Isobel: Well, I hope so. A big, strapping, muscly boy to sweep me off my feet. Yes please. I'd like a muscly boy this time.

Me: Would you?

Isobel: Please. Definitely. Pretty please.

Me: That dog's been chewing that stick for about ten minutes. You'd think he'd get tired of it.

Isobel: But you're right . . . there was so much secrecy about everything. That's the way he is. You never know for sure what he's thinking. I didn't — ever. You couldn't have, if he never told you about his dad. He's all locked up and he puts on this front all the time so people can't get at him. He thinks he's being strong . . . Nnnnn. These things are working now.

Me: I was reading somewhere recently that the more muscles someone has, the less intelligent they're likely to be.

Isobel: There's an envelope in my pocket. Can you get it out and look in it? I'm getting a really nice shimmer off those trees. You know, for a long time my mum thought I had hay fever. That was my story — 'It's hay fever, Mum.' I've always had hay fever in the summer, ever since I was little.

Me: This is his handwriting. What was in the envelope?

Isobel: Money for me. There's a wee note still in there.

Me: Is this private? Should I be reading it?

Isobel: It'll tell you about him.

Me: 'September twenty-eight. Dear Isobel. Here's another contribution to the Keep-Kitten-Out-of-Jail fund. Spend it wisely — I'll send some more when grant . . . when the grant cheque goes through next week. The things I do for you. Please don't phone. If Mark Coates or little Malone Avenue Doug happen to tell you I'm a callous swine, nod your head and say nothing. It's all a bit of a disaster, isn't it? So many regrets . . . Until we meet again some day. Love, Andy.'

Isobel: Why does he call you Doug?

Me: Don't look at me for a minute.

Isobel: Hay fever ... That's what I told her when I was all glued up. I got the idea from Owen. 'It's just hay fever, Mum, the usual symptoms.' I think Owen was pretty offended. He won't talk to me now – but that's okay really.

Me: I'll put this back in your pocket. Then I'll do barman stuff again.

Isobel: Did he get the money from you and Mark? Is that why you fell out?

Me: He's been getting it from Mark. I don't have that kind of money. But I'd have got it from somewhere if he'd asked.

Isobel: We never know what he's thinking, do we?

Me: We certainly don't.

Isobel: But we'll all be dead in a big nuclear mushroom war in a few years, so it doesn't really matter what any of us are thinking.

Me: No.

Isobel: Do you think he's serious about meeting me again some day?

Me: I don't know.

Isobel: We'll just have to see what happens, then. Put lots of Pernod in mine ... Wait and see what Brezhnev and the Americans do. Wait and see if the hunger-strike's still on in 1984. Wait and see if there's going to be anywhere left to live in when we're thirty-six.

Me: The hunger-strike's over, Isobel. Are you all right down there? Should you be drinking on those things?

Isobel: I want my baby.

Me: You mustn't do anything stupid ... He wouldn't want you to do that.

Isobel: Wait see.

Me: Just think – all our lives still to come. Onwards and upwards we go, kiddo ... Don't cry, Isobel, we'll survive. We'll listen to Joy Division and we'll survive. .

Isobel: Wait see ... mister barman ... wait see ...

14
The University of Life

An autumn Wednesday morning seemed to radiate peace and liberty, a propitious synthesis in the air that even a subterranean felt the touch of. Dancing down the escalator to the basement, where for forty minutes he had been zigzagging from the Ms to the Ts to the Ws, the embrace of the morning wafted up to him, brushed the nape of his neck and grazed the beard he was trying to grow.

The in-store stereo, manned by a cropped-haired girl in a black tee-shirt, was still playing the music of that summer – Kid Creole, Yazoo, 'Come On Eileen' – as if the city had had too voluptuous a holiday to permit October '82 its moment. I knew the labyrinthine jungle of the Bull Ring would look very different when it rained, but the two weeks I'd lived here had been a holiday – my holiday – and it would take more than an autumn cloudburst to put me on the boat-train home.

I handed *Eligible Bachelors* by the Monochrome Set to the girl at the counter and tendered the £5 note from the Lloyds cash machine. For a fortnight I had been plundering my grant cheque from that machine at 10.45 every morning;

I almost didn't have to insert my card now for it to start dispensing. *Eh-up, here comes laughing boy again — get ready with the fivers.* My four-digit card number was open sesame to the most fecund jukebox I had ever imagined — HMV alone was an irresistible temptation to a Belfast starveling — but the funds in my account were already running precariously low. *What's he buying this time, another LP in HMV or Virgin? Or will it be a Big Mac and fries at that marvellous new restaurant he's discovered near the station?*

'Are there no *NME*s in yet?' I asked the girl amiably as she sheathed my album in a polythene bag.

'They're late this week,' she replied, bored out of her mind. 'And *Sounds* — they're late too. We only have *Melody Maker* until this avvy.'

'I'll have a *Melody Maker* then. You may subtract the cost of it from my change.'

'You haven't got any change,' she said acidly. 'Pay for it or put it back.'

Paying for it, I set off in clear sunshine for the bus-stop, wondering if I would ever truly get to grips with the Birmingham accent. It had taken me six months as a five-year-old to become accustomed to Northern Ireland's *obsaluitly hurr-breeind voil soinds*, but the timbre and inflection of Brum appeared to be beyond mimicry. You either spoke like that from birth, or you never spoke like it at all. *Bicycle-ayy . . . the theeng ees, bicycle-ayyy . . . awlroit, mite!*

In splendid top-deck weather, my feet led me to the upper front seats on the Rubery bus without my brain even noticing it had stairs. Alongside the song-titles on the back cover of the Monochrome Set album was a string of lavish reviews of their work culled from American, English and

Japanese magazines, which I read and reread until a guilty feeling made me glance out of the window at the university campus coming up on the right. I was meant to have attended a Spanish lecture at 10.30 a.m.

I would tell my tutor tomorrow that I'd had a complete nervous and physical breakdown. *No, just say nervous to begin with. Keep physical in reserve.* If he asked me for a doctor's note, I would add that it was also a physical breakdown — 'you know, those ones where you can't move an inch in any direction, like for example to a doctor's surgery? Hell's teeth . . . that's tertiary education for you, eh, *señor*? But you and I are men of the world, are we not?'

Then perhaps I would scan the notice-board for a driver to London. Students drove down from Birmingham every Friday and Saturday, I'd been told, and all they asked was £5 towards petrol. Well, I knew a machine where I could lay my hands on £5 . . . It would be interesting to see Owen one of these weekends. See if he was happier. See how he was settling in at Imperial.

I jerked my head away so as not to catch sight of the campus clock tower: even after two weeks, the story of the girl still sent a chill down my spine. Kevin, our friendly volunteer student counsellor, who wore a mini-jar of Nescafé on a piece of elastic around his neck, had told us: 'The common belief is that it's apocryphal. But apparently there are folk knocking about who knew her. Postgrads and that.' A hook-nosed Mancunian on my course had loved it — a chuffing ace story, that were, Kev, give us the gory bits again, go on — but Kevin had seen me whiten and clammed up. *My thoughts exactly*, I blinked at him. *There's nothing else to add.* Girls who committed suicide were deserving of reticence, certainly more than they deserved to be a spoonful of detail in a Freshers' Week anecdote. Their deaths had been a way of saying they'd had enough of that in life. Whoever and wherever they were, as they leapt from a clock tower or sat in a park, over there where that dog is ... whatever they did, and whensoever they chose to do it, it was their way of saying Enough.

The bus wove through the dapper village of Selly Oak, home to a little record shop where I'd picked up *Quadrophenia* for £3 second-hand, and to the Shamrat tandoori across the road, where Sam Burstow, Miles Britton, Gareth Carswell and I had dined on our first Friday evening as hut-mates. Sam and Gareth were curry fanatics who could not believe I had never tasted Indian food. 'We don't have these places where I come from, but I know what a curry is for Christ's sake,' I bridled. 'I've had millions of Chinese ones, Vesta biryanis, curry-flavoured Pot Noodles ...'

'Four chicken phals it is, then,' Gareth ordained.

I should have known from the film of sweat that quickly appeared on Sam's brow that something really horrifying was going to happen when my fork reached my mouth. 'You seem to be in some discomfort ...' I began to say. No further words were possible for the next twenty-four hours.

'Can't take this youth anywhere,' I remembered Miles guffawing. 'He thinks McDonald's is a steak-house.'

The bus dropped me on the most quintessentially rural and dream-like stretch of Bristol Road South, I always felt, opposite the halls of residence. If Birmingham was not quite the England of my fantasies, this glorious cross between an evergreen avenue and a dual carriageway unequivocally lived up to the England of *O Lucky Man!* – in particular the scene where Malcolm McDowell breasts the rolling hills and looks down to see a motorway, with cars at full pelt far below.

Nissen City was, on the other hand, a functional and cheap means of housing two hundred first-year students on an accommodation complex in close proximity to the Uni. Two hundred homesick waifs streaming from their huts at 6 p.m. to share one telephone . . . When it came my turn to use it, and I read out the address for Piers to write to ('Block 39 . . . Unit 244 . . .'), he roared with laughter and said it was the bleakest-sounding dwelling he'd ever heard. His own address had the words *fir*, *Woodleigh* and *courtyard* in it.

None of my hut-mates was home. In my bedroom, boxes as yet unpacked lay on the floor next to albums as yet unplayed, while, on the desk, books as yet unread were piled on top of essays as yet unfinished. The stench of Monday night's Chinese curry was atrocious. If it got any worse – or if it had not cleared by Friday – I would have to think seriously about buying an air-freshener in Sainsbury's. I had seen one I liked, but spending my money on records rather than household luxuries was, as usual, the priority.

'It's terribly stuffy in here. Can you not open a window?'

A Saturday-afternoon packing session in September. My mother crinkled her nose at me, implying that it was not just stuffiness that had aggrieved it.

'I never open windows,' I said blithely. 'Opening the curtains is quite sufficient.'

Kneeling on the carpet with her two black refuse sacks, one for Throwing and one for Keeping, she surveyed the bedroom with a decorator's eye, seeing it in three weeks' time painted a different colour, consisting of entirely different furniture, with a different carpet covering the floor and both the windows wide open.

'Joseph Heller,' she said, examining a paperback. 'Throw.'

'Keep,' I contradicted her. 'And all those are to be kept as well.'

'Jackie Collins's *Lovers and Gamblers* . . . I didn't know you read this sort of thing.'

'What! Jackie Collins . . . ?'

Oh dear. A vague memory was coming back to me: a fourth-form winter . . . leaving a Lisburn Road bookshop rather abruptly with a rectangular bulge in my parka. 'I have no idea how that got there,' I said to my mother. 'It must have been here when we moved in.'

'Keep?'

'Throw.'

She held up a pink folder. 'The Manuscript,' she announced. '"Not to be read before December the thirty-first 1999."'

'Throw. No, keep. Put it in the Keep sack. I'll make a decision on that later.'

'You should have done English,' she said for the millionth time. 'I'm not trying to start an argument, but you should have done English.'

'I'm going to university, aren't I? Well . . . only just.'

'Oh, I think a B and two Cs is a very noble effort.' She smiled. 'Considering.'

I turned towards the window, staring at the roof where Superbird had lived, loved and died. 'If anyone's being noble, it's Birmingham for taking me on those grades. Talk about nobility. They had no obligation to let me in.'

'Ah, I remember this . . . Didn't we buy you this for Christmas?'

'What is it?' I said distractedly, watching a man get into a Citroën Diane outside number 87.

'*The Illustrated New Musical Express Encyclopaedia of Rock.* When did we buy you it? Was it Christmas '79?'

I spun round in amazement. 'Oh my good God . . .' Rushing over, I snatched the glossy paperback from her hands. I pressed the upside-down front cover to my chest, hugging it, smothering the inset photos of *Blonde on Blonde* and *Aladdin Sane* with tee-shirt cotton and rapture. 'He doesn't look a day older. A crease here, but you expect some wear and tear. Edited by Bob Woffinden and Nick Logan . . . I could never figure out who this band was on the front. Where did you find him?'

'Him? *It* was in the box I've just emptied. From the tidying-up session when we agreed you were going to have a big clear-out? Hmmm? You obviously didn't.'

Tinmeer . . .

'It *was* Christmas '79, because we got Stephen his Parker fountain pen,' she went on. 'And somebody lost his temper because we wouldn't let him watch Alfred Hitchcock. Who would that have been? Hmmm?'

Tinmeer . . .

'It was Christmas '78,' I said, opening the book. A piece of paper fell out and landed at my feet. Ever since I could remember, I had hidden pieces of paper in books. 'You even wrote it here. "Good luck at Christmas '78 . . . Hope you enjoy the pop book." My God . . . pop book. It was the bible. Tinmeer was the bible.'

I bent down and picked up the paper. I had folded it twice – lengthways first, then back over my thumbs. The handwriting was unrecognizable . . . I was forever changing my handwriting in 1979 . . . but I remembered folding paper lengthways for the duration of that year.

TINMEER'S SEMINAL TOP 10 HALCYON RULES OF CLASSIC ROCK

1. Buy Derek & the Dominos' *Layla and Other Assorted Love Songs*. It's an acknowledged masterpiece.
2. American musicians are better than English or British ones. But English or British musicians working with American ones (e.g. Eric Clapton, Van Morrison, Steve Winwood) make the best music of all.
3. Rick Grech spells his name Ric Grech, not Rik Grech.
4. John Cale and J. J. Cale are two separate people.
5. Don't listen to music for boys.
6. An encyclopaedia of rock is only as definitive as the mind of the person reading it.
7. I repeat: don't listen to music for boys.
8. I am right about the Grateful Dead.
9. Punk rock is to me something that is unknown. I am from Hamelin. Make allowances.
10. Refer to me every day until further notice. I offer you wisdom before and after school.

'What on earth is Tinmeer?' my mother asked.

'It's an acronym,' I replied, placing the Halcyon Rules between Status Quo and Steppenwolf and closing the book. 'First letter of every word. *The Illustrated New Musical Express Encyclopaedia of Rock*. T-I-N-M-E-E-R. Published in 1977 by

Hamlyn. For some reason I always thought that sounded German. Here, you can have it back now.'

'Nice colours, anyway,' she allowed. 'Throw or keep? Don't feel you have to keep it just because it was a present.'

I turned back to the window and bit my lip. September in Malone Avenue ... There would soon be a new car outside number 93 and another gaggle of nurses moving in next door.

'No, I'd like to keep it,' I said at last. 'I think I should keep it.'

Of the three English weekly music papers, *Melody Maker* was the only one I rarely bothered to buy. My precise reason for boycotting it had faded over time; perhaps it was loyalty to the *NME*, or perhaps it had pilloried Angus Young at some particularly sensitive stage in my AC/DC idolatry, or it could have been that I disliked the paper's design and wasn't too keen on the name.

Skimming through the new issue in my Nissen City bedroom, however, I found it quite readable – arguably more readable than the grandiloquent *NME*, where these days you had to stop in mid-paragraph, go back, decipher and gingerly resume. There was no deciphering necessary when I studied the *Melody Maker*'s gig guide, which was quite readable and informed me that a band called Eyeless in Gaza was playing at the Fighting Cocks in Birmingham in four days, supported by a band called Coalition of Glass.

And it was while flipping the pages of *Melody Maker* back and forth, hither and thither, thinking *oh yes, this is quite readable*, that my mind caught hold of a familiar word, then two more, then a third.

With a quickening heartbeat, I cleared a space on my desk and read the review properly.

THE SUFFRAGETTES
Belfast
A suffragette city or a city of suffering? The dribs and drabs of Belfast's teenage wildlife have descended on this tiny venue to prove the lie to Bowie's maxim that heaven loves you when you're a boy. Formerly foppish grammar schoolboys the Decadents, the Suffragettes are fronted by stick-thin Englishman Andrew Finn, a student by day and an is-he-or-isn't-he androgyne by night, whose ever-so-original Decadents (dah-ling), it can now be revealed, stole 'obscure' American psychedelic nuggets by the Seeds, Thirteenth Floor Elevators, Leaves *et al.*, claiming each and every one of 'em to have been penned by the aforementioned Finn! (What we in these parts call Doing a Midwife — don't ask.) Finn's new crew are an even damper squib, a real Ziggy-by-numbers put-on. If this is Finn's idea of post-decadence, someone should tell bassist Paul Leckie that fretless basses look and sound shit, while it's all too obvious from the *poseur* song-titles ('Heroes in Stasis', 'My Ice Melts for Kitten') that Numan, not Bowie, is what we're faced with here. When will Belfast awake to the sound of Jericho trumpets and *progress*? My money's on Coalition of Glass, who blitzed to the forefront in '81 and have just returned from a 12-month sabbatical during which they wrote not one but four crackerjack albums. Meanwhile, the drawing-board beckons for Finn and his Suffragettes.
Karl Marks

I read it once more, nodding vacantly to myself. Yes, it was quite readable. Even on a second reading, I found it quite readable. Arguably not quite as readable as the *NME*, but still quite readable.

'What we in these parts call Doing a Midwife – don't ask.'

The thing that surprised me about the feeling, I suppose, was the lack of surprise. It wasn't a feeling that said *This is a bolt from the blue*. It was a feeling that said *I've had my doubts for some time*. I recalled the quizzical looks from Lawrence to Michelle at Mark Coates's party a year before, as he played the drums on one American psychedelic nugget after another. So quizzical . . . as though he were saying to her: *These songs are all stolen, kiddo . . . just wait till I tell the Pirries*.

And I thought back to Andy's unexpected arrival at Kelly's when Isobel had her birthday drink in April. Entering the bar sheepishly, he'd given her a bottle of something wrapped in green paper and pecked her on the cheek. He was scruffy, she was pretty in her turquoise frock, but they looked like a couple who belonged together – just for a moment. Then he noticed me, smiled and came over.

'Well . . . spring is here. The sap is rising, as they say. Or whatever it is they say. Like the hair?'

'It's lamentable,' I told him. 'Is there a Cranmore Park shampoo shortage?'

'Heh . . . bitchy. No wonder you and Isobel get on so well. You being nice to her, I hope?'

'I'm trying my best,' I said truthfully. 'A friend in need, as they say.'

'Listen, I . . .' he said, looking intently into my eyes.

'Here's what I think. An honorary Dec you were, and an honorary Dec you shall remain. I do not bestow these decorations lightly. So there. And um . . .' He grimaced. 'Bit loud in here, unfortunately. You young pop kids with your Goombay Dance Band and your Toni Basil. Oh well. Listen! Best of luck in June.'

Pointing his forefingers at me like duelling pistols, he backed towards the door and made his way out. I never saw him again.

'Well, Lou,' I heard myself say aloud, 'so we finally got you in the music press. I really hope that by some unlikely series of circumstances you are on holiday in Borneo at this moment. But a dishonourable Dec you were, and a dishonourable Dec you . . .'

My voice trailed off. There were no more words, no more tears.

Which reminded me: I had planning to do for Monday. Planning and organizing and felicitous visits and sleeping arrangements to be organized and planned. I pulled down her postcard from its spot above my bed, trying to understand yet again but failing to understand yet again why she had stamped and addressed it and then posted it to me in a stamped, addressed envelope. That girl . . .

'Will be there New Street on Mon 2 p.m.-ish. I stay three days (and nights . . .). Hurrah! I look forward to see you, sir, and we have nice time. (Pls forgive bad English, I fail all exam.) Get ready for me, buster! Warn Birmingham I am coming! Can't wait to *see you* and be nice friend. I'm sure you'll be able to find somewhere for me to sleep . . . Much love. Isobel xxxx.'

That girl. It was impossible to know what was in her head sometimes. Cueing up side one of the Monochrome

Set album on my record-player, I kicked off my shoes and lay back on the bed. I was trying to remember if I'd seen any guest-houses on my last stroll up to Northfield.

Acknowledgements

The lyric couplet quoted on p. 50 is taken from 'Reverberation (Doubt)', written by Erickson/Hall/Sutherland, published by Tapier Music Corp. and recorded by the Thirteenth Floor Elevators on their 1966 album *The Psychedelic Sounds of* . . . The song 'Candy's Wrists', quoted at length on pp. 157–8, is (obviously) a fabrication on the author's part: no real lyric-writer is that bad.

While inspired in certain places by memories of a post-punk music atmosphere of the early 1980s – insofar as Belfast could lay claim to a punk atmosphere and insofar as 'inspired' is the right word for such a morbid teenage narrator – *Music For Boys* is a work of fiction, and any resemblance between any of its characters and any real persons, living or dead, is purely coincidental. *Viva* Penelope Chong Cat Ledger Andy Miller Nick Davies Kate Hyde Michelle Kane Adrian Deevoy.